So Say
Banana Bird

Jon Wynne-Tyson

So Say Banana Bird

Pythian Books 1984

First published 1984 by Pythian Books,
132 Marine Parade, Brighton, Sussex BN2 1DE

© Jon Wynne-Tyson 1984

This book is sold subject to the condition that it shall not, by way of trade or otherwise, be lent, re-sold, hired out, or otherwise circulated without the publisher's prior consent in any form of binding or cover other than that in which it is published and without a similar condition including this condition being imposed on the subsequent purchaser.

British Library Cataloguing in Publication Data

Wynne-Tyson, Jon
   So Say Banana Bird
   I. Title
   823'.914[F]   PR6073.Y/

ISBN 0 946849 00 5

Printed and bound in Great Britain

Author's Note

This is a work of fiction, but it is set in the Caribbean, which is real, and it is about human nature, which tends to be much the same the world over. Parallels are therefore inescapable, but any resemblance to particular living individuals must be deemed a coincidence.

As for the dedication, the book is for those who love islands and want them left alone; for those with doubts about today's priorities; and for all who hold differing views of where truth ends and legend begins, whether in fiction or that even stranger and more unpredictable experience we staunchly call life.

Oh, and for my wife, without whose patient succour and ruthless honesty the damned thing would be twice as long.

1

'YOUR usual table at Les Parisiennes?' Fiona asked.

Simon Loewenstein's grey eyes scrutinized the backs of his elegant hands. He wrote 'manicure' on a pad.

'Somewhere a little outside Soho might be kinder,' he said.

'Les Parisiennes would give no hint of impending change.'

'Poor Matthew Braine,' Fiona said. She was new to publishing after a sheltered year in the Foreign Office.

'Well, I'd like to break it to him gently. It can't be pleasant to feel the nudge at his age.'

Simon was in his lower thirties. The pattern of British publishing, increasingly indistinguishable from America's, was not reassuring. Anyone, any time, could be for the chop. It made for empathy.

'You can be quite cuddly - sometimes,' Fiona said.

'One tries to be civilized. Absorption by the conglomerates need not blunt the sensibilities.'

'How about the trattoria that agent took you to last week? In Tottenham Court Road. You said it was cheap.'

'Clever girl. Fix it.'

Simon sat with as much grace as the cramped surroundings allowed. Behind him two shop assistants from Heals had had to pull their seats hard in to let him through, one of them tossing his head and shoulders petulantly at the inconvenience. Simon lit a cigarette. His fingers were long and slim, in keeping with the whole.

'I do hope this won't prove disappointing,' he said. 'It was recommended. Les Parisiennes is getting a shade...' he waved a sensitive hand, '... popular.'

'Yes,' Matthew agreed, 'it is. I like it very much.'

He did not like the Trattoria Napoletana. He guessed that the unsteady bentwood chairs encouraged rapid turnround. The tobacco smoke was already making his nasal membranes prickle with alarm. He had reached a time of life when public eating was conditional upon a certain standard. The Trattoria did not set it.

In any case, lunch was a meal he could do without. He would have been quite happy to have met Simon in his office at Rupert Hamilton (Publishers) Ltd. He had always enjoyed sitting in Simon's conspicuously late-eighteenth-century room. While his own photograph had not yet been added to the rows of literary faces that looked down from every wall, it was comforting to feel they shared Hamilton's list with him. He had toyed with offering a studio portrait, feeling that after eight novels and ten years the time would never be more ripe. But he sensed it to be a matter of invitation. Why that invitation had not come, he was uncertain. If he had been told it was because bald, stooped novelists in middle life are not hard to come by, he could have understood. But Simon's gallery was proof that the quality of the outward man was no reason for exclusion.

Inflation saw them through the hors d'oeuvres, to which the Trattoria Napoletana did not accord the dignity of a trolley. Simon's holiday in South America, which had embraced both wife and children, could easily have taken them beyond the main course, but an oblique reference to the cost of education brought them on to more mutually recognizable ground, and they stayed with education through to the coffee.

'I can be thankful that at least I have no more kids at school,' Matthew said. 'Even eighty per cent on the State, it was a struggle.'

'And I see no light at the end of the tunnel,' Simon said. 'If it wasn't for our scientific back-list I think I would be very depressed about the future.'

He toyed with his coffee spoon.

'Of course, you've merged since we last met,' Matthew said. 'Hasn't that made a difference?'

It was the lead Simon had been hoping for.

'Oh, in many ways. New policies, new faces, new priorities. Cut-backs and restructurings. Reorientation at every level. Depressing. Stimulating in a way, of course, and maybe necessary. But depressing. Prompting a lot of hard decisions and some rather painful adjustments.'

'You've had three blockbusters recently. Haven't they helped?'

'Two, not three.'

'Two novels and the multiple orgasm book, surely?'

'A lot of noise was made over the multiple orgasm book, but sales have been dismal. Can't think why.'

'Maybe the bandwagon has blown a tyre at last.'

'The paperback rights went for over a million,' Simon said. There was a slightly defensive note in his voice.

'Pounds?'

'Dollars. But we didn't get a quarter of that over here, of course.'

'Even so...'

'Don't forget we have to split proceeds with the Americans.'

'How easily these details slip the mind,' Matthew said.

The moment seemed right.

'Take your own last book,' Simon said.

'I thought we might.'

Simon looked very serious.

'*Just a Silent Handshake* is a fine book. You know we liked it hugely. Hugely.'

'But the public kept their cool.'

'Well, you've seen the royalty statements. Hence the disappointment. We'd built really high hopes. We anticipated breakthrough.'

'Breakthrough? I thought *A Piece of the Action* was my breakthrough. I recall your words clearly: "This is the turning point."'

'Oh, but of course, we did well with it. Relatively.'

'We bought our house that year. Paid off everything.'

'Quite. But that was five years ago. You see, Matthew, to break into the Big League today...'

'I don't want to break into the Big League. I'm not that kind of writer...'

'I know, I know. But all criteria are relative. One has to see a pattern. The general trend must be... how shall I put it?'

'Up.'

'Well, in bald terms, yes. Declining sales graphs get these

accountant fellows absurdly jumpy. Lot of talk about responsibility to shareholders, you know.'

'The last time I met Sir Rupert he said how much he valued my place on his list.'

Simon nodded gravely.

'And Rupert doesn't lie. But since the merger he's having to stand in line with the rest of us. It's no longer a highly personalized business. We're all just employees of the holding company.'

'The sausage firm.'

'Meat packaging is one of their interests.'

'And literature bloody isn't?'

'As I say, it has to fall into line. To justify itself.'

'Make a whacking, inordinate profit or go to the wall.'

'Brutal times, Matthew, brutal times. Don't think I don't realize how you must feel about this.'

'What's the punch line, then?'

'Look, don't make this too difficult – for yourself or us. We'll want to see your next book, of course. All I am saying is that decisions are being referred; raising support for work likely to bring negative cash flow is getting more tricky; the conglomerate has to generate hype at every level; it is difficult not to follow the pattern in the States where a book is just another commodity, a deal, a package, a production. I'm not saying I like it that way, it's just how things are going.'

'And if you think you won't shift more than five thousand of my next in hardback, or make a paperback killing, you won't want to know?'

'You're simplifying a bit, Matthew, but there has to be some sort of cut-off point. There is with any property. Even with sausages, I'm told.'

Matthew pressed his thumb and third finger against his temples. Some thin, restraining cord seemed in danger of parting.

'Are these people you have tangled with so totally lacking in the civilized values that literature, the creative imagination, means nothing to them?'

'Well, let me put it this way: it doesn't come through very strongly.' Simon straightened, smiled a charming and encouraging smile, and signalled to the waitress. 'Anyway, don't let's get too miserable about all this. Maybe *Handshake* will pick up. It's simply that at the moment the powers that be are being influenced by track records, and I felt I ought to fill you in now rather than later.'

Matthew nodded gloomily.

'I guessed something of the sort was in the wind.'

Simon looked at his watch. The bright blue figures were flashing their implacable reminders.

'Got a call coming in from the States. Some Vineyard granny has produced a book with all the ingredients. Raunchy as an oyster-fed ferret. We've probably been out-bid. It's sheer Manhattan Smartass, of course, but one can't afford to let everything go to one's competitors.'

'They say aggressive marketing will sell anything. Why not hype *my* books instead of backing unknown kinky grandmothers?'

Simon smiled with wise patience.

'Now come on, Matthew, you know it isn't quite like that. Satirical fiction is a difficult field. Always has been. Fashions change. More and more that elusive *something other* has to be recognized and exploited.'

Matthew finished his coffee at a gulp.

'Like being a "personality", I suppose. God! If only I had known at birth how vital it was to be a trendy geriatric, an infant prodigy, gay, working-class, a dope-destroyed Liverpuddlian, a pissed Welshman, a randy Jew, a Russian defector, or anything on God's earth but a heavily heterosexual middle-class, middle-aged Anglo-Saxon with only orthodox inhibitions, there would have been no problem.'

'There's still time. Are you coming my way?'

'Apparently not,' Matthew said. 'Anyway, I'm due at the doctor's at three. Perhaps if he gave me a sex change...'

2

'HAVEN'T seen you much on the water this year,' Dr Trubshaw remarked.

'I've pottered over to the Island once or twice,' Matthew said. 'It's finding the time. Everything seems to take so much longer than it used to.'

The doctor nodded sagely.

'Anno Domini has a lot to do with it. By the way, did I tell you I'd changed the Folkboat for a Hillyard?'

'Quite a step up.'

'Twelve feet more overall, but only nine on the waterline.'

'Even so... Thinking of some long-haul stuff?'

'No hope until I retire. Not sure I'd want to, anyway. Getting a bit decrepit to think foreign.'

'Come off it, James, you're no older than I am.'

The doctor shook his head dubiously.

'You're as old as your bones.'

'Well, mustn't waste your time. About my...'

'Old Spofforth's bought himself a Tusker 33.'

'Motor cruiser?'

'Perkins diesel.'

Matthew looked shocked.

'Spofforth? Who keeps a Nicholson off the Hoe?'

'Says he wants to do a bit of Channel fishing.'

'He could have compromised with a Fairways Fisher, surely? Thorneycroft diesel *and* an effective area of sail.'

'Well, there you are. People do strange things, even after thirty years of cruising under canvas. He can give me ten years, don't forget. You, fifteen.'

'But still, to go over entirely to engines... Look, about this stupid ache I've been having...'

'And he won the Round-the-Island last year, too,' Trubshaw said reflectively.

'... I feel you must think I'm a hopeless neurotic.'

A quick shake of the head cleared the doctor's eyes of their far-horizon look. He leaned back in his chair and placed the tips of his fingers together. He was a bland, broad-faced man who put patients in mind of a benevolent frog. His diagnoses had no reputation for brilliance, but his deskside manner was second to none. The glass-fronted cabinet by the door held a short row of somewhat outdated medical books and an impressive selection of cups won in the heyday of his sailing.

'No, no,' he insisted, 'you mustn't think that at all. I know the Health Service is over-worked, but our role is not entirely to hand out pills and sign certificates. One tries not to lose sight of the fact that one works in a caring society.'

'If the pain wasn't in the groin I would probably not have bothered you.'

Trubshaw's chair returned to the vertical and he fingered the cards in a box file on his partners' desk.

'Here we are: Braine, M.'

He studied the card, humming the Volga Boat Song softly.

'No more trouble with those blinding spasms across the eyes?' he asked.

'Across the eyes?'

'Yes, three years ago. Suspected brain tumour.'

'No, my eyes have been all right. Who suspected a tumour?'

'You did.'

'The only thing I can remember from three years ago was a lot of back pain.'

'I've a note of that. You were worried about life confinement to a wheel-chair. Seems it was lumbago after all.'

'I haven't troubled you much since.'

'There was the throat cancer scare eighteen months ago.'

'Ah, well, I'd read somewhere one should always report long-standing huskiness.'

'Quite right.'

'But I suppose it was connected with the allergic rhinitis.'

'That no better?'

'Pretty constant.'

'A difficult area. You could try injections.'

'I'm managing to live with it.'

The doctor returned to the card.

'The last problem seems to have been your knee, a year ago tomorrow.'

'I think you were right. It was driving the new car to Wales. Beastly cramped, and a damned awkward accelerator position.'

'But the groin problem doesn't seem to have cleared up?'

'No.'

'You've had all the usual tests, I see.'

'All negative. As they were in my father's case.'

Trubshaw nodded.

'Tests aren't infallible, of course. Maybe I'd better examine you again. Just shoes and trousers, I think.'

The view under Trubshaw's elbow was of an impeccably kept strip of lawn with geraniumed borders terminating in a sundial.

'That's just the amount of garden I could do with,' Matthew said. 'I'd even settle for ten square feet of York stone and some tubs now the children have left.'

'Thankfully, Ruth loves gardening. Here?'

'No. You're lucky. I sometimes think Rebecca would be happier in a Surbiton high-rise with a vase of plastic delphiniums.'

'What if I twist the leg?'

'It feels as though you were twisting it.'

'Of course, one should sort these things out before marriage. Our own sons, if they had any sense, would look for proficiency in plumbing, electrical repairs, car maintenance, and for a love of gardens. How about if we bend your knee back on to your chest?'

'Nothing. Sometimes I wish I did have sons. I get nowhere with daughters.'

'Delightful when small, but they take after their mothers, then close ranks.'

'You're telling me.'

'Sit on the edge and I'll test your reflexes.'

Matthew's leg obediently kicked the surgery air.

'It's worst when I'm tired or tensed up.'

'Everything is, my dear chap. Do you remember old Admiral Kent? Commanded everything from frigates to aircraft carriers in his time. I let him helm my Dragon during Cowes

Week – years ago. Before the start he'd develop a twitch that would have made St Vitus throw in the sponge. All tension.'

'Well, what can I do to be absolutely certain?'

'About your groin?'

'Sometimes I wake in the night sweating with the pain of it.'

'Do you lie in an awkward position?'

'Not consciously.'

Trubshaw pondered.

'I could prescribe something. Bescott and Mainwaring have come up with an analgesic that is claimed to be very effective.'

'Who makes the claim?'

'Bescott and Mainwaring. Two-page full-colour advertisement. Convincing testimonials.'

'I don't see much point in masking the symptoms. I'm after a cure, or the assurance there's nothing the matter.'

'Come now, one must keep one's expectations within reasonable bounds.'

'I know it's stupid, but I just can't forget my father's experience. The symptoms are so similar.'

'He didn't die of it, though, did he?'

'It depends on how you look at it. He died of liver and kidney damage after resuscitation from a drug overdose.'

'I don't remember you telling me that. Trousers on, I think.'

'He had more pain than I've had, but everyone kept on telling him it was nothing. When he couldn't stand it any longer he took an overdose, but bodged it. They took him in and pumped him out and he died miserably a few months later. I went to see him in the poisons unit. I shall never forget it.'

Trubshaw nodded.

'If you're going to do it, you want to do it properly and make damned sure you aren't interrupted.'

'Ouch!'

'Felt a twinge? Probably because I twisted your leg a bit.'

'It was my zip.'

'Dreadful invention. Symbol of the times. I can't stand the press-studs on oil skins either.'

'So we're back to square one?'

'Your pain? If it's not bad enough for an analgesic, there's not much I can do. I'd sail a bit more if I were you. Take yourself out of yourself. You writer chappies tend to get a bit too introspective, you know. Too sedentary. I'm doddling down to Dartmouth the week-end after next. First decent haul in the Hillyard. I could do with a crew. Care to come along?'

'Rebecca's said "yes" to a wedding on the Saturday.'

'Not sailing people, I hope? Damned selfish to hold weddings at the week-end.'

'I've not been sleeping well. Ran out of your pills. Maybe I can have some more?'

'What do you have? Oh, yes, nembutal.' He pursed his lips. 'There's a general feeling against barbiturates these days. Would you like to try something that Pirbright Pharmaceuticals seem very happy about?'

'Another new drug?'

'Pretty new. They've stopped sending salesmen and leaflets, but their advertising continues.'

'I think I'd rather keep with what I know. I don't use them often.'

'Please yourself.' He scribbled on the pad. 'I'll make it the same number as before. Don't want to have too many of these things hanging about. Still doing any racing?'

'No, I sold my share in "Vanity Fair". Just coastal cruising now.'

'Do you know any cure for black stains on the spars?'

'Nothing short of using paint in place of varnish. You could rub down to clean wood, but it'll come back. I'm learning to live with mine.'

'If it wasn't for all this maintenance, life would be a lot more fun.'

'You can say that again,' Matthew agreed.

3

'IF you would only soak the cutlery and plates before they are washed,' Matthew pointed out, 'one wouldn't be faced with hard dry lumps on everything, and the job would be less onerous.'

'I do soak them.'

'It's hardly effective,' Matthew explained in a voice strained by patience, 'to dip the very tip of a fork's prongs into a dribble of water in the bottom of a pudding basin that is itself caked to the rim.'

'What does it matter anyway?'

'It probably matters very little in an ultimate, absolute, evolutionary sense, but it happens to matter to me because I can't stand seeing things done inefficiently. I'm not responsible for how I was brought up.'

'Neither am I.'

'All right, but it is in our mutual interest to make our marriage stagger on a little longer. I don't like dirty feeding utensils just as you didn't like me stepping out of my pants and leaving them on the floor. For years I have put my pants on a chair, so why am I still battling to get you to observe a sensible, labour-saving rule that happens - or is this the blockage? - to pander to my hang-up?'

The conversation was indistinguishable from innumerable previous occasions, and as on innumerable previous occasions Rebecca at this point went silent. Matthew, as always, found this more infuriating than even the most illogical argumentativeness.

Rebecca had been, still was, a dainty and essentially feminine woman. For that, as for her placid, limpid, heifer-like eyes, he had loved her - in due season. But priorities change. Age and familiarity modify earlier sentiments. Relationships and possessions - children, houses, gardens - speed the process; gardens - when the breadwinner's workload teams with stiffening joints to give intimations of mortality - especially. Where, in their earlier years, he had cherished a Yeatsian view of Rebecca, courting her with already outmoded snatches from 'The Lake Isle' and 'Down by the Salley Gardens,' latterly he would have felt more empathy had she possessed good, flat border feet and strong calf muscles for squatting at flower beds, and sound practised arms for pulling weeds.

'You just hate the idea of any form of change, don't you?' he persisted. 'God, what fools men are to marry pretty women. Spoiled in their youth by the bee-like devotion of horny males, nothing will persuade them in later life that a different brand of pollen is needed.'

'What *are* you talking about, Matthew? Pollen! Bees! Sometimes I think you're unhinged.'

'Why should a normal concern with cleanliness be a sign of insanity?'

'It isn't normal. You're obsessed by it. And don't tell me again that you were a pre-war, nanny-reared only-child who saw nothing of his father after the age of five, because I'm not taking over where nanny left off, and that's an end to it.'

'Nanny wouldn't have let you through the door. Anyway, I never suggested you should. All I have asked for is autonomous, voluntary acceptance of certain standards that would make our life together more supportable. God! Look at the state of this frying pan. I can hardly lift it for the encrustations.'

'So it's insupportable?'

'On the domestic, day-to-day level, it leaves much to be desired.'

'Because of your obsession?'

'It is *not* an obsession.'

'It's not normal.'

Matthew rubbed angrily at a plate. Not averse to self-analysis, he was aware that upbringing followed by an uneventful and undistinguished war in the Royal Navy had strengthened a feeling for orderliness, economy, and the equating of cleanliness if not with Godliness - for his atheism was entrenched - then at least with Humanism. Had he any truck with notions of life before or hereafter, he would have acknowledged the possibility of having been a Brahmana in an earlier existence. It was also true that by the standards of a broadly permissive British society, Rebecca was some way from being a certifiable slut. But by Matthew's criteria she nudged the borderline often and unnecessarily. Her habits at the sink, particularly in the preparation of food, were markedly relaxed. But no amount of proximity to dirty pots and pans, smeared glasses, dubious working surfaces, and damp, soiled sink cloths left folded on the draining board to breed a bacteria-mindful stench, had accustomed him to her standards of hygiene.

'The truth is,' he said, 'that you dislike housework as much as you dislike gardening, brushing the dog, deep-freezing, and writing thank-you letters, and you have learned that by showing an unflagging incompetence on all such levels there's a damn good chance I'll take over and do them myself.'

The statement was so crammed with undeniable fact that for a moment Rebecca was silent.

'You can be thankful you're not married to Lucy Wainwright,' she said.

'What the bloody hell has Lucy Wainwright to do with it? I'm thankful I'm not married to Lucretia Borgia, the Witch of Endor, or Maggie Thatcher. I'm talking about us, not about Lucy Wainwright. Lucy Wainwright happens to be a woman of proven idiocy who has romped through three husbands. She'll probably end up living with a Yorkshire Large White in the sty she has made of the very adequate house left to her by the poor exhausted wreck of her first husband whom she doubtless killed with the lethal germs bred by her unremitting slovenliness. I would have thought you could have conjured up a more self-flattering comparison.'

'If only,' Rebecca said between set teeth, clenching the tea-cloth, 'you went out to work like any other man instead of endlessly standing over me like a concentration-camp overseer.'

Matthew retied his apron strings savagely.

'It may have escaped your notice that writers do not as a rule go out to work. It doubles the overheads and makes claiming tax relief against home expenses impossible.'

'It wasn't *tax* relief I was thinking about,' Rebecca said.

'God!' Matthew said, 'this is all so trivial.'

'Exactly.'

'I don't know how you expect me to concentrate on my work when my mind has to be continually dragged back to the minutiae of domestic squalor.' He picked up a grey square of pungent cloth between two fingers and regarded it at arm's length. 'Euagh! One day they'll read your epitaph: "Bred all known germs".'

Rebecca stamped her still pretty foot on the Marley-tiled floor.

'We are not living in squalor.'

'Relatively, sectionally, we are living in rampant squalor. This kitchen and the bathroom are like something out of a post-war play at the Royal Court.'

Rebecca pushed a saucepan roughly into the cupboard below the sink, dislodging several others on to the floor.

'Men like you,' she said, 'are why Women's Lib. had to be invented.'

He laughed hollowly.

'What sort of argument is that? The old equality whine? Bloody Women's Lib. isn't after equality, which in real terms women have had in abundance for years, it's after bloody domination by a regiment of bolshy toms. If Women's Lib. have their way, women like you will end up in jack-boots shouldering rifles in the war to end all wars against the poor male mutts who have been brain-washed to feel guilt in the roles generations of women have schemed like beavers to get them to accept. Your sex has never had it so good. You are surrounded by every kind of technology to take the labour out of housework...'

'A dishwasher? Where's the dishwasher? I haven't seen one.'

'We don't need a dishwasher. Research has proved that for a family of two, entertaining less than once a week - into which category, owing to your disinclination to return more than a tenth of the invitations we receive, we undoubtedly come - a dishwasher is counter-productive.'

'Research proves anything men want it to prove.'

'This sieve's revolting. You really must buy another.'

'Anyway, technology doesn't feed you and iron your clothes and make your bed...'

'Make my bed? The flick of a duvet back on to a single, fitted, nylon sheet?'

'It all has to be seen to.'

'Of course it has to be seen to, but the point is that it's all much less of a chore than it used to be, yet you can't be bothered to keep to a reasonable standard over the few things you still have to do. It's the law of diminishing returns. That's all I'm saying. I don't see anything unreasonable about it.'

'You wouldn't. You're saying it.'

'If we can argue at this abysmal level at this stage of life, it's perfectly obvious our marriage is null and void.'

'It's only your endless criticism that provokes the arguments.'

'Now that is so typical of your dishonest reasoning, Rebecca. My endless criticism, as you call it, is the immediate and logical result of your entrenched disinclination to observe minimal standards of cleanliness. It's a simple matter of Inaction and Reaction.'

'Oh, stop being so pompous! Go away and write your book. You're just playing with words.'

'If I hadn't played with words you wouldn't even have a stainless steel sink to slop around in. That's where you're so dense. You stubbornly refuse to see that an endless succession of comparatively little things are doing as much damage to our marriage as if I walked out of this door and started banging away with Valerie Bristow in the middle of the High Street.'

'As far as I'm concerned you can bang away with Valerie Bristow anywhere and at any time as long as you don't do it in this house.'

'I don't happen to want to bang away with Valerie Bristow. I am just saying that...'

'I know what you are saying. You've said it a hundred thousand times before and it is boring, boring, boring.'

'Then the sooner you relieve me of the necessity...'

'Oh, shut up!'

'... to say it...'

'Shut up, shut up!'

'... the better for all concerned. I don't enjoy these squabbles any more than you do.'

'You could have fooled me.'

'Look, why must we go on like this? We rubbed along tolerably well when the children were still at home.'

'Only because you didn't constantly stand over me then.'

'The fact remains that things have got worse since they left.'

'If that's so, and I'm not sure it is, it's because the children at least appreciated me. They weren't endlessly criticizing. Pecking away. On and on. Over and over again.'

'As I keep on pointing out, I wouldn't have to repeat myself if you were willing to establish a reasonable routine and keep to it. *I* have to, damn it, or we wouldn't eat. That cup goes on the red hook, not the blue.'

'I only wish the children *were* back,' Rebecca said. 'It would be nice to have some affection again.' She sniffed.

'It's just as well they're not. Maybe, away from both of us, they will get a more objective view of their parents and realize that things were not as one-sided as they were encouraged to suppose.'

'Meaning what?'

'Come off it, Rebecca, you know exactly what I mean. You curried favour with both Judy and Mary from the word go. With Mary especially. You spoiled them all along the line, and when I tried to exert a little discipline or guidance you gave me no back-up.'

'Nonsense! What about when...?'

'Don't start instance-quoting, for God's sake. Of course there were times when you were cross with them, even times when you gave me a little support. But by and large those kids grew up with the carefully nurtured impression that mummy was sweet reasonableness and daddy was strict and unfair. What's more, you played it so that I was always shown to be in the wrong for criticizing you, never that I had any cause to do so. I've watched you work it, time and again, and if I'd told the children what you were at it would merely have confirmed them in their belief that I was being beastly to you. The deviousness of women is appalling.'

Rebecca's face was expressionless; her voice, when she spoke, flat.

'If only you would confine your imagination to your books,' she said.

'All right, by your standards I get up-tight too often about domestic matters, but they are not the main reason why our marriage is going on the rocks, and you know it. When the children were little I loved them dearly. I went on doing so, but it became more and more difficult to communicate with them. You seemed to grab at every opportunity to widen the gulf between me and them. I don't know how consciously you did so, but you were damned effective. Now we are reaping the reward. By damaging my relationship with Judy and Mary you damaged our own, and while I might be able to live with dirty kitchens and your general disinclination to pull your weight, I can never, ever forget that you loved neither the children nor me enough to create a happy family unit. I'm nothing to those children now. If I fell under a bus tomorrow, they'd miss me like a bad tooth.'

Rebecca spoke calmly.

'That's rubbish, Matthew. They are very fond of you.'

'Fond? What sort of a word is fond?'

'It takes more than one to create a background. If only you would once admit to being in the wrong.'

'I'm not claiming perfection; anything but. All right, you dismiss my early years as irrelevant, and I agree the whole childhood thing has been overplayed by the shrinks and the sociologists, but the fact remains that I have not found it easy to be a family man, and that must have had something to do with my not having had a very balanced background myself. I know I've failed on many counts.'

Rebecca sniffed.

'Oh, dear! So what do we do? You're saying the marriage is dead. Pointless.'

'Dead marriages don't lie down without the formality of a legal document. Even today you need some clear reason for divorce.'

'Do you want a divorce?'

Matthew shrugged. He had thought it over often enough, always returning to the conclusion that their marriage was one of the mighty majority doomed to drift rather than founder. There was no single strong enough reason to end it formally. It was not enough for incompatibility to be measured by the endless small irritations and emotional lacunae which, viewed in isolation, suggested trivial grounds, yet cumulatively could make living with another just as insupportable as the standard tabloid excuses. As for petitioning on the grounds of damaged relationships with one's children...!

He sneezed violently five times in succession.

'Have you taken your anti-histamine today?' Rebecca asked wearily.

He blew into a tissue-for-men, a box of which was permanently on the window-sill.

'I thought the dry weather was helping. I suppose it's all this tension.'

'You put everything down to tension, by which you mean me. Your allergy, sciatica, flatulence...'

'That's right! Belittle my wind!'

'Well, really, Matthew, all these ailments are just in your mind.'

'Any fool knows that flatulence and allergic rhinitis are tension-related.'

'Well, at least I don't smoke all over you,' Rebecca said. 'Which is more than could be said for your first wife.'

He rubbed his eyes. 'True.'

'Well?' Rebecca said. 'Do you?'

'Do I what?'

'Want a divorce.'

'I honestly don't know,' he said. 'What would we be divorcing *for*? As far as I know you haven't found a sugar daddy, and for my part I'm a long way from having designs on Valerie Bristow. Is there a case for parting just to be apart?'

Rebecca removed her pink rubber gloves.

'Well, one thing's for sure,' she said. 'If the decision is to be made, you'll be the one to make it.'

He undid the apron and slipped the loop over his head.

'Yes,' he said, 'I rather thought you would say that.'

4

HALF tide.

The grey Solent sea flowed silently through the mouth of the harbour, stealthily covering the shingle banks and the long humps of sand, seeping between the stiff straight reeds, filling the twisted muddy veins which branched from each creek and inlet off the main channels. In the next two hours the flooded area would double as the water found its final level, sweeping almost perceptibly over the green marshes, leaving only the occasional shingled hummock to give gulls and waders island refuge. At high tide the channels would be filled to the very verge of the roads and villages to which they led. The cycle had been repeated twice daily for centuries, since long before the Romans landed at the head of the easternmost creek and created the low-lying town whose thin spire was a landmark dear and familiar to yachtsmen.

The harbour held few craft. The schools had returned for the autumn; the holiday-makers had gone. He passed two men in a heavy clinker-built rowing boat, oars idle, drifting with the tide, their lines trailing for unsuspecting life. Staring dully across the water, the fishermen did not glance in his direction. They had little time for leisure-sailors; but in the week, and at this time of the year, the waters were free of competing helmsmen obsessed to tease the last fraction of speed and windward advantage from frail, fast craft whose slim lines and multi-coloured spinnakers pleased all but the sourest observers of others' pastimes.

He was passing East Head. More correctly, he was failing to pass East Head. His mind elsewhere, he had let the yacht creep into the centre of the fairway and was making no progress over the ground. The sloop was on a fine reach, so he trimmed her sails and pointed up out of the worst of the tide, bearing away again only when the loss of wind under the low headland began to outweigh the advantage of the slacker water. His actions were almost without conscious control, so far removed were his thoughts.

Yes, now that what had been planned was beginning to happen, his detachment surprised him. Well, better a cool objectivity than to be heading down harbour, clutching the tiller hysterically, blinded by tears, contemptible in self-pity, racked by indecision... Perhaps that was what his conscience should be telling him would be more appropriate... Did the seriousness and finality of his intention demand greater trauma...?

'Oh, belt up!'

He found few things more irritating than self-doubt. His credo, if he had one, was the pre-eminence of reason, the certainty that the human mind, given time, could cope with all problems and imponderables (which was not to deny that human affairs were a long way short of perfection).

The audible expulsion of breath was more snort than laugh, its target his familiar habit of taking himself too seriously. Well, the decision had been his; his predicament was voluntary. It usually was. Yet he was still managing to surprise himself, not least by his capacity for surprise. Ironic that a satirical writer should not have taken himself - a pretty average specimen of *Homo sap.*, for Christ's sake - more lightly.

But wasn't the satirist literature's most mixed-up hack, forever striving to keep anger and humour in delicate balance? Or was anger, in his own case, too strong a word? Had he been too content to tilt with the lance of deflation? That late review for *Handshake*, coming in the same week as the lunch with Simon, kept niggling: 'His windmills are all too small.' But each to his last, confound it! Very well, maybe he lacked the reforming passion and was content to seek the smile of recognition. Good luck, then, to those who hammered away at major issues, employing ridicule to win ground for good causes. But was literature the right vehicle for reformers? Dangerous ground. His own bent was mockery at manners, snobberies, vanities - the social satire bit. Trivial, maybe; lacking a commitment proper to the problems of the 'real world'; but what he understood. Thumping about on big crusading cart-horses was not his line. His idealism, if that was not too grand a term, sought more tidiness and consistency in human affairs; more order, commonsense. No mean goal, surely? If that wasn't enough, then bugger them.

His hand strayed to his groin. Of late, the dull ache had been more than just a night-time worry. Rebecca had said he should go back to Trubshaw, but there had seemed no point when he had made up his mind about the voyage.

He tacked, fetching the buoy accurately, confirming his instinctive assessment of the balance of wind and flood. He tacked again, aware of the hidden bank which lay only feet beyond the line of the two marks. Well, seeing how things had turned out it was appropriate he should be beating against a foul tide all the way to the harbour mouth. The story of his life. Nor was the convenient parallel weakened by the benign weather, combining the warmth of the late September sun with a light south-westerly which barely enabled the twenty-five foot sloop to make up on the two-knot tide...

No, come off it, though. That story-of-my-life tag was sheer wallow. Compared with some, he had had an easy passage. The pall of grey meaninglessness that had hung over him so long did not justify the claim of surviving any excess of storm or tempest. Perhaps that was half the trouble: too many bland calms interspersed by niggling squalls lacking the cleansing, stimulating challenge of a full gale. Maybe that was what he had needed all along: something to blow him sufficiently off course to force the charting of an entirely new future.

Too late now; and, anyway, gales just happen; nothing yet on the shelves of the microchip-shop could conjure them up at will. All right, so he was giving final proof of his innate feebleness. They'd blast his opting out as mere self-indulgence, and maybe they'd be right. Self-pitying bastard!

Another craft was approaching. A bright blue Devon Yawl running before the breeze, making good speed in the favourable tide. Its elderly helmsman, one arm resting on the tiller, took his pipe from his mouth and saluted him contentedly. Well adjusted to retirement, no doubt; happy pottering between Hayling and Bosham until expected for lunch and to cut the lawn; content to let things take their course.

He wondered idly if there was significance in his preference for beating into the wind to running before it. In his racing days most of his wins had come from making up places when under pressure to recognize and employ the subtle shifts of a head wind between the turning mark and the finishing line. Running was too easy...

Maybe the trick-cyclists (God! He must watch those dating jocularities) could make out a case for his yacht-racing being some kind of compensation. Yet he had surprised himself as much as his more intellectual acquaintances when he took to it so readily: the non-competitor, the born loner. But the pleasure lay in the sheer skill of getting the best out of a boat. Giving priority to the mere challenge of beating the competition was secondary, even faintly despicable. In any case, the very idea of middle-aged men devoting every week-end to chasing each other in small boats round orange buoys, if they really began caring about results, was absurd. It was absurd anyway, but in an idiotic world any activity involving fresh air and the perfecting of a singularly sensitive skill in pleasant surroundings must have some justification.

All right, what about the honesty bit? It *had* been a thrill on those few occasions when he had 'got a gun' at Cowes. Good atavistic stuff, directly descended from those rare moments at school when a master or senior boy had bequeathed a heady 'well done!' for some ball well placed, or tape broken. A kind of consolation prize for a life marked little by adventure and high achievement.

He tried to remember if he had cancelled the standing order at the bank for the sailing club subscription. He was sorry that episode was over. Not that he had fitted easily into the club's hearty extroversion, any more than he had enjoyed school. He had joined only because it was part of the package when his boredom with coastal pottering had laid him open to being talked into weekly, organized racing.

Yet he had had to confess to feeling some pleasure in the degree to which he had been accepted in the club. Not that he was fooling himself. The acceptance was because he was a good helmsmen, not because he was the clubby type. His pigeonhole had been comfortably, tacitly agreed. He was an introvert with extrovert leanings – a thin man with a fat man trying to get out.

He despised the schoolboy standards that judge people by their sporting prowess, but he was weak enough to enjoy being well thought of by those with whom he had little in common, even if their approval was based on nothing much more than his ability to beat them to the finishing line. It was as near as he had ever been to 'fitting in with the herd'. Rebecca had told him more often than he welcomed that it had done him a world of good to make the effort to fit in with the sailing fraternity.

He hoped he had played it the right way with Rebecca – or as right as was possible in the circumstances. He was glad the period of deceit was over. He had disliked the daily living of a lie. But, his decision made, it had seemed the only, certainly the kindest, solution.

No part of the past few weeks had been easy. Orderly, he had planned the voyage down to the smallest detail, but the problems had been many, as often psychological as material. It had been easier once he accepted the necessity to plan for others' concept of his intentions rather than for his own.

But he abhorred waste. He suffered from an instinct for economy strange, almost inimical, to a welfare-state generation whose own youth had not known the Second World War when coupons and rationing built into the civilian mentality a respect for the correct proportions of need. It was a respect that Rebecca had not often bothered to distinguish for their children from meanness.

Well, stingy he had never been, though it had certainly gone against the grain to provision the yacht for three months. But it had been essential to go through the motions that fitted his declared intention. To have set sail for the West Indies with little more than a picnic would have convinced no-one, not even someone as ignorant of sailing matters as Rebecca.

'Barbados seems an awful long way away,' she had said. 'It takes hours even in an aeroplane.'

'The thought of reaching it in a Vertue brings it nearer,' he had replied.

When he bought 'Patience' he had not bargained for the change in his fortunes as a writer, but the pattern had seemed to clarify with her acquisition, almost as though – absurd thought – she was a predestined piece in a jig-saw puzzle.

'Well, I suppose it's all for the best,' Rebecca had said.

It had meant weeks of selling it to himself as much as to her. He tried to keep it light.

'The menopause is a great time for breaking old patterns.'

'But *everything* seems to be changing. The children leaving home; the garden getting out of hand; the new boat...'

'It isn't all that new. If I'd known how the books were going to fall off I'd have put the money to better use. Thank goodness I fixed that life policy when I did.'

'You deserved the boat. You've worked hard. Sailing does you good; it takes you out of yourself.'

'Let's hope the longest trip of all brings commensurate benefits.'

He smiled now, as he had smiled then, at the absurd irony of the remark.

'Of course it will. In all that lovely sun, eating fruit and listening to your tapes, you'll write a masterpiece.'

Like the typewriter, the tapes had been a necessary part of the deception. But even at that moment, feeling guilt, he had also been irritated by Rebecca's unvoiced assumption that the little matter of crossing several thousand miles of treacherous water single-handed in a small yacht was incidental. He told himself that if his plans had matched her assumption he would have been even more put out; as it was, her lack of imagination was something to be thankful for.

Yet he had failed to resist the retort that was pointless and better left unsaid.

'I wish I had your confidence in my ability to cross the Atlantic.'

'I've not much choice but to assume you know what you're doing. I can't stop you.'

'Would you want to?'

'Not if it's what you want to do.'

'The options are limited. You have never exactly missed me when we have separated.'

'Honestly, Matthew, as someone who worships reason and self-control, why do you so often bring things down to an emotional challenge? Do you want me to make a scene and try to keep you from going?'

'That sounds like the rationalization of a lack of feeling.'

'Oh, how childish you can be! One minute you demand icy

reason, the next the kind of emotional possessiveness you say your mother drowned you in. She was right. You were a late developer and should have married in middle life, if at all.'

It had been his mother's almost last-breath comment on his deficiencies. Both she and her son had known, but on that final occasion had not again argued out, that it was another way of saying that his original sin was in not staying by her side, preferring to allow the world to pity or despise her as a woman abandoned by both husband and son.

'Don't let's start on mothers. Let's just accept that there is nothing to keep me here. Whatever happens to me, you and the children will be no worse off.'

'That sounds like self-pity again.'

'It's an admission. I have accepted that I lack the background that should have fitted me for the domestic roles. The failure has largely been mine. I've never communicated properly with you or the children. I wish I had. In all honesty, I can't say that your skill at turning every disagreement into evidence for my child-jury that I'm unkind and unreasonable has exactly helped...'

'Please, Matthew, try not to be honest just for once...'

'Look, I know I have been unreasonable at times. But don't you see that children cannot discriminate between the provocations, can't disentangle the chickens from the eggs? That's what has hurt.'

'It's pointless to rehash it.'

'Everything is pointless, which is why I'm leaving.'

'You make it sound very final.'

'I don't cross the Atlantic single-handed with any regularity.'

'All right, then, don't cross it. I don't want you to. Will that satisfy you?'

It had taken effort to alter his mood to one compatible with the fact that he had no intention of crossing the Atlantic. The idiocy of a situation in which he found himself resenting Rebecca's reactions to a non-existent future event had become an additional reason for speeding his departure.

Now that that moment had arrived, now that real physical distance was opening up between them, allowing no further quibble or accusation, he was forced into objectivity. It was Day One. There could be no turning back. If he could not resist churning it over, it had better stand up.

For a few minutes he succeeded in clearing his mind of the past, concentrating on the process of sailing; on the familiar landmarks; on the line of moored boats in the Emsworth channel; on Thorney Island's deserted hangars. But the pull was too strong.

He had been touched, slightly disturbed, by Rebecca's concern the night before. Their relationship had been for so long, at best, one of tolerant if superficial friendship that he had neither expected, nor in the circumstances entirely welcomed, her sudden almost nagging injunctions to take precautions against all those little and larger dangers that, more usually, only one truly in love, or loving, fears for another.

By morning, however, she had regained her familiar calm. When at his suggestion she had driven away from the jetty in the chilly dawn, leaving him to stow, rig and leave his mooring without the anti-climax of receding farewells, he hoped that her detachment was as genuine as it had appeared. Only a part of him - a very small and best-forgotten part - had looked for any sign that she might have driven away with indifference. But then why should she? Their earlier separations, as he had pointed out, had brought mutual relief. He had given her no reason to see this one any differently. Her need for him - such as it had ever been - was past. It was easier to part in cool friendship.

But he again fell to the task of self-conviction, mulling over his long-held supposition that it was his uselessness to Rebecca and - now that they had grown up - to the children which sealed but was not solely responsible for his determination to make the voyage. Although below-averagely ambitious in the sense of making a fortune or collecting the symbols and offices of status, he was a perfectionist in his way. What he did he wished to do well or not at all. When he had found through his yacht-racing that he possessed 'touch', that almost indefinable quality of the good helmsman, he had brought it as near to perfection as its mysterious elusiveness and his own limitations allowed. When he sensed - and, indeed, had often enough been told - that he had lost touch as a husband and father, he weighed up the case for continuing to offer second best to those he had loved as best he knew how.

His love for his children, if not articulate in their more recent years, was at least responsible. He had wanted for them the right mental and physical equipment to cope with an ugly world. But his feelings had contained an element of fear which might not have blurred his certainties about the nuts and bolts of their upbringing had his knowledge of parental attitudes been drawn from more stable experience in his own family background. If his feelings for Rebecca, lacking this element of fear, were less emotionally charged, they were out-distanced by a now forlorn hope of some degree of mental companionship. He had only recently fully and regretfully accepted that what he felt for her could not fairly be judged without taking into account that her responses to life's provocations – of which he, all right, was certainly one! – had less to do with the tranquillity of still waters running deep than with the unquestioning complacency of a puddle.

Which was not – as she had pointed out with some feeling at the end of a recent row – a very kind way of putting it. It had been a wearisomely familiar argument and it had petered out in its usual way, he charging her with lack of heart, she countering that his reverence for reason should make him well satisfied with a relationship lacking warmth.

He could see she had a point, and others would soon be telling her so more joyfully than ever. But all for which he could rightly be blamed only underlined his ability to make one monumental cock-up after another. Now, of course, he was about to be blamed for leaving Rebecca: 'Why?' they would be asking each other at the cocktail parties she could never say 'no' to, yet disliked giving, 'She's such an inoffensive woman. Poor Rebecca!'

And they would be right. There was no really bad thing about her. He was leaving her for what she wasn't rather than for what she was. He was leaving her because she was independent of him in any essential sense; because neither she nor the children needed him; and for the other reasons...

When the children were small he could never have imagined the day when their brief stays would be like the visits of near-strangers. He knew, of course, that they, like Rebecca, had cared for him in that dependent way that is the child's first excursion into love. By whatever means he might pass out of their lives, some regret must result. But their emotional centre was no longer their parents' home; that had long been little more to them than an occasional hotel with mum-comforts. Judy, after a childless first marriage she had appeared wilfully to abandon despite or even because of its material security, seemed settled at last. Although still without children, she seemed content with a husband whose difficulty in holding down a job for longer than three weeks had led to their joining some kind of commune – Matthew had never quite understood its aims and was not sure he wanted to – that was experimenting in the self-sufficient life between Cardigan and Carmarthen. Mary, more timid and conventional, and devoted to the handicapped children she was employed to look after, was implacably determined to marry a trainee accountant whose twenty-two sheltered years in suburbia had implanted a rigidity of outlook which, although not lacking a healthy disregard for parental orthodoxies, promised history's inevitable repetition.

But while flattering himself that some mild affection remained for 'poor old dad', he knew that his daughters' disinterest in himself and his work had long denied mileage to any conversation not centred wholly on themselves.

'They're finding their feet,' Rebecca had said. 'It's an egoistic time of life.'

'Egoism my arse. Egoism produces ambition, purpose, forward planning. They simply deaden their minds day in day out with this god-awful "pop". They're like zombies.'

'You were probably just as self-obsessed at their age.'

In fairly frequent moments of trying to be scrupulously fair and objective, he had considered this possibility unprompted, always concluding that the present was unique for the ruthless onslaught of commercial pressures dedicated to brain-washing an entire generation to accept and idolize the fifth rate.

'I should have played with them more when they were small. I failed to communicate. We let a vacuum develop and it was filled by the junk values being peddled to their peer group.'

'You're sounding like a "pop" sociologist. The culture of the day is stronger than we are.'

'Culture! What kind of equipment for the real things of life is provided by today's *mores*? No, we should have seen the way things were going. I blame myself – both of us. We've failed them and they are strangers, hooked to the transient and second rate.'

'You do exaggerate so,' Rebecca had said. 'They'll come through.'

'As what? People even less able than we to make a go of things?'

'Just people, in their own right.'

'Do stop thinking in clichés! Why not admit you simply don't care enough about them? As long as you have their emotional loyalty, to obtain which you'll go...'

'Don't start on that again, Matthew, please.'

'You know it's true. Look how you allowed Mary to run around in mid-winter in absurdly inadequate clothing rather than lose popularity by nagging. Result? Pleurisy. Prognosis? Permanent susceptibility.'

'What did *you* do to make her dress more warmly?'

'What could I do? They ignore me as implacably as you do. You forced me to cut off from them emotionally and to leave you to cope with them. If a skinny fifteen-year-old had convinced herself that anything bulkier than a layer of denim would expose to an agog and contemptuous world a body of gross proportions, what the hell use would it have been for me to reason or bawl for a more self-protective instinct?'

Would he have had more patience with, and time for, the family if, long before Simon's warning shot, there had not been the nagging fear that his publisher's half-yearly royalty statements were less a reflection of the difficulties of selling 'intelligent' fiction than evidence of his own slowing down, loss of elasticity, the increasing effort needed to approach his typewriter with that freshness and enthusiasm he had once known? He could almost not remember the time when the daily fund of ebullient confidence in a bottomless well of creativity was something he took for granted...

The ache in his groin had begun to throb. Sweat came to his forehead and cooled there. How ill was he? You couldn't believe doctors. Unless you turned up with something as unmistakeable as a broken neck they would either kid you along or give you a ticket for the consultants' bandwagon; and then God help you, because the quacks wouldn't until they had extracted the last extractable penny.

He drew a deep breath and shook his head impatiently, loathing his self-obsession but seeing no escape from the squirrel-wheel that had replaced a once fertile brain.

'Patience' was approaching the Northeast Winner buoy, at which point he would bring her about and sail on a close starboard reach out of the harbour. Beyond, the Isle of Wight lay two-dimensional in the haze which clung to its flanks, a vast Moby Dick silhouetted against the grey sky. The Nab Tower's visibility proved that the sea mist was dispersing. With luck the wind would fill in more positively and give him quick passage through the Solent. A final sail through its familiar waters had been part of the plan, but there was no case for dallying...

Not that all the memories were bad. There had been a time - with career ascendant, the children small - when they functioned as a family to a degree that others judged as highly successful. One of the glossies had allotted three pages to evidence of their enjoyment of each other's company from breakfast through an untypically extroverted day into an evening devoted with almost cloying cosiness and heightened reaction to reading aloud, Scrabble, and cocoa before bed. At the time it was not so far off the mark. The husband-and-father role was at its least resented. He looked back to those years with the nearest he could come to affectionate nostalgia. It was good to have been able, if only briefly, to help things to come right for them all. If only...

'Oh, come *on*!'

He said it aloud, impatient with self-pity, with the hypnotic draw of the past, and with fear of the dangers of reflection and of time's ability to soften memory and weaken resolution. But he was still within home's magnetic field.

He remembered their agreement to separate and how he, absurdly, had gone to their cottage in Wales. The story for the children and friends had been that he had to write a book needing complete freedom from domestic distraction. Only he and Rebecca knew their plan to make it a stage towards divorce; a device to get the children accustomed to his absence. But he was writing nothing demanding domestic peace because in fact he wrote best when in constant danger, even hope, of congenial interruption. Isolation and a blank sheet of paper were hurdles rather than spurs. And Rebecca, for whom radical change had always been anathema, enjoyed the separation no more than he did. She found it absurd that someone modestly competent to deal with fuses, tap washers, recalcitrant equipment, unopenable jars, and the other minor irritations of modern life, should be sitting two hundred miles away in an unheated hut (it was little more) loathing (as she rightly guessed) the creative process.

So they had come together again within three weeks, agreeing to make the best of things until some more realistic alternative presented itself. 'The children missed you, too,' Rebecca had said.

But although their separation had led to nothing more dramatic than a rather sheepish reunion, the time spent in Wales cemented his certainty that it was neither in Rebecca's interest nor in his own to see through the rest of their lives moving the pieces around in a state of joyless compromise. He thought of what might be best for Rebecca more often than he suspected she realized, with responsibility if no great depth of affection. There was twelve years between them. If they stayed together she would almost certainly find herself a widow at a time of life when the chance to remarry was slim.

So he encouraged her to develop some interest outside the home, to prepare her to fill the void she might encounter in later life. He was agreeably surprised that, despite her lack of an outgoing temperament, she enjoyed from the outset her three-day week in the dress-shop – he could not come to terms with 'boutique', which anyway seemed a short-lived phenomenon catering for women whose whims were predictable only for the insanity of their over-night changes in taste – and when after three months the Crawfords offered her a full working partnership, a big problem seemed to have been solved.

Although at first Rebecca had qualms of conscience about being away from home so much, he was content with a mid-day meal of soup or bread and cheese, preferring it to the often unnecessarily large lunches Rebecca had prepared when having little else to do. But although he enjoyed the consequent benefit of a clearer mind and a reduced urge to take a nap in the afternoons, the change brought no real stimulus to his writing. Sitting by himself at the typewriter in a Sussex village was only marginally more inspiring than doing so on the side of a Welsh hill...

He guessed he would not be shot of mental meandering until he had sailed 'Patience' out of waters so full of associations. They were beyond the harbour's mouth now, the yacht's movement subtly more lively in the slight swell over the bar. He felt the awakening of that barely definable blend of anticipation and slight unease which even experienced long-haul sailors know at the start of a voyage. His own and the vessel's responses to the challenge of deeper waters forged an empathy which seemed strangely mutual: a phenomenon which can reduce to an acceptable level the loneliness of single-handed voyaging.

The forts were clearly visible to the south west. With not long to go to high water, he had five hours of favourable tide in which to clear the Island. To enlist maximum help from the west-going current he trimmed sail for a close-hauled course into the main stream of the east Solent, hopeful of being through the forts by eleven.

He set the self-steering gear and dropped through the hatch to the small galley at the foot of the companion way. A coffee seemed overdue. On the starboard side of the cabin, opposite the gimballed primus stove and sink, a chart table replaced the locker with which 'Patience' was originally provided. Above and below the sink every inch had been utilized for storage of food and eating utensils. It had pleased him to plan maximum use of space. Because Rebecca had shown no desire to sample the unarguable miseries of a small cruising yacht built for endurance rather than comfort, he had altered and equipped her for single-handed sailing. In a craft with a water-line length of under twenty-two feet and a beam of just over seven, even a compliment of two demands a blend of temperaments few skippers can command. The vessel's five berths - two central, two for'ard where the sails, chain, spare warps and general gubbins competed for space, and a folding pipe-cot - may have looked well on the designer's plans but bore little relation to the realities of sailing life for any but a handful of masochists or the absurdly gregarious.

Not that he had made a practice of long-distance cruising. His longest trip had been to the Scilly Isles; his most adventurous, to Morlaix in Brittany. The adventure had lain in his being so long out of sight of land and coping single-handed with a rock-strewn approach, whereas he was accompanied to the Scillys by a friend whose navigational experience was considerably greater than his own. Such short journeys had taught him that in a sound craft open waters are a good deal safer than those filled by the dubious companionship of other and larger vessels; and after one hair-raising experience in fog off as prosaic if dangerously exposed a piece of coastline as that between Worthing and Brighton, he was quite ready to accept the truism that the safest waters between the Solent and the Caribbean are those lying west of the Canaries.

He made his coffee and broke into a packet of biscuits, relishing their crispness and the subtle flavour of vanilla on a palate fully ready to be tempted. Aware of how quickly in the Solent an empty sea can produce hazards, he brought both into the cockpit. The only sign of life was a cargo vessel heading up Channel. She would be two or three miles away when she crossed his bows.

He had forgotten the sugar. He returned to the cabin for the canister above the galley. It was nearly empty, so he went for'ard to the forecastle to find the Tupperware box in which Rebecca had provided six packets. It was poorly stowed on sail-bags whose smooth nylon surface would soon have rejected the box in a heavy sea. He rearranged the sail-bags, below which was a special pack he had assembled and stowed a week earlier. It was wrapped in a piece of sailcloth and several layers of plastic sheeting. He removed these carefully. Inside were plastic storage jars labelled for foods he might have been thought to need in small quantity, such as curry and dried peppers. He took up the jar labelled 'Almonds', unscrewed the lid, and shook the nuts on to the sailcloth. There were not many. An inch below the top of the jar, which was of black opaque glass, was a circle of stiff card. He removed this, then groped with two fingers in the polystyrene chips which filled the rest of the container. Carefully he took out the small black-capped bottle which was embedded in the chips. As he had no reason to doubt, it still held in perfect condition some forty sausage-shaped tablets; twice as many as he would need. Satisfied, he put the bottle back, making sure it was completely surrounded by the protective insulation, then he replaced the card and the almonds and screwed the lid home tightly before rewrapping the pack with great care to make it waterproof.

His coffee, when he returned to the cockpit, was just the right temperature for drinking.

5

CLEAR of The Needles, he set a course of 250° to keep 'Patience' well clear of Portland Bill. Even before he was through the forts the wind had obligingly backed and freshened, demanding a two-roll reef in the mainsail and giving an invigorating beam reach through waters whose memories were all pleasing. The only distraction had been the shattering shindy of a hovercraft out of Ryde and a tanker of a size to put all life-loving small-boat sailors in mind of the Collision Regulations' delicate phrase 'a vessel constrained by her draught'. The brutes needed a mile or more of water in which to slow down.

The wind, dropping as suddenly as it had arrived, left 'Patience' wallowing in an uncomfortable swell three miles south-west of the Island, a warning that the days to follow would put him through the gamut of those fears and frustrations which all conditions from foggy calms to full gales bring to a single-hander determined to cross the Channel's shipping lanes in an engineless vessel.

He put in for the night at Studland Bay – not once, but twice, victim of the wind's failure to give him the distance needed to clear the dangers of a drift towards The Needles to the east and the hazards of Portland Bill to the west. On the first occasion he quite enjoyed the memories the Bay held for him, and as he furled the mainsail in the fading light he thought about Rebecca and guessed she would be leaving home for her yoga class at just about that time. He hoped she would remember to put the cat out. Ever since the vet's injections the landing had become Tinkle's first choice for a loo when the house was empty. And then he had gone below for a paraffin lamp to hang in the shrouds, recalling Judy's view that his distaste for engines and orthodox power sources was a sign that there was hope for him yet.

'I expect,' she had conjectured modestly since joining the commune, where much emphasis was laid on alternative energy resources and minimal technology, 'it's a streak that waited to take more purposive shape in me.'

And he had thought of her fondly, for although her abstract and even mystical notions were at odds with his humanism, he was touched by her idealism if not by her choice of husband. He had always felt closer to Judy, if only because as his first wife's child she seemed to need him more than Mary who took the bulk of Rebecca's small store of affection. If his first marriage had not been a disaster of such magnitude that to that day he could scarcely bear to recall its details, he would probably have lacked the determination to stick it out with Rebecca. Maybe it would have been better if he hadn't...

On that first evening he prepared a meal, filling the cabin with the smell of food and the taped comfort of Haydn. He was surprised to find in a locker a packet of his favourite mints. When he had eaten and washed up he read for a while and began to wonder to what extent his loner temperament had contributed to the decline in interest in his books; the toadying of the rising *literati*, and the media's personality cult, were factors he had never come to terms with. Well, it was a hard world and maybe he had not been tough and egotistical enough to beat it. The manipulation of others was all very well for those cheerful extroverts who enjoyed such procedures, but it was not his scene. Doubtless it all went back to schooldays when his main aim had been to go as unnoticed as possible by both masters and boys...

Alone and on the water it had always seemed easier to view things in balance. He wondered if that was why he had chosen to bring it to a close with a voyage. He guessed it would be thought a dull, negative, lonely way of going about it. But then, if anything, what he had become was a dull man; hence, perhaps, his family's attitude to him. It is one thing to be dull, another to be conspicuously so. Possibly his working from home had been a major error. Looking at it through their eyes, his being there continually had meant that the children had seen more of him than if he had gone out to some office every day. Out at anything so important-sounding as The Office, doing mysterious and unguessable things connected with the remote ritual of Earning a Living, his absence would have been excusable, unavoidable. Fathers cannot play or frivolously communicate when at The Office. But constantly within earshot, sitting silently at a desk, sometimes to be seen wasting play-potential hours gazing aimlessly out of the window, there surely was opportunity being lost, communication deliberately avoided, love withheld.

The rest of that first evening had passed pleasantly enough. Radio Three was unbending a little with a Tchaikovsky programme, offering background rather than challenge. He cleaned the sink and chart table with a J-cloth, hanging it on the minute washing line above the galley, and was pleased to realize it was already nine o'clock and that he could soon turn in on schedule.

But his thoughts returned to Rebecca and he wondered what she was doing. At this point in the evening, since the children had gone their ways, their before-bed ritual had been backgammon. A silly game, ninety per cent chance, but as much as either had wanted so near to sleep. He remembered there had been a magnetized pocket set on board in the early days of his ownership when Rebecca had done her best to be persuaded that she might enjoy the occasional sail. He searched, finding it lodged at the back of a locker, adhered to a child's plastic lifejacket that was stiff and sticky with disuse. He set it up and played against himself until it was ten o'clock precisely.

Twenty-four hours later, after hours of drifting followed by an on-the-nose gale, he was back in the Bay. His enforced return plunged him in despair, prompting irrational accusations at a Fate determined to thwart even his urge for self-extinction. Normally, sailing time passed quickly and he had not resented changes of plan. The discipline of having to be home for dinner, for some engagement, or merely for the tyranny of his typewriter, was acceptable, even welcome. Now, with no-one expecting anything of him, on an open-ended contract with sea and sky, he wanted only to be on his way. To be once again sheltering supinely in Studland Bay was a bitter and frustrating interruption of a plan he felt entitled to see go his way.

So he turned in early, determined to be away at first light, and he kept to this plan although by dawn the wind's ferocity proved that the responsible course was to stay put. He left the bay under his smallest foresail, then came up into the screaming wind and raised a reefed mainsail before thrashing south through the pounding seas in the teeth of a near gale.

As 'Patience' bucked and butted through the breaking seas, exhilaration replaced a fear that had been rooted less in concern for life and limb than in his plans being cheated. Death must be on his own terms. To botch the whole thing would be the worst fate of all. He dreaded the anti-climax of having to give up; the inglorious celebration of being towed into port, or winched by a helicopter, or floated on to some beach in his absurd canvas coracle. If something like that happened he knew he would never regain the confidence to re-plan a solution; not, anyway, one meeting so many of the requirements for ending an affair in which he had lost the interest that is sustained only by expectation.

For an affair was how he had come to view his life; an affair with the experiment of existence; an existence that had convinced him of mankind's temporality. Surveying the natural order he had found no justification for seeking comfort from theories of humanity's special place in the scheme of things. With Thomas Hobbes, he saw life for man, as for the other animals, as nasty, brutish and short. For many, an existence so dominated by material problems that the potentialities in human life had no chance of realization; for the allegedly more civilized, hopes and energies confounded by the multiplicity of choice, the incompetence and tyranny of society's professionals and alleged experts, the obstructivism and apathy of bureaucracies, officialdom and the whole top-heavy superstructure of States welfare and dictatorial. The sheer childishness and pettiness of what he had once assumed was an adult world irritated and tired him. In youth he had noted and tried to emulate the adult characteristics in his contemporaries. In middle age he saw in grown men and women more of the child than of what should pass for the adult. The world had become puerile.

It was not how he had once felt, and Rebecca herself had accused him of inconsistency and weakness of purpose. In honest moments he had faced, though only to himself, that his personal problems had proved too strong for him and may have distorted his wider vision. By now he had done his sums, weighed the pros and cons, and like Hobbes faced that the time had come to take his last voyage, his 'great leap in the dark'. If only he could now be allowed to get on with it!

The wind moderated and he felt hungry, the more so for having skipped breakfast. He ate two massive slices of bread, baked by Rebecca and still fresh, and with them beef and liberally-applied mustard. Then he looked out the spinning tackle he kept in a cockpit locker and fed the line over the yacht's transom, watching the spinner recede and sink, winking as it began to revolve in the water's grip. He caught a sizeable mackerel almost at once. When he had worked the hook out of its mouth and it lay on the teak floor of the cockpit, he saw it was an inch longer than his boot. The light played on its wet scales, lending shimmering emphasis to the variety and vividness of its fading hues, and to the creature's still energetic will to live.

The vitality in its glazing eyes subsided as it drowned in the thin air. He tossed it into the small sink at the foot of the companionway, then let the spinner out over the transom again in case he was sailing over a shoal of fish. He could hear the mackerel thumping in the dry plastic bowl, at first with vigour, then more weakly and less often as its gasps pumped no life-giving fluid through its gills.

The wind dropped still more until the late afternoon was dimmed by a leaden sky which produced a steady, dispiriting drizzle. The sea's surface became oily and malevolent, its swell producing a rhythmic, hopeless slap from the inert mainsail as the boom responded to each slow lurch of the drifting vessel. The incessant rain sizzled softly on to coachroof and deck, reducing visibility to a level spelling real danger of his being run down. Not that this bothered him any longer; he was beyond caring.

He told himself he had been a fool to choose this way out. There had been an alternative plan. He had even selected the spot, in late Spring, when walking a familiar area on the Downs. A warm hollow on the southern edge of a stand of beech, oak and yew, still carpeted in crisp brown leaves trapped by gnarled, mossed roots on a bank thrown up to mark some ancient boundary. Screened by undergrowth and distance from the nearest footpath a hundred yards to the north, it would have done admirably, off the route even of gamekeepers and foresters. Tablets, a half-bottle of gin, 'The Pastoral' on tape, and a comatose farewell to the far-off, sun-pathed sea over a waving foreground of poppies and heartsease bordering last year's cornfield...

But something inside him had opted for an exit involving more challenge. It had seemed too easy - to settle in the warm sun, to die in idle langour among the fine grasses and the exquisite patches of herb robert whose delicate pink flower and classical foliage he sought each Spring above any woodland plant. Besides - and such considerations counted - it would have meant the distress of search and identification for Rebecca; morbid details, at least, for the children's ears; and a tedious exercise via steep fields and undergrowth for the recovery party. Added to which - to take the practical view - the pollen count would probably have made a misery of those final hours; only sailing guaranteed allergy-free action...

Sick of inactivity in the now humid cabin, he went on deck, closing the hatch after him. He stood before the mast, his legs braced to counter the movement from the swell. The cloud layer was so thick and the rain so heavy that there was no evidence except from the compass of the direction in which the yacht was pointing. The silence was absolute except for the hiss of the rain. He felt suddenly, wretchedly lonely; a new experience to someone normally content to be alone.

He raised his face to the sky so that the rain forced his eyes to close as under a shower. A stomach-pounding emptiness had settled in him; a desolation of the spirit more absolute than he had known before. The frustration of his immediate circumstances gripped heart and mind. His body ached for action and resolution. If his eyes contributed their pittance to the weather, it was not through self-pity so much as an almost unbearable desire to lose himself in that physical, purposive activity the elements denied him. The negativity of the conclusion to that purpose was irrelevant. His urge for involvement was paramount. Nothing mattered but to be allowed to complete his mission. Even if he could have been sure of being left alone for long enough, then and there, for the tablets to take his body beyond the point of no return, he would not have swallowed them. He had the right to choose...

The rain beating on to his face refreshed him, stinging his eyelids and running down his body beneath his shirt. He leaned straight-legged against the mast, grasping it behind his back with both hands and feeling himself one with the vessel in its gentle rocking. Although the frustration and futility had drained him so that he felt as empty as the sea, a calm that was almost a state of peace entered him, akin to that of a child who senses he can defy authority no further and must give in. For the moment the elements had won. In the short term, he gave them best.

His mind no longer fighting events, the absurdity of his situation struck home. There entered his mind a line from the poet whose work his aunt - a woman as fiercely committed to the notion of some higher power as his mother had been to the sterner realities of raising an only son to appreciate the need for intellectual integrity and the comforts of rationalism - had often quoted to him. His mother had done little to encourage enjoyment of her sister's fantasies, but passages from Swinburne's poem had stayed in his mind.

He began to laugh: at his idiotic helplessness in a situation in which neither technology nor the elements could be manipulated by his will; at the irony of this stage in his life when - 'from hope and fear set free' - he was powerless to get nearer the logical conclusion to his certainty of his future's futility. The rain ran down his bald high forehead and cheeks and into his mouth, and he laughed the more at the ridiculous picture he must present of a sodden middle-aged man clinging to a swaying mast and staring sightlessly at a leaden sky, roaring with inappropriate laughter.

Then as though a bored or impatient hand had turned some celestial tap, the downpour turned into a soft caress of spray. Then this ceased completely and from behind his lids he sensed a lightening of the sky. When he opened his eyes he saw to the west a thin hard line of blue above the low profile of the land, and over his head the clouds were higher and thinner. In the same moment his face was touched by a hesitant swirl of damp air, as gentle as a mother's hand on the forehead of a fretful child.

Shivering with relief and cold he went stiffly but quickly back to the cockpit to trim the sails and tiller and bring the yacht back on to her right heading with the least possible wastage of the promised breeze.

The blue band on the horizon widened, allowing the late afternoon sun to sweep the rain-grey sea on which ripples now vied for transformation into busy wavelets. As the yacht gathered speed through the suddenly sparkling water, her helmsman's earlier despair turned into a mood of exaggerated joy. He shouted into the strengthening breeze the boisterous lines of verses that would have found small favour with his aunt. He felt as he had felt as a boy, released from school at the end of term.

From then on his moods changed often, but never to such despair as he had felt when before the mast on that lifeless, rolling sea. He slept and ate and mused and played tapes, and on the first evening of escape from Studland Bay he saw low on the horizon to the north east a flashing light which confirmed his successful distancing from land. His sense of persecution had passed. He donned another jumper and his oil skins and sat on the port locker in the cockpit, determined to stare out the winking light that tried to draw his mind back to land.

But the light's mesmeric regularity cast its spell. His mind followed a dozen different paths, straying from place to place and person to person without much connecting link other than being centred on home and family. With a slight feeling of guilt he realized he was missing the company of their dog. An amiable Labrador bitch with an indiscriminate love of human beings, she often sailed with him. She had died recently, peacefully enough in old age, but it had saddened them all, himself most acutely. He had found her as a pup, nearly full grown, lying injured by the side of the road, ignored by the passing motorists. He had moved her on to the grass verge and traced a vet who lived nearby. The vet had come at once and tended the animal, and as he had felt and soothed the bruised body he recounted a stream of examples of the abandonments, ignorance and callous brutality he met with daily in his work. Matthew remembered his surprise at the passion in the vet's voice when he had said: 'Man must be to the animals what the devil was once to us, yet the poor brutes still love and trust us.'

The bitch would have been company for Rebecca. But although upset by her death, he was glad this had come before lameness and the other curses of old age had kept it an idle bundle of mute misery in the basket by the kitchen Aga. They had been through all that with the spaniel he had had before marriage. In a properly ordered world it was best for all things to die within their term.

He had never felt this more strongly than in the last years of his father's life. Stephen Braine, though of no great age, had lived beyond his own or anyone else's desiring. It had been a wretchedly protracted end, the too-familiar struggle of a strong mind in a failing body kept gratuitously alive by the technological panoply of a Nanny State incapable of imagining a fate worse than the obliteration of ego.

When Stephen Braine had worked out the prognosis for his disease, he had prayed for its ravages to be swift; he was less resistant than his son to religious consolation. His prayers had been conspicuously ignored. The disease roamed aimlessly, brutally, through his body, treated but undeterred by surgery, radiation and drugs at the whim and conviction of those whose compassion had been moulded by tradition and the law to the view that hope in pain was preferable to a dignified termination.

The physical pain had been less exacting than the suffering of his family. It had been this, not the final visible location of the disease in his groin, that had decided him that enough was enough.

For his son – in the way of children, a little inclined to take parental immortality for granted – the charade of his father's end forged an as yet unformulated resolve to cheat fate of a repeat performance. Like an untended plant growing in his brain, a determination had settled in him to avoid imposing on himself or on others a drawn-out terminal illness. Youth prompted few conscious reminders of this decision, but as the twinges and limitations of middle age brought their whispers of life's brevity, a quick departure when still possessed of his faculties became his long-term goal.

His mother had died more recently in what the ward-visiting clergyman had called God's good time. Her death only strengthened his decision to avoid at any cost being saddled with an unwanted body tormented by the plagues of approaching senility, bereft of choice, dependent upon the steely pity of the geriatric ward. On the day she died he pocketed the bottle of sleeping tablets that had been left on her bedside table at home when the doctor had decreed that only hospital could give her the terminal nursing she needed. From that moment on his determination to order the timing and circumstances of his own departure had been a straightforward matter of advance planning.

He dozed, drifting into a muddled argument with Rebecca and Judy in a snack bar he had entered en route for his retreat in Wales. The argument was vaguely about his parental qualities, though Judy was also going on at him about his lack of what she termed an all-embracing environmental concern, accusing him of complacency, of smug acceptance of man's eventual triumph over nature and – though at her age it was not how she had expressed it – others' quaint, irrational notions of destiny or purpose beyond removal of the rough edges of those material realities identified by the senses. She was waving some book at him and quoting from Shaw the question put to Broadbent by Keegan: 'You feel at home in the world then?' and Broadbent's 'Of course. Don't you?' And he was about to accuse her of naivety, of lifting words from their context, when the dream was shattered by a rogue wave which broke on the yacht's quarter and dashed spray into his face, jerking his head back painfully.

He turned on the radio, determined to stave off sleep until he had taken his last farewell of England. The winking light was further astern, lower on the dark horizon, though not yet eclipsed by it. The eastern sky held pockets of light.

He found some programme in English and tried to concentrate on it. It was a mishmash of the day's obsessions; babble about the F.T. Index, G.N.P., a nervous dollar and Iranian 'crude'; a footballer traded for many times the value in gold of his body weight; a moronic youth whose record of maiming and slaughter seemed to have been prompted by nothing but a desire to attract the oohs and aahs of television audiences thought to be insatiable for evidence of the lowest potentialities of their species; the latest example of that resentful inertia and unproductive militancy so idiotically known as industrial action; the threat and promise of the silicon chip. Greed, hate, triviality, exploitation, envy, inflexibility, fear. Media fodder of achingly wearisome predictability.

Irritated by the demand for his attention to matters no longer of relevance, he tuned through a multitude of French and German voices and found another British station. The programme was vaguely religious, though so ecumenical as to be free of any sectarian identity. A young woman with a strong Birmingham accent was enthusing about a pop singer – long acclaimed, she insisted, as The Prophet of the Sixties – who had recently felt impelled to 'get into the Christian experience' after a long absence from the microphone. She played snatches from his latest discs, one centred on the need for commitment, another on a second coming, though without clarifying the nature of the commitment or whose second coming was being celebrated. The singer's voice was high, nasal and totally unmusical, somehow reminiscent of an emasculated ferret. It could have belonged to either sex of any age, or might have been created electronically. The girl's commentary welcomed reverently the Prophet's entry into what she called his spiritual maturity. He switched off, confident that whatever benevolent Power had made him a humanist would, through religious broadcasting, do the same for others. Now that even the more poetic passages from the Bible had to be read in modern English by unisex voices nurtured in South Shields, he wondered why the Beeb any longer kept up the pretence.

It was a train of thought that had frequently led to verbal conflict with Judy. He was the first to agree that the religious experience was showing no signs of falling off. He merely queried the validity of its many forms. The search for self-awareness had been inflated into a cult showing every sign of burgeoning into a full-scale religious substitute. Hedonism had become almost a state of piety; the neo-epicurean era had arrived.

'You're getting it all muddled up, daddy,' Judy had insisted when they had last battled it out. 'You just don't seem to see that all the evils of the affluent society and consumerism and so forth are the direct result of worshipping materialism and believing that human beings can subdue nature and come up with all the answers unaided.'

'Unaided? What does that imply?'

'That the human mind alone is not capable of making sense of things.'

'There you go again. You are suggesting the existence of some higher form of mind; some notion of an outside controlling force; a God.'

'Daddy, you *know* I don't believe in an old man in a beard any more than you do. "God" is just, well, a convenience term. All I'm saying is we need to be less arrogant; we should accept... well, you know, that there just could be something greater than ourselves. *I* feel we must learn to love and co-exist with our surroundings, not exploit and conquer everything. Until then we're not going to see things straight or be really happy.'

'But look at the kind of people you claim represent such views! Freaks, drop-outs, all of them "into" crazy religions and drugs.'

'Oh, daddy, you can be so dense! That lot are as hooked by the capitalist system as your economists and industrialists and the rest. You've never even met the people who are really getting on with it.'

'On with what?'

'With New Age living.'

'Encounter sessions, group therapy, sexual liberation, rights without obligations, nihilistic anarchy posing as political maturity, the cult of the personality?'

'You see? You're just mixing up a lot of jargon and modern terms you only half understand and making a kind of poultice to slap on to something you don't really want to face, to understand.'

'I react to what I see. Your generation seems obsessed with self, avid for 'happenings', forever chasing a shallow fulfilment. Where's the global concern?'

'Oh, *daddy!*'

At this stage in such arguments Judy's voice used to turn into a frustrated squeak. Latterly she had shown more control and would either drop the subject without loss of temper or argue it out with him until deadlock was admitted on both sides. He guessed that there was nothing to be done about the generation gap, so impossibly widened by the special and sadly divisive relationship between parent and child.

Yet his daughter's patent sincerity both touched and troubled him. It worried him that she seemed to be caught up in a process rooted entirely in self-absorption and lacking that confidence in mankind's ultimate potentiality that was the most hopeful aspect of a mature humanism. Judy had agreed that they were both idealistic in their separate ways, but that his judgment of her generation was based on the media's distorted and one-sided obsessions. It was true that both he and Rebecca had fallen into the easy relaxation of goggle-boxing, as Judy called it, and nothing was to be had from that source that suggested the existence of the 'New Age' thinking that Judy insisted was growing so rapidly.

Wishing to be honest with himself and with her, he had asked himself whether he really wanted to make the effort to understand the philosophy and goals of Judy's New Age people. There was so much going on that the task of sorting out the gold from the dross seemed insurmountable. Judy was right in one thing, that the media battered the viewer with data and sense impressions, presenting so many points of view, and with such superficiality, that the net result was a jumbled vacuum of indecision, apprehension, resignation. The only specific end product he could identify was fear - fear in particular for his children, and for Judy especially now that she was tangling with abstractions about 'higher powers.' From the explosion of quasi-religious, consciousness-raising groups on the American west coast, the 'new narcissism' had devolved into a more physical obsession with the body, anything from disco halls to sex farms, and all to be taken with a po-faced reverence as though through the worship of the physical senses the great twentieth-century dream of progress was on the verge of being realized in its fullest and most desirable form. Judy had insisted that such phenomena had no place in New Age thinking, but somehow he had not been drawn to investigate the distinction, almost preferring to accept Judy's charge that he was too set in his views to want to be convinced.

He wondered if she would guess that his final voyage was - as she would surely see it - an admission of defeat. Well, in opting to join the minority who faced that, for themselves at least, the twentieth-century dream had ended, he was making a gesture which if open to the charge of conspicuous self-awareness, was at least made without harm to others. That, in this day and age of flaunted ego and frantic publicity-seeking, was at least something, and the voluntary extinction of ego was not incompatible with the humanist ideal.

But he wished he had been less critical and more understanding of what he had judged as Judy's escapist life-style. He was, after all, about to be equally – indeed, more finally – guilty of taking the easy way out. He was sorry he had not written to her before he set sail, explaining the distinctions and his motivation, but there had been the problem of timing its arrival, quite apart from the danger of it being linked with his disappearance when his body was found or assumed lost.

The wind was backing, compelling the yacht to sail close-hauled in order to retain her bearing. As it backed it freshened, heeling 'Patience' so that the receding light on the horizon could be seen only when the lift of the vessel's stern coincided with the flash. He felt a small chill across the top of his spine, though his body was warm enough under its layers of clothing. The voyage had begun.

For two more days 'Patience' butted through winds gusting force six or seven, but by evening on the second day he plotted his position as being less than sixty miles south of Falmouth; a miserable mileage from the Solent. But to be in mid-Channel and heading for the Atlantic was consoling, though his joy in escaping from Studland Bay had given way to a profound weariness born of the constant motion, lack of food, and a numbness not relieved by the varying wind's demand for changes of sail. He had not dared go below for any useful period. He remained at the tiller, dispensing with the pilot, finding some satisfaction in personal control of the boat's progress, preferring the responsibility of helming to idle, anxious wakefulness.

But mind and body have their limits. He stuck the slog into head winds through that night, dozing on the tiller, eating a little now and then to break the monotony and keep himself awake rather than from pangs of hunger. He regretted not having brought a first-aid kit, as his neck was stiff. He guessed he had jarred something when the wave had broken his dream the night before.

By morning he was sticky, dirty and haggard, every muscle stiff and aching with total physical weariness. Shipping had passed through the night, though never so near he had had to alter course. With the daylight his over-riding priority was sleep. In case the wind blew up again he reduced sail and set the pilot. Then he went below and turned in, so utterly exhausted that nothing mattered more than oblivion. He was asleep before he could zip up his sleeping bag.

6

HE woke with a start, suspicious of something wrong. For a few seconds he lay still, staring vacantly at the small inverted compass mounted over his bunk. The cabin was flooded with light. He looked at the watch he had not bothered to take from his wrist. He had been asleep for nine or ten hours. His mind not up to working out the meaning of the compass, he got stiffly to his feet, rubbing his neck gingerly, and went on deck.

The wind had moderated; the lumpy sea was empty of shipping or land. The sun's position confirmed that 'Patience', now on port tack, was sailing almost due south. At some point the wind had gone round towards the east, probably backing so as to head the yacht and put her about.

He trimmed the sails and re-set the pilot, revelling in the late afternoon sun. He had no idea for how many hours they had been on a different course, nor did he care. A massive appetite demanded appeasement. Content that the yacht was heading in the right general direction, he left her to get on with it.

Having missed breakfast, he plumped for a meal of two eggs, four rashers and as many sausages, accompanied by toast and a pot of strong coffee. Seeking a sharp knife for removing rind, he came across a box containing plasters, ointments and a selection of pills. He had never seen it before. As it included a pot of embrocation, he rubbed some into his neck. Then he noticed that the climbing plant Rebecca had given him 'for company' was drooping, so he spared it some water. Although his stomach was empty, his spirits were recovering so rapidly that his chest felt as if it was aerated, and he broke into exuberant if not tuneful song. He jabbed a tin of orange juice and drank half its contents while preparing the food.

When he brought his meal up into the cockpit, the wind had

backed still further and was blowing from north of east. He trimmed the sails and the pilot again so that his course was west of south, then he sat facing the sun, feeling on top of the world for reasons he could only attribute to sound sleep, improved weather and good food. He knew he could get away with letting the reef out and setting the genoa, but he took no action. There was no call to hurry. The story-line had been changed. Something inside him said he was on his way and was going to make it.

He had drunk two cups of coffee and eaten half his food before remembering he was not on a pleasure cruise. The corner of his mouth twitched and he reflected caustically on his decision to make his last voyage in a small yacht whose bucking-bronco discomforts should only have strengthened his resolve. Now, instead of making all speed in maximum discomfort to his logical destination, here he was wallowing in a moment of consolation that looked dangerously like turning into enjoyment. He told himself firmly that his basic conviction had not changed and that there was no crime or inconsistency in appreciating what small reliefs the world still had to offer; the man at the stake was permitted his final cigarette. Then he instructed himself to stop dramatizing and finish his breakfast, which was what he did.

He wondered without any great concern where he was. Still in the Channel, that was for sure, but whether headed for Biscay or for France he was uncertain. He hoped to leave Ushant well to port, as while its waters were unknown to him, he had heard enough of its fogs and tides to have no wish to explore the area's potentialities, and least of all to find himself between island and mainland.

He felt relaxed, fully rested, adequately fed; sapped of speculation by the warm sun; a man in control of a boat; a poor candidate for voluntary extinction.

He threw the bacon rind into the sea, and a distant gull changed course instantly, as though under radio control, swooping in low, its sharp eyes locating the rind unhesitatingly. He threw it a crust.

Christ, he thought, now I'm feeding the damm gulls as though I hadn't a care in the world. Either you're a bloody cool suicide, Braine, or a socking fraud.

Well, one more disenchanted menopausal male anticipating his natural end by a handful of months or years wasn't exactly banner material. No less than six of his friends had taken their lives for one reason and by one means or the other, and he had faced that in all honesty their deaths had affected him little beyond the initial 'God, poor old so-and-so!' and the routine condolences to the surviving spouse. Shock and surprise were energy-consuming indulgences, of suspect spontaneity in a world in which life had become cheap despite the structural indications of a caring society.

He gave the boat more canvas and went below to play tapes and listen to the radio, craving music. He took his disinclination to hear the human voice as proof he was escaping the mainland's pull.

But the wind had died with the day, and as darkness fell he was reminded of a caring world by a flashing light on the port beam. He failed to identify the flashes in Reed's, but guessed he was somewhere west of Ushant, though not nearly far enough out to achieve without possible interruption what had seemed to be a simple enough objective. Studying the manual he realized the profusion of alternatives when, without certainty of a vessel's position, it came to identifying lights off the hazardous north-west tip of France.

His spirits dropped with the wind. Such breeze as remained was fitful and variable in direction, teasing him with alternate hope and frustration. Eventually, soon after midnight, it tired of the game and became positive, but to remind him of the pecking order went back to its old quarter and blew from the west. He cursed his luck, but with the strength gained from the day's respite he accepted the challenge philosophically. Not wanting to stay in the shipping lanes with the constant worry of a lee shore, he resigned himself to another session of battling into the wind.

The character of the sea had changed. The short, sharp waves of the Channel had given way to the long, heaving waters of the ocean's swell. 'Patience' had become an even more insignificant piece of flotsam in the deep, rolling troughs which, lit by the moon, took turns to cradle her in rough indifference, the ever-alternating silver and black of their surface emphasizing the cold inhospitality of limitless sea.

As the night wore on the wind rose again – a gusty, blustering, capricious wind that lacked consistency of speed or direction. The waves crested in response to its bullying, creaming over the yacht's deck and soaking him in spray. Wearing his safety harness, he reduced sail, reefing the main again and setting the number two staysail; not because 'Patience' was unable to carry more at that stage, but because he could not be sure of having the strength and stamina to go forward to change sails again in the kind of blow he feared might be on the way.

The pilot was coping poorly with this confrontation with head winds and disturbed sea. The water's surface seemed not to have adjusted to the wind's change of direction. So he helmed the boat doggedly all night, going below only to make coffee and bring some chocolate bars into the cockpit. He told himself he should be becoming acclimatized, but he felt wretchedly tired by dawn. The contrary seas had brought back the queasiness he thought he had conquered, and he shivered in the thin dawn air.

He calculated he had put another twenty to thirty miles between himself and the French coast, but he judged from the shipping seen during the night that he was no distance into the Atlantic.

The wind was still rising. Fearful for the mast, he dragged himself forward and again reduced sail. The troughs were so deep that the shrieking of the wind in the rigging rose and fell with the vessel's undulating progress between peak and trough. He had never known such seas before and was awed rather than frightened by their magnificence. There seemed less malice in them than in the shorter, choppier, more aggressive waters of the English Channel. It was as though the vast ocean was so indifferent to the intrusion of his tiny shell of timber and steel that it was content to accommodate the impertinence of its presence, as a river will carry a straw. He remembered Judy telling him how she had watched a beetle struggling against the current in the stream that ran along the boundary of their cottage in Wales. Eventually, exhausted, it had ceased to resist and let the water have its way. The stream carried it on to a stick lodged between boulders, where it rested until finding the strength to crawl to safety.

Once again, sheer physical exhaustion was beginning to outweigh every other consideration. Below, every movable object was enjoying a life of its own. His mind felt battered and fragmented by the incessant rough and tumble, but he guessed the wind was blowing six, gusting seven or eight, and he willed the energy to keep one step ahead of the worsening conditions. So he went forward again and removed the mainsail completely, replacing it with the trisail and storm jib. He was surprised by his ability to make the changes on the bucking, steeply angled deck, though the work took him twice as long as it would a younger man.

Uncertain of how the pilot would respond to so little canvas, he stayed on the tiller, keeping the yacht into the seas, half fascinated, half unbelieving, at her ability to weather such conditions. Much of the spray was coming from blown crests, and the surrounding waters were so torn by the wind's fury that it was like ploughing through a vast bowl of disturbed cream.

What he had read about but never experienced started to happen. The water's turbulence was being flattened by the wind, which now sustained a thin high scream in the rigging. 'Patience' sailed for long moments almost serenely through the gale-flattened waste. But the wind was blustering, bullying and unsteady in direction, and every now and then the vessel would shudder from the combined blows of the elements as though struck by a vast mallet.

He recalled calm articles in yachting magazines by hardened sailors claiming that there is little to worry about in heavy weather once sails are off and the vessel is well clear of land.

As though to encourage decision, an enormous wave broke over the yacht, stopping her in her tracks, leaving her wallowing and out of control.

'All right, bugger you!' he shouted into the wind. 'Have it your own way!'

He went forward again, too exhausted to bother with his safety harness, and fought with the wind and the drenching spray for the chance to remove both sails entirely. It was the longest and most dangerous twenty minutes of his life, the removal of one shackle taking five minutes, but he stripped the vessel and stowed the sails, then lashed the tiller, leaving 'Patience' to lie ahull with the wind on her starboard beam, heeled over with her gunwale awash. The sea was now completely white in the storm's grip. There was nothing more he could do.

Exhausted to the point of being unable to stand, he went below, closing the hatch behind him. Conscious of, but indifferent to, the chaos of the cabin, he fell on to the port bunk without removing his oilskins. He lay wedged between the mattress and the padded side-panel, listening to the screaming shrouds, his mind in suspension, too drained for fear or sleep.

7

IN that no-man's-land between sleep and consciousness, doubt and reason make feeble but unsettling contest. With the passing of uncounted hours, the disordered processes of his tired mind were penetrated by awareness that the conditions were moderating. To escape the conflict and uncertainty that had crowded his withdrawal from physical activity, he heaved himself off the bunk, pulled back the hatch, and put his head into the still boisterous wind.

Its direction had not changed and was steadier. He knew 'Patience' could carry sail again, and something about the sky suggested the effort would not be wasted. But in mounting the steps he had caught sight of himself in the small mirror above the sink, and before anything else he knew he must wash, shave and recover some semblance of order and routine. While the kettle boiled he stowed displaced equipment and wiped up the grisly remains of a shattered honey jar. He did not enjoy the task. An early and abiding minor neurosis was his dislike of coming into contact with things sticky. Judy and Mary had not been slow in appreciating the potentialities of this weakness, and in their teens found ways of taking fond revenge for childhood mealtimes dominated by a damp flannel.

He had forgotten the steadying effect of shaving. The ritual of brush and lather, not impossible now that he had found his sea legs and the yacht was riding the swell, was a soothing, mind-clearing experience. His beard was tougher than he had expected. He took his time, achieving a smoother finish than usual, and felt equipped to cope with the day ahead.

Having survived the worst conditions he had yet experienced at sea, he was able to look out over the ocean with a feeling if not of mastery, at least of some confidence and familiarity. He had a childish desire to tell someone he had pulled through, as if to release the small quiver of excitement that had entered his stomach when the reality of his survival came home to him. As he cleaned his shaving brush, he dabbed at Rebecca's plant, leaving a blob of lather on one of its leaves. He remembered the children's giggles when they were small and he tipped each expectant nose with a soap-laden brush.

Back in the cockpit he drew a deep breath, then looked over the yacht's mast and rigging, checking and approving, as the body of a woman may be surveyed after first and satisfactory intimacy. It was as though he were relinquishing a battle in order to enter into a relationship, for he had decided while shaving that he would no longer fight the elements. He would bear away from the wind, even if that meant closing with the land, sailing 'Patience' comfortably until the right circumstances came together. Owing to the deception necessary to hide his intentions, he had plenty of provisions. There seemed nothing inconsistent in deferring his plans by making a roundabout and more civilized journey to his destination.

So with a reefed mainsail and second staysail he gave the wind best, reaching south towards the sun at a good pace. He maintained this course throughout the day. In the afternoon, looking up at the sky, he saw a tiny speck of moving light. A Boeing, perhaps, at some 37,000 feet, setting its 500 miles per hour against the Vertue's three knots. As evening fell, the wind backed, so he bore away and made his bearing 120°, indifferent to shipping and the approach of land. A new mood was upon him, one familiar to those to whom the elements have proved their mastery without withholding mercy. He slapped 'Patience's' coaming, feeling, absurdly, almost ashamed of himself for having earlier wished he had chosen a stiffer, more comfortable boat than a Vertue.

He had lost all sense of time and position, and when he saw the thin evidence of land against a sky already warning of approaching dusk, he felt curiously indifferent to its identity, content to wait until shore lights gave him some clue to his whereabouts.

As day gave way to evening, the lights began to reach him with their messages. As 'Patience' responded to a perfect beam breeze of ten to twelve knots, he sat in the cockpit and studied his Reed's, not too concerned with accurate plotting of his position. But the answers came almost too easily and he was sure he was approaching the peninsula between Carnac and Quiberon, beyond which lay the intricate waters of the Golfe du Morbihan.

Feeling no urge for complicated navigation with night falling, he decided to come up into the wind a few degrees, away from the French mainland, to lay Sauzon on the offshore island of Belle Isle. He had never visited the island, though a well-heeled friend had once offered him and Rebecca a trip there in his old Hornet Moth biplane. It could have been a good holiday, coming at a point in their marriage when they needed to get away, but the weather had deteriorated and their journey had begun and ended at Panshanger where the small 'plane was kept.

He judged the distance between Quiberon and Sauzon to be about that between Hayling Island and Ryde, and the thought was somehow homely and reassuring, diminishing any qualms about finding the entrance to Le Palais, the small fishing harbour on the island's east coast.

He hoisted his courtesy ensign and Q flag and tidied up below. In the sheltered lee of the island 'Patience' made light of the final hour, and they made a good landfall, entering the harbour between the narrowly set moles when the life of the small town was at the evening's height; which was not to say much by comparison with more sophisticated landfalls, but there was no lack of movement and people on and off the water.

By nine-thirty 'Patience' was lying between a Belgian ketch and a British Contessa, stern-on to the south mole. The Contessa's skipper had come on deck to help with a line to the quay while his wife stayed on board to play the fenders between the two vessels. When 'Patience' was secured fore and aft they introduced themselves as Roger and Jill Armitage.

'You'll find this a wet billet if it blows up from the east,' Armitage warned. 'Don't leave your hatches open when you turn in.'

'Do customs find me, or I them?' Matthew asked.

'They'll probably be along. We were treated to a glance through the hatch and a couple of grunts.'

He asked where Matthew hailed from and said he had been in

the Solent only a few weeks earlier. They exchanged notes while Jill Armitage fixed some drinks which it was just warm enough to enjoy in the cockpit of the Contessa. The name on the yacht's dodgers was 'Pact II'.

'She's not quite in your class, of course,' Roger remarked, 'but we've had some good moments in her up till now.'

The last three words seem to hang in the air. Roger struck Matthew as a rather cold fish, but the judgment was perhaps prompted by the other's pale blue eyes which seemed disinclined to look directly into his own. He guessed the couple to be around forty.

'Are you all right for food?' Jill asked, as they finished their drinks.

Without waiting for his answer, Roger said: 'How about joining us for dinner? There's a quite decent place overlooking the outer basin. I daresay you won't want to start provisioning after a long haul.'

It seemed to have been more or less decided what was for the best, but the idea of escaping the confines of 'Patience' for a few hours had its attractions. He felt he had been at sea for weeks.

'We must make it Dutch,' he said, 'if you don't mind my repaying you when I've drawn against a credit card in the morning.'

'Forget it,' Roger said. 'Be our guest.'

The dinner increased the sense of unreality that had settled in him. The noise, the foreignness, the heightened response to the smells of food, bodies and tobacco, conspired to draw him back to a world he should have done with. The couple seemed glad of his company, showing interest in the Vertue, even envy.

'You carry no engine, I see,' Roger remarked.

Matthew chose a piece of cauliflower from the plate of *crudités* the restaurant had provided unasked. Its flavour was so sharp and cleansing that it was some seconds before he stopped chewing to answer.

'Engines aren't my scene. I had one once in a twin-keel tub with a length-to-beam ratio of three to one and the sail area of a beginner's dinghy. I spent hours tinkering and cursing. It drove me to make a solemn vow that if ever I cruised seriously it would be without an engine.'

'You certainly keep the Vertue very clean and spare,' Roger

said. 'In the brief glimpse I got inside I couldn't even see an echo-sounder.'

'A ten-fathom lead is more reliable. Apart from that, a Walker log, standard and hand compasses, a barometer and a Hurst plotter about see me through.'

'No radio?'

'Just a portable domestic set for home waters.'

'But for coming this far, surely a Heron...'

'You're probably right, but it's one more thing to go wrong. If you start to rely on crutches you can't stand when they break.'

Bloody hell, he thought, they're getting a picture of a highly-experienced ocean helmsman, contemptuous of navigation aids, at home on lone waters with only the wind on his cheek and the stars to guide him.

'I just don't have much of a *rapport* with technology,' he explained. 'But I know my limits. The self-steering gear is a concession to age.'

Jill's eyes were shining a little. They said 'Modesty becomes you.'

'I don't know how you manage,' she admitted. 'I'd not be very happy sailing offshore without the diesel.'

'You can wet your pants sailing with one,' Roger said. 'Especially when you have come to rely on it and it breaks down in an onshore gale.'

Matthew nodded. 'Life holds fewest shocks for those with the least props.'

He smiled, feeling slightly protective towards Jill and noting her prettiness when she smiled back. Her mouth was mobile, sensuous, and he wondered if her habit of drawing her tongue across her teeth preserved their whiteness from her incessant smoking. Her slightly freckled face was not free of lines but they were few enough to suggest character more than age and he guessed she had been very beautiful.

'We're just doddlers,' Roger said. 'I sometimes think we should take on more of a challenge than coastal pottering.'

'We might if you didn't devalue yourself so much,' Jill cut in sharply. There seemed more irritation than loyalty in the statement. 'Roger's a fine seaman,' she said to Matthew, 'but since he retired we seem to have just drifted about.'

'We agreed...' Roger began, then went quiet.
'Coastal pottering can be pretty challenging,' Matthew said.
'Do you always sail by yourself?' Jill asked.
'A lot of the time. My wife wasn't... isn't very keen.'
'They either are or are not,' Roger observed. It seemed an obvious remark.

They exchanged inevitable notes about homes and families. Jill and Roger's children were living abroad.

'It can leave a bit of a gap,' Roger said. 'Jill and I have been sailing around for the best part of a year. Nothing very adventurous. Just getting the feel of our new-found freedom, so to speak.'

Jill stubbed her cigarette, flattening it more than the others in the already well-filled ashtray. She lit a replacement. Matthew had not noticed before that her hands had a slight shake. She was slim and tense and he felt she was full of a bottled-up energy.

'Have you thought of making the crossing?' he asked Roger.
'The Atlantic? We all think of it. But it's a bit of a step and it might be rather foolish in our present boat. She needs a lot done to her.'

He ordered a fresh carafe of wine. Matthew was beginning to feel wonderfully well fed, a little light-headed, tremendously tired. The contrast with the past few days was considerable and at the back of his mind he was disturbed at having allowed such a revision of his plans.

'Where are you bound for?' Roger asked.
'I thought I might head west,' Matthew said, hoping he did not sound too casual about it.
'Shouldn't be much of a problem in a vessel like yours. Where are you thinking of fetching up?'
'I thought the Caribbean. Barbados, I suppose. Not very original, I know,' he added, again conscious of oneupmanship.
'That would suit me,' Jill said, gazing dreamily across the room through her cigarette smoke. 'To be in the sun after this damn-awful summer...'
'I sometimes think,' Roger said evenly, 'that people make a mistake in seeking happiness by changing their geography.'

Matthew felt he was on the fringe of an old contest.

The evening slid by in a haze of wine, slowly consumed food

and barely remembered chatter. It was clear that Roger half regretted having sold his printing business. But it had been, he said, at the right time. The reason for his wanting to retire so early was not given, but the impression was conveyed that it was best for them both to get away at that stage of life. It became clear that Jill's view of the 'right time' was not her husband's. For Matthew the evening was marred only by a feeling that it was his presence alone that discouraged a quarrel, but he was too well wined to let it spoil so good an evening. He noticed that whenever Roger irritated his wife she would take a grissini from the pot on the table and snap it into little pieces. She got through all the grissini in the course of the evening.

For his part he talked more freely than was his custom. The tiredness, the new surroundings, the company of people he would never see again, combined to break down any inhibitions. He did not reveal his planned ending of the voyage, but he saw no harm in admitting that purpose in family and working life no longer motivated him. It was the first time he had felt it was safe to confess this to others, but his admission was not followed up and Jill turned the subject by declaring herself intrigued to meet a writer after years of hearing only about the manufacturing side of the printed word. Neither she nor Roger seemed to have read any of his books, but that was a cross he had long learned to carry.

He hardly remembered the walk back to their boats. He was not so much drunk as smitten by the full weariness of reaction. Jill pointed out where to buy croissants, but he only half took it in.

'A Vauban fortress,' Roger remarked as they walked below towering walls. 'Quite a feat. By the way, if you want to do anything to the boat you can lie up here and dry out at low tide.'

At the stern of the Contessa they parted.

'It was an excellent meal,' Matthew said. 'I'm most grateful.'

'You'll get a good kip,' Roger predicted. 'We'll try not to disturb you. Don't forget your hatches.'

Sleep came quickly, free of any anxiety about weather or destination. Cradled in the harbour's slight and even swell, 'Patience' rocked him gently through the night.

When he woke it was broad daylight. Through the solid teak hull came the muffled sounds of a world fully awake. Voices, the putter of engines, the cries of gulls, and from further off the hooting of vehicles about their business in the narrow streets.

He lay there for ten minutes or more, thinking idly of the previous evening and of the preceding days' frustration and discomfort. Fed, rested, secure in harbour, it was not difficult to extract some retrospective pleasure and even self-congratulation. To have gone further than the north coast of France, and single-handed at that... well, for some it might not have seemed out of the ordinary...

He got up and looked through the port window of the doghouse at the Belgian boat. There was no sign of life. Then he peered through the opposite window and saw that the Contessa's berth was empty. He supposed she had been taken into the inner harbour for some jobs to be done.

A shave was the obvious priority, and he enjoyed every minute of it, listening to a French radio station blasting out music that he suspected his children would have assured him was 'pop', but which was somehow acceptable.

It was a fine morning, promising warmth and a fair breeze. He had thrown back the doghouse hatch before shaving, and the sun poured into the cabin, warming his bare skin as the razor traced its familiar routes. He was surprised by the depth of his tan. Then he told himself he was beginning to find compensations a shade too easily and must be on his way.

A woman's voice hailed him, and with his face still half-lathered he put his head through the hatch to see Jill. She was alone on the quay.

'Can I come on board?' she asked.

'Of course.'

He compressed the starboard stern warp with his foot to bring the yacht nearer to the quay. Jill stepped aboard gracefully.

'Thanks.'

She seemed nervous, almost agitated, and drew deeply on her cigarette.

'If you don't mind,' he said, 'I'll just finish shaving.'

'Go ahead. I'll sit in the cockpit.'

He sensed she was in some kind of trouble.

'Sleep well?' he asked casually. '*I* went out like a light.'

'No,' she said, 'we had a hell of a night.'

'Did it blow up? I'd have slept through anything.'

'It blew up all right,' she said, 'but below deck, not outside.'

'Oh! I'm sorry.'

'He's gone,' she said.

'Yes, I see you're off your mooring.' The tone of her voice caught up with him. 'Gone? You mean left harbour?'

She nodded. 'That's right.'

He joined her in the cockpit, drying his face with a towel.

'Without you?'

'Well, obviously.'

'But why?'

'It's been coming. We had an almighty row. I'm surprised you slept through it.'

'He'll be back.' He patted her knee stiffly and smiled, wanting to keep it light. 'Lovers' tiffs...'

She exhaled smoke violently. 'It was no tiff. This has been brewing for months; years. It's the parting of the ways.'

She pointed to a small suitcase between the port dodger and the coaming.

'That's mine. I left the boat and spent half the night walking across the island, trying to calm down; trying to sort things out. He must have put it there after packing some of my things.'

'I'm sorry.'

'I'm not. Not really. It had to come and I wish it had been sooner.'

'Look,' he said, 'I've not had breakfast, and I don't suppose you have either. Why don't you find some croissants and milk while I just tidy up below? I'll get some francs and repay you later.'

'Don't be silly,' she said, and departed readily. Her small, slight figure, dwarfed by the background of the fortress, might have been that of a child on an errand.

He cleared up and made coffee. When Jill returned they had breakfast in the cockpit in the mid-morning sun, buttering their croissants generously and using several small flat tubs of cherry jam.

He did not want to seem to be probing.

'These late September days can be wonderful,' he said.

She managed a small laugh and he smiled apologetically.
'Where's he making for?' he asked.
'I wouldn't know.'
'But you had plans?'
'We were going to La Rochelle for a few days. It's the furthest south we've been; a nice town.'
'So he may put in there and wait for you.'
'I tell you, it's over. We are not children. When Roger makes up his mind, that's it.'
'Perhaps one shouldn't shut doors...'
'The kids were all that kept us together. It's a common enough situation.'
'So what are you going to do?'
'Go home, I suppose. My sister and her husband are living in our house until they go back to Australia, but there's room for me.'
'What does Roger think you are going to do?'
'We didn't discuss it.' She chain-lit another cigarette, throwing the butt over the side. 'Do you know what his parting shot was?'
'I might have if you hadn't taken me to such a good restaurant.'
'He said "Get a lift with Matthew to Barbados if you're so bored pottering with me."' She smiled. 'Don't worry, I'm not asking for that.'
He licked his fingers. The jam was runny in the warm sun.
'It... it isn't... it's just that my plans are still a bit... well, fluid.'
'Forget it. It was his idea, not mine.'
He worked at his fingers with a handkerchief.
'But look here, I'd certainly be very glad to take you as far as La Rochelle.'
'What would be the point? It would only mean a longer journey home.'
'I just feel...'
'I know, you think Roger will be waiting for me.'
'You can't rule out the possibility.'
She looked at him quizzically; an assessment.
'All right,' she said, smiling. 'Thanks! It's a lovely day for a sail, and let's face it, I've nothing better to do.'

She opened her suitcase and checked its contents.

'The bastard! He might have included my make-up bag.'

They had lunch in the town after she had shopped and he had got some francs. She insisted on sharing the cost of the food and wine, but the bulk of her purchases was clothing.

'You'd think he'd have thought to leave me a change of underwear and a jumper or two, wouldn't you?' she said, but otherwise she said nothing more about Roger. There seemed to be a lot more inedibles than a change of underwear and a jumper or two, but he stowed the bags philosophically. He admired the effort she was making to seem cheerful, and her manner was so natural that they might have been old friends planning a weekend cruise. She looked so much younger than her age that he rather enjoyed being seen with her, feeling slightly dashing in his role of rescuer.

Customs proved as sketchy as Roger had predicted. They set sail before three in a steady west-sou'-westerly breeze. When 'Patience' had cleared the south-east tip of the island, they sailed on a comfortable reach to keep well clear of St Nazaire. There was a lot of shipping around, so Matthew was not sorry to have a crew. He could see that Jill knew more than to sit around being a passenger, and he thought how different things might have been had Rebecca shown more of a feeling for messing about in boats.

'We were in these waters at the end of May,' Jill told him. 'Gale-force winds from the east, and they got stronger at night. Only Les Sables d'Olonne and La Rochelle offer protection from easterlies. That's how we got to know La Rochelle.'

'I can see you've picked up quite a lot about sailing,' he said.

'Well, be warned. I daresay my experience is a good deal less than Roger's.'

She smiled. 'And you haven't even an engine, so I may get scared out of my life.'

'Or lose it.'

She shrugged. 'That seems to have happened already.'

There was no other vessel within two miles.

'If you'd like to take the tiller,' he said, 'I'll get some coffee.'

'No, let me.'

He had a very tight, efficient routine for managing the galley, and a place for everything.

'The stove can play up a bit if you don't know its ways,' he said. 'It's no trouble, really. I'm sure you'd like to get the feel of the helm.'

She showed no sign of feeling thwarted. He made the coffee, using a French brand Jill had brought, and they sat in the cockpit and talked. The conditions were ideal. 'Patience' rode slowly over seas whose long green folds were reminiscent of the South Downs. He set the pilot, showing Jill how it was done.

'Do you have a name for it?' Jill asked.

'For the pilot? No.'

'So many people do. We met one man, a single-hander like yourself, who called it The Management. He had escaped from a very bossy wife and said it made him feel at home but with the choice of going manual at a moment's notice. Roger calls ours Emmeline. I don't know why.'

'I'm not keen on anthropomorphism.'

'I can't blame you; it sounds as though it could be nasty.'

She asked him the kind of questions most writers find congenial. They discussed his career, how he began, the ups and downs of the free-lance life, dependent on inspiration and the receptivity of publishers. She asked few direct questions about his relationship with Rebecca, but showed interest in his plans for the voyage. He sensed puzzlement at his inevitable evasiveness, but rather enjoyed sustaining the element of mystery. It was a long time since so much interest had been shown in himself. He warmed to her, and physically she was growing on him.

They spun for fish over the stern and caught their dinner. Jill seemed happy for him to do the gutting and cooking and they ate in the cabin, occasionally checking on the shipping situation. The wind dropped and backed with evening until 'Patience' was ghosting along at less than one knot for La Rochelle.

'Are you happy to share watches?' he asked.

'Of course.'

'She's not a difficult boat to handle. Well balanced.'

'I can see that.'

'If you are uncertain about anything, just let me know.'

'I'll think I'll be all right. Really.'

'Fine! Well, I'll take the first watch.'

Leaving him on the tiller, Jill got ready to turn in.

'Take whatever bunk you like,' he called down to her.

She re-entered the cabin from the forecastle, nearly undressed, and the firmness of her slim body surprised him.

'I'll take one of the forward berths,' she said. 'I've re-stowed to make room.'

He let her sleep on beyond the agreed four hours, and she appeared without prompting as the dawn rose like brush strokes on the eastern horizon. She wore a thickly-knit, barley-coloured roll-neck jumper under her red light-weight sailing smock.

'I'll make coffee and put some brandy in them,' she said. 'It's chilly.'

'I reckon we've covered about forty miles since Le Palais,' he said. 'The wind has shifted again and we're heading due south.'

With one of them recovering from sleep and the other ready for it, they drank their coffees in near-silence.

'All right,' she said when they had finished, 'you go below. I'll cope.'

'I had to use the signalling lamp for a coaster at about two,' he said, 'but it's almost light enough not to need it now. I expect you know about beaming the light on to the main...'

'Yes,' she said, 'I do know.'

'I dowse the stern and side lights promptly to save fuel,' he said. 'I'm afraid you have to lower the masthead light by halliard. It's battery-powered.'

'I'll manage.'

'Well, I'll go below,' he said.

With the water remaining in the kettle he washed up their cups and wrung out the J-cloth after mopping up the sugar Jill had spilled. He closed the locker door she had left open and emptied the saucer she had used for her last cigarette.

He slept solidly for three hours. When he pushed back the hatch, Jill was looking through his binoculars.

'You're just in time to shave and get breakfast,' she said. 'The wind has backed a lot, so we should be able to get in quite easily.'

'Get in? We can't be there yet.'

'Not La Rochelle. Port de la Meule.'

'Port de la what?'

'Meule. On the Ile d'Yeu. Look.' She handed him the binoculars.

'You've been here before?' he asked.

'Years ago. When I first knew Roger.'

The island seemed about five miles long. He had never even heard of it.

'Do we *want* to put in?'

'*I'd* like to,' she said. 'It's a heavenly spot, but the wind isn't often right for an approach. It was May when we went there, after three days at sea. As we neared land, the air was warm, perfumed by gorse and honeysuckle.' There was a lyrical quality to her voice.

He shaved and made a kind of kedgeree from eggs and the remains of the fish. Jill had disconnected the pilot and seemed happy on the helm, so he passed the food up to her and joined her in the cockpit.

A mile or two offshore she swore she could smell the gorse and honeysuckle again. He thought the season was wrong, but did not say so. The ruined castle to which she drew his attention was certainly picturesque in a stark landscape that spoke of ceaseless wind and salt air.

'Is the island inhabited?' he asked.

'The main port is on the other side. Port de la Meule is just a tiny fishing harbour with some pretty little houses nestling above it in the valley that crosses the island.'

The harbour was about a mile beyond the castle, and they anchored by bow and stern in its narrow entrance, below a small headland. The squat white tower on the rocks hardly ranked as a lighthouse, but it was in scale with the rest of the place, which was Lilliputian. The only other visible craft was a fishing boat with two or three dinghies nuzzling her starboard planking. Half way up on the opposite cliffs was a small white-painted chapel of attractive simplicity.

'You see,' Jill said happily, 'it *is* lovely.'

They brought the bedding on deck to air, then saw to some of the maintenance and cleaning inseparable from the freedom of sailing. By mid-day they were hungry.

'Some fresh bread wouldn't come amiss,' he said, throwing what they had left to the gulls. 'There's no mileage in a baguette.'

'It's a pity you don't carry a dinghy,' she said, almost reprovingly.

'It's the space problem. But there's a collapsible coracle affair up for'ard under the gubbins. Good enough for paddling a few yards.'

She brightened at this, finding and setting up the coracle with quick efficiency.

'We need quite a few things,' she said firmly.

The coracle demanded skill from a single user, an act of faith from two. They left it on the rocks above high tide then walked up the cliffs to the chapel which was as simple and scrubbed inside as out. The houses in the village were also painted white, with coloured doors, reminding Matthew of a stop-off in Bermuda on his way to the States some years earlier. They found two restaurants and a general store. Jill plumped for a picnic - so forcefully that he ruled out cost-saving as the reason - and they bought bread, Bonbel cheese, butter, a *pâte à tartiner aux noisettes*, some Vittel water and a bottle of wine.

'The castle is only a mile away,' Jill said, as though their destination had already been discussed and agreed.

They met no-one as they walked along the clifftop. Although there were few trees, plants were abundant among the rocks. When they reached the castle they were more than ready for lunch and Matthew suggested they ate it below the ruins in a hollow sheltered from the wind. But Jill was firm almost to the point of petulance.

'It's much nicer on the ramparts. Just there.'

Matthew had to agree that the setting was very romantic. By now he suspected that he was participating in some form of re-enactment.

When they had eaten Jill said she would show him the castle. It was pretty dilapidated and Matthew could see most of it from where he was, but he followed her obediently, responding with the proper amount of respect to her assurance that it was eleventh-century.

'Oh, and look,' she said with delight, pointing into a pit at the base of the main tower, 'the cannon is still there!'

There was indeed a cannon, looking extremely heavy, and it was clear that at some time the ground floor of the tower had succumbed to its weight.

'It would be,' he said.

The cannon had been joined by surprisingly few modern artefacts and Matthew was again able to agree sincerely that it was a really most attractive spot.

They climbed as high as they could round the outside of the crumbling tower and Jill held his invited hand for a shade longer than was necessary. On the way back to the boat she took his hand again, on the even slimmer pretext of negotiating a small decline which in fact he found rather difficult himself, and the link was broken only when she wanted another cigarette.

'You oughtn't to smoke so much,' he reproved.

'Now don't spoil things,' she said. 'It's been a lovely day so far. You know, you should come and write a book on this island. So much peace and quiet.'

'I'm through with writing books,' he said.

He spoke what came into his mind, not really intending his response to be a subject for discussion.

'Through? Why?'

He shrugged. 'Maybe the well's run dry,' he said.

'At your age? Nonsense!'

'I don't know that age is all that relevant. Other factors count.'

'But why?' she persisted. 'You can always get ideas from other people; even from their books. Some authors have never had an original idea all their lives. It didn't stop them from churning out books.'

'I think maybe I've got bored; a bit out of touch, perhaps; anyway, the old fire is lacking.'

She took his arm.

'Come on,' she said, 'this is no way to be talking on such a happy day. Things go in phases. You'll see.'

When they got back on 'Patience', a line over the side solved the problem of dinner. With potatoes, a can of peas and some fruit they ate adequately, sharing a bottle of the white Macon Jill had bought in Le Palais. It was, as she had promised, every bit as good as a Chablis of twice the price.

'I suppose we might have bought a lobster from the fishermen,' he remarked. 'I should think they get some whoppers in these waters.'

'You haven't a big enough saucepan,' she said, 'and, anyway,

I can't bear to cook them myself; it seems so cruel.'

'It's no less cruel if you get someone else to do it for you,' he said.

'Maybe, but I don't see it happening.'

'That's adding cowardice to cruelty.'

'All right, but I still think it's beastly.'

'The world is here for us to use,' he said.

'If you start to quote the Bible,' she said, 'you can find an excuse for anything under the sun. It's another sign of cowardice to defend one's failings by quoting respectable texts.'

'I wouldn't dream of quoting the Bible. I subscribe to no religion.'

'Oh, well, we shan't argue about it,' Jill said. 'It really has been such a lovely day.'

She put the dirty dishes into the sink.

'I find it best,' he said, 'to soak them first in a bucket of sea water. It conserves the fresh.'

They had agreed to make an early start in the morning. He let her wash up because she seemed to want to. He hung the paraffin lamp in the shrouds and tidied up on deck. When he returned to the cabin Jill was wiping over the surface of the table.

'Does this thing lift out?' she asked.

'If you want it to.'

She looked at him, a hint of amusement in her face.

'I think I do want it to.'

'The bunk opposite your own is about the only place to stow it.'

He took the rag from her and wiped round the sink, then rewashed the top plate in the stack.

'Don't you bother with washing up,' he said. 'I've a very simple system. It's no trouble.'

'Let's go on deck,' she said.

The air was still and the moon bright. The chapel on the hill gleamed softly and the light at the entrance to the harbour blinked with faithful regularity over an empty sea. The chill of the late September evening was reason enough for Jill's closeness to him. They went below.

She began to undress.

'You could put the mattress on the floor,' she said.

He felt a slight annoyance at being taken aback by her directness, but it had been a long time...

'But I couldn't read the compass from there.'

She smiled.

'You don't need to, do you, when we're at anchor? In any case, your sense of direction will take care of itself when we are together.'

It was as she had said.

8

IT was a perfect autumn morning. They left Port de la Meule before a light following breeze. Clear of land the pilot was trimmed to give a comfortable beam reach on a course of 170°. Jill's eyes were moist.

'It was the last place we were really happy,' she said.

She had been as subdued as he at breakfast and he had supposed she was equally tired. He had been unprepared for her ferocious energy. At first he had submitted gladly enough to the almost forgotten thrill of abandonment, but she had enticed not only performance but an encore. Several encores. Their narrow bed, hardly more than coffin-width, lacking elbow room, allowed no space for separation, for recoupment of energy. When, in the small hours, she again sought his arousal, his response had been minimal; with Rebecca, months could go by... He would not at all have minded returning to his solitary berth, but he told himself she had been through something of a shock and that it would have been churlish not to see it through. As they ate their breakfast in the cockpit, his limbs were so shaky that his coffee was in danger of spilling. He had had to stand up and gaze keenly shorewards as though intent on some weather sign, steadying his hands by leaning on the doghouse.

He found himself thinking about Rebecca again. Not with any particular guilt, but rather to recall that even in the heyday of their marriage she had preferred the passive role. He remembered regretting it occasionally at the time.

'With any luck,' Jill said, 'we shall be there this evening.'

She had had her fourth cup of coffee, held in hands as steady as rocks. Any sadness at leaving the island had been replaced by an obvious desire to reach La Rochelle. Her suggestion that they replace the number one staysail with the genoa for added speed was almost an order.

'We're in three, gusting four,' he pointed out. 'The mast isn't the strongest point in Vertues.'

She blew smoke at him impatiently.

'I thought they could go anywhere, take anything.'

'You can over-canvas any vessel.'

Her expression lacked patience with an uncalled-for timidity. With the uncertainty of a middle-aged man long unaccustomed to the role of lover, he assumed she had not found the previous night satisfactory. He said as much, his tone apologetic.

'Oh, don't be absurd!' she said. 'What a really rather insensitive remark!'

He drew comfort from what he supposed might have been a back-handed way of confirming he had not done too badly, and left it at that.

A little later the wind died completely. Jill appeared restless. She made several rather challenging remarks, all with a slightly sexual connotation, as though to provoke him. The night had left him with no reserves. He had left the breakfast dishes to soak, but made no effort to stop Jill washing them up.

He did his best to turn the conversation to impersonal and general topics, but she met with thinly veiled irritation his every remark, whether a request to thread a sail needle or a solicitous suggestion that she have a little rest or another cup of coffee. In time she accepted the coffee, and he had one too, though with no feeling of need.

He remembered some tag about the most important equipment for a small yacht, after a decent set of sails, being a sense of humour. Rebecca had at least shared his view of the absurd and they had often agreed that without it they would long since have separated. True, in recent years she had told him that his own sense of humour had been overtaken by a range of inadequacies he had quite failed to recognize, but he put that down to her lack of satisfaction with a marriage both accepted had lost its spark.

Suspecting that Jill's mind was on her husband, he tried to draw her out. The discovery that few human pleasures exceed talking about oneself had become part of his stock-in-trade; even dealing with daughters' adolescent tantrums was made easier by asking them about themselves.

It worked for a time. Once Jill overcame her suspicion that his concern was mere idle curiosity, she was not all that different to Judy and Mary. Indeed, in her review of life with Roger Armitage she surpassed them, both in depth and range of detail. Her interest in himself was now confined to his role as captive ear; it was as though their night's intimacy had forged a different relationship, entitling her to relax and chat as to an old and patient friend. No response seemed required other than the occasional attention-confirming 'Really!', 'Good Lord!' or less specific grunt, though she sometimes sought comparisons by probing questions about his own marriage. On the still but heaving sea, surrounded by the utter silence of deep water and limitless sky, her monologue of domestic complaint and emotional regret began to weary him. Too much of what she said and asked pushed him back into a past he was trying to forget.

By mid-morning she seemed to have talked herself dry and suggested they have a drink. Gin, not coffee. As his wine merchant had given him a case of so-far hardly touched spirits it was difficult to expect mileage from the plea that daytime drinking made him tired and had been inconsistent with creative writing.

They sat in the cockpit, stranded in calm sea. He gained relief from Jill's soliloquy, resumed with the aid of the alcohol, by a search for the cocktail biscuits Rebecca had given him to celebrate his arrival in the Caribbean. He kept quiet about the champagne that had accompanied them.

'Do you know,' she resumed as they nibbled the biscuits, 'at one time he said I had no feeling for the earth?'

'Who? Roger?'

She nodded impatiently. 'You see, he got this self-sufficiency thing some years before he retired.'

'Oh, yes?'

'The children were still at school. The flower beds had to go and he grew vegetables in every nook and cranny. Our garden is much too big. He bought a huge deep-freeze - six feet long - and expected me to keep it permanently filled. He said it cost a terrible lot to keep the empty spaces frozen.'

'We have a deep-freeze too. Not quite as big as yours.'

She was not interested in his deep freeze.

'It was dreadful. I spent half my life picking and tailing beans, podding peas, and cutting the good bits out of hundred-weights of maggoty apples. He wouldn't use sprays.'

'It's a short season, of course,' he put in. 'One does have to go all out when the produce is there. I think we felt that getting good food into the children made it worthwhile.'

This had in fact been his argument, not Rebecca's. With the garden stiff with sprouts, cabbage and the Jerusalem artichokes he loved and Rebecca hated, she was apt to return from the supermarket with six aseptically clean leaks wrapped in cellophane.

Jill drained her glass and refilled it, the proportion of gin to tonic more generous than the time before. Her incessant smoking was bringing back his allergic rhinitis. For years his nose had reacted to household dust, pollens and tobacco smoke, but his solo voyage had so calmed his membranes that even the restaurant on the Belle Isle had provoked no response.

'Even when the children had left, he still wanted it filled. Because of the cost of the empty spaces.'

She stared gloomily across the quiet water, looking years older than when she smiled. He supposed her metabolism was affected by alcohol. Rebecca hardly touched a drop, having come from a long line of drunks.

'Maybe I ought to be thinking about lunch,' he said. 'You stay here – and smoke.'

He dropped down into the cabin, sneezed violently several times, and wondered despondently what might cheer her up. The coffee cups they had used earlier were still in the sink. They were slopping about in a cold brown gravy with a black dishcloth he did not recognize. Closer inspection proved the dishcloth to be a pair of panties which in the right context could have been sexy. He squeezed them out and put them in one of the cups on the draining board, then drained the sink, wiped round it with the J-cloth, and put the kettle on. His mind shelved the problem of what to do about the panties and returned to the task of feeding their owner. He remembered that Rebecca had suggested some tins of asparagus for celebrating his crossing of the line. When he pointed out that he would have to be about a thousand miles off course to be able to cross the equator, she said they might come in useful anyway.

The problem was to find them. The unsorted stores were kept forward, so he spent some time shifting sailbags and other tackle. He found the asparagus tins in a cardboard box with soap powders, some packets of 'Tissues for Men,' and a fortuitous bottle of already-mixed French dressing.

Coming back into the cabin he called out to Jill:

'Which do you prefer with asparagus – oil and vinegar or melted butter?'

There was no reply. As she was not in the cockpit, he ascended the stairs and looked forward, for a second alarmed by her apparent disappearance. Then he saw she was huddled up in the pulpit, lying on a sailbag, hugging his bottle of gin. She looked at him with dull disinterest, and when he moved nearer he saw that the bottle's contents were appreciably less.

'Asparagus,' he said. 'Do you like French dressing or butter?'

Jill crouched lower, clutching the bottle to her breast as though to suckle it.

'Go away!'

'How can I go away?' he said irritably. 'This is a twenty-five foot yacht. Do you want butter or dressing with your asparagus?'

'I hate asparagus. It makes your pee smell.'

He felt he was dealing with Mary again, in adolescence.

'Well, you've got to have something, especially as you've drunk half that bottle.'

'Now I shpose you're grudging me a little drink.'

'Don't be ridiculous.'

'Why isn't there a radio on this boat? I'd like some music.'

'You might be able to get something on the transistor.'

'Where is it, then?'

'If I get it, will you tell me what you want to eat?'

She only looked at him sulkily, her eyes in poor focus, so he went back into the cabin and collected the transistor. She did not thank him, but found a station producing a distorted jumble of jungle pop, made worse by being given maximum volume.

'Well?' He had almost to shout to be heard.

She regarded him reproachfully, tears threatening.

'*You* should know what unhappiness is like in a woman,' she said.

'My wife never went on like this,' he answered tartly. 'She held her liquor and she didn't stir her knickers in with a lot of dirty crocks.'

The tears broke and he left her to get on with it, thankful he had not yet pierced the tin of asparagus. He decided plain, wholesome food would be best for the woman, so cooked potatoes and opened some corned beef, making soup for a starter so that he had an excuse to get her back into the cockpit as soon as possible. While she drank the soup, after protests that called on techniques of hoaxing and coaxing forgotten since Judy and Mary were small, he washed panties and coffee cups.

'Anyway,' she called down, somewhat sobered by the soup, 'no one ever calls them knickers these days. If you use words like that in your books, no wonder people think you out of touch.'

'I'm not out of touch,' he replied angrily, 'least of all with you. I hope you're going to eat this food now I've been to the trouble of preparing it.'

She ate resentfully, as though in feeding her he was offering a personal slight. Rebecca and the children at their most irritating paled by comparison. She seemed determined on squabbling and he found himself arguing on familiar topics, but she showed even less respect than Rebecca for the rules of commonsense. She returned to her husband's urge for self-sufficiency, producing statements of such intolerance and exaggeration that he began to counter them with a passion that would have made him *personna grata* with Judy and her husband in their Welsh community. The air was so still that her tobacco smoke hung heavily, as if they were sitting in a small room. She smoked not only between courses but during them. His eyes itched violently and he rubbed them with the back of his wrist while he ate. He swallowed an anti-histamine pill, fearing a sleepless night.

'God!' he said at length. 'Is Roger as hooked on that disgusting habit?'

The sudden change of topic took her by surprise.

'No. Why?'

'The poor bastard,' he said irritably.

'Does it worry you, then?' she challenged.

'I'd have thought it was bloody obvious...' he began, but gave up and stacked their plates instead. 'Coffee, or would you like some fruit?'

'Coffee. Strong.'

He was thankful that with food inside her she could at least state her preferences.

As he descended the steps 'Patience' rolled gently in a sudden puff of wind. Coming unexpectedly it was enough to take him off balance. He landed clumsily, one of the plastic plates spilling Jill's left-overs on the chart table. He cleaned up the mess with a J-cloth, relieved they had not had French dressing after all. When he came up with the coffee it was obvious they were in for a quick change in the weather. Dark clouds were approaching rapidly and the air held that indefinable promise of worsening conditions.

'I'd better shorten sail,' he said.

'Drink your coffee first,' she said. There was a note of authority in her voice. 'It won't come that quickly.'

The wind blew up to force five at an amazing speed, but Jill had no difficulty in matching his every move to make the boat snug and seaworthy in the face of the impending gale. The wind had gone round to the south west, but as yet the sea had not responded.

'I think it's going to blow up harder,' Jill said. 'We'd better head out into the Bay while we still can. It'd be asking for trouble to run for shelter to a windward shore.'

He was glad she had the sense to see this. He noticed that her eyes were bright again, her lips slightly parted from exertion. Years seemed to have dropped from her. She puzzled him. He had met some women, usually younger, who were as good as many men in a crisis at sea; but most of them had been built on lines that would have inspired an Epstein – strong-limbed girls to be seen in marinas and ports the world over; bleached, bronzed and jolly good chaps to have about a boat; game for anything, but possibly not valued over-much sexually by the habitual cruising male whom he had long tended to categorize somewhere between latent homosexuality and the over-extroversion of the emotional non-starter.

They brought 'Patience' round on to the port tack, Jill slamming the runner into place with impeccable timing, he trimming the yacht's pilot as she cut into the mounting seas. For the next few hours Jill was the best of companions, her conversation centring on cheerful memories of sailing, holidays and the earlier years of children. But it was a wet sail, and tiring, in the gusting wind, which died gradually until no more than a force two; but the swell stayed, making the ride lumpy but without challenge.

They went below and removed their oilskins. Jill's roll-neck jumper was wet, and she took it off with a quick experienced gesture, shaking her hair loose as the garment slid off her head. She was wearing no brassiere or vest, only pants too brief for utility. She was as unselfconscious as if he had been her husband.

It had always surprised and worried him how few clothes his daughters wore.

'Oughtn't you to have more on?' he said, steadying himself as the yacht rolled. 'It's not that warm.'

She laughed and looked at him with her head on one side, half-profile, the whites of her eyes and the set of her lips provoking. He was suddenly conscious of his tiredness.

'You can be quite funny,' she said cryptically. 'Come on, try to relax for once. In a silly sort of sea like this we can't stand around making conversation.'

She pushed him out of the cabin, took the mattress from the bunk and laid it on the floor. Then she grasped his hands firmly and drew him back into the cabin, pulling him down on to her as she sank back on to the four firm inches of plastic-covered foam rubber. Before he could adjust to this change in her mood she had opened his zip deftly and wrapped her slim firm legs round his hips. It was the last thing he had been expecting, but spontaneous desire has its own crude logic. Her body was so demanding that capitulation came rapidly and they abandoned 'Patience' to the uncomfortable swell outside.

9

'YOU'RE just not interested, are you?' Jill demanded. 'That's the whole truth of the matter – you are just not interested.'

'You're like a bloody barometer,' he complained, 'except that when the glass is high you create storm and depression, and when it's low you come alive.'

'Now you're evading my question. Why not just admit you've lost interest?'

'Because I haven't. Wasn't I proving it twenty-four hours ago? It's just that I find this long-distance stuff pretty tiring, and after heavy weather I daresay one's body needs to relax.'

'Exactly.'

'There's relaxation and relaxation. Sex is more tiring for a man than a woman. He has to give more.'

'Now where are we? Biology or psychology?'

'I wish you'd stop trying to make me rise.'

'So you have indicated.'

'You know what I mean. This calm has lasted a whole day and we've done nothing but sit and drift and argue...'

'If you insist on denying me a tiny drink...'

'After your last performance, can you blame me?'

'Ah! Now you're going to throw that in my face.'

'One learns by experience. You can't hold your drink, so you're better off without it. That's all.'

'You sound just like Roger.'

'I can believe that.'

'You're disgusted because I drink a little? Is that why you repelled me just now?'

'Of course not. I just can't perform non-stop. Your endless smoking is partly to blame. Anti-histamines make one tired. Anyway, I didn't think you wanted it unless you were stimulated by hairy conditions.'

'Is sex the only thing you can imagine between man and woman?'

'Then what are you after? Scrabble? Backgammon?'

'There is such a thing as civilized intercourse.'

'Quite.'

'I mean conversation, sharing, companionship, a little warmth and tenderness. Affection's possible without going the whole hog.'

'One thing leads to another, which is all very well now and then, but I'm... well, I'm not as young as I was.'

'What has age to do with kindliness and communication?'

'But you're so argumentative and abrasive in anything less than a force five. There seems to be no happy medium between your god-awful moods and having it away. I wouldn't at all mind civilized conversation.'

'Has it ever struck you that perhaps you just don't know how to handle women?'

'Frequently. But my problem at the moment is woman singular, not plural. You're a creature of moods and I just don't have the skill to talk you through them. I'm sorry.'

She looked at him and compressed her lips, then nodded her head.

'I'm sorry too. I suppose I have what's known as a low boredom threshold. Since the children left home I have needed stimulation to feel alive.'

'Oh, well,' he said, mollified. 'I'm not easy either.'

Her arms had been across her chest while they sat facing each other in the cockpit. She lowered them and stood up.

'I'll get a meal,' she said. 'Everything's worse on an empty stomach.'

'Well, if you're sure...' he said. The memory of her panties was still strong.

She busied herself in the galley, making more noise than seemed necessary. He guessed she was switching her attentions to inanimate objects.

'No salt!' she said. 'Bloody marvellous! Honestly! Of all the things to be without on the surface of an ocean...'

But he could tell she was bantering rather than spoiling for a fight.

'I don't use salt,' he said. 'There's pepper, but I don't use salt.'

'You'll just have to tell me,' she said.

'Tell you what?'

'If you don't want it.'

'It?'

'If you don't want me to encourage you to make love to me.'

'Oh, that! Oh, well, yes, right, thanks.'

'You haven't much stamina, have you?'

It was a statement rather than a question, made without intent to provoke.

'I have for my own kind of routine. The last few days have been somewhat exceptional, one way or another.'

'Well, we're not going to make La Rochelle to-night,' she said, 'that's for sure.'

'The wind's come up a bit.'

'With a force two dead on the nose, it's hopeless. The weather isn't settled. It could blow up again.'

He had learned to respect her predictions. He pondered on whether to let her handle the boat by herself in the next blow so that he could store some energy for the ensuing lull by getting some sleep. He had no faith in the truce lasting.

'So where do you reckon we are now?' he asked.

Her reply was not the consciously inadequate feminine contribution of a woman happy to be put in her place by male superiority.

'It would help if this boat was equipped for more than fair-weather sailing in a marina,' she said briskly, 'but by D.R. since our last fix I'd say we are about thirty-five miles west-sou'west of Les Sables d'Olonne. You don't do nearly enough navigation.'

'I've had some distractions,' he reminded her. 'I wasn't doing too badly before you came on board.'

'Anyway – skipper,' she said, an edge of challenge to her voice, 'what's the programme to be?'

'Why don't you tell me?' he invited. 'In the long run we'll end up doing what you decide.'

'Well, I don't recommend making for the coast until the weather's more settled, so why don't we press on at about two-twenty degrees and take advantage of the wind shift? It'll probably veer again before long, and by then we shall at least have made good to the south.'

'But you want to join up with Roger again..?'
She smiled at the anxiety in his voice.
'Don't sound so worried. He's probably not there anyway.'
The thought of that worried him even more.
'He's probably covered in remorse by now,' he said.
She ignored the remark.
'What I'm not clear about,' she said, 'is where you were making for in any case. Obviously not for Barbados.'
'Why do you say that?'
'I was looking through your charts while you were asleep. Anyone seriously set on crossing the Atlantic...'
'I'd made no hard and fast plan.'
'Then you are much more relaxed than you appear, unless you have suicidal intentions.'
He guessed it was said facetiously, but it put him on his guard.
'How's the food going?' he asked.
'All right.' She pumped the stove for greater heat. 'I don't think you have the least intention of going to the West Indies.'
Challenge again, a query over his character, his ability...
'So what *am* I doing? Chunting up and down the Bay looking for abandoned wives?'
'Ouch,' she said without real reproach.
'Well, honestly, you do ask for it.'
'From time to time,' she agreed.
'If that egg's for me,' he said, 'give it five minutes - actual boiling time.'
She laughed. 'There you are! A man who is that precise about his egg doesn't set off on a four-thousand-mile trip without more preparation.'
'I've spent a lifetime being fully prepared. Maybe I was due for a holiday.'
'Not from habit patterns. They're built in long before one reaches your age.'
'What have I done to deserve this motivation study?'
'Women are inquisitive creatures. We like to understand people.'
'All right, if you're so ruddy sure you know my intentions better than I do, you'd better let me drop you off at Corunna.

Or wherever we choose to put in,' he added, protecting his options.

'All right,' she said cheerfully, 'that'll do nicely.'

It was all of two hundred and fifty miles, a far greater distance than he had ever sailed out of sight of land, but she was so matter-of-fact in her acceptance that he knew he was committed.

The wind had dropped again by dusk but was enough to draw 'Patience' through the water at two or three knots. As the light faded, his hope that Jill would keep off the bottle was dashed by her reminder that the time was right for a jar. She had tried not to rile him, so he lacked the anger to prolong prohibition. Her choice was again spirits and he took a larger tot than usual for himself, feeling that to join might be easier than to beat. She returned to her probing.

'You just don't seem the sort of person to go on a trip lacking purpose or destination,' she said.

'Why not leave it that I'm ... escaping?'

'From what? Prison? Debtors? Over-work?'

'Just life, maybe.'

'Bureaucracy? Regimentation? Red-tape?'

'That could be part of it,' he agreed. 'Do you know, it took nine months' hassle with the planning people before we could put a dormer in the roof? By then the builder's quote had nearly doubled, the windows we needed were out of stock, and winter had arrived. Whatever you want to do, there's some little Hitler whose job is to bug you.'

'Roger takes the view that a half-dozen bottles in the right quarter is life's best lubricant.'

'It's knowing the right quarter. I'm hopeless at corruption. I applied for our rateable value to be lowered. We offered the valuation officer coffee and a ginger biscuit. He refused and put up the R.V. by fifteen quid for a shed he said they didn't know about. The power to corrupt is built in. Take our local traffic warden. We've double yellow lines everywhere. People we know give him cigarettes, cakes, the odd pheasant, and so forth. I can't bring myself to join them. So when Rebecca goes shopping, we get tickets.'

'You're a kind of idealist,' she said. 'I can tell.'

'Life's a bit like the late-night films they show on television in the summer – you keep on thinking that they must get better.'

'Do you and Rebecca fight a lot?'

'Not much. We've developed a kind of live-and-let-live relationship. It was easier once the children left home.'

'And you're bored with each other?'

'I suppose so.'

The immediate past had made him less certain.

'Well, you're obviously not inseparable,' she said tartly. She drained her glass and poured another drink. 'What about the children?'

'What about them?'

'Are you interested in them? Concerned?'

'I have been, but it's clearly not mutual.'

She looked gloomily out through the hatch at the darkening sky. The wind had dropped again and the yacht was hardly moving through the water.

'Join the club. Ours are the same. I think I only agreed to come away with Roger because I was sick of an empty house and of waiting for some evidence of still having a family.'

'It can be worse for the mother,' he conceded.

'And when they do come back it is only when something has gone wrong. Did I tell you about Belinda?'

'I don't think so.' He felt very tired and could have got by without knowing.

'She met this sociology student at East Anglia. Why's it always sociology? Marxist, of course, and terribly progressive. No question of marriage. He said anything but a free relationship was a positive immorality. They shared house with another couple; squatting, I think. The man was Polish; an acupuncturist. He said he preferred Belinda to his mistress – you don't say "mistress" these days, do you? – and we had the two of them home for the week-end. You could tell they both wanted marriage at heart, but Belinda was full of the other boy's fears about intellectual dishonesty. They insisted on 'talking it through 'till my head swam. Now the four of them are in Israel. God knows why, or what they're doing. What with that sort of thing and Christopher's disastrous marriage to a girl he met in Boots, a prolonged voyage seemed attractive. If you can't *tell* your children anything, or be useful to them, there's no point hanging around living off memories.'

'True.' He drained his glass and refilled it. 'Very true. It's being wanted that is what it's all about.' He stumbled over the sentence and felt obliged to repeat it more slowly.

'It's all so different when the children are young. When they need you.'

'God, yes! But when you feel the whole world can get along without you...'

They pondered silently over their glasses.

'Why don't you use salt?' she asked suddenly.

'Salt?' He frowned. 'It's supposed to be bad for arthritis.'

'Have you got arthritis?'

'My mother had it.'

'Why do you keep feeling your crotch?'

'Do I?'

'I thought at first I was disturbing you,' she said, 'then I guessed the reason was less flattering.'

'My father got cancer down there when he was about my age.'

'And you think you're going to?'

'I suppose I fear the possibility.'

'Roger's a hypochondriac too. All men are.'

'And all women generalize about men.'

She lit another cigarette moodily.

'It's the pill, I suppose.'

'What is?'

'Why grandchildren don't appear. In *our* parents' day one would get married, and within a year or two, by accident or design, there would be children. The young just don't seem to want children these days. Roger, of course, says it's just as well with the population problem.'

'Isn't that a rather selfish attitude? Expecting grandchildren to keep one amused?'

'All life's selfish. It's selfish to have children and to want to share theirs. Even to love someone is selfish, I dare say. Why should I be different?'

'This is a cheerful conversation.'

She held out her glass. 'Fill it up, then.'

'I doubt whether it will help,' he said, but topped up for both of them.

She drank the contents almost at a gulp, then put her head between her hands and groaned.

'If only I could sleep!'

'You don't do badly,' he said.

'I'm a wreck on anything less than eight hours. Roger's got my pills, blast him. What have you got on the boat?'

Without thinking he said: 'Nothing except the nembutal...'

'Just the thing,' Jill said. 'I've a good relationship with nembutal.'

'I don't think...' he began, then remembered that eight hours of deep sleep was just what he needed.

'Where are they?' she pressed.

'It's blowing up a bit,' he said. 'Let's shorten sail first and both turn in. Into our bunks,' he added, stressing the plural.

'I get the message.'

'Sorry, didn't mean to over-do the isolationism bit, but you said you were tired.'

'I'm hellish tired. Nothing's worse than being becalmed.'

'Why don't you take the port bunk, opposite me? It's more comfortable than being up forward.'

On deck, reducing sail, his head cleared and he cursed his carelessness in letting on about the nembutal. But a proper night's sleep was unbelievably tempting.

'That should do,' he said, 'in anything short of a storm.'

'It's not very seamanlike to have no-one on watch,' she said.

'I know,' he said, 'but there's no shipping about.'

He turned the lights on and they went below. Jill declined cocoa but greeted the nembutal like an old friend.

It was so pleasant to be alone in his bunk without fear of interruption that he was asleep within seconds.

The gale was short, sharp and memorable. The yacht lurched and bucked, the oddly jumpy motion doing more to drive him from his bunk than the shrill of the wind through the rigging. Jill did not stir. He went on deck and removed all sail, leaving the boat hove-to with everything closed up.

He lay on his bunk, hoping for sleep but no longer sleepy. After about an hour he was dozing off when a freak sea struck 'Patience', rolling her right on to her side with such force that Jill was tipped out of her bunk above the leeboard and landed on top of him. The yacht righted herself so abruptly that before Matthew, winded and bemused by the impact, could grab Jill, she dropped back on to her own bunk, limp with uninterrupted sleep, her fall broken neatly by the padded side-board.

Worried that she might have been injured, he leaned across and shook her shoulder, but she was quite unconscious, her face tranquil and relaxed. He strapped her in with the canvas bunkboard and did the same for himself, lying like a boxed egg, feeling his chest gingerly for broken ribs, before eventually dropping into nervous slumber punctuated by nightmares and moments of wakeful anticipation of a further knockdown.

The next day, until she examined her bruises, Jill refused to believe him. By the evening they were both so stiff that for several days he was under no pressure to squander his physical energies.

10

IT was neither Corunna, Vigo, Oporto nor Lisbon. Confirming the unpredictability that is the only certainty about voyages under sail, weather and circumstance kept them well away from land for the next nine days.

By the dawn of the tenth they were agreed that they must be seventy or more miles off the Portuguese coast, but log failure and a plotting error on his part cast doubt on their latitude. She was for 38.5°, he for 37.5°. Backing her own calculation, Jill said they were less than a day's sail from Setubal where she and Roger, on a motoring holiday, had stayed in a *pousada* converted from an old fortress overlooking the Rio Sado.

'The dining room overlooks the town and the fishing harbour. The sardine fleet is very picturesque. At night it's like being in an aeroplane above a sea of lights. It was one of our happiest times together.'

'You can cut the commercial,' he said crisply. 'We are not going to make any more nostalgic returns to the haunts of your *temps perdu*.'

Their relationship, after so many days of intensive co-existence, had much in common with long-marrieds. Bickering relieved the pretence of compromise. The conditions outside, a source of challenge and exasperation, were matched below deck. By and large, hers was the challenge, his the exasperation; but although he did not recognize it at the time, he had learned more about heavy-weather cruising since she had joined him than from all his jollies in and around the Solent.

They had had three days of gales, but now the sun was shining, hatches were open, the wind had dropped. 'Patience' was moving quietly through the water in a steady six-knot breeze. Warmth in the air hinted of better things to come. They were at breakfast in the cockpit; it was usually their best time together; Jill was still sedated.

'I will say,' he remarked, 'you're a jolly good sort to have around in a crisis.'

'Oh, God!' she said. Still sedated, her smile lacked sparkle.

'No, I mean it,' he insisted. Although he preferred to bear the brunt of the domestic chores, in navigation, weather prediction and general alertness she had shown great capability. Her healthy nervousness about the lack of an engine could have saved their lives, for left to himself he might well have tried to make landfall in conditions he subsequently agreed could have spelled disaster.

'Have you learned it all from just pottering around with Roger?' he asked.

'Heavens, no! He probably wouldn't have proposed to me if I hadn't been thrown into a Seaview at an early age.'

Alert to the dangers of the calmer conditions, he steered the conversation away from autobiography.

'So here we are, well down the Portuguese coast. Are you still for carrying on to the Canaries?'

'We might as well. Things couldn't be more sordid below, but we have enough provisions.'

'They're not that sordid. I've kept on top of them.'

Although the past few days had often been fraught with irritation and, at times, stark fear, he had made a kind of adjustment to her presence. Although the calm days had on balance been worse, provoking the all-too-familiar alternative outlets for her energies, they had been few, and by giving her unrestricted access to the nembutal he had made up on his sleep and established a workable rhythm.

'There's not a lot of choice about where we go,' she said, 'unless you change your mind about Setubal.'

'I'm not keen on back-tracking,' he said.

She shrugged, throwing her third breakfast cigarette over the side.

'It's your yacht. The Canaries will do me. It's a pity your chart's so small-scale, though. You are extraordinarily underequipped.'

'Some people have sailed round the world on a school atlas,' he said. 'If Cook navigated the globe with a chronometer and a sextant, I ought to be able to manage.'

'Oh, well,' she said, 'I've got to repair the storm jib. Why don't you air the bedding?'

He noticed that Rebecca's plant was wilting with neglect. He watered it and removed some dead leaves, feeling oddly guilty.

Twenty-four hours later he was regretting they had not put in at Setubal and parted company. The wind dropped steadily through the day, and by nightfall they were rolling in an oily and windless swell. As the return of her boredom threw up recognizable signs, he played Debussy and Schubert and suggested cards. She sought no such distractions. Eating little of the meal he prepared, she drank so heavily that by eight in the evening she fell into loud sleep. He prepared 'Patience' for the night and was about to turn in when she woke and began to abuse him for refusing to put in at Setubal. He tried to calm her but she was determined to work up her grudge. At mid-night, under no provocation other than what he saw as his impeccably logical analysis of her unreasonableness, she hit him with the frying-pan. He held her wrists, but she broke away, cursing, and hurled a copy of Reed's at his head. It made good contact at so short a range, drawing blood above his left eye. This seemed to calm her a little and she took to her bunk, swallowing another of his nembutal pills with the dregs of the gin.

'For God's sake,' he said, 'you'll kill yourself one of these days with a mixture like that.'

She turned her face to the hull angrily, stuffing the bottle of tablets under her pillow.

'Who's to care?' she said.

'You could think of others,' he replied.

For the next twenty-four hours the wind stayed light and Jill kept to her bunk, her arms hugging her body, from time to time crying and moaning. She ignored him when he spoke to her and would eat nothing. He wondered if she was having a nervous breakdown and what he should do about it. In the end, seeing no alternative, he left her to get on with it. Two days after they had discussed making for Setubal, the wind returned, light at first but soon settling to a steady force four from the north east. He guessed they were in the Portuguese trades at last. Adopting Jill's suggestion for when they had a light following wind, he set the masthead genoa and trysail. The pilot liked this arrangement and 'Patience' made good progress with the minimum of fuss. He tried to persuade Jill to come on deck and enjoy the idyllic conditions, but she moaned unintelligibly and asked for another box of tissues. He looked at her face and its fast-shut eyes, deciding she did not look all that ill and had better be left to snap out of it. He remembered Judy's insistence that the best cure for most things is to fast or take nothing but liquids. Jill, in her fashion, had obeyed both these directives.

They passed close to a French warship and he thought of signalling a request to report his position, but by the time he had remembered where the flags were and which he needed, the ship had passed. He doubted in any case whether Rebecca would think to seek such information. She preferred to believe all was right with the world until proof to the contrary was overwhelming.

With Jill out of the way, and the rig suiting the conditions so well, he began to enjoy his sole command. The horizon was empty of shipping, the yacht dead on course, so he made coffee and drank it in the cockpit, nibbling Rich Tea biscuits contentedly and studying the pilot chart for the North Atlantic. It had not really dawned on him until that moment, unruffled by his companion or bad weather, just how far they had come. A spider with cold feet seemed to run down his spine. They were making it! He had sailed – all right, *they* had sailed – God! a thousand miles or more; many more in actual distance travelled; and in a tiny, bucking, exhaustingly tender five-tonner across some of the worst water in the Western hemisphere.

He studied the chart. Three hundred miles to the Canaries. Madeira, he realized, was a good deal closer. About a hundred miles closer. If they changed course now they would lose hardly any mileage by the diversion. In fact, yes, better than that, he would try to fetch Porto Santo, just for the navigational exercise, after which Madeira would be a piece of cake. With wind and current in their favour, he could see no problem. Jill couldn't object; indeed, as she was it seemed the only responsible thing to do.

He altered course and trimmed the sails and pilot. Then he sat back again, treating himself to a second coffee and the rest of the biscuits, and dwelt on the past few weeks. They seemed more like months. It took a certain effort to consider why he had set out from Chichester Harbour on his final voyage. Summoning all the conviction he could muster, he told himself that although he might be deriving some satisfaction from the way things had panned out, nothing had basically changed. There was no reason, his mind insisted, for altering his original plan. All right, so he had postponed them, so he had had to adapt them a little, but in the end he would have to confront the facts of a life that was not worth prolonging. That, after all, was what he had decided when in normal circumstances and a normal frame of mind. This business, this little triumph of surviving a long haul in open sea, was a personal matter, a one-off. It would cut no ice with the rest of the world, and even for him could be only a source of temporary satisfaction. Meanwhile, he concluded, taking the last biscuit and dunking it appreciatively, there was nothing for it but to press on and get the present ambition out of his system. His swan song. Yes, it made sense.

It was late morning and the sun was pleasantly hot. 'Patience' was still sailing fast and without fuss, almost as though scenting warmer climes and friendlier seas. In the following breeze he could have read a newspaper without the irritation of blown pages. He had almost forgotten Jill's existence when a short cough reminded him he was not alone. His slight pang of guilt at having left her for so long was tempered by the lack of any solution. He was considering whether to go below and make another attempt to communicate when she appeared through the hatchway, the paleness of her face emphasized by the colour she had applied rather carelessly to her lips.

He eyed her warily, rejecting the thought of asking if she felt better, as he could see several ways in which she might take against the question.

'The rig you suggested is working well,' he said.

She looked around and sniffed the air, like a mole after winter.

'Feels good,' she said.

'Warmer by the minute. Would you like a mattress on deck?'

'I've had enough of lying down. Where do you reckon we are?'

She slumped on to the seat opposite. He decided to keep quiet about their change of course.

'Less than three hundred miles to the Canaries.'

'God!' she said, 'I *have* slept.

'Hungry?'

'Sort of.'

'Sit here while I get something to eat.'

She didn't argue, taking his place and tilting her head back with her eyes closed to take the full comfort of the sun.

He opened a tin of pilchards, for which she had earlier admitted a curious passion. Then he wondered if they would be too rich on an empty stomach, so he served them with plenty of crispbread. She ate with relish, silently. With the coffee she settled back and closed her eyes again, as though greedy for the sun. Without opening them she said:

'I'm afraid I have rather put you through it.'

He had never been able to take an apology without feeling guilt.

'Oh, well, takes two,' he mumbled.

'It's nerves, I suppose; and being frightened.'

His instinct for accuracy overcame caution.

'You've as steady as a rock in heavy weather,' he protested. 'I'm the one who needs his hand held.'

'Not inside. That's why I drink a bit. Alcohol is wonderful for reducing wave height. Better than oil.'

He was not so incautious as to remind her that her drinking came in the calms. He guessed it would be better to tell her about Madeira than let her find out, and the mood seemed favourable.

'I thought it might be more seamanlike to make for Madeira,' he said casually.

Her eyes went to the compass with heavy-weather alertness. To his surprise she smiled.

'To shorten your agony?'

'Not at all,' he protested. 'But if you aren't feeling too good...'

'I'm all right. I go through phases. Roger called them my turns. Something to do with the moon maybe. O.K., let's press on for Madeira. As a matter of fact I had a rather super holiday there once.'

'Oh, God!' he said to himself. 'You fool, Braine, you total bloody fool.'

'As a child,' she added. 'With a great aunt. I expect it's changed a bit since then.'

For the next twenty-four hours Jill was as pleasant as when they first met. Taking neither spirits by day nor nembutal by night, she read, navigated, and when unable to find anything else to do insisted on touching up the varnish work. She seemed keen to put in more time in the galley, so to keep things sweet he let her have her head. She did not complain when she caught him surreptitiously giving the crockery a second wash, nor when he replaced the J-cloth before going over the sink and working surface after her. But after that her interest in the galley seemed to decline and he gradually took over all the preparation and clearing away of meals.

Apart from being asked incomprehensible questions by an Italian ketch bound, they suspected, for the Mediterranean, the days were uneventful, though on the day following Jill's recovery they nearly ran down a large basking shark. It took avoiding action in the nick of time, then cruised companionably alongside, its nose opposite the yacht's stem, its tail by the cockpit. They regarded its dorsal fin, which was above the level of the deck, with some apprehension and were not unduly sorry when their company bored it and it dropped astern.

'Wants to bask again, I suppose,' Jill said. 'What a tedious life. No challenge.'

Perhaps because the shark had made her nervous, or perhaps because the wind had dropped and they were making no more than two knots under the genoa, she began to show signs of restlessness again. Dreading a return of the previous days' pattern, he prayed for more robust conditions.

'We ought to sight land tomorrow,' he said, feeling as he had on long car journeys when the children were small. Games had been needed to pass the time away. 'Why don't you choose a cassette and surprise me?'

She looked at him quizzically.

'It's all right, you don't have to keep me amused.'

The night was starry and clear, the sea like a mill-pond. The genoa was idle, as lifeless as a punctured balloon. Except for the occasional gluck of water on the hull and the plop of a leaping fish, the silence was absolute.

'Oh, God!' she said, 'we could lose wind for days.'

'Are you keen on backgammon?' he asked nervously.

She bridled. '*Keen* on backgammon? Do you mean you want to play it?'

He shrugged and pulled down the corners of his mouth.

'Not particularly...'

'Then why suggest it? Why don't you do some writing or read a book if you are bored?'

'I'm not bored. I just thought...'

'That I was.'

'Well, you did say...'

'Look, don't patronize. Let's just relax, shall we? The last thing I want is to be in the way.'

He wondered idly if she was the kind of woman who deep down craved regular beatings. Roger's disappearance had long been understandable. It was a grim choice for any skipper - perpetual force eights or a crew moaning like a foghorn. He was determined to keep the peace without recourse to sex or drugs for what might be their last day together. His body and nerves had hardened since leaving home waters, but he was of an age to be convinced of limits.

'I think I'll get my head down,' he said. He wasn't particularly tired, but it seemed the only way of removing the provocation of his availability. 'Will you be all right for a few hours?'

'Of course,' she said. 'I owe you a few watches.'

He was surprised she had noticed, and as he fell asleep he counted her better qualities with some genuine affection.

When he awoke, Jill had repaid him more than two watches. It was dawn and conditions seemed ideal, which was to say that 'Patience' was bowling through the water and he could hear Jill singing. He stuck his head out of the hatch and looked around. The yacht was charging along at a speed of which he had not thought her capable. The crests of the high following seas were being blown by the strong wind into a mobile mist that sparkled in the sun. As the bigger waves caught up with the boat, she surged forward, almost surfing.

'Real colour-supplement weather!' Jill shouted.

She had abandoned the automatic pilot and was keeping

'Patience' under expert control, her eyes shining and her hair blowing in the wind. The genoa was still set, and as the yacht raced down the larger waves she tried to plough through their leaders as though impatient to ride over their crests.

'Christ!' he said, 'you'll break the bloody mast.'

'Rubbish!' she replied cheerfully, avoiding a broach-to with a deft flick of the tiller, 'you've got twin backstays and double spreaders. I knew you'd been under-driving her all along.'

'At least let's change down to the number one jib,' he pleaded. 'You'll drive her to the bottom if you're not careful.'

'It's eased off if anything,' Jill said. 'At four this morning it got quite sporty; force seven at a guess.'

'Holy Mary! he said, paling. He went below with the excuse of wanting to shave. What the eye didn't see... When he re-appeared he brought his binoculars and scanned the horizon anxiously for sight of land. The blown spume gave poor visibility.

'We'll find it,' Jill said exuberantly. 'Meanwhile, enjoy yourself. You don't get a sail like this every day of the week.'

'You can say that again,' he said, once more scanning the horizon.

'If you won't have a Brookes and Gatehouse on board...' Jill said teasingly. He had never known her so maddeningly cheerful.

As they rode a high crest Porto Santo appeared briefly exactly where he had hoped it would be. He shouted with triumph and Jill smiled at him with what seemed to be congratulation. The rugged blue-grey shape was only a few miles from their bow.

'This calls for celebration,' he shouted.

He went below and returned with an appropriate bottle and two tumblers.

'Pour mine,' Jill commanded. 'I don't want to miss a moment of this sail.'

'You better hadn't,' he said fervently.

They passed along the north coast of Porto Santo and rounded the island's western tip. He expected to see Madeira, whose mountains exceed six thousand feet, but nothing was visible. He laid off a course to pass its eastern end by a safe margin in case of any deviation by the Canaries current which Jill pointed out ran between the two islands. While doing this piece of navigation he noticed a great shelf in the sea bed between Madeira and the Islas Desertas to the south-east.

'The depth drops rapidly to over a thousand fathoms from fifty,' he said. 'With the south-bound current sweeping over it, we could have a rough passage.'

'O.K.,' she said reluctantly. 'Legitimate panic-stations. Number one jib at your convenience.'

The passage proved fast and uncomfortable and they sighted Madeira when no more than two miles off. The pilot had warned that thick weather was a feature of those parts. As they approached the ocean 'step' the passage was even harder going, but the wind had eased and they could enjoy the spectacular natural features of the island.

'Think of being driven on to those great rocky cliffs,' he said.

'If you want me to dwell on those lines, you'd better splice the mainbrace again. Take a few fixes. Distances can be deceptive and I don't know these waters.'

The thrill of both seeing and smelling the land again was so powerful that he felt light-headed.

'There's nothing like it,' he said.

'Like what?'

'Making landfall with the feeling that one is discovering a place for the first time.'

The remark produced a flood of reminiscence from Jill for whom landfall held a mystique superior even to the excitement of fast sailing and heavy weather.

'It's what it's all about,' she said happily.

'You must have some Hawkins or da Gamas in your ancestry,' he said. With landfall a near certainty, he felt almost affectionate towards her.

'I have,' she said. 'Three admirals and an arctic explorer. On my father's side. My mother didn't like the water, but she was a great balloonist in her day.'

'You might have warned me,' he said.

Soon after they rounded the tip of Madeira, dusk fell, and as 'Patience' sailed into the island's lee they were nearly becalmed. But as though anxious not to spoil their day, a gentle if variable breeze held up for long enough to ghost them gently towards their destination. He busied himself preparing ship, making ready anchors, tidying sails, looking out warps and fenders, and finally hoisting the Portuguese ensign on the starboard spreader, the Q flag to port.

By himself, he would have hove-to and awaited a friendly tow or a pilot. He mentioned casually that 'Patience' carried a G flag. But Jill would have none of such cowardly schemes to diminish their arrival. While by the light of a torch he made what sense he could of the too-small chart on the bridgedeck, Jill sailed them carefully past the twinkling shore-lights towards Funchal. At shortly before nine they entered harbour and were quickly closed by a motor launch prominently marked 'Pilotos.' Only then was Jill prepared to admit that some assistance might be welcome. With difficulty they conveyed that 'Patience' carried no engine. They were taken in tow and led into a corner near the town quay. The bower anchor dropped and the Pilot's launch took the kedge and laid it astern.

'Well,' Jill said, 'that wasn't so difficult, was it?'

'Actually,' he said, 'the one thing that racing a keel boat does for you is to teach you to pick up a mooring without an engine.'

'You must show me next time,' she said.

Shore sounds drifted pleasantly on the night air. They sat in the cockpit and finished their work on the mainbrace. The lights of the port swept up into the mountains.

'This is one of the most romantic landfalls I have ever made,' Jill said.

He drained his glass. The underlying threat seemed almost acceptable.

11

THE Customs launch arrived tactfully after breakfast. Little interest was shown in the remaining stocks of spirits and cigarettes. The health clearance obtained in England was waved aside, presumably on the basis that survival in so modest a vessel was proof enough of physical fitness.

The coracle covered the sixty or so yards to the steps of the quay. An amused boatman lifted it on to the steps and tied it to a handrail, making gestures that implied the need to prevent it blowing away. The massively-built stone quay rocked so violently that Matthew felt like sitting down, but by the time they had found the post office in the compact little town their land legs had returned.

'I must cable my sister,' Jill said.

The clerk spoke good English and the matter was quickly over. Matthew noticed that Jill's message announced arrival and ended 'further cable follows.'

'Are you going to mention you are no longer single-handed?' she asked.

'Who to?'

She looked surprised.

'Your wife.'

'I don't think she'd be interested,' he said.

'So what are you telling her?'

'I wasn't going to bother.'

'Not bother? What, not send a cable at all?'

'No.'

Her irritation returned with wifely suddenness.

'Don't be so bloody silly. Of course you must send the poor woman a cable. You left her nearly a month ago.'

It was preferable to give in than to explain. He pondered, then wrote:

'Madeira first port of call. Hope all well. Matthew.'

Jill vetted it.

'Inaccurate, brief, and you've forgotten "love", but I suppose it's better than nothing. Now you can have a hair cut and go to the chandlers while I top up the stores. Then we can meet at that café for coffee at eleven.'

When she joined him she had little shopping, but her hair and face had undergone major overhaul. It seemed tactless to remark on the improvement. A couple took the next table.

'Bloody hell,' he said. 'The Jacksons.'

'Shush,' she said. 'They'll hear you.'

'He's the end. Vast gin palace; motor, of course; known everywhere between Birdham and the Isle of Wight; has crewed in club races at the height of the season and thinks he knows it all.'

The man saw him.

'Hello, mate,' he said, 'where've you wafted in from?'

His moustache suggested over-ripe nostalgia for a good war in the R.A.F.

'Hello,' Matthew said coldly. They had never been within a mile of mateyness. The hearty, approval-seeking extroversion of those in the Jackson mould had helped Matthew's transition from racing to solo cruising. He made the introductions, ignoring Jackson's opening question.

'Douglas and Ellen Jackson. It is Ellen, isn't it? Jill Armitage.'

'Well, well, well,' Jackson said. He eyed Jill professionally. His wife was a quiet, dismal little woman with a handshake suggesting total disinterest or advanced ill health. 'When did you fly in?'

'I didn't fly,' Matthew said.

'Ah, cruise ship,' Jackson said knowingly.

Noticing the look he gave Jill, Matthew felt the words 'shipboard romance' could have appeared in a bubble over his head.

'I sailed here,' he said firmly.

Jackson's eyes widened. He had once made Dartmouth by sea.

'Sailed? I thought you were strictly a round-the-buoys-and-back-for-tea man.'

'Surely you knew I'd been cruising for several seasons?' Matthew replied irritably.

'Well, yes, piddling about the Solent,' Jackson said dismissively, 'but no long-distance stuff. What did you come in?'

'The Vertue. I don't have a choice of yachts.'

'You're joking! No offence, old man, but that little job isn't fit for more than a Channel hop on a fine day.'

'Vertues have circumnavigated the globe,' Matthew said stiffly. He knew it sounded pompous and that Jackson was thinking 'Yes, but not by you', but the man got under his skin.

'Well, I'll be buggered,' Jackson said.

'Douglas,' his wife said.

He turned his attention to Jill.

'You a sailor too, then?'

'In a small way,' Jill admitted.

'And off a boat?' Jackson persisted.

'Right.'

'But a proper one, no doubt.'

'Very proper. A Vertue.'

'There's a lot of Vertue about,' Jackson said, sniggering.

'It's the same one,' Jill said, impatience thinly disguised.

'Oh, ah, yes,' Jackson said, sitting back and looking sideways at his wife.

'She has helped me down from the Belle Isle,' Matthew said.

'Of course,' Jackson said, 'wherever the Belle Isle may be.'

'We flew,' his wife said. 'We've been here a week. At Reid's. It's my reward for never seeing Douglas at summer weekends.'

'You *could* see me,' her husband said, 'if you weren't so set against sailing.'

'You know I don't like the movement and the engine noise,' Ellen said, 'and I've nothing much in common with all those people you ask down.'

'You've still got your motor boat, then?' Matthew questioned, determined not to call it a yacht.

'No time for anything more time-consuming,' Jackson said defensively. 'You know how it is with a staff to look after and all that.' His tone changed to one of solicitous enquiry. 'Tell me, how's the little woman?'

He had met Rebecca only once, early in Matthew's racing days, when she occasionally helped to entertain visiting teams. Matthew guessed that Jackson did not remember her name.

'Which little woman do you mean?' he asked innocently.
Jackson puffed out his cheeks.
'Who do you think? Your wife, of course.'
'Oh, my wife,' Matthew said, surprise in his voice. 'As far as I know she is in the pink.'
'Glad to hear it,' Jackson said unconvincingly. 'She'll be joining you, no doubt.'
'I doubt it. I'm moving on.'
'After selling the boat? Bloody boring to bash back against wind and tide.'
'On, not back.'
'The Med.?'
'West.'
'What, all the way across?' Jackson said unbelievingly. 'To the lands of rum and ginger?'
'That's the general idea. Via the Canaries.' All of a sudden, he really wanted to.
'Well, I'll be...'
'Douglas,' Ellen said.

'I almost enjoyed that,' Matthew admitted as they walked back to the quay. 'Nosey, conceited bastard.'
'If he's a representative example of your friends,' Jill said, 'I am more sorry than ever for your wife.'
'He isn't, and what do you mean by "more than ever"?'
'Well, you *are* a bit of a sod, aren't you?'
'Why should you say that?'
'I'm an expert sod-detector.'
'Just because you're sour about your husband leaving you, there's no need to take it out on me.'
'No connection.'
'What have I done, then?'
'Look, I don't know your wife and I accept you may be bored with each other, but you have two grown children and have spent most of a lifetime together. She is bound to be worried at not having heard from you for several weeks – especially if she knows you sailed off under-equipped and are not exactly the Francis Chichester of five-tonners.'
'So?'
'So you weren't even going to send her a cable.'

'Supposing,' he said, 'just supposing I wasn't going to go back to Rebecca. Supposing I had planned to do a Roger?'

'Let's suppose, then. It's more interesting than backgammon.'

'Wouldn't it be kinder just to disappear? Or would she prefer an interim report of my being safe and sound, and then to hear no more?'

'That sounds made up as you've gone along; under pressure. Anyway, surely you'd still write to her, even if from Barbados with a planter's punch in one hand and some dusky maiden in the other?'

Almost angrily he said. 'Things won't work out like that.'

She looked at him speculatively.

'You're not just a sod, you're an odd sod. But I suppose I've got to make the usual allowances for a writer's temperament.'

'You *do* that. It's high time *you* began to make some allowances for *me*.'

They spent the next few days sight-seeing. Jill insisted on treating them to a self-drive car and they spent a night in a *pousada* in the centre of the island. He felt it might make amends for his refusal to stop off at Setubal. He was not resistant to the comfort, good food and wine, nor to Jill's ability to make love independent of force eights.

Back on 'Patience', they enjoyed the choice of fresh food, especially the bread, fruit and vegetables. Funchal's harbour was a busy, interesting place. Matthew indulged a sense of immense superiority over the visitors brought ashore in launches from the cruise liners. In this, as in other respects, Jill stayed true to type in being quick and capable in cutting him down to size, but he did not resent her ability to give as good as she received, even quite enjoying being put in his place. Now that he was not sharing her attention with 'Patience', he found her acid and accurate in many of her assessments of him; if the pleasure was somewhat masochistic, at least she was showing in him an interest he had long felt to be lacking from any quarter at home.

She said nothing about flying back to England. He wondered why, but said nothing; for some reason he found it hard to analyse, he was quite happy having her around. The relaxing days they spent on Madeira made him realize he had not felt so fit for years.

They were enjoying the panorama of Funchal from a belvedere high to the west of the town.

'It's been fun,' Jill said.

'Not bad,' he agreed. 'We've... sort of adjusted.'

'I suppose at our age one leaves a good few things unsaid.'

'I haven't noticed you miss many,' he said, smiling. She was better company on land, but no less quick to assert her rights and emphasize his obligations. He supposed that in a gruesome fashion beyond Jackson's imagining, it had been a shipboard romance.

'It's difficult to stop being a wife,' she said.

'I don't mind that,' he replied. 'Old patterns die hard.'

She looked down to where the houses of Santo António, snug in its valley, clustered round the white church like day-old chickens round a mother hen.

'Why doesn't one pull out and live somewhere like that?' she said. 'Away from all the stress and strain of modern life.'

'What, you? With no challenge? You'd be bored out of your mind within three weeks.'

'You're probably right. People get addicted to civilization. They may not like it, and it drives them into early graves, but the alternatives are not for the majority of us.'

'I'm not sure that I'm in the majority. I've had the rat-race along with the rats.'

'You really ought to get a light-weight hat,' she said. 'Sun stroke in the middle of the Atlantic can be no fun.'

He had been quietly amused and rather touched by the way Jill had begun to slip in small pieces of advice – usually quite tactfully – about crossing the ocean. But at times his responses caused her to look at him curiously – a summing-up, conclusion-making look he had often seen on Rebecca's face. He wondered how much she had guessed.

But in the days ashore he had seldom resented her renewed interest in himself and his plans. He continued to guard the secret of his ultimate intention, but the questions she asked about his marriage soon uncovered his belief that his decline as a writer had much to do with what had gone wrong between himself and Rebecca. But even as Jill drew such matters out of him, he felt a loyalty towards Rebecca and sought alternative explanation for his feeling of having outlived his *raison d'etre*. So he made more of his fear of old age, of ill-health, of the children's disinterest in him.

It was Jill who, after a pleasant two weeks on the island, suggested they leave for the Canaries. He made no objection. She had begun to be impatient with him again, though over small things and in a kindlier, almost motherly way, with less of the sex antagonism she had shown on their voyage.

The barometer was rising. Jill topped up the provisions with fresh food while he walked along the front to the Harbourmaster's Office for a forecast. A call to the Meteorological Department confirmed that a low had just passed; the outlook was winds of force four from the north west.

'Just the job,' Jill said.

She was waiting for him on the quay with a pile of stores including a flagon of Verdelho. The boatman who had helped with the coracle on the first day, ran them out to 'Patience' - stores, coracle and all. They gave him cigarettes and two bottles of beer and he retrieved their stern anchor and warp and passed them aboard with a lot of smiles and, they supposed, good wishes. Matthew took the tiller and sailed 'Patience' towards the harbour mouth under headsail alone. It was early afternoon.

'Three hundred miles,' he said. 'Under. Shouldn't be any problem.'

Jill looked sad.

'That was a lovely fortnight. And nice people.'

'Not sorry to see the back of the Jacksons,' he said.

'Not everyone's a Jackson,' Jill said, 'and we only met them twice.'

'I'm quite glad to be away, even so,' he said. 'Islands can get a bit claustrophobic.'

'You don't really like people very much, do you?'

'I've tried to. It's not so much that I don't like them as that I don't feel part of them, I suppose.'

'Only-children often have that problem,' she said. 'They try to put all their eggs into one relationship, which is tough if the relationship doesn't work out.'

He was disinclined to pursue the matter. He was not quite

sure what he felt. Physically more fit, yes, but somehow inclined to live for the day and the day alone.

'Don't let's discuss it,' he said. 'I'm a self-pitying sort of sod and better not encouraged.'

She squeezed his arm but said nothing.

The breeze was fresh, even in harbour. Clear of moorings, Jill raised the main and set the genoa. Clear of the outer mole, 'Patience' romped away at six knots in a big beam sea. Their spirits rose as they made good time southwards under pilot through the sparkling water. Clear of the island, the wind settled down to a steady force five for the rest of the afternoon, moderating in the evening. They had been warned to set their course well west of the Selvagems, an untidy and rocky group of uninhabited and unlit islands.

'I think I'm going to bring up,' Jill said.

'I thought you might. You've not said a thing for half an hour or more.'

'Neither have you.'

'I may be following you.'

She was ten minutes ahead of him, which rather pleased him.

The night was starry and clear. 'Patience' moved at four knots under genoa and trysail. At dawn the wind backed to the west. Mid-day brought a little rain and the afternoon proved exhausting. The wind altered strength and direction repeatedly, demanding constant changes of sail. But they covered nearly a hundred and twenty miles in the first twenty-four hours. On the evening of the second day they needed storm jib and trysail. Slacks, pullovers and oilskins were welcome against the chilly air, and when the wind veered north again they spent an uncomfortable night, 'Patience' rolling vigorously in an aggressive beam sea. The log showed they were south of the Selvagems, but they did not turn south-sou'-eastwards towards the eastern tip of Tenerife until dawn. It had been an unusually tiring sail for both of them.

'We're too soft from shore living,' Jill said ruefully. 'And I've news for you. The ruddy loo's blocked.'

The following afternoon brought sight of Tenerife. Matthew was for making Los Cristianos their landfall, having heard it was a small fishing village. Jill had heard otherwise.

'A man in St Malo said it's a whopping great resort now and

miles from the airport. It might be more sensible to make for Santa Cruz.'

'I have a feeling we're not going to like it as much as Funchal,' he said.

They rounded the tip of the island in brilliant moonlight. This put them into an unpleasant sea for a time, but once into the lee of the land they almost completely lost wind. Jill prepared fenders and warps and hoisted the Spanish ensign and Q flag while Matthew stayed on the tiller. He was determined to enter unaided, and after sailing through a strange area of what appeared to be overfalls they made a simple if slow entrance and cruised gently round the huge harbour with no idea of where they were expected to go.

'People,' Jill said softly but without rancour, 'who go to sea in small under-equipped boats...'

A pilot boat roared past them without as much as a wave, and eventually they picked up a mooring off what was unmistakably the Yacht Club. They had hardly had time to furl the sails before they were hailed by a surly boatman in a dinghy. With his one-and-a-half-horse-power outboard he towed them noisily through the close-moored trots to a battered and rusty forty-gallon oil can. It seemed an ignominious reception and they rewarded the man with cigarettes, beer, and restrained gratitude.

The stove's cheerful hissing soon dispelled the feeling of anti-climax, and they washed and changed their clothes while the beef and yams were cooking.

'Not bad,' Jill said, tipping some Verdelho into a jug. 'Nearly three hundred miles in little more than two days. You realize something?'

'What?'

'This is your point of no return.'

'How do you mean?'

'Once you leave the Canaries in a sailing boat there is only one way to go.'

'Oh, well,' he said, 'I'll think about that tomorrow.'

'You've done so well to date that the rest will be a piece of cake – even though you do insist on going one worse than Cook.'

Further up the harbour a night-shift was playing raucous

tunes on steel plate. When this ceased they were conscious of a sighing sound, so sinister it made Jill nervous. They decided it had to be some natural phenomenon to do with the wind in the surrounding hills. The yacht's gentle movements as she aligned herself to the vagaries of wind and tide brought peaceful sleep, though not before Jill had invited an encounter in which a singular tenderness on her part made it memorable for him.

The morning proved Tenerife a comedown after Madeira. Craggy mountains of barren rock rose in grotesque shapes to the north-west, more cruel and harsh than the sweeping wooded heights of Madeira. To the south-west lay the city of Santa Cruz, a vast expanse of modern buildings overlooking the enormous port. The long outer mole was lined with ships of every kind, class and nationality, with others lying to the oiling berths outside the harbour. 'Patience' seemed the only British yacht in sight.

Their mooring was at some distance from the palatial Club Nautico. The yacht's 'yellow duster' brought no response from the pilot boat which was busying itself in all directions. As they were finishing breakfast in the cockpit a faint hail of 'Señor Capitano!' came over on the breeze, and Matthew's binoculars revealed on the Club frontage a portly khaki-clad figure whose gold braid epaulettes gleamed impressively in the rising sun.

'So much splendour will expect abject submission gestures,' Jill warned.

'It's a hell of a haul for the coracle,' he muttered.

Rehearsing the full range of his Spanish vocabulary, Matthew worked the coracle over to the shore.

'Buenos dias, Señor!' he said, giving his all and pulling the coracle up after him.

The Port Captain, surveying the modest craft at Matthew's feet, seemed to grow in size and joviality. Waving aside passports, ship's papers and the impressive green card issued in Madeira, he wrote the yacht's name and statistics on a piece of paper. After a testing series of handshakes which at one point Matthew feared might turn into warm embraces, formalities appeared to be over.

The Club Nautico was somewhat over-powering at close quarters, offering a choice of split-level swimming pools, squash courts, sauna and highly polished terazzo floors for elegant leisure. The club was deserted except for the Commodore. His command of English faltered at the concept of a coracle, but after visual introduction he offered the loan of a dinghy for transporting the provisions needed for Matthew's voyage into the west.

He rowed back to 'Patience', the collapsed coracle lying across the gunwhales. Jill looked upset.

'What's the matter?' he asked.

'Matter? Nothing. Why?'

'You look a bit... off colour.'

'I'm fine. Feeling a bit end-of-the-affairish, perhaps. I've always preferred beginnings to ends. Anyway, I know you don't want to hang about, so let's provision you.'

It was a pleasant walk along a front planted with trees and shrubs clamorous with birds.

'That reminds me,' Jill said, 'I must get you some salt.'

'Salt? I don't use it. I told you.'

'You must in a hot climate, especially if you can't get fresh food for a long period.'

He shrugged. 'You're the boss.'

'And that hat. You should have reminded me in Madeira.'

'It's certainly not bad weather for mid-November.'

Jill sighed. 'I wish I could afford to stay here for a week or two.'

They sent cables. His was voluntary this time, reporting arrival and adding 'love'. He did not read Jill's.

The supermarket could have been in Brighton or Boston except that the prices, generally lower than in Madeira, were in the local currency. On their way through the Club Nautico on their return, the Commodore told them to make use of the facilities.

With the help of a long hose Matthew filled the water tanks. He hung mesh bags full of oranges, lemons, apples and onions in the forepeak. His supply of fresh bread was more than he would be able to eat while still edible, but it seemed a forgivable luxury.

After lunch aboard they returned to the club to shower and for Jill to wash some smalls furtively in one of the many awesomely gleaming washbowls.

'I suppose I should have gone to a washataria,' she admitted, 'but it seemed such a waste.'

Carrying the damp garments in a plastic bag, for courage to beg storage had failed them, they went into the town again to see what the free port had to offer. It was a mecca for the technologically minded, catering for yachtsmen for whom engines and navigational equipment were nine-tenths of the battle and the pleasure. Neither saw anything they really needed except for a jumbo-sized pack of brightly-coloured lavatory rolls.

Back on the hard, hot pavement in the broiling sun, conversation difficult above the din of traffic, they looked at each other gloomily.

'Well, that's about it,' Matthew said.

Jill nodded. 'Los Cristianos might at least have been prettier,' she said.

'The view from the breakwater could be good,' Matthew said. 'We'd see more of the hinterland.'

The view was the best thing they had encountered so far, apart from the showers at the Club Nautico. They were strolling back towards the promenade, looking idly at the large yachts moored stern-on, when a voice called Jill's name.

On the stern of a fine ketch a tall, slim man with wisps of grey hair below his yachting cap had his arm up in graceful salutation. The ketch was all of eighty feet with teak decks and a hull of such gleaming perfection that it might have been painted that morning. Forward of the leather-covered wheel a wide, open cockpit was filled with dark blue mattresses and cushions with white piping.

'No idea you'd be this far south,' the man said. 'Come aboard.'

The long telescopic gang-plank had a stainless steel handrail and its own lighting system. They left the plastic bag and the pack of toilet rolls on the aft deck by a massive winch and accepted iced vodka martinis which they drank lounging on the comfortable mattresses. Not a square inch of fibreglass or marine ply was visible. Teak and stainless steel abounded.

'What a boat!' Jill breathed with undisguised reverence.

Iain Vesper-Strathclyde nodded. Contradiction would have been absurd.

'Got a bit tired of the old Nicholson Forty-eight,' he

admitted. 'Thought I'd go back to the real thing while I could still afford it. More maintenance and crewing problems, of course, but she handles marvellously well.'

His face had the deep, permanent tan of men who can afford unlimited time in the more romantic parts of the world. It was lined in all the right places but was too lean to have sagged beyond a hint of good-living. His nose had the aquilinity of the improbable beings common to the pages of women's magazines.

Envy had never been one of Matthew's more troublesome vices.

'A beautiful vessel,' he said sincerely.

'What do you sail?' Iain enquired.

'A Vertue. Not quite in this class. Teak, though.'

'Oh, but yes, yes, yes, yes, yes!' Iain said. 'Superb little craft! Go anywhere. The quintessence of five tonners.'

The charm was heavy, but for the moment Matthew warmed to the man.

A white kitten skittered into the wheelhouse, chasing or being pursued by its own shadow.

'Seamew,' Iain introduced. 'All the makings of a good crew, but her claws are into everything.'

Jill clucked at the kitten who looked at her blankly with round blue eyes.

'You've just arrived?' Iain asked.

Jill picked up the kitten who kneaded her forearm with small needles.

'Yes. Well, last night.'

'Then for goodness sake, you must come to dinner. Both of you. It will take Arianna only moments to bike into town for some more lobster.'

'You're married?' Jill asked with what Matthew took to be either surprise or disappointment.

'Bless you, no! Arianna is our galley-slave. She and Jean-Jacques have been with me since Cannes and do almost everything. Mind you, on a yacht of this size we could do with another hand. We are pressing on to Panama as soon as the Wildensteins join us, and Max is no Slocum.'

'Wildenstein the publisher?' Matthew asked.

Iain nodded. 'I expect them tomorrow.'

Matthew had never met Max Wildenstein, recently elevated to the peerage, but he remembered the recent fuss when his firm had paid the biggest advance ever for a first novel destined to be the hype of the decade.

'It's very kind of you,' he said, 'but I think I must hit the sack really early and get a decent night's sleep. We've just provisioned my boat and I'd like to make an early start.'

'Well, I know there's nothing much to keep one in Santa Cruz,' Iain admitted, 'but are you sure? We could eat quite early.'

'No, really, I think I should press on and not upset your routine.'

'And what about you?' Iain asked Jill, offering her another cigarette from a silver box divided into compartments for French and Turkish with tips of various colours. 'Good Lord, I haven't even asked what you are doing here, where you are staying, or anything. Typically me. Full of my own doings.'

'It's a long story,' Jill warned.

'I felt guilty about accepting,' she said.

'I wanted you to,' Matthew said stoutly.

A part of him had counselled against depriving her of an evening whose equal could not be found below deck on 'Patience'; another part felt that the resistance she showed to Iain's invitation could have been stronger.

'I've nothing smart enough to wear,' Jill said. 'Iain sets terribly high standards. I shouldn't have accepted.'

They were walking back to the Club Nautico. The sun was a little less hot; the trees' longer shadows gave more shade; the end of something more than just another day was within sight.

'You had the opportunity to refuse.'

'Well, it's a bit difficult. He knows Roger quite well...'

'Does that matter now?'

'Perhaps not, but there are other complications.'

He shrugged. 'Oh, well, it's no business of mine. I shall be quite happy with flying-fish sandwiches and the Verdelho.'

She squeezed his arm.

'Look,' she said, 'we've got to be sensible. This is where we planned to go our separate ways. It's been fun, but I can catch a plane from here and I must get back and sort my life out.'

'Of course,' he said. 'That was the plan.'

'You go on back to the boat. I saw something in the town that I think would do for this evening.'

When she called from the club frontage he rowed ashore to collect her. She had bought shoes as well as a dress.

'I needed them for the 'plane anyway,' she said. 'Roger took nearly all my things with him.'

While she dressed he stowed gear and provisions. The packet of salt Jill had bought was big enough for an army. He knew they had to part if his plans were to go ahead, but he felt slightly sick and knew that this had little to do with fear of the long haul ahead or of having to come to terms with his old decision.

When she was ready for shore he rowed her in. He said she looked terrific, and meant it. Her deep honey tan was a match for Iain Vesper-Strathclyde's and her make-up took ten years off her age. She had packed her suitcase so as not to hold him up in the morning.

'Don't wait up for me,' she said.

He assembled the coracle which he had put into the dinghy and returned to 'Patience'. He ate all the scraps he could find and drank more Verdelho than his palate required. He turned in early, against all reason feeling as wretched as hell.

He did not stir until dawn. As consciousness seeped back and he remembered the day's programme, he wanted only to be up and away as soon as possible. But he made himself lie in while the light strengthened, not wishing to disturb Jill in her forward berth after her late evening. When he could stand his thoughts no longer he got up quietly and put his head through the hatch for a feel of the weather. He noticed that the dinghy was not tied to the stern, then a hail from the shore drew his gaze to Jill's slim figure approaching the frontage to the Club Nautico.

As he waited for her to reach the yacht he felt angry; in some way deceived. She came alongside and handed him the dinghy's painter.

'Sorry,' she said. 'I hope you haven't been waiting for me.'

'I've only just got up. I assumed you were on board.'

'People from other boats joined us. It went on so late I thought it would be unfair to disturb you. I knew you wanted to make an early start, so I crept out of my cabin without waking anyone.'

He knew he had no reason for feeling resentment, so made the best of it.

'Oh, well, you'll be wanting your suitcase.'

She stood up in the dinghy and came on board with the help of the shrouds. He went below to collect her suitcase from the port berth. She stayed in the cockpit looking oddly awkward and out of place in her expensive dress and pretty shoes.

'Do you know your flight time yet?' he enquired.

'No. I must finalize things.' Her eyes failed to meet his by a matter of inches.

He put her suitcase in the dinghy, forward of the centre thwart.

'Will you thank the Commodore for me? I don't think I need go ashore before leaving; I saw to the formalities yesterday.'

'Of course. I'll row myself back. Don't you bother.'

He pointed to a small cardboard box and a supermarket bag on the aft seat of the dinghy.

'Are those yours?'

Jill stepped over the guard rail and lowered herself into the dinghy.

'It's for you,' she said. 'A present from Iain, if you like.'

As she passed the box up to him there was a squeak from inside. He opened it. Seamew blinked up at him, such brain as there was still dulled by sleep.

'And here's some tinned food,' Jill added, hastily pushing the supermarket bag through the guard rails. 'She only likes one variety.'

He gazed at Seamew blankly.

'What the hell shall I do with it?' he asked.

Jill had undone the painter and was placing the oars in the rowlocks.

'We all need something to look after,' she said.

She rowed away quickly, leaving him holding the box uncertainly. He closed the lid and gazed after her. She shipped an oar and blew him a kiss. Faintly her last words came to him:

'Don't give up, will you?' And then: 'And remember the salt.'

A small wind riffled across the water from the mountains, thin and chilly at that early hour, turning the yacht's bow a little towards the mouth of the harbour; a reminder that he had business in deep waters.

12

HAVING no large-scale chart of the island, he was anxious to clear it before dark. At 10 a.m. he cast off from the rusty drum, feeling more unsettled and alone than at any time on the voyage. As he cleared the outer mole the sun emerged, glinting on the windows of the tall white buildings of the city of Santa Cruz and illuminating the conical tip of Pico del Teide. Behind the 12,000-foot peak a black sky reminded him that he had obtained no recent forecast.

Outside the harbour 'Patience' butted into a light head wind, but during the early afternoon a breeze came off the land, aiding gentle progress along the coast under main and genoa. The yacht finally cleared the southern end of the island at 17.30 hours, when the wind fell right off then gradually filled in from the south east. Their course was 230° true, which would keep them well clear of the island of Hierro about seventy-five miles away.

The night was cold and wet. It seemed absurd to be due west of the Sahara Desert and yet to need thick pullover and oilskins. Just before midnight the wind backed to the north and freshened and he made good progress on number one jib only.

He slept better than he had expected and when he woke the wind had gone light, what there was coming from the south west; then it went altogether and he ate breakfast in the cockpit on an ocean of the deepest blue and in increasing heat. He thought about Jill and knew he was missing her, but comforted himself with the reminder that in such conditions she could be absolute hell. He was annoyed for wanting her to be there. He wondered if she had slept with Iain the night before and was all the more irritated at caring. He preferred to think of her on the plane back for England and hoped there would be a reconciliation with Roger.

There was a scratching on the companion way and the kitten appeared, blinking into the morning sun. Perhaps because the motion of so humble a craft alarmed her, Seamew had not yet proved to have the crew potential Iain had predicted. After a bedtime saucer of milk she had seen the night through in her cardboard box, so quiet as to be forgotten.

Matthew looked at the creature apprehensively, wondering what additional problems its presence might bring. He offered her a small piece of crust with butter. She nosed it, then looked up at him and mewed indignantly.

'If you're hungry,' he said, 'you'll bloody eat it.'

Seamew splayed her legs more widely as a slight lift in the sea rocked the boat, and mewed again, more demandingly.

Matthew looked the kitten in the eyes severely, finding more power in their innocence than he knew was in himself.

'Oh, all right,' he said weakly, 'it's milk you're after, is it?'

He got up and dropped through the hatch into the cabin. His bare feet discovered a small pool in the middle of the floor. He frowned, suspecting that the night's rain had found a point of entry through the doghouse roof. Then the more likely answer struck him.

He preferred dogs to cats but knew the basics of their training were much the same. He reached into the cockpit and took Seamew round her small middle, lifting her down into the cabin. Dapping the kitten's nose into the pool he said 'Aaaaagh!' in a tone of extreme disgust. Then he patted the furry bottom, said 'Aaaaagh!' again, and put Seamew back into the cockpit. But on a small boat it did not seem sensible to leave matters there, so he mopped up the pool with some sheets of newspaper, keeping them flat, and returned on deck. He laid the newspaper on the coachroof, immediately aft of the mast, and contrived to hold it down with a length of stretchcord tensioned between the mast and the grab-rails on the roof. Then he went back for the kitten and placed her squarely in the middle of the soiled paper, this time gently pushing her head towards the paper to make the message clear. He stroked her fur to show that ill-feeling was not uppermost.

'You do it *here*,' he said firmly. 'Sorry there isn't a properly equipped powder-room on *this* vessel.'

Seamew gave no indication of understanding the situation,

but walked to the edge of the coachroof and collapsed carefully on to the side deck a few inches below. She then padded towards the cockpit, looking distrustfully at the surrounding waters as though shocked by the vulgar proximity. Only when the canvas dodger on the aft rails cut off her view of the offending element did she climb back into the cockpit with some sign of confidence.

Matthew followed and found the kitten's head hanging over the washboard at the cabin's entrance. She was clearly unaccustomed to such dangerous drops after life with Iain Vesper-Strathclyde. Matthew tipped her gently over the edge and she landed on the first step, legs wide apart, with a protesting squeak. Matthew followed and poured some milk into a saucer. Relieved that an intelligent appreciation of her needs was at last being shown, the kitten drank the lot. She then sniffed at the site of her earlier misdeed and positioned herself on target. Matthew grabbed her hastily and shot on deck, ignoring indignant protest at so gross an interruption of a private requirement. He placed the kitten firmly on the paper and stood back expectantly. After what it was difficult not to interpret as an inner battle between resentment and primal need, Seamew contributed to the dampness and then went a stage further. When she had finished and had tried to scrape newsprint over the soiled area, Matthew tore off the top two sheets and threw them over the side. He returned to the cockpit with a sense of achievement.

With so far to go before there could be any facing up to the purpose of his voyage, it was frustrating to be drifting on the windless sea. The morning wore on interminably, and a descarded beer can, thrown overboard at eleven, was still alongside at mid-day. A fish with unusual markings cruised round 'Patience', seemingly enjoying her shade.

It was not until after midnight that the breeze returned; positive and from the north, it later veered and enabled him to set the trade wind rig for the first time. A small flying-fish came on board and he gave it to Seamew who showed no interest until it was cooked in a little milk.

The wind kept up for the rest of that day, pushing 'Patience' along at five knots. In the evening he hoisted the masthead light and reduced sail to genoa only, fearing to be over-canvassed through the night. He retired early, weary from the extra work of being solo again. Seamew was already asleep on the forward berth Jill had first occupied. He had stowed sails there, and the gap between two of the bags offered a very snug corner for a kitten disinclined to make constant adjustment to the roll and pitch of a small yacht.

For days after, life was largely a matter of routine involving his still basic navigation, twice-daily bilge-pumping, clock-winding, barometer readings, log entries, maintenance of lamps and stove, and the arrangement before turn-in of torch, knife and other gear in case of emergency. Establishing in Seamew's small brain the need for orderly routine was a further demand on his time and imagination, but a workable symbiosis – if such a term was applicable to so one-sided a relationship – was established after about a week.

It was not until the eighth day that he realized he had not seen a single vessel since losing sight of Tenerife. More was involved than recording an idle fact. Before arrival in the Belle Isle, the nearness of land and shipping had ruled out serious thought of the mechanics of his ultimate purpose. With Jill on board there had been no alternative to pushing it into the back of his mind. After a week on a seemingly barren ocean he realized that the moment of truth need no longer be delayed. A full night in the Atlantic, with no riding light, offered the maximum chance of pulling off his plan without the dreaded interruption that psychologically as much as physically would be worse than a declining quality of life. Yet he hesitated, and knew that his hesitation must be analysed...

He told himself he had not considered that the challenge might become an end in itself, affecting his resolve to take the action that at the time had seemed logical and timely. He had under-estimated his capacity for adjustment, assuming – inasmuch as he had thought through his psychological responses – that discomfort, danger and loneliness would combine with life-weariness to make a drugged drifting into final sleep a welcome relief. His toughness and resilience surprised him, making him unsure of being sorry or glad that the logistics and rigours of the voyage had weakened resolve. Leaving the Solent – with the frustration, despondency and seeming futility of living so close in time – his plans had seemed logical, desirable, clear. Now, he had been got at by events and no longer knew his own mind.

He tried to weigh the probabilities. He might find the present run before the trades so boring that after a stern course in self-reminder his original rational frame of mind would return. Or, with so much ocean still ahead and so ill-equipped for major crises, he might run into conditions that would revive determination to see his plan through. Equally, circumstances might be so beyond his control that his fate was no longer a matter of choice. Examining these possibilites he recognized that each depended on circumstances outside his control. He lacked – yes, there was no doubt about it – he lacked the will to determine the outcome.

'All right,' he said defiantly to Seamew who was making a good job of a leg that seemed as clean as the rest of her, 'we'll leave it in the lap of the gods.'

He wished he was not missing Jill. Remembering the early days of their trip, when her behaviour had made life with Rebecca almost a nostalgic memory, he had mixed feelings of guilt. He pondered Jill's likely impression of him. Had she despised him? Pitied? He was a feeble man when all was said and done. Feeble husband, feeble father, feeble in life and work generally, as events had proved. Feeble sailor, even, compared with Jill, though at this stage in the voyage with something on the credit side.

He squared his shoulders, determined not to return to negative introspection. He would give the present routine a few more days; see how he made out; wait, as one so often had to wait in the role of writer, for inspiration for the next chapter...

In the way of the lonely, he had always found comfort from routine. There was a kind of security in the daily ordering of trivial events: a small world of one's own to measure against the vacancies and manipulations in others' lives.

The routine proved less predictable than he had supposed. Over the next few days the wind's changes in strength and direction proved the fallibility of those pundits who held that the east-west crossing on that latitude was a monotonous doddle. With his inborn respect for the correct procedures, he made many sail changes, noticing how his judgments and anticipation had sharpened over the weeks and how much more easily he could cope with the work involved. For nights, to ensure good sleep, he usually set the trisail with genoa or number one staysail. This lost some speed, but removed fear of accidental gybes. Gybes still came, but were less alarming than when under a full main. In one day he made 140 miles and began to regard less than 120 as a near disaster.

He played a lot of tapes and noticed how his reactions had changed. Vivaldi had long been one of his favourite composers, yet *The Four Seasons*, even with James Galway the flautist, proved thin and unsatisfying. Mahler, at least admired, now seemed neurotic and uneven. Some, but not all, of his Mozart tapes paled into insignificance against Beethoven.

He began to find more satisfaction from reading than from music, deriving deeper pleasure from texts he had read without particular response in earlier days. In Conrad's *Nostromo* he read and re-read several passages, finding particular affinity with those on solitude:

> ... the truth was that he died from solitude, the enemy known but to few on this earth, and whom only the simplest of us are fit to withstand...
>
> Solitude from mere outward condition of existence becomes very swiftly a state of soul in which the affectations of irony and scepticism have no place. It takes possession of the mind, and drives forth the thought into the exile of utter unbelief. After three days of waiting for the sight of some human face, (he) caught himself entertaining a doubt of his own individuality. It had merged into the world of cloud and water, of natural forces and forms of nature. In our activity alone do we find the sustaining illusion of an independent existence as against the whole scheme of things of which we form a helpless part. (He) lost all belief in the reality of his action past and to come...
>
> Not a living speck, not a speck of distant sail, appeared within the range of his vision; and, as if to escape from this solitude, he absorbed himself in his melancholy ... But at the same time he felt no remorse. What should he regret? He had recognized no other virtue than intelligence and his passions were swallowed up easily in this great

unbroken solitude of waiting without faith... His sadness was the sadness of the sceptical mind.

He found much the same thinking in Bernard Moitessier, and as with his responses to Conrad was now more in agreement than at issue with their evaluation of scepticism, their qualified respect for intelligence *per se*. A part of him particularly enjoyed recalling passages from Moitessier's logbook when that great single-hander, instead of returning to Europe to complete his passage in the 1968 non-stop round-the-world race, decided on a second lap:

> I have no desire to return to Europe with all its false gods. It is difficult to defend oneself against them – they eat your liver and suck your marrow and brutalize you in the end... To leave Europe and then go back again is senseless. Like leaving from nowhere to return to nowhere... I know that life is a battle, but in modern Europe this battle is idiotic.
>
> Make money, make money – to do what? To change your car when it is still going well, to dress 'decently' – this word makes me laugh – to pay an exorbitant rent, to pay for the right to moor one's boat in a port for almost the price of a servant's room in Paris, and perhaps one day to have a television; pushed, forced, ordered about by those false gods... I am going where you can tie up a boat where you want and the sun is free, and so is the air you breathe and the sea where you swim, and you can roast yourself on a coral reef...

But he found it unsettling to focus too long on the writings of those still open to enchantment by the world. He rediscovered the word-spinning of Saul Bellow, granting the accolade of marginal scoring where, in *Humboldt's Gift*, Charles Citrine's arguings with Renata provoked metaphysical speculation on the probability of Hereafter. He responded to the supposition that oblivion is all we have to expect of the big blank of death.

> What options present themselves? One option is to increase the bitterness of life so that death is a desirable release. (In this the rest of mankind will fully collaborate.)

But when the page presented a further option he decided it

was time for a cup of coffee and closed the book.

He spent time tending Rebecca's plant, proud of its survival. It had seemed to pick up again since leaving Tenerife. Although 'Patience' had taken on a character and identity he had never found in her during his short cruises in home waters, there was a lifelessness in steel and wood that was somehow relieved by the plant's thrust for growth and change. The sea's remoteness from life familiar to man was in itself a challenge, and the company of plant and kitten was strangely pleasurable, especially once Seamew had accepted the routine of sleep, play, the daily ration of tinned cat food and milk, and the aft-of-mast duty area.

The spinnaker had come into its own. One day he lost its boom, which flew from its socket when the boat came beam-on to a sudden squall. After that he used a boathook instead, which bent alarmingly but seemed to do the job.

Apart from such small incidents and the frequent sail changes, life was so uneventful that his log bordered on the cosy, being full of domestic data concerning the ways and whims of Seamew, a bird that spent a night in the cockpit, the growth-rate of Rebecca's plant, an improved method of catching rain water in the mainsail, and some mild self-criticism after running out of J-cloths.

When the gale came he was at first sufficiently unconcerned to notice, almost feel smug about, his calm adjustment to its demands. Because he had mended and tinkered in response to his perfectionist urge, he felt confidence in the yacht, her equipment and himself. As conditions worsened he was curiously excited by the realization that he was not seriously frightened. Alert, calculating, but no longer convinced of his inability to take all reasonable precautions, he recalled how on leaving the Solent and running into his first taste of really bad weather, he had under-canvassed the boat; how, later, Jill had scorned his excessive caution. Now he felt competent to stretch 'Patience' to the full, to relax enough to let the yacht do the job she was built for, to play his part in a spirit of guiding co-operation rather than apprehensive restraint.

The gale continued for twenty-four hours under an ugly, overcast sky. When the conditions became too much for the number three staysail and trisail, he stripped the boat and hove to on the starboard tack, wary and tired but not seriously perturbed.

'Patience' drifted like a cork, alternating between the relative quiet of the troughs and noisier exposure on the crests. Although seas were breaking over her, he preferred to stay in the cockpit to 'know the enemy.' Seamew thought little of the motion, and her face appeared above the companionway washboard. He could see though not hear a long, protesting comment before the kitten disappeared to her berth, clearly wanting no part of the current action.

The wind continued to rise. The sea became white with foam and boiling crests of water. 'Patience' was heeled over with her gunwhale awash. He guessed they were in the grip of a force nine and wondered if he should lay out a sea anchor.

Now there was something about the whole feel of the sea and the sky that was different in character, in threat, to anything he had previously experienced. The wind's increase was not steady or in gusts from a single direction, but first from one quarter and then from another. It was like being caught by a mob of vicious thugs who aimed blows and kicks from all directions, whirling their victim to face punishment from every side. Again and again 'Patience' was spun like a top, and below deck everything capable of movement was sent flying. He considered trailing warps, but feared that the lack of consistency in wind direction might entangle the yacht in a cat's cradle of rope.

Fear stirred. The sea was responding to the changing directions of the wind, threatening to sweep over the vessel from any quarter. The conditions were not only beyond his personal experience, but he could not recall reading any account of how yachts had survived such circumstances. Winds strong enough to blow the tops off waves, creating relatively flat seas, were one thing, but the seas surrounding 'Patience' were twenty or more feet high and in the contrary gusts were not only a mass of foam and crests but were beginning to tumble in from every direction as though the yacht had reached the converging point of several mighty rivers.

Instinct rather than reason, which had now become almost impossible in the screeching, buffeting fury of the storm, drove him to follow Seamew's example. He checked that the helm was lashed down and the boom securely in its crutch, then went below, closing and bolting the hatch after him. There seemed no alternative but to sit tight if not dry and let the elements get on with it. Someone had said – was it after the 1979 Fastnet? – that the best liferaft is a sound boat.

Lying in his berth he read, as best he could in the violent motion, a passage from Hiscock's *Cruising Under Sail* in which a Vertue was reported as running before a force ten under bare poles, kept stern on to the overtaking sea in case of a broach-to. The situation in which seas converged rather than overtook, treating a boat as a cork would be treated in a tin of paint being shaken in an automatic mixer, was not satisfactorily covered except by the elegant concept of the 'impossible situation'.

He knew he had done the right thing in going below. Seas were breaking right over the yacht, washing from stern to bow and from bow to stern. Water found a thin crack between the main hatch cover and washboards, spurting into the cabin with incredible force, soaking everything and adding to the mounting humidity to create a fine mist. The compass above his berth was in such a constant and violent state of readjustment that it was pointless to try to work out in which direction the yacht was facing at any one moment. The only question of relevance was whether or for how long she would survive. He told himself that maybe this was it; that he was to be spared the need for decision about time, place and method...

When the seas were stern or bow on, the yacht's motion was relatively steady; when beam on, her rolling was so violent it was all he could do to stay in his berth. The canvas bunkboard, useful in moderate conditions to prevent a rude descent to the floor, was now taking strains never imposed on it before. He wondered whether the weight of his body would rip the canvas or tear the holding rope from the eyes at either corner. The danger of his being hurled bodily out of the berth was now so great that he knew he had somehow to lash himself down to the berth. He found a way of bringing the canvas across his body at a sharper angle, tying the rope ends at lower points to the ribs that held the hull, so that the canvas made a kind of strait jacket, pinning him to the berth like a voluntary Gulliver.

He lay there, in suspended belief in the yacht's ability to withstand the brutal pounding from ton upon ton of water. The shindy of plastic crockery, tins, bottles and anything else not actually nailed, screwed or tied down to its appointed place, increased as each shaking and battering found more defects in his preparations. A heavy can of corned beef from one burst-open locker became his best guide to the yacht's motion, rolling the length of the cabin floor when 'Patience' was stern or bow on to the seas, and from side to side when the seas were beam on.

With nothing better to do, and dazed by the constantly changing motion, he began to count the seconds the can took to roll from one side to another. The slower journeys suggested longer troughs in the boiling waters outside, the can's faster progress was a response to the terrier-and-rat shaking the yacht received when gripped by the opposing turbulence of sea and wind.

He was muzzily measuring the can's progress from side to side when he realized it had missed a return journey. In the moment in which his tired brain tried to analyse this, half supposing the can to have been interrupted by some heavier piece of equipment, the cabin grew suddenly dark and he was aware of being held by the canvas as though face down in a hammock. He was looking down, not up, at the roof of the doghouse. Brief though the experience must have been, he hung there for what seemed an eternity, idiotically, helplessly, gazing down at the white paint of the roof, listening to the crack and rattle of stores and equipment thudding down to join the can that had found a new area for exploration. Water polluted by the contents of broken bottles and spilled tins drenched him as the yacht made her turn, and a stream of indignant, terrified squeaks from Seamew punctuated the cacophony of what he indifferently, almost with relief, concluded was his last taste of life.

Then, as though bored with holding her pose, 'Patience' completed her 360° roll, pitching as she turned. For an instant he was aware of the renewed shindy of equipment falling back from the roof, then any further assessment of the situation was violently interrupted by a numbing blow on his head. For seconds his mind fought to retain consciousness and he felt his eyes fluttering furiously to stave off the blackness which seemed to be pushing up behind them; but the odds were too heavy and he succumbed almost gladly to the undemanding condition of oblivion.

13

THE sea was as bleak as glass, as lifeless as coal, its surface so hard and smooth he knew it would support him as he set off down the long ocean pathway by which he had come. He glanced back only once at the frail vessel which had taken him so far into the west. It seemed to be sinking, though whether into the sea or over the fast-receding horizon he could not tell, and he increased his pace until the steel-coloured water sped beneath his feet as fast as the road had flown through the hole in the floor of his father's old car long years before – a more pleasingly frightening gauge of speed than the trees and hedgerows.

Smudges of grey appeared on the pale horizon, but he was not seeking to return to islands and he left them behind in no more time than it took to respond to some faint dictate of the heart.

And then he had arrived at a door, blue-painted and unexceptional except for its size, with a brass knocker familiarly far above his head. He reached up to the knocker and managed to lift it with the middle finger of his hand, but he could not raise it high enough, and the tap it gave was too small a sound to bring an answer.

Now it was within reach, but he knew he was not expected there at that time. He moved on at a different level of awareness, into a street entered with joy at being new to man's estate, free of choice, with all of a thousand long tomorrows in which to find a way and a purpose.

The narrow street was a kaleidoscope of people and traffic, the people all sizes and shades of skin and many speaking words he could not understand. Small shops catered for every need. The aroma of roasting coffee beans came from a doorway;

from another the fragrance of spices and herbs, jarred and bunched above cool shelves of cheese, prepared meats, and tinned and bottled delicacies from all quarters of the world. Patisserie windows invited inordinate consumption of cakes and pastries, their price beyond his pocket, their artistry deserving a respect more devotional than greed. The smells of garlic and French cigarettes, the clip of horses' hooves above the horns of cars, then a long street with barrow upon barrow stacked high with fruits and vegetables with all the colours of a paint-box. Shrewd, humorous Cockney faces offering barter and bargain to the quarter's residents; to sensible land-ladies from less colourful districts; and to the poorer or more knowing housewives from Battersea, Lambeth, Kensington and the suburbs of Hampstead and St John's Wood.

Chinese waiters chattering on the kerb; dust-adoring London sparrows tilling the summer gutters with their wings; lean, cunning cats curled into cool corners out of the sun's rays, one eye watchful for the hundred dangers besetting those with so many lives to spare; bored, drained faces of women beyond youth's caring, inviting instant love in dingy attic rooms; young men passing them by, some without a glance, some refusing with the confident smile of those not needing to pay so directly for relief from nature's goad; old men furtively assessing risk and value, some being led away obediently, gaze lowered, trailing the temptress like small boys following their teacher on a not wholly pleasurable outing.

The scene dimmed, fading into a less nostalgically sensual mood, fraught with uncertainty and lack of purpose; tedious war years in which the automatic heroism of being in uniform was inwardly set against the conviction of personal and corporate futility; years of search for identity and credo; the rejection of imposed notions of something beyond the seeming certainty of intellectual concepts; the eager acceptance that man's condition was destined to be governed not by any more irrational visions but by an endlessly fluid and inescapable state of division, leading (though who could say when?) to a more sanely ordered future.

But now as then, all that middle phase was in some respect unsatisfying, lacking that central piece of the jig-saw that was the key to the whole, and his journey quickened, reaching a confused crescendo in the breakdown after his first marriage foundered on the rocks of inexperience; the nightmares of obsession and depression, the irrational fears, the exhaustion of mind and body, the inexplicable certainties of self-extinction comfortably if not comfortingly labelled 'anxiety states' by the ones who claimed to know...

The metallic surface of the water began to craze like a shattered mirror, then broke into jagged, threatening splinters below which he felt rather than saw a turbulence it lay within his will to accept or reject...

And then it was as if he had entered some quiet harbour, a hurricane hole of the mind, and his fears and worries became the concerns that go beyond the squirrel-wheel of self and are more urgent and real for being centred on those for whose future one is more alert than for one's own. For all its unrequited needs and uncertainties, a more tranquil period of consolidation in marriage, appreciative of the company of someone offering at least peace and reliability after the turmoil of an impossible, near mind-destroying liaison; consolidation in work, providing an adequate if not remarkable living, but at least a reputation for competence in a field of his own choosing; finally the discipline and coalescence, the ego-levelling joys and tender agonies, of small children, with all they bring to shield the shielding from realization that their need and vulnerability could one day become the responsibility of themselves or some other.

The eye of the camera panned more slowly, images crystallizing into a few hard, in-focus memories, seen without the colours that only seldom infuse dreams. Yet the clarity, though lending significance, did not stay but gave way to a fluid *mélange* of memory and insight in which Rebecca and the children were seen in double and yet varied image, as though transparencies of the same subject were imposed one on the other only to be processed to produce variations in what he knew was one and the same.

Rebecca in first focus, pretty and anxious to please, but out of depth with someone whose errors of judgment and priority had created the turmoil in which she had found him; her later, more supportive role, accepting its limitations and concentrating on the provision of such props as were within her imagination and competence; her cool reliability and integrity over matters vital to the background against which he had been able to rebuild his life and give to his writing a form that finally brought recognition and security.

The essentials of their life together, stripped of habits and expectancies that were the measure of their separate deficiencies, came back into sharp focus, showing what had made the backbone of their relationship, emphasizing what should have been cherished above the non-realization of a reciprocity granted to few.

Then the focus was on Mary: briefly, succinctly on all he had loved and perhaps taken too much for granted in her early years when she was the almost alarmingly appreciative and affectionate child whose gentleness and consideration won every heart; for longer, on the later period when he had too often succumbed to the irritation of seeing in her much he could least easily accept in her mother. But now he was seeing her as it were through a filter, viewing highlights before invisible, conscious that shadowed areas held more depth than he had supposed, seeing the person behind and beyond her adolescence with all that that period spells in disappointment and uncertainty for child and parent alike.

Judy: the difficult one, the unpredictable. The child most affected by his own deficiencies. The one not more loved for being more worried about, but more in mind for being less capable of being taken for granted.

And of a sudden he seemed tuned in less to what he had hoped for in his children, for that had been ill-defined, than to what he might have learned from them had he been able to stand far enough back to view them in perspective and proportion instead of with the anxious proximity that is the blinding and distorting penalty of parental love.

As though a key linking a lock's parts had turned in his mind, he identified with Judy in her attempts to come to terms with the chimera of romantic love. Unlike Mary who was blessed with wanting more to give than to receive, Judy had had to learn the hard way that there is little true love on the level of person to person that is not a preparation for sacrifice.

Mary, so level-headed and even-hearted, had seemed to move with enviable ease into the state of being in love, conscious of no problems that could not be solved by the gentle understanding and fond patience that was part and parcel of her nature. But Judy, nearer to him in reaction and expectation, had always striven, often clamorously, to bring about change; insistent on her story-book illusions being realized, but employing mind more often than heart, tense with determination to create and consolidate patterns to fill the voids of which she had convinced herself. Impatient with reason's inability to realize her dreams, she had been quick to expect, to demand, to blame, and so slow to love, though cursed with a heightened sexuality which craved the shadow before the substance had been touched by the sun. Mary, seeing in men little of importance to her heart that was not what she would later see in her own children, loved them for their inadequacies, for the dependence that invited the concern and pity without which love is nothing but a mocking word for Nature's tediously predictable plan.

The camera began to recede, offering a final glimpse of Rebecca as he prepared to sail away. Then he saw himself as from above, tending the plant she had given him, pondering that he might have blamed her for a monotony that was in his own cautious, routine-dominated make-up, holding her in some way responsible for the dullness he had found preferable to challenge, just as perhaps he had all along blamed those nearest to him for somehow depriving him of youth's celebration of being alive. His mind came within sight of acceptance that the *Weltschmerz* born of his sense of failure and redundancy was as much the product of an inability to forge and maintain relationships in a spirit of undemanding love.

The journey came to an end inconsequentially with Judy in their garden, looking up from an old brick path where she was studying quick red spiders the size of poppy seeds and reciting almost defiantly a long-forgotten poem by Yeats beginning 'A pity beyond all telling is hid in the heart of love', and then telling him crossly he was a rudimentary environmentalist, but in a tone suggesting there was hope for him yet.

Then he had a vivid, immediate glimpse of her, holding up a white kitten which was mewing stridently...

14

HIS return to consciousness could have been days or hours after his memory of the storm. More time passed before he summoned the strength and inclination to release himself from the canvas. The incentive to do so was less his own condition – though he felt a morbid interest in identifying what had hit him and to what effect – than the weakening mews which suggested the kitten was abandoning hope.

He sat on the edge of his bunk, feeling sickeningly dizzy, his head throbbing. Gingerly he fingered the wound in his scalp; the blood was encrusted. Muzzily surveying the chaos on the cabin floor, he guessed that the can of corned beef had been his undoing. But his body's bruises suggested that more than one missile had found its mark.

Seamew, putting a hopeful interpretation on the sounds aft, found strength for more frantic appeals. He stood up, good intention fighting the powerful disincentives of his aching head, blurred vision, the long slow swell in which 'Patience' wallowed, and a floor calf-deep in shattered and displaced equipment. Broken glass, sodden books, cushions, matches, backgammon counters, sail battens, soap, crockery, food and a multitude of other domestic and nautical bric-a-brac were washing about between the berths in an indescribable pool of spilled milk, orange juice, alcohol and sea water. The roof, bulk-heads, lockers and all visible surfaces were streaked and daubed by an indecipherable combination of fluids and solids.

He was relieved to discover that his binoculars had escaped serious damage. They were the best money had been able to buy when the advance on his most successful book had prompted Rebecca to encourage him in one really extravagant indulgence.

He looked at himself in a piece of shattered mirror and was

repelled by a bloodstained, haggard face sporting several days' growth of beard. With a muttered 'yuk!' he threw open the hatches, suddenly avid for fresh air in the humid, stale, stinking cabin. The movement made his head throb with renewed violence, and he sat down again and pressed his fingers hard into his temples. He remembered the box of pills and embrocation Rebecca had put in the boat. He found it jammed under the galley and swallowed a couple of 'Veganin'.

Seamew's calls were by now frantic. He moved forward but could not see her. A further cry revealed her behind and half pinned down by a sailbag that had been catapaulted into the forepeak. The kitten's matted fur suggested she had received her fair share of airborne pollutants. He replaced the sailbag in its old position and transferred the animal to her favoured hideout. From there she blinked at him, indignation and expectancy nicely blended in her comments.

'Sorry, mate,' he muttered.

Worried that no carton of milk had survived, he searched among the debris, finding almost nothing in its accustomed place. To his relief, several cartons were still intact. He found a reasonably clean saucer and gave Seamew a generous helping, then opened a fresh tin of petfood, the remains of the last having added strength to the evil mixture in which he was wading on his errand of mercy. Double rations seemed justified. Seamew wolfed the lot, then spot-squatted with sudden urgency. A reminder course in toilet training seemed untimely. With so much going on, her contribution was neither here nor there.

He was upset to find Rebecca's plant floating, soilless, between galley and head. Only then did he muzzily recognize that the water's presence might mean that 'Patience' had sprung a leak and that he must lose no time in pumping the bilge and checking the hull for damage. But first he put some pieces of the plant into fresh water, hoping it might strike roots.

The bilge proved almost too much for him. The pump quickly clogged with debris and he had to clear it several times. The physical action, although tiring, helped to clear his mind. He saw he must get more method into restoring order in the boat. He piled all the loose gear on to the bunks and threw everything broken or ruined overboard without leaving the cabin. He knew he would have to go on deck before long, but was apprehensive of what he might find. Through the murk of the starboard window he had already noticed a tangle of stainless steel wire hanging over the side of the yacht, and he had a pretty good idea what that meant.

He realized that his weakness might in part be due to not having eaten for a long time, so he opened a tin of beans that was floating to hand and ate them cold with a teaspoon while pumping, gripping the tin between his knees. The level of the water sank slowly but encouragingly.

The monotony of the task freed his mind. He wondered what day it was, but his watch lacked a date dial and he doubted whether he would find the log in any condition to provide a clue. He had no idea for how far, how long or in what direction 'Patience' had been driven in the storm. As she was some thirty degrees off course he guessed that the pilot had been damaged.

When the pump's loud sucking noises proved it was taking in more air than water, he steeled himself to go on deck. Evidence for his fears was abundant. Not only was the pilot's vane shaft twisted and its gear wheel stripped beyond repair, but the mast had snapped at the top spreaders and hung forlornly to starboard in a tangle of stays and halyards. The log had gone, and his concern to give plausibility to his plan had not run to carrying a spare.

The sight was so daunting, so apparently final, that in his weakened condition he could think of nothing more positive than to go below and pump the bilge again. He drew no comfort from the audible proof that no more water had collected, but continued dully and slowly to work the handle, his confused mind trying to take stock.

His body began to utilize the food he had eaten. He stopped pumping and moved about the boat, at first pointlessly putting things back in their remembered places, then finding a sponge and filling a bucket with water and moving methodically from stem to stern, cleaning all surfaces before refilling lockers and shelves with the salvaged remains.

The activity was soothing, providing temporary purpose in what had seemed a totally impossible and irrecoverable situation. As his mind hardened he began to turn over the solution to the external damage. He could see no way of repairing the vane. In any case, the priority was that the boat be restored to a condition of some manoeuvrability, as while the storm had given way to a light wind that was filling in behind 'Patience' as though to encourage her to resume course, he had no control over her progress until some kind of jury rig had been devised.

Almost his last discovery among the chaos was a small black-capped bottle of opaque glass lodged in the lowest point of the bilge, near to the inlet of the pump. The jolt this gave him was harsh and unwelcome, compelling him to face once again what had already edged back into his mind. It was as though geography and circumstance had combined to offer him the perfect conditions for carrying out his plan. His brain ticked them off with implacable logic:

He was alone and far from land.
He had not seen a ship in days.
His yacht was disabled.
He had only to restore some of the mess inside, perhaps contriving some damage to the rudder, to show every justification for abandonment.
He should wait for evening, take to his life raft with pills and a bottle of gin, then as consciousness faded start a slow puncture in the raft so that his body, with some winch handles tied to his feet, would be taken to the bottom.

The perfect plan! That way, even his slight worry that suspicion of suicidal intent might affect Rebecca's insurance claim would be done away with. Things could not have come together at a better time.

But it was his mind talking. The missing element was proving stronger than reason. He sat on the edge of his bunk gazing fixedly at the bottle of barbiturates. It would be so easy, so irrevocable, to down the lot, to quell doubt and argument by action no more demanding than swallowing half a dozen oysters. Well, this was, or should be, *it*. He had no excuses left.

Except Seamew, of course. He explored the possibilities of this line of retreat, but it did not stand up to logical analysis. If he left plenty of food, milk and water in the cabin, she should survive until the yacht was found. Should? Maybe 'should' wasn't quite good enough...

He told himself that he must allow time for determination to return with opportunity. He went back to the calming if pointless employment of working the pump, arguing with himself furiously, muttering aloud as his arm punched the handle rhythmically back and forth. He remembered the part that alcohol played in so many of the suicides of the experts, the doctors. Of course! He was far too sober to carry through his plan. If there was one occasion in his life when he was justified in breaking his rule about daytime drinking, this was surely it!

He had two unbroken bottles of gin. He opened one and poured a generous measure, then lay on his bunk sipping, running over yet again the excellent reasons for not backing down. On a stomach empty except for a few beans, the gin soon took effect.

'Look,' he argued with the unconscious Seamew, 'there's no bloody point in putting it off any longer. Even if we make it, nothing'll've changed. I'd never wind up to it again, mate, never. Anyway, Christ! – think of the anti-climax if we went home. Bloody pointless marriage, bloody useless career, health packing up, everything up the spout. What'd be the point?'

To this and a good deal more Seamew made no response. As a second and third measure of gin overpowered the beans, he thought about Rebecca and the children and their old dog and his parents. The sadness of the world and his part in it overtook him.

Seamew, her shattered tissues recovering through deep sleep, was rudely wakened by a hand stroking her fur emotionally, almost roughly.

'Poor little cat!' Matthew said thickly. 'Poor bloody little animal.'

The poor bloody little animal purred mildly, as though to prove there was no ill-feeling at the interruption, then closed its eyes firmly. There was nothing in the small world of the ginger kitten that it wanted more than long, undisturbed sleep.

'Poor little brute!' Matthew emphasized.

The kitten pushed its head deeper into the fur on its belly. It was unaccustomed to so concentrated an aroma of undiluted alcohol.

Matthew made his way unsteadily back to his bunk. His head was swimming, but pleasantly, irresponsibly, without the pressure of doubt or fear. He staggered to his feet again and put his head through the hatch, looking round him at the sea whose gentle heaving so remarkably matched the current performance of his head. Against the bleak vastness of the ocean his little life was losing all importance. To have planned and agonized over its ending had been a conceit, the puny gesture of an insignificant atom whose staying or passing was of no more concern to the material world than the death of a beetle or the fate of a blown speck of dust.

Right! He'd take a few of the tablets now, then if he felt the same way a little later he'd get out the life raft, leave Seamew fixed up with food, see to it that everything looked ship-shape... no, that was the wrong word; wreck-shape, then; and after that...

Where had he put the bloody bottle? He searched feverishly, suddenly afraid that in his stupor he had dropped it overboard, stepped on it... He found it lodged between the mattress and the edge of his bunk. He sat down and looked at the small dark shape lying in the palm of his hand. His body swayed from the waist up with more than the movement of the swell outside. All right, then...

He unscrewed the cap, telling himself that in any case he should have checked that the contents were dry. The contents were perfectly dry. All five capsules.

Five!

For a second his mind broke through the surface of his near-stupefaction like a fish leaping. Five! For Christ's sake, there had been forty - twice the dose that suicide reports had made clear would do the job. His head swam with the combined force of his intoxication and the shattering implications of his discovery. Had he under-estimated Jill's capacity for the things? Had she taken some with her? All right, so at one stage his sole aim had been to escape the scenes, sleeplessness and sex, but surely to God she couldn't have got through thirty-five capsules...

He sat there for a long while, pondering, his brain mulling muzzily over the facts, taking tangential excursions down pointless paths of speculation, but forced each time to return to the central fact that conjecture could get him nowhere. Five capsules would not be enough, and that was that.

He lay back on his bunk, feeling it would be appropriate to give himself up to despair. He gazed at the cabin roof, inviting lamentation at the savagery of fate. But even with the help of the gin that was flowing through his system, his heart refused to respond correctly. There was no doubt that the dominant emotion was one of relief. It was sweeping through his mind like a wave.

He went on deck and held on to the broken mast. The horizon was bare. The air was warm and humid, the breeze gentle and steady, perfect for blowing them towards - what had Jackson called them? - the 'lands of rum and ginger'. A fat lot that conceited bugger knew about anywhere west of Madeira...

He went below. Seamew was awake and greeted him in a voice that for once seemed unloaded by thought of self. He tickled her under the chin and she lifted her small head, closing her eyes appreciatively. He tended Rebecca's plant, removing some dead leaves he had not noticed before, then breaking in half some of the longer shoots so that none had to support too much growth while making roots.

He went back on deck and put the jar of shoots in the cockpit for some fresh air.

'Get yourself a load of that,' he said.

Then he began to look through his books for some hints about jury rigs.

15

THE rig may not have looked much, but it was effective for running before the wind. The worst bit had been getting up the mast in the heaving sea to work on its shattered tip. It took him most of the day to reposition stays and shrouds, to lash a block to the broken spar for the main halyard, and to make the other adjustments necessary if 'Patience' was to continue under reduced main and foresails. By booming out the headsails and getting all he could from the heavily reefed main, he coaxed little less speed out of the boat than before the capsize. Cautiously, he tried bringing the yacht up into the wind, finding it possible to beat and come about after a fashion, but he had not been able to devise a way of restoring the runners and felt more comfortable with the breeze aft.

Loss of the pilot was serious. He experimented with lashing the tiller and found that in a steady wind 'Patience' could be tuned to keep very closely to the set course. This was a great relief but had limitations. On the third night after the storm he woke to find the course so altered by a major wind shift that they were on their way back to the Canaries.

But he knew it was more important that he slept and kept on top of things psychologically than worry about how long it might take to reach land. Jill had more than adequately topped up his stores for the crossing. Even with the losses since capsize, he was equipped for several weeks' survival.

His navigation now centred on little but the compass. It seemed pointless to bother any longer with fixes or to try to estimate the miles covered daily. He kept 'Patience' on the course he judged might bring her to Barbados, then fought worry. He had little choice.

There grew in him a peaceful resignation that was almost

contentment; he was more relaxed and unconcerned with the future than ever before; curiously indifferent to the problems and personal limitations that had prompted his voyage. Twice in his life – once when in hospital, earlier when he had joined the Navy – he had experienced a strange sense of relief at his lack of responsibility to do anything but obey orders. The feeling had been one of self-abnegation, almost loss of identity. His present indifference to past and present dangers seemed of a similar order. He found comfort in a sharply heightened awareness of personal insignificance in the wide waste of water that was so utterly beyond the control of his will and wisdom. It was a kind of courage.

He recalled a sharp exchange with Jill about courage. He had quoted someone as saying that bravery is a generous word awarded, often posthumously, to those in whom stupidity exceeds imagination. She had lectured him on the dangers to spontaneity and emotional development of (as she called it) over-intellectualizing, berating the deficiencies of those who set too much store on reason and will. He argued with her, but with less conviction than when Rebecca had made similar charges, and over the weeks he had remembered with dwindling disagreement her statement that too much self-control and self-awareness could prevent going with tide and wind even on the little things, the things best given in to.

But self-awareness had become a habit and he could not resist analysis of the changes taking place in himself. With his writer's interest in the appropriate phrase he dated these changes as Before and After Capsize.

Five days 'A.C.', the wind strengthened and veered and he was obliged to test the yacht's ability to point into it if he was to hold his course. She was noticeably slower than before. Once, he luffed up as far as he could, and because she was making little speed she went into irons and then bore off on the opposite tack. He let her gather speed, then again put the tiller down so that she came up into the wind. At this she shook her sails like a dog shedding water and bore off on the old tack as though anxious to oblige a master who did not really know where he wanted to go but deserved to be humoured.

Later that day the trades returned. He was able to lash the tiller again and leave 'Patience' to get on with the job with minimal supervision. He played his tapes and spent much time sitting in the cockpit drinking tea or fruit juices, nibbling at food when he felt like it, and musing with - as he realized - much less tension and self-pity. He scanned the empty sea impassively, unconcerned by the thought that he was of no more importance in that still untamed waste than a weevil sitting on a cork. He diagnosed his mood as a coming to terms with life, though more for the reason that he could accept his involuntary role in existence than that he had to prove or achieve something specific. He told himself it was a mood that would disappear if ever he made land and returned to the rat-race, yet he felt that his *Weltschmerz* would never again plumb the depths of despair he had known 'B.C.' He was pleased to find that the shoots from Rebecca's plant were beginning to produce roots.

He recalled many past moments and moods, but less resentfully, more objectively, than before. It was as though events 'B.C.' were reordering themselves in proper ranks of priority. He thought fondly of the Sussex countryside that had for years been his sheet anchor. He recalled random moments in his career such as the Oxford think-tank to which, as a committee member of the Society for Improved Racial Relationships, he had been asked to contribute; he remembered his amusement and irritation at the way the panel's academics, all so enormously pleased with themselves, had played with concepts and juggled with words to the almost total neglect of the problems that had brought them together. He recollected his disappointment - doubtless childish, but real enough at the time - when in the early days of knowing Rebecca they had been separated for some months, and how on the way to meeting her after what had seemed in those days so long a time, he had stopped at a fair and won a squeaking toy dog. He had given it to her and then lost sight of it until nearly four months later he came across it under a pile of discarded clothing earmarked for a jumble sale. Rebecca had never been a rewarding person to give things to, and her response to those early tokens of affection had played its part in the deterioration of their relationship. But although he now knew that she would not have changed in this or other respects, he found himself searching for the factors in her own life that had made her the person she was, just as he had done with more seeming success when he was first in love with her and before the irritations and disillusionments of their years together had blunted his responses and obscured the early vision, overlaying that frail compound of hope, dependence, physical love and determination without which marriage loses all meaning.

He thought of Judy and Mary, but less of the gulf that had seemed to separate them than of how they were coping with their own problems; thinking of them as people in their own right; wanting for them success in those problems of life and relationships that had so clearly defeated their father.

The days passed uncounted, their sameness producing a routine which combined with his peace of mind to magnify the small satisfactions of eating, drinking, bucket-showers of sea water, tinkering with the yacht, communing with Seamew, and watching contentedly the ever-changing pattern of the sky. He experienced none of the agonies of solitude some single-handers had written about. He was in a state for which he could find no better description than that of being in tune. Even his sole ambition to reach the Caribbean was muted and free of tension. He had a fresh zest for living, but it was controlled and without frenzy, enhanced by the realization that if it persisted and he reached land he would not have lost face by surviving; he had, after all, put it about that the West Indies were his target...

The almost continual warmth and following wind told him he could not have made any major error of calculation. 'Patience' seemed as relaxed as himself, needing few adjustments to her tiller, creaming through waters whose blues and greens by day and phosphorous beauty at night reinforced confidence that he was sailing in the right general direction.

Flying fish would land on board, sometimes being caught by the sails and dropping on deck, sometimes hitting the coach-roof or stanchions. He retrieved them, sharing the sea's gift with Seamew, but one day he found himself studying a fish that landed by the forward hatch. He noted the helpless lifting of its strange 'wings' as it sought to return to the life-giving sea. He picked it up, feeling the tremulous proof of its humble being, the vibrating will to survive, and in what might have been idle curiosity he held it over the side, watching the eager response of its fins to the dousing of a passing crest.

There came into his mind, independent of any train of thought, something Judy had quoted – Schweitzer? Schumacher? Shaw? She was always coming up with a new one: 'Nothing is bringing civilization to an end more quickly than man's belief in his role of predator.'

He let the creature go and saw it flash back to its fishy routine where, no doubt, it would before long fall prey to something no more congenial than man or cat. It didn't seem much of a contribution. But he felt a small tinge of pleasure that the action would have pleased Judy, perhaps brought them a little closer.

He recalled criticizing her concern for animals and of warning her that anthropomorphism would only make her own life more difficult. He remembered how she had rounded on his reasoning when he responded to a news item with the judgment that some murdering guerilla or otherwise euphemized thug had 'behaved no better than an animal'. His moment's empathy with the returned fish made her recollected reaction more acceptable: 'Honestly, daddy,' ('honestly' was a favourite), 'people always try to pin on animals the bad things in themselves. If we saw the good qualities and the rights of other species we might begin to behave better to each other.'

He went below and opened a tin of sardines for himself and Seamew. And then he began to laugh and would have liked to share the moment with Rebecca.

16

THE grey smear on the horizon did not change shape with the other smears he knew must be clouds.

'The presence of cloud betokens land,' he quoted to Seamew. But although birds and two absurdly courting butterflies low on the water had signalled its proximity, he was surprised by how calm he felt to be at last so near his journey's end.

Barbados? Impossible to tell. But some assumption was better than none. With only an hour or so to sunset, and remembering from books how few lights the night yachtsman had to help him in those seas, he altered course several degrees to the west in case conditions worsened and he reached the island in moonless dark.

'Better to overshoot than pile up on some rock, eh, Seamew?'

The kitten was resting up after her last meal and in no mood for navigational speculation. Wedged between her beloved sailbags she was an appreciably larger animal than when she first came on board. She roamed the boat to the manner born, no longer apt to splay her legs and go boss-eyed when 'Patience' bucked and rolled in heavy seas.

'If we see some lights,' he explained patiently, 'we'll take it from there. If we don't, we'll press on until we know we must have cleared it, then point up a bit to the north and hope to fetch St Vincent or St Lucia.'

Seamew voiced no objection.

'You might bloody say something,' he said. Talking to Seamew was a one-sided indulgence.

He was soon thankful he had borne away to leave the island to starboard. Sheeting rain began to fall, entirely obscuring any sign of land, and they were driven on blindly by a force five wind in uncomfortable humidity.

By eight in the evening he guessed the island could be to starboard, but any hope of detecting lights on shore was ruled out by the constant rain. Uncertain of the tidal drift, he was worried by this sightless progress through unidentified waters, so he stayed on the tiller, determined to keep a constant look-out.

Conditions worsened. At midnight he had to reduce sail to storm jib only. He began to regret not having hove to for the night, making landfall at his leisure in daylight. But he knew he must by now have passed the island, so he kept to his plan and altered course to bring the wind on to the yacht's starboard quarter and give her a more northerly heading.

His relaxation began to leave him. He realized that the days - or was it weeks? - of uneventful routine had dulled his reactions. If the island had not been Barbados, what other might it have been? He knew from his inadequate small-scale chart that the alternatives were many. He started to dread the anti-climax of coming to grief at this, the possibly final stage of his voyage. It was too late now to lie a-hull, for with several hours of night to pass he could too easily be driven on to some windward shore with little hope under the cumbersome jury rig of beating back out of danger.

His tiller hand was clammy with a tension from which he had long been free; his eyes ached from sustained effort to penetrate the driving rain; he mouthed self-condemnation of his idiocy in letting himself into an impossible situation.

He was toying with the idea of turning the boat round and trying to short tack until daylight by the route he had taken, when with a suddenness he could measure in seconds the wind dropped and the sea moderated to a lumpy swell. It was as though he had sailed into the shelter of some harbour. His mind, in a confusion of apprehension and uncertainty, groped for explanation of so abrupt, so uncanny, a change. The only one that made sense was that the yacht was protected by land. Realization of what that 'protection' could mean brought a prickle of fear to his spine. How near to the shore were they sailing? What was its nature? Could he so hopelessly have misjudged his distance from the land he had seen in the afternoon? Was he running in its lee?

As though he had been prepared for the first act of drama by the elements' overture, the rain eased to a soft drizzle, and to starboard and high in the torn sky the moon sought a pathway to the sea. The gap it found in the scudding cloud was quickly obscured, but not before revealing that something more solid and immobile than any cloud had obstructed its beam. His heart turned over in an onrush of fear. He was in no doubt that he had glimpsed the peak of some great face of rock and that it was towering almost directly above the boat. They were in the lee of land and so near to it that his teeth were on edge in anticipation of imminent disaster.

He remained seated in the cockpit, rigid with fear and uncertainty, so taken by surprise that the appropriate action was beyond his reasoning. The moon appeared again, this time more brightly and through thinner cloud, and now he saw that the rays were falling between twin peaks, confirming their alarming height and proximity. Below them, in the shadowed waters either side of the beam, he could detect nothing.

By now the jib was doing little work in a wind that had fallen to scarcely more than a directionless disturbance of the air. Assuming he was sailing parallel to land but could be running into shallows or a headland, he raked feverishly through the cockpit lockers for his lead-line, recalling seeing it in the chaos after the capsize.

By the time he found it the moon was winning over the cloud, framing a range of almost theatrically craggy peaks high above the shattered tip of the yacht's mast. Clouds were still being driven at speed above the peaks; the wind's roar, eerie and forbidding, was dauntingly audible on the sheltered water below. Peering into the darkness across the swell, he could just detect the creaming of foam at the foot of the cliffs. The way the water broke suggested that rocks and boulders studded the shore.

He scanned the dark land for any sign of lights, but there was none. It seemed clear, now panic had passed, that he had sailed into the lee of some deserted headland, though of what island he had no idea.

His lead-line showed a considerable depth. As 'Patience' was making slow progress along the shore, he kept her going, anxious to maintain momentum in a situation where the wind's help might fail entirely. The depth below the keel grew less but was still too great to ensure good holding for the yacht's anchor line. He realized he was pouring with sweat, not only from the airless humidity in the lee of the land but because his imagination had had time to list the possible dangers.

He was wondering whether to abandon the thought of an anchorage and try instead to get away from the shelter of land into open water again, when the moon won her battle and bathed the black sea in full and ungrudging light. Her help arrived not a moment too soon, for directly ahead lay a shining platform of rock, and behind, jutting well beyond the yacht's course, a sharply inclined promontory which seemed to mark the further end of the range of peaks.

The depth gave hope that if he let out all his warp and chain the anchor might hold. He struggled with the ties holding the anchor to its chocks, cursing that he had not troubled to evolve a quicker system for its release. When he lowered it over the bow, 'Patience' was barely fifty yards from the rock. He prayed that they were above good holding ground.

'Patience' swung into what little wind was coming off the land, then backed off until the rock was on her port bow. The line held, the position of the rock not changing in relation to the promontory beyond. His lungs filled with a sudden huge intake of air, as though he had not drawn breath for a long while. A great elation filled him; he wanted to celebrate. To drink a toast to arrival in the small hours of some undated night seemed staid and inappropriate. Since he was wet with exertion and recent fear, he chose to jump ungracefully over the side of the boat into the gently heaving water which glimmered with phosphorescence. Its clean coolness cleared his mind and invigorated his body, and he began to laugh in celebration of survival. He reviewed all that might have happened in the past few hours, but his panic was over. He swam alongside 'Patience' and patted her hull, suddenly filled with a sense of gratitude and pride which his mind told him was absurd.

Anxious complaint from above his head confirmed that his departure from the place of duty had not been appreciated. He clambered aboard.

'Sorry,' he said, chucking the kitten under the chin, 'I didn't know you cared.'

They shared some food and retired to their separate bunks. Seamew drifted quickly into untroubled sleep, but he lay awake for hours, his mind racing with achievement, yet puzzled by the where, the when and the how of his arrival.

Because his dreams were full of re-enactment he awoke in full daylight with no certainty of where he was; his first thought was that he was somewhere in the Atlantic and that 'Patience' was running before the wind under her jury rig. When memory returned he lay only for seconds before succumbing to curiosity to survey his landfall.

The view from on deck made him catch his breath, not only because of the almost miraculous set of circumstances that had spared him from disaster and provided so perfect an anchorage, but because the wild and awesome solitude was overwhelming.

The cliffs ahead and to starboard were almost as precipitous as they had appeared under the moon's light. If not of quite so great a height as he had supposed against the backdrop of a torn night sky, he guessed that the tallest peak almost directly above the boat could be little less than a thousand feet from the sea's surface. The rock was grey, he supposed volcanic, relieved here and there by drifts of green and streaks of white. The white patches were explained by the countless birds – gannet-like creatures he took to be boobies, and a few more graceful and lordly birds with sharply angled wings and forked tails that flew at a greater height, remote from the more gregarious boobies.

For a full twenty minutes he stood in the bow and watched the wheeling birds, studying the forbidding background to their plunging and soaring responses to the invisible pockets and currents of air that played about the peaks and escarpments.

But although he had achieved landfall, he had not landed. He was intensely interested in identifying the island, to confirm whether it was the tip of a much greater land mass or some huge offshore rock. Although the quickest answer might have been to up anchor and try to sail round the promontory, this would mean coming up into the wind and putting to her first real test the yacht's ability to beat under jury rig.

He longed to feel dry land under his feet, to know the childish satisfaction of being able to say 'I've done it!' He wondered whether the coracle could be worked to shore but decided to swim there as unencumbered as possible. Although the sea was still swirling between the rocks, the swell seemed gentle. With the fear of sea-urchins, born of a long-distant encounter in the Mediterranean, he put on sailing shoes and plunged into the water in bathing trunks; in the small inner pocket he took with him a folded plastic bag and a strong rubber band.

The distance was not too taxing in the warm, buoyant water, but the problem of getting ashore seemed greater at sea-level than from the yacht's deck. He floated watchfully just beyond the line of the swell's assaults, deciding on the best place to scramble up the steep approach. He felt a stinging across his shoulders and trod water, cupping some in his hands. It was alive with tiny jelly fish hardly larger than pin-heads. He chose a stretch of the shore where the rocks were small, then timed his approach so that the surge carried him with alarming speed towards them, stabbing down frantically with his feet to find the bottom. He failed and was drawn back into the boiling water. He thrashed clear of the groundswell and paddled around gasping with the wasted effort, awaiting a further chance; when a large swell receded with what seemed enough force to produce a strong return flow, he swam with the advancing water and stumbled desperately through the small boulders to the brief margin of fallen scree which was the nearest the precipitous cliff could offer to a beach. He sat there for several minutes, his head between his knees, asking himself why at his age he was being such a total bloody fool. But elation underlaid self-criticism. He had landed! If a whale now plucked him from the shore, nothing could alter the fact that he had made landfall in the Caribbean.

But it was not the spot he had selected from the yacht's deck. That had been at the foot of a gully which was now to the north of his landing, the far side of a sharp prominence of rock. With careful timing he managed to reach the other side without being drawn back into the greedy swell, and he found himself looking up from the foot of the shale-filled cleft at what seemed an impossibly steep ascent.

He wondered if the dizziness he felt was proof that he had already over-taxed his strength, then he put it down to the weeks at sea. The air was cool and almost still at the foot of the ravine and he knew that if he was going to climb it he had to get going before the sun's heat dissuaded him.

The gully's grey shale, was loose and abrasive. Large boulders had embedded themselves in the shale and it proved all too easy to start a local but nevertheless dangerous landslide. He moved from the centre to the side of the gully, working up it where some of the rock was lodged securely against the gully wall and where scrubby plants and the occasional spindly bush provided unstable but welcome foothold. It was hard going and he slipped and slithered many times until his limbs were bleeding from numerous small cuts and grazes. Disturbance of the shale produced clouds of choking, powdery dust.

After about half an hour he turned and looked down the ravine, then wished he had resisted the temptation. 'Patience' already resembled a wooden toy moored in a blue tin sea and the steepness was more apparent and more frightening from above than from below. He wondered how on earth he would ever make the descent, but the speculation was a pointless demand on his concentration.

Fifteen minutes later he reached a barrier of huge rocks that seemed insurmountable, for both sides of the gully were still almost perpendicular. He found a cleft about a foot wide between two of the rocks, and by jamming smaller pieces into this he made a crude and precarious stairway that enabled him to get a fingerhold higher up and pull himself, panting with the exertion, to a point from which the final scramble to the top of the overhang was just within his ability. He sat there for a while, his head bowed and swimming, gasping with exhaustion and longing for a drink of water.

He stood up, ruefully contrasting his wobbly feeling with how he had been after Jill's method of relieving the tedium of calms. Well, it was said that intercourse used as much energy as a brisk five-mile walk, so there was no cause for despondency; in calorific terms the carnal equivalent of the climb was a full night of group-sex.

The way ahead was slightly less steep and green with vegetation; but the green was a thick forest of calf-high, jointed cactus plants which he supposed were some form of prickly pear. 'Prickly', as he rapidly learned, was a genteel euphemism, for the plants fragmented at a touch, distributing clumps of barbed, needle-sharp spines that were almost impossible to remove from clothing or skin.

It seemed absurd to have got so far only to be defeated by a plant, but without a stick or other weapon there was no arguing with the cactus. The highest peak was still a long way off and he could see no way of approaching it from the south side of the ravine where the steepness was too much for anything but the boobies nesting on the sparse flat bushes whose roots writhed out of the vertical face of the cliff.

The left side of the gully was filled with loose shale in which the cacti had found no hold. It was the only possible route, though the angle of incline was even greater than lower down. He felt his way up with infinite care, keeping well to the side away from the waiting cacti, catching at the smallest hold in the harder rock, at times slipping back a few inches, his groin aching with fear. If the shale started to slide there was nothing to check his fall; at best he would be torn to ribbons by the cacti before coming to rest on the overhang. Sweat poured from him. Even as a young man he had never been much good at heights.

The sides of the gully became less sheer and began to flatten off to the north to merge into the steep but feasible flank of the peak. He saw with relief that its greenness came from the low, almost leafless bushes on which the birds were nesting, and from smaller more succulent-looking ground plants that had managed to find moisture in the arid surface of the rock.

But the angle was still daunting, allowing no margin for error. He found a thin winding track between the bushes and a little later saw in the distance a long-bearded goat climbing with effortless ease the face of a smaller peak that seemed to mark the northernmost tip of the headland and to be separated from it by a deep ravine.

A flatter patch enabled him to stop and lift his eyes from their unceasing quest for a safe foothold. 'Patience' was now out of sight, but on the northern horizon was the unmistakable outline of a sizeable island. This knocked on the head any possibility that he was standing on Barbados, for he knew no other land was that near. Could he have made such good speed that he had reached St Lucia? A quick calculation confirmed the impossibility of this if the island he had seen the previous afternoon had been Barbados. His one hope of an answer lay in reaching the further side of the peak.

The shimmering blue sea held no trace of shipping. The other island was too distant to detect any sign of human occupation.

It would not have been difficult to sell himself the fantasy that he was the last man alive in a mysteriously abandoned world. Even the hum of some far-off aeroplane was lacking. His imagination stirred, but he remembered several long-gone books of similar theme and was in no condition to explore a new angle. What was more relevant was whether he was going to survive the next few hours of clambering about in a terrain unsuitable for anything but a deranged goat. That he had not yet suffered a massive 'coronary' from the combination of gross exertion and stark fear told him he was in fair nick for his age.

Very slowly he worked his way round the flank of the peak, eventually experiencing the relief of the breeze on his hot skin. As the sea to the east came more into view he could see the grey mass of another island, much the same distance as the first. He knew it was the island he had supposed was Barbados and he wished he had his small-scale charts of the Antilles with him, as he could not remember the lay-out of the islands well enough to work out his probable whereabouts.

His way was barred by the lower fringe of another large stand of cactus. He had to descend some distance in order to skirt this, but then the going became easier and he was able to climb again, seeing no major obstruction between himself and the peak. The sun's position told him he was on the north-east flank.

As he climbed, the sea opened up to the east and south, proving he was either on a narrow headland attached to a landmass of no great height, or had landed on a small island. By the time he had reached the peak there was no doubt that he had made landfall on an island no more than a mile long and a few hundred yards wide.

The view from the summit was awe-inspiring, of such solitary magnificence that his mind found no more inspired description than the tired *cliché* 'indescribable'. The blue of the sea was of a depth and richness beyond the scope of any painting or photograph. It glistened and sparkled with life and movement under the constant caress of the trade wind and the hot sun. There was still no sign of human life, not as much as the sail of a yacht, and it astonished him that the scene should lack abundant evidence of man's appreciation of so paradisal a playground.

He basked in a solitude that brought peace rather than loneliness. Under the sky's vast vault the wind sighed and roared across the harsh volcanic rock, yet although it challenged his foothold on the peak he felt no threat from it. It was as though, in conquering the island's summit, he had overcome something in himself; it was as though – he fought the notion with his intelligence, but it did not wholly admit defeat – he had been brought there for a purpose. It was a different kind of remoteness from his weeks at sea, and heightened by the fact that he did not even know what day of the month it was – and only by deduction that the month must be December.

In the midday heat fewer birds were flying; their nearest nests were on the stunted bushes that clung to the sheer west face of the cliff below. He backed away from the edge, his groin tightening again at the few friable inches of rock separating him from a conclusive plunge of many hundreds of feet. 'Patience' was a tiny model at anchor in an improbable sea. He wondered how the kitten was taking his absence, then why at such distance, in so euphoric a mood, he should have thought at all of a handful of furry animal a thousand feet below.

There was something almost bewitching, mind-blowing about the halcyon remoteness of his communion with sea and sky. The gist of a passage from Conrad came to him: '... his own individuality... had merged into the world of cloud and water, of natural forces and forms of nature... he lost all belief in the reality of his action past and to come...'

He shook his head, as though fighting the effect of some insidious drug, though the effect was an elation – an elation he could only partly attribute to landfall and ascent. He had never experienced such a lifting of the spirit as in the lonely timelessness of his surroundings. It was a joy enhanced rather than modified by a humbling awareness of his ludicrous insignificance in the scale of things. It was not the first time he had experienced that strange reductive yet comforting reappraisal of his own individuality, but now it had returned at a new and indefinable level, so stilling the processes of his brain that he stood on the summit for unmeasured minutes in an almost trance-like state of peace with himself and his surroundings.

Only when a high, wheeling bird emitted a thin drawn out mew did his mind click almost audibly back into reluctant action; he could not stay there for ever...

From the little and gentle climbing he had done in the past he knew that descent, unless helped by ropes, could be more taxing and dangerous than assault; and that it would take longer.

As, unwillingly, he began the downward journey, he noticed, set into the rock only a foot or so lower than the peak on which he had been standing, a small piece of piping. A long stick was lying nearby, its source puzzling, for no tree he had seen on the island could have produced such a branch. Feeling slightly self-conscious, like a schoolboy drawn to some game of his juniors, he trimmed the thicker end of the stick by rubbing it against the rough rock, then jammed it into the piping, wondering if he would be able to see it from the yacht.

If he ever reached the yacht...

He must have retraced his route too sharply to the north, for he found himself on a rather wider track than before. He had no way of telling whether it had been made by goats or men, but from the lack of the familiar artefacts of an industrial civilisation he plumped for the former. The track led him towards a wide stand of the same explosive cactus he had met earlier. He was about to retrace his steps and seek an alternative route when he reached a turn in the rock and came across the mouth of a cave, protected almost to its entrance by the sentinel cacti.

At first, after the blinding tropical sun, he could see only a few feet into the entrance; but after sitting on a ledge of rock a few feet inside, grateful for shelter from the unremitting heat, his eyes adjusted, confirming that the cave was of considerable depth. He ventured a few more feet, revelling in the coolness. His eyes reached their limit of adjustment and he shuffled each foot forward in turn, keeping his head slightly bent, for the cave's height was no more than that of an average man. When he could no longer see his hand before his face he stopped and turned, looking back as down the wrong end of a telescope to the entrance of the cave. The silence was absolute.

It was broken suddenly, alarmingly, by a scratching sound near his feet, as though something was being scraped across the floor of the cave. He froze, his mind flying to thoughts of scorpions, tarantulas and snakes. Before he could collect his faculties for flight he felt a hard something moving slowly across his right foot. He forced himself to keep rigidly still, fearing that the smallest movement might provoke attack. The weight left his foot and he peered at the ground, bent almost double, but could see nothing. Whatever it was was shuffling towards the entrance, and by squatting lower and following the scratching with his eyes he was able to make out a dim shape the size of a child's football in silhouette against the fierce disc of light. He breathed a deep sigh and made a quick mental inventory of the possibilities, selecting with qualified relief a hermit crab of uncommon size. At least, he supposed it was uncommon. Not over-anxious to put the cave's potentialities to the test, he followed the creature cautiously, pushing forward rather than lifting each foot, for fear that he might step on something capable of lethal reaction. As he neared the entrance he saw the crab move to the side of the cave into the shelter of a small angle of rock, and he sidled round it gratefully, relieved that there was to be no confrontation.

The oven-like heat outside brought an involuntary gasp. It seemed insane to contemplate returning to the boat in such conditions, but the descent had to be made in daylight, and the thought of a night in the cave held little appeal; in any case, there was the kitten...

The return was frightening and exhausting, exposing him to the full glare of the afternoon sun. The gully lacked the smallest breath of wind. Its descent took him two hours, some of which time was spent stuck in positions of fearful immobility, uncertain where next to place foot, hand or bottom. Resting on a ledge of rock he found a thin deposit of gritty soil. He scraped this up laboriously and poured it into the plastic bag he had brought with him, sealing the neck with the rubber band.

He arrived on the narrow fringe of shale and boulders, lacerated, bruised and dizzy with exhaustion and over-exposure. His feet were hot and throbbing, their blisters aggravated by the sharp grit that filled his shoes. He staggered into the swell that creamed through the rocks, indifferent to further injury, intent only on reaching water deep enough to allow his torn, dirty body to float in coolness and regain energy for swimming back to the yacht.

Seamew's head greeted him through the guard-rail. Her comments were critical rather than welcoming. The effort it cost him to climb aboard did nothing to modify his companion's assessment of the situation. The kitten had never been left for so long without the back-up of human services and for all her short life she had been a stickler for routine.

In self-defence as much as from obligation he laid on milk and food before sinking on to his bunk triumphant, grateful, contented, and with an achingly deep appreciation of home comforts. Within seconds sleep had hit him like a friendly sledgehammer.

17

WHEN he woke it was dark. His limbs ached abominably. Before his mind checked in, he turned over and willed his body into accepting further sleep, instructing his brain to wake for the dawn departure that would ensure maximum daylight hours in which to make final landfall.

The island sheltered the yacht's anchorage from the morning sun, but when he woke again he knew from the quality of the light that it had risen an hour or more earlier. He was so stiff that he had to roll off his bunk and break his fall with his right leg. He investigated his blisters; they were fairly sensational. He made his way painfully on deck and climbed carefully down the rope ladder into the cool sea, treading water and making slow sweeps with his arms to bring some mobility back to his limbs. The water felt wonderfully good on his smarting feet, after their first reaction to the salt. As he climbed aboard he made sure that only his insteps touched the rungs. The bag of soil was where he had left it in the cockpit. He got a tumbler and selected the best-rooted shoot from Rebecca's plant, then poured the soil in round it, making sure that the tender white roots were undamaged before moistening the soil and firming it.

He ate muesli for breakfast; there was nothing else. He would have given a lot to be able to add fresh fruit. As he ate he studied his maps, understanding Jill's surprise at his ill-preparedness. He could reconcile the position and apparent size of the surrounding islands with only one conclusion – that his landfall had been on the small and seemingly uninhabited island of Zafada. This was only just acknowledged as existing on the 1:1,000,000 scale map of the Lesser Antilles which had been the cheapest way of covering the area of his alleged destination to satisfy those at home.

'That was Monesterio we overshot,' he informed Seamew.

He remembered it had been the objective of several yachtsmen he and Jill had spoken to in Santa Cruz, where the talk had been of the charms and facilities of Monesterio's Port St George. With the repairs 'Patience' needed he knew he must aim for the dockyard haven made famous by its association with the British navy in the eighteenth and nineteenth centuries and its reputation as one of the best hurricane holes in the Caribbean.

'Monesterio it is,' he told his crew. 'The silly sods don't show Port St George on our map, but it's somewhere between Newport and Morant Bay.'

Seamew seemed content with his decision. His own slight qualms at sailing 'Patience' to windward were much reduced by the good fortune that had stayed with him until then. The one big decision still to be made had to wait until they had cleared the lee of Zafada and found the true wind.

Raising the anchor required less effort than he had expected and 'Patience' backed slowly off the land as he raised jib and reduced main; this brought the yacht stern-on to the island as small eddies of wind played with the sails, filling them positively as they cleared the headland. He was elated to discover that he could point up well enough to make several degrees good to the east of true north. He looked back, trying to detect the stick he had planted on the summit, but the distance was too great and he did not bother to use his binoculars.

He remembered that Jill had scrounged some old charts from Iain Vesper-Strathclyde, and on looking through them found one for the area Sombrero to Dominica. Although its scale of 1:475,000 was of limited navigational use, it showed the worst dangers, promised lights along Monesterio's north shores, and confirmed the position of Port St George.

'I know you don't care,' he told Seamew, 'but I reckon our course has got to bring us almost level with Guardo so that we can beat back to clear the east end of Monesterio by a good margin, then run before the wind for Port St George in some sort of style. If this weather holds it'll take us about twenty-four hours. Okay?'

His chart warned of a two-knot current setting predominantly westward, so he chose a course of 30° north to be sure of leaving Guardo to windward with something in hand in case the weather did an about-face. 'Patience' managed this with gratifying ease and might have improved upon it, but there seemed no point in trying to make landfall before morning. The waters were so free of shipping that he decided to go below during the night, leaving the boat to manage on the lashed tiller.

His calculations came right. The day produced a steady wind with just enough cloud to give respite from the sun. He saw only two yachts and a very distant steam vessel whose course soon took it out of sight. The night was clear with so many and such brilliant stars that the later moon did little to increase the light. His first tack was at dusk when he judged that on a course of 120° they would leave Guardo's White Horse shoals comfortably to port and sail through the night, making the final tack at least twenty miles east of Monesterio. He knew he was leaving exaggerated margins for error and accident but was anxious that nothing should go wrong at the eleventh hour.

'Breakfast in Port St George,' he promised Seamew. 'With any luck we'll find some fresh bread and be able to open that tin of chunky marmalade.'

Seamew seemed unimpressed. As a companion for someone who had always rejected anthropomorphism she left little to be desired.

'And maybe they'll have some milk,' he added.

The last carton had run out three days before and Seamew took a poor view of the evaporated alternative.

The night was uneventful and he slept well. When he came on deck his view of Monesterio on the starboard quarter was reconcilable with the smear of land he had seen ahead of him on the afternoon before his arrival off Zafada.

He gybed and set off down-wind for Port St George, then prepared a breakfast from all the bits and pieces needing to be finished.

'When we arrive,' he told his crew, 'we'll stock up with everything we like best. Make a list and pass it over.'

He had begun to crave fresh food. With the prospect of being within reach of alternatives to the tins, dried foods and made-up concoctions, hunger took on a new meaning. He had always taken food for granted; a source of fuel; necessary, but low among the priorities. Now he began to plan meals, daydreaming of exotic fruits and vegetables, unusual fish, English biscuits and even plain bread and butter.

His chart's scale gave little impression of the approaching coastline. He decided to sail to a bearing of 240° until far enough off shore to clear the island on a due westerly course, then to keep a look-out for a white house shown as 'conspic.,' and hope for a fix on the radio mast in the south-west corner of the island.

In the event, cloud over the higher land prevented identification of the mast, but he thought he had spotted the white house and closed with the shore a little to make sure of locating Morant Bay. The chart showed a more than adequate depth of water along the south-east coast of the island, so he sailed a mile off, aware that from then on there was no alternative to the simplest visual navigation.

Morant Bay opened up and surprised him by its lack of development except for what looked like a hotel beyond its western headland. Earlier, in small bays, he had caught glimpses of buildings, and here or there a yacht confirmed he was arriving at one of civilization's more romantic outposts; but the seaward approach suggested none of the vulgarities and congestion of a resort island. He realized that he knew almost nothing about Monesterio, never having been to the Caribbean or even considered the possibility. Of Barbados he had learned no more than seemed necessary to claim it as his destination.

If he had his facts right, the entrance to Port St George was only about three miles away. He began to work up a small panic about over-shooting it and having to find some way of beating back to the entrance against wind and tide. The thought of circumnavigating Monesterio a second time held no appeal. Well, he could always drop anchor and seek a tow; but that would be anticlimax. He wanted to make it without help; all the way; even to the last few hundred yards...

He cleared a prominent headland and looked back into what appeared to be a creek rather than a bay. The chart's scale was too small to be clear about this. But so far as he could tell there were no more bays or inlets between the creek and Port St George, only high land shown as Cape Tabitha. He had a vague recollection of the name Tabitha Heights in connection with Port St George.

Like a somewhat incongruous answer to prayer another yacht appeared, under motor and heading towards him, her deck and cockpit alive with young bronzed flesh. Seeing his jury rig one of the crew hailed him from the bow, holding gracefully to the boat's bare forestay, the epitome of youth and virility in the Attic style.

'Had a small problem?' the young man called. His accent did not quite match the classic impression.

'Am I right for Port St George?' Matthew yelled, desperate to get the basic question settled before wind and engine noise drowned conversation.

'Sure,' came the cheerful reply. 'Just keep going, then take a right.'

'Any identifications?'

'Sorry?'

'Identifications!'

The yachts were passing each other, the distance between them no more than forty feet.

'Samson's Columns,' the other shouted. 'Can't miss 'em. Plain as your arse.'

'What the hell are Samson's Columns?' Matthew bawled.

The breeze and the engine conspired against him. Only 'Have a good day' came down wind, and a friendly wave.

He decided that Tabitha Heights were to starboard already and that Port St George could be just round the corner. He hoped that Samson's Columns were not half-submerged rocks in the yacht's path. Twenty minutes later 'Patience' rounded a headland and he saw that the land fell away sharply. The water was still deep, so he kept within a hundred yards of the shore, anxious not to miss what might be a narrow entrance. Then they were in the lee of the headland, almost without breeze, below a cliff curiously shaped by wind or water to resemble pillars.

The yacht inched forward, perhaps helped by tide as much as wind, and beyond low-lying land to the west he could see the tips of masts. There seemed no entrance to the harbour, but as 'Patience' crept along the shore he realized that the land to the west was a fortified promontory beyond the harbour mouth and that the cliffs they were passing fell away to a drift of half-submerged rocks marking the eastern shallows.

As they passed the cliffs into more open water the wind picked up again, but the land had caused it to change direction and it was coming from the north, threatening to blow them away from the harbour entrance. He pointed 'Patience' up all he could, hoping the tide might help them in. But the boat continued to drift across the approach and he feared either being put on to the fortified headland or forced to bear away and continue his journey west. He was damned if he was going to drop anchor and wait for help...

The wind began to veer. His heart leapt and he coaxed and teased 'Patience' to point up, mentally back to the days when he would strain every nerve to clear the leeward mark of a finishing line. She responded amiably and without fuss like the thoroughbred he knew her to be, and they edged almost casually into the calm waters of Port St George, though leaving the rocky tip of the western headland mere feet to port.

But there was no time to bask in self-congratulation. The harbour was small and he was heading into waters crowded with anchored craft. He chose an area large enough for manoeuvre, came into the wind, dropped the mainsail and ran to the bow, cursing for having again forgotten to prepare earlier for dropping anchor by releasing it from its chocks.

Chain and rope whistled down but stopped abruptly, indicating a depth under the keel of no more than five or six feet. He let 'Patience' drift slowly back with the wind until he was within twenty feet of a large, square craft several decks high, bristling with aerials that looked like fishing rods and fishing rods resembling aerials. A squat stump carried a variety of flags, radar scanners, antennae and other static and revolving devices suggesting that below decks everything that could possibly be done was being done, electronically at least, to retain a firm hold on the logistics of the *dolce vita*.

Dwarfed by this pleasure dome, 'Patience' lay humbly at anchor while her skipper lowered the foresail and set fenders against the collision dangers of a crowded anchorage. Seamew, in a mood of untypical alertness, stumped up and down the deck as though on the look-out for old friends. Matthew guessed that smells from other craft were getting an atavistic reaction from an animal bored by the monotony of below-decks cuisine. Certainly his own nose had been sharply conscious of land smells from the moment they had entered harbour.

He walked back to the cockpit, Seamew following and now loud with suggestions. A short, big-bellied man had appeared on the lower deck of the pleasure dome, his matted chest and legs many shades paler than his face which was red with over-indulgence in tropical sun.

'Hi, there!' the man said.

'Hello!' Matthew replied reservedly. There had not been many occasions in his life when he had recognized in a stranger the components for lasting friendship, and something told him that this encounter was going to be par for the course.

'You made a good job of that.'

'There don't seem to be any laid moorings,' Matthew said.

'I mean your rig.'

'Oh, that!' Matthew said. 'I didn't have a lot of choice.'

'Never happened to me, but my wife's cousin now, his broke off six feet above the deck.'

'Must have raised some problems,' Matthew said.

'You gotta believe it,' the man agreed.

'It happened to me on the way from Tenerife,' Matthew mentioned casually.

'That's how it goes; *and* at night; *and* when you're outa beer; *and* when you're sick enough of your wife's yack about hurricanes to want for nothing but dry land and the company of men.'

'I've come across single-handed,' Matthew said, hoping that by the flatness of his tone he would not be judged as seeking to impress.

'What's the matter with you guys?' the man demanded. 'You're *all* doing it solo. Mind, it costs an arm and a leg for *one* to stay in this god-damned island, never mind two. My wife, she eats all the way down from Chesapeake. Sick as a dog she is at first, but she adjusts. By the time we get here she's carrying so much surplus it's all the supermarket can do to keep up with her.'

Matthew wondered what data might be on offer if he really dug for them.

'There's a supermarket, then?'

'Kind of; kiddy-size; over the chandlery. You gotta go into town for anything fancy.'

'I could do with a loaf of bread.'

The man laughed, a process indicated less by sound than by the undulations of his stomach.

'I like that! Jeeze, but I like that. Hey, Amy!'

A woman whose brightly coloured leisure wear did nothing to disguise her weight problem, emerged reluctantly from the wheelhouse.

'Hey, Amy,' the man repeated, 'this guy here, he's just come in. Know what he said?'

'No, Lou, how would I know what the man said?' Her voice was weary with long-exerted patience. 'Tell me.'

'"I could do with a loaf of bread", that's what he said. How do you like that? All the way across and he could do with a loaf of bread.'

'Is that what you wanted me for, Lou? Did I get out of my chair for you to tell me the man wants a loaf of bread? Listen, why not just give him one out of the freezer?'

A plaintive note came into her husband's voice.

'Yeah, well it's good, isn't it? All the way across, then "I could do with a loaf of bread". Not steak or lobster thermidor or scotch on the rocks... There are times I just don't understand you, Amy...'

He followed his wife into the wheelhouse, loud with explanation.

Matthew had meant to ask about entry regulations but decided to find out by going ashore. Rubber dinghies powered by outboards were plying busily between yachts and the quayside. The driver of one was so taken aback by the sight of Matthew working his coracle that he changed course only just in time to avoid a schooner that was manoeuvring under powerful engine to moor stern-to at the wharf reserved for the larger visiting yachts. The landing point for dinghies was indicated by a board with yellow letters on a black background. Beyond, across a pleasant green, a handsome brick building of Georgian proportions looked out over the harbour. Between the landing point and the first of the large yachts, access was up a sloping ramp, which was ideal for the coracle. The quayside was of weathered brown stone, and as he stepped ashore

Matthew trod on a flat green paper Christmas tree about five inches long.

A girl in her early twenties was passing, her minute bikini cherry-red below a diaphonous white garment that billowed in the breeze.

'Can you tell me what day it is?' Matthew asked.

The girl glanced at him, surprised, and he supposed she was assuming it was an unimaginative attempt at a pick-up.

'I've only just got in,' he added hastily.

'It's December the twenty-seventh,' she said, not slowing her approach to the dinghy in which a lean young man of about the same age awaited her.

The thought that he had stood on the summit of Zafada on Christmas Day was illogically pleasing.

A flagstaff marked the centre of the green which was surrounded and crossed by stone paths. Another large building lay beyond the flagstaff, built of the same brown stone and verandahed, with grey doors set regularly in the white walls behind the black and white balustrade. On the path below, under shade-giving trees, fruit and vegetables were laid out over several yards of the worn turf. Matthew walked slowly past them, reminded that there was nothing he wanted more than to get his teeth into fresh fruit. An elderly black woman was sitting on the stone steps leading to the verandah.

'Everything nice,' she said. Her smile was like a gash in an old boot. 'Everything nice.'

'Yes,' Matthew said. 'Very nice. I want some. But I haven't any money yet.'

The woman pointed across the green.

'You want money, some person there can help you.'

The simple timber building she had indicated seemed to be the focal point of the quayside's activity. He walked over, appreciating the feel of soil beneath his feet, and saw a board announcing it to be the pay office, which he assumed had to be taken at its historical rather than face value. People were using the door at the top of a flight of steps, and he mounted them; it was the supermarket. The black woman at the desk looked too harassed to welcome questions unconnected with trade, so he descended and entered a door surrounded by boards announcing yacht charters and the elsewhere existence of a

Cable and Wireless Office. There were piles of letters and packages on the counter; the girl behind it was fingering her plaited hair, gazing into the far distance as if a thousand miles away.

'I have just come in,' Matthew said. 'I wonder if you can tell me what the landing regulations are.'

The girl blinked, as though woken from a dream. Her glance suggested she found him no substitute.

'Yo' jus' landed?' she said dully.

'Yes. I'd like to know about customs and that kind of thing.'

'If you' jus' landed yo' bes' go back,' the girl said.

'Go back?'

'Yo' no supposed lan' till customs men clear yo'.'

'But don't they need to be told?'

'Boats mus' anchor in Liberty Cove, den customs go see dem,' the girl explained, plainly weary of dealing with idiots.

'How long is it before they come out to you? To me, I mean.'

The girl shrugged. 'Mebbe half a day; mebbe two.'

'Two days?'

She nodded slowly.

'Good God!' The discussion was clearly not going to mature profitably. 'Oh, well, where's Liberty Cove?'

Her arm lifted reluctantly and pointed in the general direction of the Caribbean Sea.

'Dat's where yo' should be,' she said severely.

'I anchored where I could,' Matthew explained. 'I sailed in under jury rig, single-handed, and had little manoeuvrability.'

For the first time the girl actually looked at him, for perhaps as long as two seconds, and Matthew was uncertain whether her expression confirmed distaste, uncomprehension or total disinterest. Whatever else, it was not sympathetic admiration.

'Yo' bes' go back to yo' boat,' she said dismissively.

Matthew felt he had been labelled as a potential trouble-maker. Another enquirer was asking if a parcel had arrived for him. Matthew took some comfort from the fact that although he looked like a Viking chieftain at the peak of virility, the girl showed no more animation.

He returned to the dinghy wharf and worked his coracle slowly back to 'Patience' against the steady breeze. There was no sign of life on the pleasure dome. He spent the next two hours cleaning and tidying below and on deck. Seamew was vocal for attention and a taste of shore life, but he put her off with promises and small pieces of cheese for which she had developed a liking.

After another hour he saw the dome owner going aboard from a dinghy. He was not agog to re-open the relationship, but proximity brought obligation. He waved and the dome owner responded.

'Can you give me the right time?' Matthew called.

'Nearly two thirty.'

'And the day of the week is Tuesday?'

'Sure! Where you been? The moon?'

'I told you. This is my first proper landfall since Tenerife. I had a knock-down. Unconscious.'

'Oh, yeah, sure,' the dome owner said. 'You had problems. Waddya mean – "first proper"?'

'I went ashore on a small island some way from here. Uninhabited.'

'Uninhabited?'

'It's called Zafada.'

'I heard of it. Ain't been there.'

Matthew was glad to know this. He had developed a proprietary feeling for Zafada. The thought of the dome owner anchoring off it was somehow distasteful.

'Landing's pretty well impossible,' he said.

'So if it's uninhabited, where did you get clearance?'

'I didn't.'

'But you're cleared now?'

'No. I'm waiting for them to turn up.'

The dome owner's expression suggested that had his face been capable of paling it would have done so dramatically.

'You mean you've been ashore without the okay from Big Daddy?'

'Who?'

'It's what we call the guy. Captain White. Head of the dockyard gestapo. Man, take my advice. Don't cross that bastard. When Big Daddy reaches you, you ain't been climbing around any offshore islands, see?' A jerked thumb indicated the shore. 'They can be a cussed bunch of bastards when they're so minded. They won't like it if they know you been ashore already.

They won't like it one little bit.'

'Well, I landed just now to look for them,' Matthew said. 'I assumed they'd want to know I was here.'

'Ker-*rist*!' the dome owner said devoutly. 'You've landed *twice* without 'em knowing? They'll crucify you.'

'What is this place? Alcatraz?'

The other's gesture spoke volumes.

'But I'll tell you this,' he said, as though rounding off a longer discourse, 'they're bureaucracy mad. Every goddam device for bringing creeping paralysis into the affairs of men has been thought up on this island. If you're minded to breathe, you can bet your bottom dollar they'll want a form signed. In quintuplicate. You gotta believe it.'

After weeks at sea, civilization's petty irritations seemed outweighed by pretty girls, fresh fruit, earth beneath the feet...

'It's such a fantastic feeling to have arrived at all,' Matthew said, 'that they're going to have a hard time spoiling it for me.'

'Sure,' said the dome owner lugubriously, 'sure.'

Two hours later 'Patience' was boarded by Captain White and a silent aide. Apart from requiring assurance that Seamew's port of origin was in the U.K. - a detail about which, in view of the kitten's radiant good health, Matthew felt entitled to take an affirmative view - the Captain did nothing to deserve his reputation. Some admittedly tedious forms had to be dealt with in triplicate, but after being assured that Matthew had neither firearms, contraband nor drugs hidden about the boat, the policeman chucked Seamew under the chin jovially and departed.

'It wasn't all that bad,' Matthew told the dome owner as he paddled past for the shore twenty minutes later.

'Did you tell 'em you'd already landed?' the dome owner demanded.

'They didn't ask me.'

The dome owner looked disappointed.

'Guess even Big Daddy has to have an off day,' he admitted grudgingly. His face brightened. 'Wait till you meet 'em in the post office.'

Matthew paddled in to the wharf, checked that the 'everything nice' lady was still in business, and made straight for the supermarket, salivating slightly at the thought of the meal ahead. As he reached the top of the steps two women came out of the door which they shut behind them. He pushed it, but it was locked. He saw a notice board at the foot of the steps on the side furthest from the yacht charter office. It told him that the supermarket closed at four-thirty and would be open from eight-thirty to twelve the next morning.

He wandered round the corner of the pay office and had a glimpse into the chandlery before the door of this too was shut by a tall, loose-limbed man with spectacles and a pleasant, weather-beaten, indecisive face. His floral shirt looked new but his shorts had the frayed, comfortable look of very old friends. Matthew knew he was English before he opened his mouth.

'Sorry,' the man said. 'Hope you didn't need anything too badly.'

'I'm after food rather than equipment,' Matthew said. 'I've only just got in from Tenerife.' He offered his hand. 'Matthew Braine.'

'Peter Richardson. Welcome to Port St George.'

Another man joined them, walking briskly as though unaffected by the climate. He was short, gnomish and red-complexioned; his face showed impatience to be elsewhere.

'Tom Riley,' Richardson introduced. 'Tom runs the brokerage business here.'

Riley nodded curtly but did not offer his hand.

'Is there anywhere I can get a meal?' Matthew asked.

'Of course,' Richardson said. 'The Captain's Arms will fix you up.'

He had the look of someone who had passed a trying day.

'Is it far?'

'Follow that path, leaving the Naval Museum on your left, and you'll see a board.'

'What does one do for money here? I've only English pound notes and a credit card.'

'Here,' Richardson said, producing some grubby notes, 'have these. Sixty E.C. dollars, sometimes called beewees. Give me ten pounds for them as security, but let me have them back later. Only E.C. or U.S. dollars are accepted in Monesterio. The banks are in Campbelltown.'

He loped off with the relaxed, unselfconscious gait that is the British give-away in all corners of the world. Riley went with him, talking fast. His bearing was tense, apprehensive, even fearful.

Just walking around was helping Matthew to throw off his post-Zafada stiffness. He wandered along the wharves looking at the boats moored stern-to. They varied from modest forty-footers with the look of vessels whose owners knew the oceans, to unrepentant gin palaces whose ensigns suggested that their possessors were flown from Europe and the United States to enjoy brief interludes from fortune-hunting in the hands of paid skippers. Nearly everyone was young, bronzed, bleached and in exuberant health. Many of the girls had tough faces and sturdy bodies made for winching and sheeting, but a few were shatteringly pretty and dressed in what was obviously idiotically expensive sail-wear. The voices were largely American, but French, German, Scandinavian and Australian origins were also apparent. After twenty minutes of observing them he began to experience small shots of relief when able to detect men of his own age.

In case the 'everything nice' lady also decided to shut up shop, he returned to the green and bought a pineapple and enough bananas, paw-paws and mangoes to feed a crew of six. He calculated that the pineapple would have cost no more in Harrods. Returning to the yacht, he worked the coracle with extra care in case the precious cargo was lost. Realization that he had brought nothing of interest to Seamew turned into guilt when her face appeared through the guard-rail registering – if his imagination was not getting the better of him – anxious enquiry.

As he climbed aboard he remembered Captain White had said he should pay port entry fees, but as nothing had seemed open he decided to wait until the next day. He gave over the rest of the afternoon and evening to making everything shipshape. He made long overdue repairs to the head, galley and locker doors strained during the capsize, then up-anchored and let 'Patience' drift towards the quay through a gap in the moored yachts, re-anchoring at a distance that brought the quayside within reasonable reach of his coracle.

The best he could do for Seamew was to trick up her evaporated milk with a little treacle, open her favourite fish-food tin, and make promises for the morrow.

He ate some of the fruit and wondered why he had spent a lifetime indifferent to food. The most memorable was the pineapple – a slim, tapered variety that made its price seem almost reasonable.

He made a list of the things he had to do, heading it 'New mast', and because he had given Seamew extra rations to ensure a full if not wholly satisfied kitten he was able to turn in early without fear of disturbance from a plaintive crew.

Sleep came less easily than off Zafada. Music, laughter, dinner parties and drinking sessions on neighbouring boats continued for hours after the early fall of darkness. Outboard engines and the slap of halyards on metal masts added to the indiscriminate orchestration of human enjoyment. But his stomach and mind were in reasonable harmony; when sleep came it would have taken a hurricane to wake him.

18

CONVINCED that the pleasure-dome owner was a born pessimist, but not wishing to put local bureaucracy to unreasonable tests, he went ashore at eight-thirty the next morning and found the post office. It was at the north end of the verandahed building which a notice board announced as being erected in 1815 as officers' quarters and in need of restoration; contributions were invited.

In the post office a white-uniformed official dealt with the formalities with an efficiency that gave no substance to the dome-owner's dire warnings. Matthew was given a bill to take to the paymaster below the police station near the dockyard gates, and as he approached he was greeted by a hand which, if not at the salute, was at least evidence of Captain White's continued cordiality. Above the waist the Captain seemed off duty; his tee-shirt read 'Here comes trouble'.

The paymaster did nothing to break the lyricism of Matthew's introduction to Monesterio's officialdom; he left the building feeling a free and contented man. A sudden warm pang of affection for Rebecca swept over him, compounded a little of conscience at being in such an idyllic spot in the middle of winter when she was probably ankle-deep in snow; Rebecca had an insatiable craving for hot sun. He had thought of her even on Zafada. It was as though renewed contact with land was enmeshing him in those fragile strands of memory so easily parted by a prolonged voyage.

He would write to her. He returned to the post office. The man who had dealt with him was busy with a German yachtsman. Language problems seemed likely to prolong matters. A girl he took to be the official's assistant was at her desk behind the counter. Lovingly and with almost studied slowness she was eating a grapefruit with a tea spoon. From the pleasure it gave her it might have been her first introduction to the species. She smacked her eminently smackable lips over each slowly-chewed segment. Removing the pips from her mouth with a stroke of her yellow-palmed hand she placed them carefully on a telegram form with long black fingers as though intending to preserve them as a memory of better days.

Respectful towards what seemed an occasion near to ceremony, Matthew stood by the counter and watched this performance for a full five minutes. The grapefruit was only half consumed and the male clerk was still the wrong side of the language barrier. Despite liberal inclinations Matthew experienced a twinge of Anglo-Saxon impatience.

'Could I possibly trouble you for a stamp?' he enquired. 'I'd also like to send a cable.'

The girl withdrew her gaze reluctantly from the object of her desire and looked at him reprovingly with big slow eyes.

'Ah mus' finish mah fruit,' she said.

He waited a further five minutes while she finished her fruit. When he had paid for his stamp and sent a cable to Rebecca, he left the post office with the feeling he had been judged a man in need of a better sense of the priorities.

It was nine and the supermarket had just opened. It was already hot and he was thirsty. Beefy Australians and Germans were jostling for first choice of tins from the large refrigerator, drinking from them on the spot as though their lives depended on instant gratification. He chose a tin picturing pineapples, oranges, pears, cherries and other more exotic fruits. The contents were described in bold letters as 'Fruit Punch'. He stripped the ring off and poured the cold liquid down his throat. The coolness was welcome but the taste drew his attention to the small-print analysis of contents. These included most of the chemicals he had ever heard of and a number new to him. The consumer was assured of '10% real fruit juice'. He had noticed white palings enclosing a garbage area beyond a line of three restored capstans. He left the supermarket and consigned the tin and the balance of its contents to its ripely smelling confines, then returned to replenish the stores on 'Patience'. It was pleasant to find Rich Tea biscuits in good supply. He overreached his sixty Eastern Caribbean dollars and had to put three cans of beans back on the shelves in order to leave enough for a bus fare into Campbelltown.

When he returned to the quayside he was helped to get his box of stores into the coracle by a solitary young black who had been practising bowling and batting motions unequipped with bat or ball. The looseness of the boy's limbs and trunk was remarkable; his joy in the mere repertoire of movement was pleasing to watch.

The journey back to the yacht against a wind that had freshened was still long enough to cover him in sweat. He had noticed that the south end of the officers' quarters consisted of lavatories and showers. He decided to use the shower before going into Campbelltown. Mosquitoes had forayed successfully for his blood during the night, making the thought of cool water doubly attractive.

Seamew's reaction to the carton of seriously preserved and strongly fortified milk fell short of ecstasy but she submitted when convinced that choice was not being offered.

'You're to look after the boat and behave yourself,' he instructed. 'I'm going into town and if I see anything you'd like I'll bring it back. For Christ's sake,' he added as he got back into the coracle, 'stop talking to that bloody cat.'

He walked through the dockyard towards the gates, enjoying a more relaxed look at the buildings which had been so tastefully restored and put to new use in their historic surroundings. Beyond the wide, airy mast house and the joiners' loft he noted to the right of the dockyard gates a passage-way to the Captain's Arms. At its entrance bead-sellers were arranging their wares. He resolved to try the inn that evening, to celebrate his arrival with a touch of style.

Outside the dockyard gates the breeze blew coolly between the high brick wall of the inn and the cut-back rock on the other side of the long approach road from the car park to the west. Below the rock, behind a narrow containing wall on which they sat, several women offered fruit and vegetables. Asking the price of some of the fruits, he appreciated the psychological advantage held by the 'everything nice' lady on her quayside pitch.

No bus was waiting in the car park, so he sat on the end of the containing wall where trees overhung the rock. An orange van roared into the park in a cloud of dust, discharging a remarkable number of people from its battered rear doors. A grubby card behind the windscreen read 'Campbelltown', so he boarded the van and sat on the long side-seat. Three Americans and an Italian followed, sitting opposite him; they were clearly off boats and he wondered if he smelled as much as they did.

The driver returned and closed the rear doors before jumping in and roaring off so violently that his passengers slid down the shiny seats like beads on a tilted abacus. The lack of side windows spared their nerves a lot of punishment, but the road surface made their teeth chatter like castanets, and until the wisdom of keeping jaws clenched had dawned on them, each time the wheels thunked into a deep pot-hole the snap of meeting molars was like being closeted with a bevy of angry turtles. Through the murky windscreen Matthew caught glimpses of children and chicken scattering like blown chaff before the van's horn-happy approach.

'Jesus!' said one of the Americans, who kept a hand near his jaw as though fearing separation from his dentures, 'it must have been some ride before they invented pneumatics.'

His bleached denim shorts were so worn that no logical explanation accounted for their staying on his hips. Only the Italian's scanty clothing suggested he cared about style, but their grease marks indicated deep involvement with engines. He was the least disturbed by their driver's road technique.

The bus could be successfully hailed from any point on the road. It seemed full by the time they had gone two miles. As they hurtled alongside a wide stretch of water, the elderly black woman next to Matthew said it was Newport Harbour. At the village that followed, five more blacks and a pretty white girl in very brief, ready-frayed shorts got on. Everyone inched along the benches and somehow the new arrivals were fitted in. Some of the black women looked at the white girl without enthusiasm. The road surface had improved, but now and then the driver tested a pot-hole whose depth might have been expected to detach the body of the van from its chassis. The clatter of the engine, which held all the complaint of machinery that had been pushed to the limit for many times its normal life-span, was accompanied by incessant jungle pop from a radio tuned full blast. The noise, combined with the swaying, bucking motion and the frequent sickeningly sudden stops and starts, produced a kind of trance among the white passengers. The blacks seemed unaffected, their bodies responding instinctively to the varied motion. A number of the young men who got on were carrying expensive radio recorders on their shoulders, each producing maximum volume but pressed against their ears to ensure full value. Their eyes were unseeing, glazed, as though high on drugs. Only when the van's radio showed no sign of letting its audience down were the individual sets turned off.

In Freeman's Village, and again in Wilberforce, more people got on. Extra seats appeared out of nowhere and filled the gangway. The hip bone of the thin black woman on Matthew's left contrasted with the rubbery fullness of a girl, hugely in child, dressed in a dazzlingly yellow and red dress and head-scarf on his right. Her body transferred to his a glow that did nothing to make the journey more comfortable. He put the temperature in the bus, despite an open window near the driver, at something over a hundred.

'It's a pity,' he said to the thin woman, 'they can't have windows that open in the rear doors.'

'In the summer maybe. Now, in winter...' She shook her head, her lips pursed in disapproval.

The cheerful congestion of the villages was a far cry from the staid calm of Sussex. Most of the homes, many painted in bright clashing colours, were little more than the sheds to be found at the bottom of English gardens. Their haphazard proximity to the road proved that individual impulse ruled firmly over any instinct for planning. Small tracks led to higher ground where the shacks and huts were gradually swallowed by the verdant postage-stamp gardens full of bright flowers, banana and coconut trees, and bare earth over which goats, chickens and an infinite number of unkempt dogs, many about to whelp, roamed at will. Men lounged on steps and against walls; women head-carried their burdens, their backs straight as pokers; slow pregnant girls, their zombie-like expressions showing total abandonment to nature's plan, moved reluctantly out of the path of traffic; children, most of them too small to be at school, out-numbered even the goats. Everything and everyone looked aggressively healthy and well-fed; the whole scene reeked of unbridled fertility and carefree adjustment to the fecund scheme of things.

'A pity Rousseau didn't come this way,' Matthew said to the American in the threadbare shorts. The man stopped chewing gum and looked at him blankly.

'Come again?' he invited.

'Rousseau,' Matthew repeated. 'Henri Rousseau, the primitive painter. I was saying it's a pity he couldn't be here. He might have made something of it.'

'More than I can,' the man said, looking through the windscreen with distaste. His jaw rhythm returned.

Each village appeared over-stocked with churches: Seventh Day Adventist, Baptist, Episcopalian, Jehovah's Witness, Moravian, and some Matthew had never heard of. When the van's radio, perhaps hoping to respect some balance between temporal and spiritual, delivered a song with remote religious undertones, the female occupants began to hum and croon in accompaniment, their corporate swaying putting further strain on the non-participating passengers' hip joints and shoulders.

Beyond Wilberforce few people boarded, but it was not for want of willingness on the driver's part. When a woman with three worn tyres sought entrance, Matthew assumed that the limits would at last be seen to have been reached. But the driver let her in cheerfully and the passengers tucked the tyres under their feet like footstools.

As the bus neared Campbelltown the roads deteriorated again. On the outskirts a middle-aged Asian boarded. He was cheaply but neatly dressed, very clean, in a tight dark suit. He carried a flat black brief case with bright metal trim which he rested on his knees. The pretty girl in shorts was opposite him. He had large melting eyes which he fixed on her unblinkingly like a spaniel wanting a walk.

The terminal was between the market and Campbelltown Harbour on a wide area of dusty ground. When the rear doors were opened a welcome coolness swept into the van. The passengers queued outside the van to pay the driver; the fare of little over one bee-wee for the ten or more miles they had covered seemed remarkably good value, for all that a journey on the trans-Siberian railway might have been less exacting. Matthew noticed that as the Asian alighted he held his briefcase flat across his thighs; or as flat as was possible in the circumstances.

On the waste area by the road coconut sellers were slashing the ends of their wares with bush knives and finding ready buyers for the milk inside, which was drunk on the spot from the big green husks.

The morning was well advanced and the market's peak had passed. He looked in at the fish market and peered into deep round baskets holding multi-coloured creatures of all shapes and sizes. Some were round and as flat as plates, others triangular with a flat base like full purses of shining silk.

He walked on into the town along a street that climbed gently towards the centre. Cars, cycles, people, goats, dogs, chickens and every imaginable form of human litter, much of it abuzz with flies, made an odorous and noisy tapestry of uninhibited life. Every ear between the years of fifteen and thirty-five seemed to be glued to a radio, each station producing much the same music as the next. Matthew wondered if a holiday in Monesterio, had he ever been able to afford it for the whole family, would have cured his children of their obsession with pop. It was a pointless reflection; like most of their contemporaries they appeared to be entering adult life with a total disinterest in classical music and he had almost stopped agonizing about it.

He tried three banks before finding one prepared to accept his cheque card. The doors were about to be closed when he was at last successful, but even so he had to wait twenty minutes in a queue that wound like a snake to the counters. The bank was staffed by cocoa-coloured girls in coffee-coloured dresses, some of them very easy on the eye.

Money in his pocket brought a further stage of relaxation. He explored the town, trying to keep to the shady side of each street. Apart from the banks, post office, two supermarkets, British Airways and a few other buildings, the town was a ramshackle hodge-podge of mostly timber buildings with deep gullies at the sides of the steepest roads, which were those running down to the harbour. An attractive cathedral with a cool wooden interior dominated the town and gave a view of cruise ships in the harbour, their presence accounting for the many pale whites who were wandering around looking ripe for rip-off. Despite the squalour every black looked fighting fit, well dressed, and almost as relaxed and contented as the people of the villages. The façade, he told himself. Reserve judgment.

He asked a chemist for something to stop mosquito attacks and was advised that only a body spray called 'Scram' was really effective.

'I'll have a tin, then,' Matthew said.

The chemist pulled a face.

'The tourists, they've taken every can.'

'Can't you get some more from your suppliers?'

The man shrugged.

'It's the season, you see, sir. There are so many folk around.'

'Don't your suppliers realize that and send you more at the busy time of the year?'

'They don't see it that way, sir.'

It seemed pointless to analyse the reasons. He tried five other shops. They were all out of 'Scram'. He bought some witch hazel so that he could at least ease the after-effects. It was very expensive.

He remembered his promise to Seamew to buy some fish. He was assured that the market was his only hope, but that it was now too late. He returned to one of the supermarkets at the bottom of Steep Street and bought a packet of fish fingers, telling himself that at least Seamew would recognize it as something entirely different. On a stall outside newspapers were for sale. The English papers were ten days old and cost about a pound. He decided that no permutation of the wheelings and dealings of politicians and trade unionists was likely to merit such expenditure, so bought instead a local paper, *Labour's Voice*, for thirty-five cents.

As the sun's heat grew less he wandered through streets on the north side of the town, intrigued by the overhead wires heavily festooned with some form of plant, like baggywrinkle on a ship's shrouds. Even there, in what might politely have been called the residential side of the town, there was still no sign of the human wretchedness that might have been expected to accompany the dilapidation and stench. Feeling – absurdly, he told himself – almost cheated of something, he walked to the bus terminus and found a van going to Port St George. This time the bus had a side door and forward-facing seats, some of which folded down into the gangway so that any further overflow could be accommodated only by hanging for dear life on to rails either side of the entrance. He had forgotten that Campbelltown would have a rush hour like any other capital city. From the start of the journey he was wedged so tightly between bony pelvises and broad black shoulders that his chest had a little more room for the act of breathing if he hunched his shoulders and put his arms out in front of his body. Since this was more or less the appropriate position for reading a newspaper, he decided to tackle *Labour's Voice*.

The front page was headlined 'The Rape of St George' and subtitled 'Threat to Our National Heritage.' The first few lines suggested he had stumbled on evidence of the frustration, misery and injustice for which his trained British conscience had been on the *qui vive*. 'In Port St George,' the report read,

> 'the ripple of discontent is spreading and gaining momentum. The Monesterio dockworkers, beadsellers, laundry-ladies, hotel maids, waiters, taxi-drivers, Policemen and Harbour Officials are no longer happy to play second hand and fourth fiddle to the outside squatters and get-rich operators who for decades have held sway in the world's finest old Naval Dockyard. The Czars of the Dockyard have wheeled and dealed in contraband yachts and consumer goods whilst making their millions and apparently convincing successive administrations and the Port St George Trust of their sincere love of history!!!!!!! and all Monesterovians!!!!!!! The rank and file, however, the grass roots, the sons of the soil, the voters in this country, are not so easily convinced that all is well in Port St George, their heritage.'

He read on. If spelling, syntax and even meaning left something to be desired, it was good rabble-rousing venom in the true tradition of the gutter press, and Matthew could appreciate it from a professional point of view if not with any inner conviction that it could be more than some exercise in political leverage. The article went on to slam the 'unlicensed, unregistered and clandestine yacht brokers' and the 'self-styled Professors of Archaeology, sending off their millions directly to their overseas banks.' 'The yacht-broking rip-off,' the paper screamed, had to come under control, for the 'Czars' made no direct contributions to the economy. 'So who the hell,' the piece ended poetically, 'are these unwanted, un-needed parasites to complain about holes in the road and garbage on their doorsteps. Ah we sons of the soil and the sea say to ah deh people go away and na come back...' It was signed by 'Dockyard Dan the Jumbie Man.'

Because the door of the bus had been kept open by the hangers on, such air as he had been able to pull down into his constricted lungs had been more wholesome than on the outward journey. Feeling semi-pulped by the half hour of vibrating intimacy with the hardened bodies of the sons and daughters of the soil and the sea, he alighted in the dockyard car park more than ready for the shower he had forgotten to take earlier. The water was cold and so refreshing that he wondered how he had managed without one for so long.

Seamew accepted the fish fingers with reasonable grace and seemed willing to settle down for an early night. Matthew felt like a rest himself and followed suit. When he woke two hours later it was nearly eight and dark except for the light from the stars and moon. Rebecca had insisted he took a new shirt in which to celebrate the opening of the champagne, so he put it on, reserving the wine for when he might have more appreciative company than Seamew. Uncertain how dressy they might be at the Captain's Arms, he wore a pair of long trousers but decided that a tie was more than would be expected. He rubbed witch hazel into his bites, the worst being on his calves where the brutes had accurately located the chief vein near the surface of his skin.

He paddled to the wharf. On some of the yachts moored stern-to, meals were under way. Lamps swung lazily from booms above chatting groups, providing enough light for the ritual of eating but too little for loss of privacy to the world beyond the confined cosiness of cockpits. Some of the lamps were enclosed in shades punched with holes, and their slight movement in the breeze cast a dappled, wandering light that baffled identification of faces. Matthew felt half attracted, half repelled by the scene, ill at ease in being part of a display of conspicuous wealth and idleness, but not immune to the atmosphere of cheerful togetherness. He walked through the dockyard fighting pangs of a loneliness he had not experienced in his weeks at sea.

The beadsellers had departed; on the other side of the gates a group of taxi-drivers was laughing, arguing and throwing dice below a tree in front of the paymaster's office, risking small portions of what they had earned by returning the day tourists to their cruise ships for the next excursion to some fleetingly glimpsed paradise.

The passage led him to a scene of such charm that he stopped to admire it from beneath a helpfully labelled neem tree. The inn lay ahead at the end of a path some forty yards long. On the left of the path, against a high brick wall, bougainvillaea and several varieties of hibiscus made a colourful backdrop to a wide area of grass in which a few short-trunked coconut trees rustled in the breeze. Surrounding the grassed area on three sides, and dramatically flood-lit, were more than a dozen enormous stone pillars some twelve feet in circumference. Their bulbous tops suggested they had been capped against erosion, though the weather had taken great bites out of some of them. He counted seventeen. The open fourth side of the rectangle gave on to the water, as did the stepped terraces to the north of the stone and brick inn. Eucalyptus and other trees whose names he did not know swayed in the warm air over pillars and terraces; the uncountable stars, less changed by the passage of history than anything on which they looked down, completed a setting made for opera or classical drama.

He walked slowly down the path toward the invitingly open door, above which in the shingled roof an unshuttered dormer displayed illuminated beams. A small board on one of the pillars confirmed they had once supported the sail loft above a boathouse built in 1797, and that the loft had been destroyed by earthquake in 1843. Along the line of pillars nearest to the inn, and within the original confines of the boathouse, was a narrow wet-dock with ring bolts set in the stone walls. This too was flood-lit to great effect.

He entered and asked at the desk if he could have dinner. A middle-aged, good-looking black woman in spectacles and a long dress said she would do what she could, but that usually it was necessary to book. He went to the bar and asked for a rum punch, looking round from his stool at the crowded lounge and the full tables beyond. Tall louvred doors opened on to the terrace and he walked out on to the highest level which was clearly used for dancing. To the right, at a table against the wall, a man younger than himself was drinking from a tall glass. Above, a tree with fern-like leaves responded delicately to the breeze. Matthew felt the bark of the slim trunk with his hand, admiring the beauty of the foliage.

'Casuarina,' the younger man said.

Matthew looked round the terrace, suspecting a greeting to someone he had not seen.

'Casuarina,' the other repeated. 'The name of that tree. You seemed interested.'

'Yes,' Matthew said. 'At home I study trees in a very amateur way. You know what a vareity we have.'

'There are times when I'd gladly exchange a hundred palms for one honest oak.'

Matthew laughed. 'What a very English statement. You been here for long?'

The other smiled. 'Not really. I suppose I sounded like an expatriate of twenty years' absence. But long enough.'

He was slim, fair-haired, with a mouth and eyes suggesting a sense of humour. Matthew put his age in the mid-thirties.

'Matthew Braine,' he said. They shook hands.

'Sebastian Rutherford. Bit of a mouthful.'

'Don't let me disturb you.'

'Not at all. Are you waiting for a table?'

'Yes. The lady said she'd do her best.'

The other nodded.

'She has her problems. Why not join me?'

'Are you sure?'

'Please.'

'I don't mind waiting.'

'I'm by myself. I'd be delighted.'

'In that case...'

Matthew sat down. Sebastian smiled.

'Strange, isn't it,' he said, 'how formal we still are?'

'Old inhibitions die hard,' Matthew agreed. 'Are you on holiday? Working?'

He studied the other's face. Despite the younger man's casual, almost facetious way of speaking, there was a tenseness suggesting effort was needed to communicate and seem at ease. His good features were marred by a gauntness his next words explained.

'A working recuperation, I suppose. Past errors and omissions caught up with me. I allowed a perceptive G.P. to persuade me that a winter in surroundings entirely different might cauterize the nerve endings and turn me right side up.'

'Is it working out?'

'I think so. I paint furiously, read voraciously, consume moderately, hit the sack early, rise with the grackle birds, and in short lead a life of unrepentant selfishness and aimless contemplation. I shan't stick it much longer. And you?'

'I arrived by boat.'

'Not cruise, to judge by your colour.'

'A small yacht. Solent, Tenerife, Monesterio, with a short stop on a rock called Zafada.'

'Zafada!'

Sebastian seemed about to say something more, but took another sip from his glass and murmured a non-committal 'Well, well!' Matthew changed the subject, still disinclined to have others' knowledge of Zafada confirmed.

'You paint, you say. Canvases, I take it, not boats?'

'Humble sketches in pen and colour wash. Depressingly uninspired.'

'For a living?'

'No, architecture is my field. Small practice in Fulham. Fortunately I've a partner who copes in my absence.'

The woman Matthew had spoken to came out on the terrace.

'Ah, Esterlyn,' Sebastian said, 'Mr Braine has joined me. I hope that's all right.'

'That's okay, Mr Rutherford. You want to eat now? I'll have the girl bring you the board.'

'Esterlyn's a nice lady,' Sebastian said. 'It can be tough running a hotel in a predominantly yachting area, but she does her best.'

'She has the setting on her side; no colour-brochure could do justice to it.'

'It's as attractive by day as by night.'

A waitress in a canary-yellow overall had moved a blackboard into the beam of a lamp hanging below the trees. The menu was written in chalk. Fish predominated.

'I can recommend the snapper,' Sebastian said. 'It's pleasant enough if you are not expecting Solent standards.'

They gave their orders and Matthew settled back contentedly.

'This is very pleasant,' he said. 'I was expecting to have to celebrate on my own.'

'Your birthday?'

'No, but I only arrived yesterday and this is my first real meal. I wish now I had brought the champagne my wife said I must drink on arrival.'

'Keep it for another occasion,' Sebastian advised. 'This hotel hasn't yet got round to the excellent Californian wines that are the best alternative to the absurdly priced French stuff they try to flog you, but a bottle of the South African Chablis will do us very well.'

Matthew slapped his neck and examined the palm of his hand hopefully.

'Missed it,' he admitted ruefully.

'They're bloody awful,' Sebastian agreed. 'I've developed a strong admiration for the Jains since coming to this island. I'm caviare to things that bite, though I've built up some immunity by now. But as Peter Richardson says, when they smell new blood you might as well expose your limbs and let them get on with it. They fall about laughing at nets, screens and aerosols.'

'I've met Richardson. Seemed pleasant. Easy going.'

'Very. His wife too. Well, you have to be here. If you're the tense type you'll be carried off within weeks with the screaming heebie-jeebies.'

'What's their background?'

'The Richardsons? Peter and his brother Donald sailed over in the late forties with their father, meaning to go on round the world. They were so intrigued by Port St George, which was rotting steadily into the ground, the concern of no one, that they have been here ever since. Old Captain Richardson retired and went back to the U.K.'

'They restored the place?'

'They didn't have the means for that, but certainly their interest in the dockyard, and the chartering and allied business they built up, helped to put it on the map. A few years after they arrived the then Governor lent weight to create The Port St George Trust. The Trust is now run by a British couple living in the dockyard under the aegis of the Overseas Development people at home.'

'Seems a very happy arrangement. So the island owes quite a debt to the Richardsons?'

Sebastian smiled.

'You might think so.'

'That's a rather ambiguous reply.'

Sebastian grimaced.

'Few things on this island are what they seem,' he said.

'So I gathered from a paper I was reading this morning.'

'Local?'

'Yes. *Labour's Voice*.'

'Ah!' Sebastian said. 'I can imagine.'

'Are you living in this hotel?' Matthew asked.

'Good Lord, no! I couldn't have afforded that for a whole three months. No, I'm in the village about a mile away, in a timber shack under a hot tin roof. The sort of place one passes thankfully, marvelling at others' capacity for the simple life.'

'Any services laid on?'

'On and off. One learns to take nothing for granted on Monesterio.'

'I don't know that you are exactly selling me the place.'

'It isn't as bad as it sounds. When the water is not turned off, there is water – of a kind. When the electricity is not turned off, there is electricity. Which is to say that to-day there is neither water nor electricity for the second day running, which has something to do with my blowing a sheaf of bee-wees in my friendly neighbourhood hotel.'

'The hotel seems all right for the services.'

'They're equipped to cope with the logistics. They have their own generator and water storage. But one gets by. Candle-light has its charms and makes for early nights.'

'I have oil and candles on the boat for choice,' Matthew said. 'I'm not engine-minded.'

'We share common ground,' Sebastian said. 'Within reason I enjoy the uncluttered and independent life. Our numbers, I think, are growing. The chore of looking after possessions is becoming insupportable.'

'One of my girls is always lecturing me on those lines,' Matthew said, 'and I go along with her about the disease, if not the cure. The inefficiency and deviousness at every level, from the bureaucratic to the cultural and academic, make one wish that some more simple system *could* be made to work. Have you kids?'

'Things haven't worked out that way. I nearly married, but it didn't come off. The breakup was part of the background to my coming out here.'

'A good spot for regrouping.'

'You haven't told me what you do,' Sebastian said. 'Most people fill you in within two minutes once they are off the home patch, so my patience is under strain.'

'I've lived by writing for a good many years.'

'The past tense. Are you into something new?'

Matthew hesitated. 'The future's uncertain.'

'You can say that again.'

The waitress brought their meal. Time passed pleasantly. From discussion of the agonies of creativity they moved on to architecture.

'Have you been to the big city?' Sebastian asked.

Matthew stirred his coffee. 'Campbelltown? Yes.'

'It's about the most broken-down capital in the Caribbean, but no one can deny it has character.'

'I walked round it this morning.'

'The best method,' Sebastian said. 'You get the feel of a place through your feet. Tomorrow, if you've nothing better to do, let me show you some of the trees in the dockyard. Then if some bread and cheese in my shack would suit you...'

'Delighted.'

'Ten? Here?'

'Fine.'

'Then if you don't mind,' Sebastian said rising, 'I'll shoot off home. The doc said nine-thirty for lights out, and I try to oblige.'

They shared the bill and Matthew stayed on under the stars, sipping a liqueur. He was already a little in love with the place and could imagine how Rebecca would have reacted to it. He wished she could be sharing it with him...

He shivered, not because of any cooling of the trade wind

that blew over the terrace, but because of a sudden and seemingly unprompted reminder that came with as much force as a blow on the head. Was he a charlatan, a poseur, a fool? He had no right to be sitting contentedly under a tropical sky toying with a Tia Maria after a pleasant dinner in congenial company. He should be, for God's sake, a cleanly picked skeleton at the bottom of the Atlantic, well on the way to being forgotten by friends and family with more ego-centred things to do than sustain a mood of mourning for a man who had decided rightly enough that his useful and purposive life had come to an end. Nothing had changed, neither himself nor the world he had sailed from. Yet here he was, by no means suicidal, healthy, well fed, and not beyond feeling some quiet pleasure in having completed single-handed – well, mostly single-handed – the longest voyage of his life. He had arrived in one of the most romantic harbours in the world after a creditable journey without, patently, making too many major blunders. So what? What the hell was he doing, sitting there savouring the recent past and contemplating a routine for the future that most would see as a rather splendid holiday . . . ?

'You're a bloody fake,' he said aloud.

The people at the next table stopped talking, as though tuning their ears, then took up their conversation again.

He rose and walked down the flood-lit path into the shadowed passage to the dockyard gate. The taxi-drivers were kicking a screw of paper, their long loose arms seeming independent of their bodies. He walked past them into the village of St George and took a small rutted road that wound up to the right through wooden shacks and past a church whose open doors revealed walls of celestial blue. He turned right again at the top and kept on climbing, leaving the dwellings behind, walking slowly, hardly conscious of his route. The clean, warm wind was so refreshing he could have walked all night. After about an hour he came upon the roofless remains of an impressive arched building, bathed in the bone-white light of the moon. He had met no one. The road ended at some ruins within whose perimeter a rock-paved platform overlooked the dockyard, a fairyscape of lights. In his solitude something of the peace that had come on the summit of Zafada returned to him, a state of total acceptance, a harmony of the soul. The lights on the moored yachts far below were the only evidence that this island was not equally his own. He turned full circle, his head back, humbled by the countless profusion of the stars, then looked out over the dockyard again to beyond the harbour's mouth where the sea receded into unbroken darkness, defeating his eyes.

19

HE was woken by Seamew's urgent reminders that breakfast was overdue. He lay still, uncertain whether his walk had been dream or reality. The best way to settle the matter was with his binoculars. By the time he was on deck he was fairly certain it had been no dream, and when his glasses located the arches on the top of an overlooking hill he realized he had walked to Tabitha Heights.

He gave Seamew her breakfast, abstractedly, his mind taken up with seeking a reason for his lapse from rational control. Leaving Seamew with twice her normal ration he returned to his bunk and tried to work back to what had prompted the sudden rush of self-criticism and uncertainty. He attempted to recapture the mood in which he had left the Solent, his real intentions before the encounter with Jill, his subsequent frame of mind when the challenge of the crossing had proved so destructive of rational thought about anything but the short-term obligation to achieve a tangible, geographical objective.

He concluded that the answer was just that - the focus of his energies had been temporarily diverted; a decision made in a more rational and realistic mood had been eclipsed by a later, atavistic obsession with survival. It was like thinking about a different person. The question now was whether the old mood, the old reason, would return, and with sufficient force. He could come to no more definite a conclusion than that he was in a state of transition and had no choice but to carry on, day to day.

But he went on mulling it over, feeling irritated at not being able to leave it alone. He chastised himself with reminders of the agonies of mind experienced by Donald Crowhurst before finally abandoning 'Teignmouth Electron.' Had he himself suffered one tenth of what that deranged man had experienced?

Like hell he had. Had he even known the psycho-spiritual moods of Bernard Moitessier, the single-hander who had written of his fear, after months alone, of being plunged once again into the idle chatter and trivial concerns of his fellows? He had not. All right, he had been through a rough period after the capsize, but recovery had been rapid; shamefully rapid. He had stepped ashore with no more apparent hang-ups than if he had crossed the Channel from Dover in a ferry. So far from being fundamentally repelled by the people about him, his writer's eye had soon begun to study and enjoy the change of scene. The voyage had sharpened his reactions. He had recovered a zest long forgotten.

He got up from his bunk.

'We'll just have to see,' he told Seamew, defensively. 'We're not all made the same and we shall just have to see.'

He shaved and decided on breakfast at the Captain's Arms, suspecting he had had too much of his own company in the confines of a small boat.

The laid tables were all occupied, but where two had been put together to accommodate six people the night before a couple were sitting. Matthew sat at the far end from them, his faintly apologetic smile a substitute for interrupting their conversation with a 'Do you mind?'

'I guess you can't expect them to accept stoop labour,' the man was saying. 'Not in this day and age, Millicent.'

'It's not stooping to serve you breakfast, Howard,' the woman replied. 'I can't see no shame in that. We have waitresses back home, don't we?'

'We've got to try to keep in step with change, Mill. You know what the Book says - the old order perisheth...'

'But all I wanted was toast - and some coffee.'

She noticed Matthew's poorly disguised pretence to be unaware of their conversation.

'We've been waiting fifteen minutes for someone to take our order,' she explained.

She was a small, dark woman with a worried face and hair thinner than seemed fair for her age. Her husband was light-complexioned, even sparser on top, with spectacles and a self-effacing, mild expression that suggested a lifetime of trying to do the right thing. He half rose and offered his hand.

'I'm Howard L. Norton. This is my wife Millicent. We are from Idaho. A pleasure to meet you, sir.'

'Braine. Matthew Braine. From England.'

'I would have assumed that, sir.' Howard assured him courteously.

'My!' his wife said, 'but have you gotten yourself a swell tan! You been using a sailboat?'

'Yes,' Matthew replied, 'I have a boat here.'

'Millicent means a Sunfish – you know, kind of a flat board with a single sail.'

'Oh, those! No.'

'They are kind of scarey,' Millicent agreed. 'Like, take off with you.'

'I sailed over from England,' Matthew admitted.

'You did?' Millicent said admiringly. 'Fantastic!' Like her husband, her skin had a paleness that suggested she had not yet taken the comings and goings of the dockyard for granted.

'Direct, sir?' her husband enquired.

'I stopped off in Madeira and Tenerife. Oh, and Zafada.'

'Zafada!'

A chord seemed to have been struck. Howard Norton looked interested.

'Have you met the king?' Millicent asked.

It seemed an odd switch.

'We have a queen,' Matthew said, 'not a king.'

'I meant of Zafada.'

'Zafada?'

'Sure. The island has a king. They told us so when we flew over on Eastern.'

'It isn't inhabited,' Matthew said. 'Just a lot of birds, some goats, that kind of thing.'

'There's a king even so,' Millicent said, rather as a small girl might defend an attack on fairies.

'You've got to believe it,' her husband said.

'On my chart it says it belongs to the U.K.,' Matthew said, 'which would mean it is a possession of the British Crown.'

'Oh, well, it's a kind of legend thing,' Millicent admitted. 'Goes way back. Sort of ... how did they put it, Howard?'

'An intellectual aristocracy. Something to do with a writer guy whose father claimed the island for him back in the last century. Then the boy grew up and wrote books - science fiction stuff, some of the earliest.'

'And made writers and other famous people into dukes and duchesses and the like,' Millicent added. 'Kind of romantic.'

'He must be dead by now, then,' Matthew pointed out.

'Oh, there's been two kings since then,' Millicent said. 'The present one is a young Britisher. They say he's on the island right now. This island, I mean. I'd like to meet him. We don't know any kings.'

'What is his name?' Matthew enquired. He had remembered Sebastian's stifled reaction to his mention of Zafada.

'We don't know,' Howard said. 'It seems he keeps a rather low profile.'

'Someone did say,' his wife put in. 'A kind of quaint name - you know, old fashioned - but someone was talking.'

A waitress came to their table, her walk slow and her demeanour reluctant. Her carriage and curvature suggested fairly advanced pregnancy. She gazed at her pad blankly as though spiritually no part of the action.

'Ah!' Matthew said cheerfully. 'Breakfast!'

'You want to order?' the waitress enquired in tones that discounted the probability.

'We'd love to,' Matthew said with an encouraging smile that was not reciprocated.

The waitress made a laboured note of their requirements and walked slowly off in a direction that seemed remote from the kitchens.

'I reckon part of the trouble,' Howard said, 'is that the gratuity is built into the bill. No incentive to give personal service.'

'Now in Italy,' his wife said, 'they really turn you on. You remember in Venice, Howard? They smile and look happy and make you feel special. At the end of the meal you *want* to leave them something.'

'Until you see the bill,' her husband said.

Another couple approached the table. The man had a thirty-year-old face; a fifty-year-old's pot hung over the top of his shorts. His companion was a few years younger but her figure suggested she was no more calorie-conscious. Their faces were set in a mould of wary disgruntlement as though few years had taught many lessons, none of them casting a good light on the established order of things.

'They don't seem willing to set another table,' the man said. 'Mind if we join you?'

They sat either side of the table between Matthew and the Nortons, looking at each other as if to confirm that the day had started as they might have expected.

'Are you staying here?' Matthew asked, taking on the role of ice-breaker.

'For the shortest time possible,' the man said. 'Until our boat gets in.'

'Ah!' Matthew said. 'Chartering.'

The man looked at him coldly.

'The boat is mine. My skipper was late out of Barbados and should arrive this evening.'

'Matthew Braine,' Matthew said. He waved a hand towards the other couple. 'Howard and Millicent Norton.'

The man raised an arm in general salute, with a weariness that suggested it cost him a lot of effort.

'Hi!' he said bleakly.

His wife said nothing, but bit savagely at a piece of dead skin at the side of a finger nail and glared into the middle distance. Matthew sighed and looked away across the terrace and the water on which boats were slowly coming alive. The night had been humid and windless, but now the surface of the harbour was beginning to ripple before the rising breeze whose caress had already set the fronds of the casuarina trees in motion.

'Our name's Farrer,' the man said, but he clearly didn't think there was much point in divulging the fact. Matthew guessed New York or Chicago, but not for any very informed reason.

Farrer flicked his fingers at a passing waitress and said 'Hey, *miss!*'

She ignored him.

'Hey, miss!' he roared. 'I'm speaking to you.'

She walked on.

He moved in his chair as though held by inescapable bonds. The girl returned slowly, in her own time.

'Yo' wan' somethin'?' she enquired dully.

He glared at her with undisguised dislike. Her eyes suggested she was too disinterested to reciprocate.

'I'd like breakfast,' he said. 'For both of us. If it wouldn't be too much trouble.'

She pouted and moved on.

A thick-set man, hunch-shouldered, plodded lugubriously past their table to where a woman sat below the top terrace. He wore a tee-shirt and a pair of long pants covered in brightly-coloured flags. On the back of the tee-shirt were the words 'Another day of bloody paradise'.

'Gee,' Farrer said, pressing his middle fingers to his head, 'I was sure loaded last night.'

His wife shrugged and attacked another nail, her eyes fixed abstractedly on the calabash ash-tray on which her husband's cigar smouldered, sending tendrils of acrid smoke in Matthew's direction.

Matthew decided to leave the ball in the Nortons' court and subsided into speculation. He told himself few people were at their best at breakfast and that holidays tended to attract hangovers. As for the waitresses, pregnancy in that climate couldn't be a heap of fun...

After some minutes in which little was said, the breakfast arrived; unevenly toasted French-type bread, overdone very lean bacon, pale watery eggs, coffee; all nearly cold. Almost simultaneously small birds appeared – finches and a bevy of black and yellow birds of engaging boldness with downward-curved thin beaks. The dullest of the finches was dark brown with a rust-red bib smaller and less showy than the full dress shirt of the British robin. They too were tame, some willing to take crumbs from Matthew's fingers.

'Does anyone know what the yellow ones are called?' he asked.

'Banana quits,' Howard said. 'Seems unlikely, but that's what some guy said.'

His wife dropped a sachet of sugar and one of the quits immediately stood on it and began to peck at the paper until seen off by a jet-black bird the size of a starling, but with a bright yellow beady eye.

'A grackle,' Howard said. 'I asked that too.'

The grackle took over the sachet and with a few practised jabs of his bill penetrated to the contents. The quits and some finches stood around respectfully, awaiting their turn.

'Not so different from us, are they?' Millicent remarked.

Matthew agreed. The other men said nothing. There seemed to be a general consensus to preserve silence. Two quits bolder than the rest sat on the edge of the sugar basin and consumed vast quantities with a healthy greed that seemed to defy current notions of the dangers of refined foods.

With half-an-hour to go before he met Sebastian, Matthew said he had bread to buy and left the table, paying his bill at the desk inside the hotel. Breakfasts were clearly not the best meals at which to sustain belief in the *dolce vita*.

'First, an apology,' Sebastian said. 'I'm worse than average about names and I didn't immediately make the connection. You wrote *The Liberty Boy*.'

'An early effort,' Matthew said. 'Best forgotten.'

'It was most amusing. It's a wonder the Establishment survived. But I suppose you are right; it was rather a young novel.'

'I'm not sure the later ones were more mature. They have sold no better.'

'Then they were probably more mature. Maturity brings less commercial values into play when a civilization's running downhill. What are you working on now?'

'Nothing,' Matthew said. 'Nothing at all.'

'Ah! A creative pause. Whose expression *was* that?'

'Hitler's, I think.'

'Pity.'

In the harsh daylight Sebastian's face showed lines and hollows not commensurate with Matthew's assessment of his age. It was a face that had known suffering, yet there was a determination which dispelled earlier conjecture of weakness of purpose or opinion.'

'That's a fine tree,' Matthew remarked.

'By the museum? A sandbox. I heard one of the taxi-drivers telling a cruise-ship fare that Nelson swung on it when he was small. Nonsense, of course. The man didn't come here until he was twenty-six. Incidentally, he loathed the place, especially the mosquitoes. If they'd had "Scram" then, the whole course of British naval history might have been totally different.'

They walked towards the water.

'Do you think this place may give you any ideas?' Sebastian asked.

'For a book? I doubt it.'

Sebastian looked at him curiously.

'You sound almost...' He stopped.

'Almost what?'

'No, forget it,' Sebastian said. 'It's rather a nerve on such short acquaintance.'

Matthew smiled. 'Now who's being British and reserved?'

'All right. Well, it was almost as though you were reluctant about the thought of writing.'

Matthew stopped and fingered the leaf of a tree by the officers' quarters.

'Mango,' Sebastian said.

'To be honest, I think I'm written out.'

'Believe it or not,' Sebastian said, 'even architects can have these dark nights of the soul. I sometimes think I shall never again raise the talent for a bigger challenge than a dog kennel.'

'My last three books have been flops,' Matthew said. 'Rather marked flops.'

'That could have something to do with the maturity we were discussing just now. You may have shot ahead of your readers.'

'I wish I could think so. If the critics are to be believed, I am merely repeating the pattern less effectively.'

'This is a bitter lemon tree,' Sebastian said. 'Dull, isn't it? But look at this, a frangipani. The leaves and trunk are splendid. A pity it's not in bloom, but this is after all what they darkly term winter.'

'I wish you had read one of my later books,' Matthew said. 'I'd have valued your opinion.'

'I did dip into *A Mixed Reception*, but then nervous troubles caught up with me and other things took precedence.'

'Did you get as far as the house-party when the Minister of Trade was trying to make his number with the hostess?'

'I did, and enjoyed it. Your social commentary is pleasantly acid. We share a contempt for pomp and circumstance which, if I dare say so, is more common at my age than at yours.'

Although Matthew found the views of his juniors more to be dreaded than those of his contemporaries, he persisted:

'So on the basis of what you have read of my stuff, what is

your frank, off-the-cuff, top-of-the-head, no-holds-barred opinion of my decline and fall?'

'I'm sure you're exaggerating, but if you want to know what left me just a shade disappointed it was that you too often let sarcasm stand in for anger.'

'My windmills are too small?'

'I suppose you could put it that way.'

'Someone else did. It stuck.'

'And hurt. Obviously.'

'Yes.'

'Critics can be bastards,' Sebastian said. 'Every Sunday at home I weep buckets for authors, especially when it is perfectly obvious that the reviewer has not bothered to read more than the blurb and the first chapter. But in your case I feel your talent is not being fully exploited. You write so well, but I think your subjects are often not worthy of their treatment. Is that too bloody rude for words?'

'Not at all,' Matthew said, 'but what it boils down to is that I have been written off because I lack commitment; a readily identifiable political slot. I suppose I'm vaguely left of centre, but maybe I don't show it strongly enough.'

'I don't know that it's necessary to take a narrowly political stance,' Sebastian said. 'My feeling is that you are a disappointed humanist, that you have been content sending up inadequate humanism, not humanism's inadequacy.'

'It's a nice distinction,' Matthew said, 'but I'm not sure I'm fully tuned into it.'

'You might not think it from the leaf,' Sebastian said, 'but that one is a lilac.'

Matthew took him out to look over 'Patience', whose line and compactness Sebastian admired with genuine and perceptive enthusiasm.

'I would rather like to try living on a boat for a time,' he said. 'I have sailed on friends' but never owned more than a dinghy. Come and see my jungle hut.'

From the car park beyond the Captain's Arms they drove into St George in a buggy-type vehicle, open at the back and sides, no doors.

'A Bustler,' Sebastian said. 'Quite handy for this climate. On the steamier days one just lifts one's elbows like a frigate bird and cool air hits you where it's needed most. But the hiring costs me twice as much as my shack, and the firm's lack of maintenance is horrific.'

His shack was impressive only for its cheapness compared with the Captain's Arms. Of timber construction with a crude block-built kitchen and bathroom at the rear, it was close to the road and airless. Wooden and curtained divisions created a living room and two small bedrooms, in the larger of which Sebastian slept.

'I use the smaller one for dressing and gubbins,' he said.

Despite its obvious disadvantages, the relative spaciousness after weeks on 'Patience' was attractive.

'If the idea appealed to you,' Matthew said, 'we might switch homes for a while. I wouldn't at all mind being shore-based.'

'You may not find it all that quiet for your writing,' Sebastian warned.

'What writing?'

'How about tomorrow, then?' Sebastian said.

'The only thing that worries me is Seamew. She wouldn't last long from what I've seen of the local competition.'

'If she's a normal cat she'd rather stay where she is. I like animals. If she'll accept me I'll be her willing slave.'

After a light meal Matthew said he would walk back to the dockyard 'to get the feel of the place through my feet'. As he strolled down the dusty road, narrowly escaping death beneath the wheels of two insanely driven cars of indeterminate vintage, he told himself he was going a funny way about cultivating the art of detachment. He reminded himself of his resolution not to force the pace; to let the future decide itself...

On a section of broken wall by the side of the road a large green lizard was contemplating a dusty leaf. Its mouth opened briefly and the insect that had been on the leaf was no longer there. The lizard looked at Matthew, its iron jaw registering nothing that was not conveyed by a beady eye. Matthew remembered he had forgotten to tell Sebastian that Rebecca's plant had earned a spell ashore. In the climate of Monesterio he guessed it had a sporting chance of outstripping its old vigour.

The lizard's stiff predatory pose had relaxed, and so far as was possible it looked pleased with itself. As Matthew passed, it tilted its shining green head and winked. Even in the middle of winter there was a lot to be said for life.

20

THE mosquitoes – so small, quick and virile – had little in common with the lumbering jumbos of England. Settling on only two surfaces – himself and dark backgrounds – the Monesterion mosquito lacked the sporting optimism of its temperate cousin who could be relied upon to rest obligingly on plain light walls where the chance of flattening it with a rolled newspaper was at least fifty-fifty.

He sat in the cockpit awaiting Sebastian, abstractedly scratching his legs and observing the ceaseless activity on the quayside. The thought of staying outside the dockyard, safe from constant intimations of mortality in the shape of bronzed, bouncing young, as slim and spare as rapiers, all life before them, was not without appeal. There was something mildly depressing about their hearty sameness; even the not-so-young did little to give a balanced reminder of human potentialities.

A burly man in a white tee-shirt and dangerously brief shorts slowly crossed the green. His walk was stiff with implied aggression, his rigid trunk swaying rhythmically on scarcely flexed legs, his arms slightly raised from his sides as though prepared to punch something: the archetypal Main Street cowboy, postured to remind the rest of the world not to push him too far.

A British boat had moored nearby, crewed by four men in their late twenties or early thirties, and two girls. They were having breakfast in the cockpit. After a windless night the breeze had not yet filled in, making conversation possible.

'How's it going at home?' Matthew called out.

'Gold's taken off again,' the dark-haired man replied.

'Not happy about Equities, though,' his taller companion added, spreading his toast from a flat white pot of Gentleman's Relish.

'Weather grim, I suppose?' Matthew said.

'Pretty awful when we were last in touch,' replied the youngest-looking.

'Makes one feel a bit guilty,' Matthew said smiling.

They looked at him blankly.

'Gather the dollar is improving for us,' the darker one said.

Matthew sensed an urge to return to familiar ground.

'Things seem a bit expensive here,' he said.

'Known for it,' the fair man agreed. 'Gather the duty-free in Tortola repays a visit if one's here any length of time. Bit of a haul, of course.'

'You're here for the winter?' Matthew enquired.

'Eighteen months,' the dark man said.

'All of you?'

'Except Lucinda. She's due back at the F.O. in March. Work, you know.'

'Ah, yes,' Matthew said. 'Work. Nice for the rest of you, though.'

'So little moving,' the tallest man said ambiguously.

'Everything's very uncertain,' Matthew agreed.

'Difficult to make any firm moves,' the fair man said.

'Got to mark time,' said the taller.

'Right,' said the youngest.

News of Britain exhausted, they returned to their breakfast. Matthew would have liked to have seen some old Sundays for the book and theatre pages, but he guessed that only the financial sections might have survived the trip across.

'If it's all the same with you,' Sebastian said, 'I would be very happy to pay the bit extra and have "Patience" moored stern to the wharf.'

They were completing their second journey to the quay by coracle.

'Of course,' Matthew said. 'Good idea. If I'd known how things were going to turn out I'd have brought a dinghy.'

They found a slot for 'Patience' among the smaller boats to leeward of the garbage area. Sebastian showed by his handling of warps and fenders that he knew a little more than he had made out.

'They'll let me bring the Bustler into the dockyard to pick up this stuff and dump my own,' he said.

'I feel I should contribute to the rent of the house,' Matthew said. 'It must be costing you a lot more than it takes to keep a boat here, and the amenities are greater.'

'Not at all. If I had to charter a yacht to live on, it would cost many times more. Call it quits.'

The transfer to the boat was completed by eleven; the Bustler was loaded with Matthew's needs for the house. He had covered Rebecca's plant in a large plastic bag in case of wind damage on the drive into St George.

'Phew!' he said. 'I'm a bit sticky.'

'Elevenses,' Sebastian said firmly.

'Captain's Arms?'

'Where else?'

They walked to the inn. The taxi-drivers under the tree near the gates were clustered excitedly round a warri board. The speed with which brown fingers flipped brown seeds into the dark board's bowl-shaped receptacles, and the chattered comments of the contestants, baffled the onlooker.

'I've tried to master it,' Sebastian said, 'but those boys take me to the cleaners every time.'

A dark cloud brought a sudden shower. The taxi boys rushed for cover.

'You'd think there'd been a fall-out warning,' Matthew said.

The tables on the terrace held small pools of water. They sat inside on a settee, which made catching the eye of a waitress marginally easier.

'I hope you don't mind,' Sebastian said, 'but I've accepted an invitation on your behalf. You can easily say no.'

'Sounds exciting.'

'They're a pleasant couple. Youngish, dedicated, doing a difficult job. A bit culture-starved and keen to meet you.'

'I'm not sure I rate as culture. Who are they?'

'Bill and Rosemary Watkins. Bill is employed by the Overseas Development people in London, as I think I mentioned. He runs the Port St George Trust. They live above the naval museum.'

'Does the Trust have the Monesterion government's blessing?'

'Well, put it like this: Bill has the power and contacts to influence grants and suchlike.'

'And of veto?'

'In a sense. His brief is environmental, conservational; to protect the dockyard area against too much visual and commercial exploitation. He walks something of a tightrope.'

'I can imagine. He must have nerves of steel.'

Their attention was diverted by a man at the desk. His face held a tenseness peculiar to male tourists about to be relieved of large sums for a no more tangible end-product than leisure.

'It was only five nights,' he said throatily, 'not six.'

The desk-girl's reply was inaudible, for she was still seated, but the tourist performed an interesting full body turn with his arms outstretched and his closed eyes turned on the ceiling. It could have been the remembered execution of a dance step once seen in Greece or Spain, or it could have been the needful measure of an American executive mindful of blood pressure but desperate to release tension. The man's circuit completed, he lowered his arms and head, took a deep breath and leaned over the counter. He spoke in a voice of controlled evenness, his posture suggesting an improbable meekness and cordiality.

'Listen, dear,' he implored, 'we have been through all this before. Like I told you, I fixed it with the good lady who is manager here. I told her on Wednesday we would be leaving this morning.'

Whatever response he received was clearly unsatisfactory. His knuckles grew noticeably paler and he began to rise up and down on his toes.

'Now you listen to me,' he said, 'and listen good. I have spent five nights in this hotel. Five whole nights and five whole days. Right? I have endured five whole days of slow, surly service. Right? I have endured five whole days of fighting the flies off my food before they wolfed everything down to the salt. Right? I have endured five whole days *and* nights being eaten by the most goddam savage horde of insects I have met since Nam. Right? I have plugged my ears and swallowed massive overdoses of barbiturates in order to grab a pitiful few seconds of coma in the noisiest room this side of Alaska. Right? For this hysterically fun-packed rip-off I am resigned if not enchanted to pay according to scale. Right? But I am not, repeat not, going to pay you for a further day of undiluted enjoyment I haven't even had.'

'As it has stopped raining,' Sebastian said, 'how would it be if we took our coffee outside? I find this kind of thing a little depressing.'

The table below the casuarina tree was drier than the rest.

'I felt he had a point about the slow and surly service,' Matthew said. 'The waitresses give you the feeling they'd really rather plant a bush-knife between your shoulder blades than bring you a lime squash.'

'Part of the trouble is the yachting fraternity, with all due respect to your ancient calling,' Sebastian said. 'The boats bring a mixed lot, some expecting a little hero-worship, some mannerless bullies after their third beer. And the high season brings too many. The girls here are still unsophisticated; they can't make fine distinctions. One boorish honky means we all get labelled.'

'Yet the villagers look cheerful enough.'

'*Joie de vivre* seems in inverse ratio to involvement with the whites – except for the taxi-boys, most of whom are so pleased to be in control of an engine and to be paid for it that they're a class apart.'

'I've begun to wonder what they are supposed to be escaping from when they make it to the West, but maybe I haven't been around long enough.'

'Maybe,' Sebastian said. 'It depends how sold you are on the idea of conspicuous equality. The blacks are worked on from all sides. It's bad enough that they're persuaded happiness is junk food and domestic technology, without their own politicians vote-snatching by whipping up envy with the glib tactics of material comparisons. The black's being weaned from the life he can cope with, understand and enjoy, and turned into a bewildered, resentful sub-consumer.'

'You're quite a political animal,' Matthew remarked.

'Only in a rather negative sense. Politics poison the soul. But you see things more clearly in a small place like this. Population pressure, for instance. One finds the confidence to extrapolate, to homologize.'

'Better for the tourist soul than endless price comparisons and tracking down the largest steaks, I suppose,' Matthew said, smiling.

'Well, this isn't my first visit. I've spent enough time here to get beneath the surface, but not so long as to start taking things for granted. It's easy to forget first impressions, yet they are often accurate.'

'True enough. I once wrote a novel after spending a week in Jersey. Not a very comparable island to this, maybe, but just about everything was going on.'

'Perhaps history is about to repeat itself,' Sebastian murmured.

Matthew stirred his coffee vigorously.

'What's all this about you being King of Zafada?' he asked.

Sebastian grimaced.

'You've heard about that, have you?'

'Two and two have come together.'

'All a load of crap.'

'Untrue, you mean?'

'Well, Zafada exists, as you know; and it's true I took on - because it was wished on me - this kingship thing. But all it means is that I'm the literary executor of the previous so-called kings who were both writers, and it's administratively convenient for the literary executor to inherit the kingship. And there's some publicity value.'

'You say "inherit"...'

'My father was the last "king".'

Matthew snapped his fingers.

'Of course! Christopher Rutherford. The poet. He wrote some fine stuff back in... well, I liked a lot of his work.'

Sebastian smiled.

'The thirties were his best decade. As you obviously know, his talents didn't survive the war.'

'There was a biography of him. I read extracts in one of the Sundays. One felt the author knew him almost too well for his own comfort.'

'He did. To spare you possible red ears I'd better confess I wrote it myself under a pen-name.'

'Very professional writing. Yet you say you're an architect.'

'Thanks for not saying "only an architect". I'm a bit of a dabbler, I'm afraid.'

'Rutherford's decline interested me. I wish I'd known him.'

'It depends which "him" you chose. Family money and a liking for the hard stuff can be a fatal combination.'

'You clearly inherited a lot from him, and I don't mean money.'

'The distillers got the bulk of that.'

'You're certainly no dilettante. Your book proved that.'

'I enjoy work, yes, but a friend once said I have *survived* being able to do what I want, rather than exploited it.'

'You don't have to work for a living?'

'For a living, no. For something more important, yes. The blessings of modest material security are mixed, however. It enabled me to make minimum effort in some directions, maximum in others. Result: a rather messy life and too much self-searching. But if I'd been born to more staid and stable parents...'

'Speculation about what would have happened had one gone the other way at the tee-junction gets no one anywhere.'

'Too true. Anyway, that's why I'm lumbered with Zafada.'

'You don't own the island, physically?'

'Hell, no! The Brits pinched it long ago, and lacking a bigger gun boat than the late Victoria Regina, old Scully, the first king, could only write angry letters to the F.C.O. Scully and his descendants might have had some moral claim to the island, but morals don't come into it when a desirable Caribbean rock is up for grabs.'

'What made it desirable?'

'Guano. Very old guano. Phosphate deposits, in more commercial terms. As many as two hundred people worked the seams at one time, but it all packed up around the first world war; a hurricane was the final discouragement.'

'It's a good story, though,' Matthew said reflectively.

'You told me when we met that you put in there.'

'Yes. I... I thought it had a rather special atmosphere. But then I'd been through a pretty rigorous few weeks one way or another.'

'It seems to take different people in different ways,' Sebastian said. 'I suppose I have a special feeling about it myself, doubtless because of the connection with my father.'

'Did he ever go there?'

'Never. He didn't inherit the "kingdom" until after the war, and by then his drinking had got on top of him. The only use he made of Zafada was to make a bit of an ass of himself by playing along with the more sensational Sundays when they felt like doing one of their king-of-an-island stories. It was pretty sad, really. Instead of being remembered as a first-rate writer, he chose to die a down-market king.'

'Those who knew his work will remember him for that.'

'I suppose so. Oh, well, doubtless Zafada has provided a spot of light relief in a dreary world, but it's also inclined to become a time-consuming bore. I kept quiet about inheriting the "kingdom" until Patrick Scully's books started to make a come-back and I thought the publicity might help sales. But the media focused on the giggle of my being king of an island and hardly mentioned Scully, let alone his books.'

'You sound a somewhat reluctant monarch.'

'I am. Out here I try to keep the profile as low as a beetle's sneakers. Two tourists heard about it last week and kept me talking so long they missed their cruise-ship. They had to stay over before flying to Guadeloupe, so refusing dinner with them was difficult. The man was in motors somewhere in west London. He was quite offended when I wouldn't dish out a dukedom. His wife tried to bribe me with what she described as a metallic chestnut "roly-poly" at a special price.'

Matthew laughed.

'It's a pity it's gone sour on you. Your a-political stance is just what a king needs'.

They finished their coffees and walked to the car park, Matthew stopping outside the gates to buy some bananas and sweet potatoes.

'Anyway,' Sebastian said, 'kings should be supra-political. I'm that accursed thing, the intellectual floating voter, beloved of no man and the bane of candidates.'

'Join the club,' Matthew invited. 'I've been a total abstainer in the last two elections.'

Sebastian sighed.

'Well, I know it's considered a naïve point of view, and you may write me off as a precious and unrealistic dilettante after all, but political hang-ups strike me as the most hopeless of any, being based on the impossible dream of politics – which increasingly means party-politics – being enough to alter the nature of man.'

'But what else is going to? Flower-power or whatever it's

currently called? My daughter was into that and now she's tending a bean row in darkest Wales.'

'Watch it,' Sebastian warned, 'you'll get me started.'

'I can take it.'

'Then hold on to your salt-mill. Look, however much it may smack of élitism to say so, the problem we are faced with is qualitative. The young know that - or the best of them do. If, instead of being a lukewarm segment in a literary legend, I had the monarchial muscle to pull in something bigger than a cut-price Rolls, I wouldn't frigg around assenting to parliaments on the present pattern.'

'You'd become a benevolent dictator.'

'No way. I'd elect the best minds among the educators, philosophers, poets, craftsmen, and commonsensical men and women generally, and brief them to honour - and be seen to honour - only those values which recognize man's proper place and responsibility in the scheme of things. From that nucleus of better minds might emerge the structure for true government.'

'Might.'

'Might. A bloody big might. But it's more likely to do so than our present system of electing third rate people to represent the wishes of constituencies who vote them into power because of assurances that their greeds, habits, envies and hatreds will be pandered to.'

'And you reckon that the world's Napoleons, Hitlers, Castros, Ayatollahs and Amins would come along with you?'

'God knows. All I'm sure about is that nothing less than something on those lines can reverse our descent to the termitary or the holocaust. If the lead was given, I've still just enough faith in our species to believe that in time other rulers and governments would recognize a genuine commitment to a less cynical pattern.'

'But in the short-term...?'

'In the short-term, of course, the so-called realists and manipulators who hold power today would fall about with laughter.'

'And that would be that,' Matthew said, smiling.

'Ah! But if I were a big-time king,' Sebastian replied, tweaking the brightly-beaded top-knot of a small girl whose wiry black hair was laboriously braided into an elaborate maze,

'I'd be dictatorial enough to ship the schemers and disbelievers to Zafada and sit them on the summit in the hot sun and cool breeze. And when they had gazed at and been gazed upon by the thousands of booby birds and had come to their senses, as all must if they spend enough time in such a situation, only then would I readmit them to responsible citizenship.'

'A romantic and appealing notion,' Matthew admitted, 'but unlikely to be welcomed as practicable.'

'All the very best notions have been romantic and impracticable,' Sebastian said. 'That's why, in the end, they are adopted. It was someone's dream that landed man on the moon; the technology was incidental.'

'You should give up buildings for books,' Matthew said. 'You've a nice turn of phrase. How about fiction?'

They slid into the Bustler.

'I wouldn't have the discipline. It's easier to yack than to get things on to paper. Anyway, no one publishes you if you don't conform to the prevailing *mores*. I lack the necessary *nostalgie de la boue*.'

'But the size of the windmills wouldn't frighten you.'

'It's the publishers they'd scare. No, I know my limitations. I'm one of the many who have to be content with being a catalyst through others. Through influence rather than power.'

He turned the Bustler's ignition key.

'Pity,' Matthew said. 'People who see things straight ought to come out with them.'

'That's for the likes of you to do. For those with the power to communicate.'

For a second and third time the Bustler's response to the key was a thin whirr.

'Such is the answer to omniscience,' Sebastian said. 'Can you give me a push? Since hiring this toy for an astronomical sum I have had six breakdowns, five punctures and three replacements. This is the one I had originally, now supposedly bug-free.'

Matthew pushed. When the engine fired Sebastian kept it roaring while Matthew got back in. The Bustler covered the mile to the village in a sequence of tongue-biting bunny hops.

'After about three miles it usually settles down a little,' Sebastian said, 'but I seldom do more than a mile at a time.'

They drew up outside the bungalow. Sebastian left the Bustler a few yards further down the road at the top of a slight rise.

'It makes a push-start easier,' he explained. 'When I told the hirers the battery was flat, they told me to park on the top of declines and to rev before switching off. Anyway, welcome to Buck House.'

'Not its real name, I take it?'

'No. Peter's little joke. He's a duke, by the way. Zafada duke, of course. Been there more than anyone. When he gives his weekly archaeological tours he plugs Scully, hanging it on the Zafada story. The tourists love it, especially as they can see the island from the hill where Peter finishes his tour.'

'Do the locals know the legend?'

'Some of them. It's a part of the island's history; in some of the school books.'

They unloaded the car.

'Right,' Sebastian said, 'I'd better push along and see to things at my end. Sorry the fridge is so noisy, but the motor's pretty ancient and the door fits so badly that it works overtime. When icicles push the door open, you have to defrost it.'

'Don't forget your radio.'

'You're welcome to it; I have another. You can get World Service at seven and eleven most days, but there's precious little else to justify the cost of the batteries.'

He left, taking Matthew's copy of *Labour's Voice*. As it was nearly mid-day Matthew turned the radio on to accompany his unpacking. Above the crackling a deeply sincere voice was saying 'British Airways. We'll take good care of you. When you are going to London on business, you like to fly in style. Who cares? *We* care. We'll fly you 747 style with music and movies all the way.' This threat was overlaid by lyrical female voices which echoed the caring theme with musical accompaniment. The commerical over-ran the opening words of the international news that followed. Although it came from London it centred on Africa, the Middle East and the United States and had nothing to say about the United Kingdom. He switched off.

The silence was quickly filled by a variety of alternatives including passing shoulder-borne radios blaring 'pop', strident voices conducting conversations at the seemingly pointless expenditure of decibels, barking dogs, and the engines of cars and lorries moving at speeds in no way related to the surface and narrow width of the road outside.

Buck House was not over-endowed with cupboard space and drawers. He followed Sebastian's example and used the single bed in the smaller room as a display area offering instant selection of shirt, socks or underpants.

He examined the kitchen. The single tap produced water, the gas stove was in business. He opened the cupboard doors below the working surface on the right of the louvred window. Its battered saucepans and frying pan were pitted and grey, but when he looked over the large pile of similar utensils in the next section it seemed like girlish neurosis to have reservations about the first. Fat silverfish melted into the cupboard's recesses. He closed the door, not doubting that Sebastian had met the same problem and scoured his minimum requirements.

To the left of the window was a pair of rough doors held together by a top bolt. To open them a many-punctured insect screen had to be removed. The doors faced south and when he flung them wide a flood of light and warm air entered the small kitchen. A portly lizard on the stone steps outside gazed at him for long enough to make an objective assessment, then slid prudently out of view. The outlook was across a paddock towards Newport Harbour. In the paddock a lean horse saw him and snuffled a hopeful greeting.

Already a subscriber to Sebastian's view that the climate demanded a high proportion of salad and fruit, he washed a lettuce under the tap. The water was warm and yellow and the flow was unsteady, as though there were blockages in the pipe. It did not look too appetising and smelt slightly stagnant. Sebastian had said there was a tank of rain water under a floor board below the sink. The area below the sink was enclosed by two doors. He opened these and lifted the loose board at floor level. A small cloud of mosquitoes zoomed out and distributed itself on walls and ceiling. Suddenly conscious of a hundred tiny eyes, and slapping at real or imaginary settlements on his legs and arms, Matthew dipped a saucepan into the pool of water whose surface was about a foot below that of the floor. The water came up cool and clear and was obviously grudged by the small frog that swam in it. Matthew replaced the frog in the tank and poured the water into the hole left by the lost spout of a kettle whose whistling days were over. He was not being fussy about the frog, but Sebastian had advised boiling any water that did not come out of the tap, and not using more than he could help of the water that did. 'It won't kill you,' he had promised, 'but it would not get by in Evian.'

A voice on the small verandah fronting Buck House said 'Hullo, there!' He opened the door.

'I'm on my way home for lunch,' Peter Richardson said. 'Sebastian said you'd moved in. Wondered if you'd like to come up for coffee when you've finished your meal.'

'Great,' Matthew said. 'Others' coffee always tastes better than one's own.'

Peter gave instructions for finding them and left in a Landrover with big, powerful tyres.

It was hot and airless in the house. The fine nylon curtains over the louvred windows hung motionless. He felt sticky all over, as though thinly coated in jam. It seemed a good moment to christen the shower. The fittings in the bathroom were encrusted with lime and heavily pitted like the aluminium kitchen utensils, but the water was getting through. He removed his shorts and tee-shirt; the shirt was a very restrained one he had found in the chandlery, sporting nothing more original than a jolly jack tar sitting on a lobster pot. He stepped into the well. A frantic clattering round his feet drew his eyes to what he took to be a cricket of tropical proportions making rapid circuits. He went back to the kitchen for a saucepan and put this in the path of the cricket who ran straight into it at full tilt. Matthew looked over the rim of the saucepan cautiously. Recovering from its headlong impact, the cricket began to move again, fast, clawing at the side of the pan. The noise of its feet on the metal put Matthew's teeth on edge. He shook the saucepan from side to side to discourage it getting a grip and rushed to the front door, opening it with one hand while maintaining the vital panning movements with the other. He reached the rail of the verandah and tipped the cricket into an oleander bush, feeling shaky. Spiders were his chief horror, but large armoured beetle-like creatures ran them a close second. He was suddenly aware of three pairs of round white eyes set in black faces regarding his nakedness from the road. Then the three girls pushed their hands over their mouths and walked on giggling and chattering like a trio of brightly feathered birds.

When he had confirmed he would be alone in the shower he turned it on. The water, yellow and warm, was no shock to the system. Then it turned colder, presumably after exhausting pipes exposed to the sun. He felt wonderfully refreshed and invigorated, drying off by walking about the house naked so as not to work up heat again by towelling.

When he had eaten he set off for the Richardsons. Although 'only a mile', the first half of the route was along the dusty road towards the dockyard, the second a steep ascent of a track whose surface made the Richardsons' investment in a Land-rover understandable. The final incline ended in a cattle grid beyond which opened out a pleasant garden with steps leading across a lawn to the house above. A lean-to, open-sided garage housed the Land-rover and a Bustler. A mobile of pieces of pottery, an old clock, some coral and a spoon hung from a tree by the foot of the steps.

Peter introduced his wife, a tall, pretty woman in her forties, with a slight American accent. Peter had met her when her father chartered a Richardson yacht twenty or more years ago. Betty served coffee and brownie cake on the terrace overlooking Newport Harbour. The low terrace wall was covered in cannon balls, broken bottles, corals, conch shells, and innumerable sherds and other artefacts. They discussed these, Peter's eyes shining with the light of the devotee.

'Let me show you my spanner,' he said.

From behind an apricot-coloured bougainvillaea on the north-west pillar of the house he produced a huge rusty spanner nearly three feet long. Matthew did his best to share the other's enthusiasm.

'It came from Zafada,' Peter explained. 'Probably pushing a hundred years, maybe more. Left there when the mining was abandoned. The king said I was to have it when we went there last Spring to plant his flag.'

Matthew laughed. 'You really planted a flag?'

'We certainly did. Several of us.'

'Do you mean that Sebastian came all the way from England to do that?'

'Yes, but not at his expense. There's a Texan millionaire

who's Scully-crazy, and he financed it; a larger-than-life character who has made his pile and owns a whole museum of priceless modern paintings. He's determined to keep the legend alive.'

'Who were the other... people who went over on this mission?'

'A Harvard professor, a National Trust man, a junior minister – all solid citizens.'

Matthew tried to visualize a boat-load of middle-aged eccentrics clambering up the precipitous face of Zafada with a flag. The idea took some digesting, but it explained the pole he had found on the summit.

'Must have been fun,' he said. 'I suppose.'

Peter's eyes shone with memory.

'I found a nineteenth-century bottle; the Harvard bug-man got pretty excited about some of the fauna.'

'And three of you nearly got killed by rocks,' Betty put in, as though this had added to the enjoyment.

Peter smiled happily. It clearly had.

'And you met no problems?' Matthew asked, remembering his own ascent.

'The main one was with the government,' Peter said. 'They weren't too keen about it.'

'You mean they took it seriously, the flag-planting and so forth?'

Peter nodded.

'Fairly seriously, and they didn't even know about the flag beforehand. As it was, they delayed the trip and caused a lot of extra expense to the entrepreneur. They even shipped over a bunch of Rastas ahead of us, armed with bush-knives. For security.'

'You're joking!'

'It's a different culture,' Betty said. 'They don't have quite our sense of humour.'

'So I gathered from a local newspaper I was reading the other day,' Matthew said.

There was a pause.

'We've only heard about it so far,' Peter said. 'We don't normally read that paper.'

'Would you like to see the house?' Betty asked. 'People are

sometimes quite interested to see how we live out here.'

Looked at realistically, the asbestos-roofed bungalow was little more than a shed consisting of four stone pillars with an in-filling of timber walls. An hibiscus-fringed picture window overlooked the terrace and harbour; large unglazed openings to east and west of the matting-floored living area funnelled the welcome breeze; a simple bedroom and bathroom led off the living area; there was a fan over the open-topped four-poster bed. Needing to use the bathroom, Matthew found it difficult to reconcile its almost masochistic lack of sophistication with the 'raj-style' accusations in *Labour's Voice*. The small kitchen and a tiny workshop cum bedroom were lean-to additions on the west and east sides of the house, and a small but attractive garden wandered further up the hill to the Richardsons' guest garden-room – a three-sided shed overlooking the harbour and furnished with two beds, a Victorian washstand and a dilapidated wicker chair.

In the living room, hanging from a large fish hook, a mobile of shells, corks, a green bottle and dried seaweeds moved lazily in the breeze. The wall space between the windows and openings was filled by an ancient upright piano, simple hung rugs with bird feathers pushed into their weave, an old map of Monesterio that was losing out to termites, row upon row of books, and shelves and cabinets overflowing with artefacts labelled by hand in inks faded into indecipherability. Above a desk built of old pieces of timber was a shelf crammed with pieces of pottery, china, and the bowls of clay pipes. Matthew examined one of these.

'If you'd be interested,' Peter said hopefully, 'I could show you some better examples.'

Matthew declared an interest.

The tour covered not only the living room, but the bedroom, workshop, bathroom, garage and an outhouse. They ended up in the kitchen, not because there was room there for further artefacts among the bottles and jars of herbs, spices, grains and pulses, but because exhaustion had prompted thought of tea.

'We could go on the terrace,' Betty said, 'but you might like to sit at the window.'

Below the glassless opening was a long counter which doubled up as a working surface. The view was of the headland west of Newport Harbour, seen through a fragrant canopy of creeping plants and sprays of bougainvillaea. At the first appearance of more brownie cake a hopeful contingent of finches and banana quits arrived, so sure of themselves that they perched on the sugar bowl and accepted crumbs from open palms as by long habit.

They returned to the living room with its shabby settee, old rocking chair, and coffee table which must have been all the rage in the early 1950s. The one good piece in the room was the large round dining table which could seat ten or more on the rush-covered chairs. Peter invited Matthew to sit at this, then showed him with infectious enthusiasm the beginnings of his library catalogue. As large portions of many of the books had long since gone into the tiny maws of the termites, Matthew felt unvoiced admiration for Peter's faith in the future; they discussed the merits of the Dewey system and Matthew admitted he had long intended to get his own books file-indexed and into some kind of order.

'If you felt like a swim on your way home,' Betty said, 'there's a quite pleasant beach nearby. You turn left instead of right at the end of the track beyond the grid.'

He found the beach. It was fringed by an invasive plant with round flat leaves and ground-hugging tendrils which squirmed across the white sand as though avid to enter the sea.

At one end of the bay a group of young blacks threw themselves about in the shallows, leaping in the air and falling on to the water in sheer exuberance, their audience themselves. Two white girls, topless, wandered to the blacks' end of the bay and began to oil themselves, massaging their breasts from below so that they showed cupped and glistening to best advantage. Matthew was mildly pleased that the blacks seemed to find the gentle waves more stimulating. For himself, he swam away from that end of the bay, not because exposed breasts in the strong, flat sun held any particular interest, but because he felt inexperienced at showing indifference.

He walked back to Buck House slowly, tired but refreshed. There was someone on the veranda, bent over the rail, writing.

'Good Lord!' he said.

Jill looked up.

'Hi, sailor! I was just about to leave you a note. The woman opposite said you were probably with the Richardsons, or swimming, but it sounded rather far to walk and I've a 'plane to catch.'

'I don't know any woman opposite.'

'Black lady with small children.'

'They're all black round here and the children are legion, but I've not spoken to any of them.'

'Oh, well, I thought I'd try to find you.'

She offered a cheek and he kissed her awkwardly. She was deeply tanned and looking lovely.

'It's awfully nice to see you,' he said.

'I was beginning to wonder.'

'Sorry! It was such a surprise.'

'So was seeing "Patience".'

'I was dismasted and blown off course.'

'So I've heard.'

'And you? I thought you were flying home from the Canaries.'

Jill looked sheepish.

'Iain said he could do with another hand for the crossing to Panama.'

'I've news for you. This is Monesterio.'

She looked at her watch.

'I've a few minutes if you'd like to ask me in.'

'Sorry, I'm just not adjusting.'

He made tea.

'I'm glad you're writing again,' she said, looking at his typewriter.

'Just a few jottings.'

She noted the empty draining board, the hung J-cloth, the carefully made bed, and smiled.

'Still running a tight ship, I see.'

He grinned. 'Leopards. But how come you've put in here?'

'Long story. Hairy crossing; fantastic blows; Iain nervy under pressure. Pretty impossible all round.'

He opened a new packet of Rich Tea biscuits and listened to her tale. She seemed very happy, relaxed, vivacious. He shifted in his chair, finding his thin cotton shorts suddenly rather tight.

'Anyway,' Jill finished, 'I'm so glad *you* made it.'

'Poor old Iain,' Matthew said, his voice not redolent of sympathy.

Jill laughed. 'In that boat, and with all that equipment!'

He poured another cup of tea.

'Couldn't you... stay?' he asked.

She smiled and touched the back of his hand as he passed her the cup.

'I really must go.' She looked at her watch. 'My God, I certainly must! I've only about twenty minutes to get my things off the boat and grab a taxi.'

'There's a plane back to London several times a week.'

'Roger's meeting me. It's all fixed.'

He tried to look pleased. 'Reconciliation?'

'He wants us to have another go. He's found a little business we can run together. Oh, and he's sold the deep-freeze.'

He walked back to the dockyard with her. They parted at the gates.

'Well,' he said, 'I hope it all works out.'

'And for you.'

'By the way, did you take pills on Iain thing's boat?'

'No,' she said, 'I felt, somehow, too needed.'

'I know what you mean.'

'The sea can give you such a different perspective.'

'True.' The subject no longer held much interest.

'Did the kitten help?' Jill asked.

'Help? Yes, I suppose so.'

'Good. Sorry I was a bit of a cow at times.'

'You weren't. I wish you hadn't to go so soon.'

She kissed him affectionately.

'Ring us when you get back,' she said. 'Bye!'

He arrived at Buck House hot and sweating again. He showered, concentrating the cool water frontally. As he lay on the bed he thought about Jill's crossing with Iain Vesper-Strathclyde. A smug smile settled on his face. He gazed at the ceiling, appreciating the soothing stirrings of a breeze through the louvres...

'Thought I'd have to break the door in,' Sebastian said.

Matthew stuck his middle fingers into the corners of his eyes and pulled his hands down over his cheeks.

'Sorry,' he mumbled. 'Must have dozed off.'

'No matter,' Sebastian said. 'Punctuality isn't expected on this island, and it's only drinks.'

Matthew began to dress.

'I was with the quote self-styled Professor of History unquote,' he said.

'That was some article,' Sebastian said. 'I gather another instalment is due tomorrow.'

'It was so incredibly full of hate,' Matthew said. 'And the racial bias was quite frightening.'

'It's difficult at times to separate the two. In the case of the dockyard one has to remember that yachting and the trades that go with it are traditionally whiteman pursuits. So the envies thrown up by the signs of conspicuous wealth the yachts bring with them can easily seem to be directed at the honkies. Assessment of the actual racial bias is something one has to make individually. You'll probably have drawn some conclusions of your own before the evening is over.'

'People here certainly seem to keep their tabs on you,' Matthew said. 'The woman opposite told a friend I was with the Richardsons. I hadn't even spoken to her.'

'The bush telegraph beats anything the Post Office can lay on,' Sebastian said. 'I say, you keep some grand friends. That fellow's yacht has been given a prime berth next to the pay office.'

'He's no friend of mine,' Matthew said. 'Just a chap who knows a woman of my acquaintance.'

'I thought she was rather pretty,' Sebastian said.

The Watkins' apartment was more considered and better equipped than the Richardsons'. It was furnished with restful good taste in the late Georgian style, but lacking ostentation. A tape recorder played Bach quietly through discretely placed speakers. The acoustics were good below the timber ceiling. The room was square and flanked on two sides by a verandah to which access was through large sash windows open to the evening breeze.

'A delightful ambience,' Matthew said, with polite sincerity.

'All Rosemary's doing,' Bill said with quiet pride. He was of middle height with whitening hair and a jutting beard that was still an unrepentant ginger-red. His eyes and bearing suggested a fiery nature and tireless energy; his voice had the enthusiasm and forcefulness of a man whose inner convictions affected all his judgments. Matthew detected dedication and earnestness, but perhaps not a keen sense of the absurdities of life.

'It has a restful, timeless atmosphere,' Matthew remarked, 'as though you have been here a long time.'

'We've only been married five years,' Rosemary said.

She had a soothing, gentle voice, and Matthew could well believe it when told she had been a nurse. She was small and pretty, wearing a loose cotton dress that was so effective in its simplicity that he needed Rebecca on hand to judge whether it had come from the top end of Liberty's range or from the women who sold locally-made dresses by the dockyard gate. Rosemary asked him all the right questions about his voyage to Monesterio, and after two gins and tonic he was in a mood to deceive himself that not everyone who came to the apartment could be so fortunate as to prompt such a felt concern and interest.

Another guest arrived, and with a slight shock Matthew recognized Captain White. The delicacy of the surroundings threw the size and manner of the extroverted policeman into heavy relief.

'We meet again, suh,' the Captain said, enfolding Matthew's hand in a huge black fist. It was one of those grips that have to be returned quickly and so far as possible in kind if the bones are not to be heard crunching under the pressure.

'Small world,' Matthew said lamely, wishing to God the Captain would let go.

'Yo' havin' fun?'

'Everyone's been most kind,' Matthew assured him.

'Yo' know the island?'

'Not before I arrived, no.'

'Fine place, man, an' dis...' the Captain stabbed a thick finger at the floor '... dis li'l ol' dockyard here is where is all goin' on.'

'You must be kept busy,' Matthew guessed.

'Fren', it never stop. Ah'm tellin' yo', at dis time o' de yeah Ah don't know wedder Ah'm a man or a yo-yo. In an' out dem boats like a mad ting, Ah can tell yo'.'

'Do you get a lot of problems?'

'Problems?'

'Contraband, marijuana, illegal entry, that kind of thing.'

The Captain's small eyes narrowed.

'Con'raban'? Ganja? Waddya know 'bou' dat, man?'

'Know?' Matthew said hastily. 'Well, I don't know anything about it except in general terms.'

'How yo' mean, g'nl terms?'

'Well,' Matthew said, floundering and suddenly, absurdly fearful that he might be turning pink, 'I mean I know that things like smuggling go on in ports the world over, and I was wondering whether you have any particular problem in that way.'

'Why yo' wanna know, man?' the Captain persisted, clearly not at the root of the mystery.

Matthew was wishing he had kept the conversation to the weather.

'Being something of a writer, I am always interested to know about others' jobs and that kind of thing.'

'Yo' ain't got no partikler reason fo' askin', den?'

'No,' Matthew said. 'No, none at all.'

'Cos if yo' have,' the Captain said, lowering his voice perceptibly, 'dere's always sometin' can be arranged.'

'Arranged?'

The Captain nodded, the nod of a man of the world in company with another.

'In dis life, man, dere's always ways yo' can make tings easier for yo'self.'

'Yes,' Matthew agreed, now totally out of his depth. 'I suppose so.'

'Yo' jus' come alon' an' see me any time,' the Captain said. His hand swept laterally through the air. 'Any time.'

'Thanks very much,' Matthew said.

Bill Watkins joined them with three men who had just arrived. The tallest was tastefully attired in a loose, florally trimmed pirate-shirt with a thin gold chain which looked well against skin several shades paler than that of Captain White. On his right was a shorter, heavily built man, as dark as the Captain, with a body as square as his face. The third man was small and thin featured and could have had Spanish blood in his veins. His quick sharp eyes summed up Matthew in a glance and his smile held little warmth. The taller man was introduced as Oslin Stedmore, Minister of Public Works and Communications. Matthew guessed, more or less correctly, that the others were his bodyguard and fall-guy. The Minister offered a cool pale hand of normal grip. The pressure of his bodyguard's hand was a brave imitation of the Captain's. The fall-guy's hand slipped in and out of Matthew's almost without trace.

'Oslin and I are always getting our heads down,' Bill Watkins said.

The Minister nodded. 'That's right, Bill.'

'I suppose,' Matthew said, 'that environmental problems come within your jurisdiction.'

'Mr Braine,' the Minister said smoothly, 'they are with me night and day.'

'You can't rest in this job,' Bill said.

'The dockyard is extremely attractive,' Matthew said sincerely. 'You seem to be doing a wonderful job.'

'When you've been around a bit longer,' Bill said, 'you'll notice some of the problems we are facing.'

The Minister nodded sagely.

'Litter and so forth?' Matthew hazarded.

He had noticed that paper plates and discarded bottles kept in step with any efforts that might be made to clear them up.

Bill's gesture seemed to brush this problem aside as of almost no consequence.

'Look at the skyline,' he said darkly.

Matthew peered through the windows into the soft night, loud with chirruping insects. He could not see beyond the subdued lighting which suffused the room.

'Development?'

Bill and the Minister nodded. Rosemary had joined them with Sebastian.

'I'm afraid,' she said in her gentle voice, 'that Donald has sub-leased some land up there.'

'To a certain English lord,' Bill added.

Matthew caught a whiff of something more than factual observation.

'An' odder rich pipple,' the Captain put in.

'I think I know what you mean,' Matthew said.

On his way out of the dockyard he had winced at the brightly-painted, horrendously designed house on the hill off to the right. Its roof zig-zagged and had white-painted barge boards. Below, the vertical rails of a verandah suggested a huge mouthful of teeth. It was as though a sea monster from the recent best-seller was about to descend on the dockyard, scooping all before it into its cavernous mouth. It was all the more apparent for being on its own on the hillside, surrounded by bare rock with no relief from foliage or other properties. In his own mind he had named it 'Jaws'.

'Ah, you've noticed,' Bill said. 'Right on the skyline.'

'Well, I meant the house a little further down towards the water,' Matthew admitted. 'Obviously pretty new.' He laughed. 'Rather like a shark about to swallow its prey.'

A silence fell on the room. Even the night insects seemed to have taken time off from communication. Sebastian coughed behind his hand, his eyes moving from one face to another. Rosemary looked into her glass, twirling it by the stem, and her husband's body tensed like a pointer. The Minister looked at Matthew, his expression registering nothing whatsoever, and his subordinates stared across the room into the night as though their minds were elsewhere.

The moment was broken by the ship's bell which visitors had to ring at the top of the stairs if they were not well enough acquainted with the Watkins' dog McAlister to survive his partiality for living flesh.

'Excuse me a moment,' Rosemary said with evident relief. She left the room hurriedly.

Matthew said the first thing that seemed in any way relevant.

'I suppose you need a dog in a place like this,' he managed.

'Need?' Bill said cautiously. He seemed in doubt about what Matthew might say next.

Matthew saw the chasm at his feet and rapidly rephrased his thinking in three different forms, coming out with:

'All the visitors from cruise-ships. I daresay you get the odd rough diamond among them.'

The quintet in the background came to a stop and Bill crossed the room to replace the tape. Rosemary re-entered with a couple of unmistakable British origin. The man was of powerful build with heavily overgrown eyebrows. His eyes, when visible behind a pair of spectacles of less than recent styling, were keen and intelligent. His features were strong, but the passage of time put the observer in mind of granite which was a little over the top. His wife was as tall as Betty Richardson. Intelligence and a sense of humour showed around mouth and eyes. Their presence imposed an unspoken hierarchy.

'This is Sir Alfred and Lady Bishop,' Rosemary said. Perhaps so that there should be no misunderstanding, she added: 'Sir Alfred is adviser to the British Government in matters of economics and the environment.'

Introductions were made, leaving Matthew with Sir Alfred and the Minister. Sir Alfred showed an immediate and intelligent interest in the Minister's role and responsibilities. His questions struck Matthew as being clear and straightforward, but Oslin Stedmore appeared to be having some difficulty with them. None of his answers seemed to match the questions and his responses were non-committal and monosyllabic. After a while Sir Alfred brought his questioning down to a level where the answers would have been available from a copy of *Whitaker's Almanack*.

'Now your constituency,' he said, without condescension but with a slow kindliness such as a teacher of eight year olds might have employed with a shy newcomer to the class, 'how many voters are there?'

The Minister moved his feet uneasily.

'In round numbers,' he said, looking over Sir Alfred's left shoulder as though seeking inspiration from the tastefully coloured birds that were part of the wallpaper, 'I don't know that I can answer that.'

The quiver of an eyebrow was the nearest that Sir Alfred's face came to registering surprise. He heaved a quiet sigh and chose another tack.

'Have you any children of an age to be striking out on their own?' he enquired.

He had struck oil at last. The Minister had thirteen children and he proceeded to give Sir Alfred a close and detailed account of the age, sex and developmental status of each and every one. Matthew, feeling that Sir Alfred could be trusted with the new formula, crossed the room to join the others. Rosemary was charming Captain White and the Minister's aides with a friendliness and warmth of interest Matthew concluded ruefully was as impartial as it was sincere. Sebastian and Lady Bishop were laughing quietly together in a corner near one of the loudspeakers.

Another couple arrived, apologizing for lateness. American, he was elderly but sprightly, though no match for his wife who it turned out ran a chain of boutiques on the island. Mrs Cornelius made it clear they had retired from Manhattan to their Green Hills holiday home but that she had decided work was much more fun than fun.

'It was Nöel Coward used to say that,' she admitted. 'He had a house on Green Hills for a time. It's a very select estate.'

She asked Matthew if he had a wife and whether she would be coming out to join him. Matthew replied with a yes and a no and Mrs Cornelius looked disappointed. Then with some skill she brought the conversation round to her husband's trousers which she said were of pure sea island cotton and could be obtained in her shops.

'They're a little pricey, of course,' she admitted, 'but if it's quality you're after these days...'

Her husband was interested to know what Matthew wrote and seemed inclined to talk about his library of books on the Caribbean and Central America. Mrs Cornelius did not allow too much of this; it was clearly a topic lacking mainline relevance. Before managing to separate Sebastian from Lady Bishop, Mrs Cornelius established that Matthew had no immediate plans to leave the island.

'We're not in our house presently,' she said. 'The high season is so exhausting socially we're lying low in a little place right by here. It's so nice meeting with you. You must come over. We'll be in touch.'

Matthew in turn assured her he would call in at her Campbelltown boutique.

With the feeling that his earlier gaff, whatever it had been, would make his departure acceptable, Matthew told Sebastian he would walk back to Buck House for an early night. Sebastian allowed him to insist upon this, indicating with the merest flick of an eyelid that he wanted to continue his conversation with Sir Alfred.

Feeling dispirited by an evening that had gone flat, Matthew walked home under the high moon along the dusty road. The night was strident with crickets, frogs, barking dogs, and the cocks who greeted every minute as though it were dawn.

21

IT had not been a quiet night. Although the refrigerator was noisy it did little to drown the shindy of innumerable cats who fought and yowled below the open louvres. Dogs from near and far conducted a night-long competition to have the last bark, and whenever a car screamed at manic speed through the village the entire canine population rose as one to voice protest and challenge.

It was early apparent that the bungalow next door was rented by the crew of a yacht, for at two in the morning they arrived in a state of alcoholic solidarity, seemingly determined that no party once begun would end on a dying fall. A tape recorder turned on at full blast provided the background for incessant door slamming, the crash of falling bottles, and an almost constant stream of such venomous variations on the sexual proclivities of Jesus Christ that it was difficult to imagine what was happening to lend fuel to so much over-reaction. When a tape came to an end, the voices also ceased, and for the few seconds until another tape took over it was possible to hear the frogs and crickets chirping and croaking regardless in the surrounding gardens and mangrove swamps. The raucous conversations of the villagers had made sleep difficult earlier on, but local bedtime seemed at a reasonable hour. Matthew wondered that the villagers made no complaint about the yobs next door, but hoped that the soundness of their sleep was preventing too close an evaluation of the superiority of the Western lifestyle.

At four in the morning he was sticky with the exertion of turning on his foam bed to find a position that would block at least one ear from the worst of the cacophony outside while at the same time giving his body a chance to come to terms with the faulty areas in the pocketed and disintegrating mattress. He padded into the kitchen in bare feet and turned on the light. He had the momentary impression that the floor was covered by a sheet of black polythene. Then the sheet appeared to be flicked away from him under the sink and cupboards as though by a hidden hand.

His weary mind settled on the truth of this phenomenon and he left the ground with a falsetto 'Euaaaaagh!' Then reason told him that the cockroaches were no keener than he on confrontation and that his bare toes were under no real threat. Nonetheless, he was shaking a little as he poured himself a glass of tepid yellow water, leaning forward to the tap from the middle of the small kitchen.

A shower was the next priority. He returned to the bedroom, put on a pair of plimsolls, and cautiously felt for the bathroom light switch through the curtain which filled the opening between the rooms. The bathroom seemed free of livestock apart from a mosquito which, disturbed by the moving curtain, danced provocatively in and beyond the thin beam from the naked 25-watt bulb. It took him nearly ten minutes to get the creature into an air space where visibility allowed for effective swatting.

When he had showered he rubbed himself from head to toe in the cheap white vinegar Sebastian had said went some way towards easing the itch of stings received and thwarting the promise of those to come. Smelling like a pickle factory he pulled the thin sheet up to his chin as the cocks' intensified welcome to the true dawn was being added to the sad braying of a hundred donkeys on their tethers in the surrounding hills.

When he woke at eight the human world outside, except for the bungalow next door, was in full swing. Cars, lorries and earth-moving equipment with huge tyres and throaty, powerful engines, were coming and going without the benefit, it seemed, of a single silencer between the lot of them. Harsh voices called, laughed and argued, and a woman opposite, who appeared from the Coca Cola notice by the door to be living in some form of bar, was bellowing 'Viiiirgil' and 'Ann-Mareee' at a group of children playing ball at hideous risk from insanely-driven vehicles horning their way through the village from both directions. Young men were walking around with the inevitable radio clamped lovingly to their large ears. The only explanation for the volume being turned full on, Matthew supposed, was that they were stone deaf from a lifetime of excess decibels or generously determined that the rest of the world should miss no particle of their enjoyment.

He groaned, sat on the edge of the bed, scratched his limbs, counted the proof that not all Monesterion mosquitoes minded a touch of vinegar in their cocktails, and went wearily into the bathroom for another shower. A knock brought him to the front door where a bearded Australian asked if the crew of 'Puritan' could be found there. Matthew directed him next door, hoping the Australian would not succeed in penetrating his neighbours' drunken slumber. He returned to the shower, looking forward to the grapefruit he had halved and coated with brown sugar before putting it to cool in the refrigerator the night before.

Refreshed, he filled the kettle and put a match to the gas stove. There was a short weak hiss, then silence; the lighted match waved hopelessly over the rust-encrusted jets. He shaved in cold water, soaping his face several times. It was not the same. Even in 'Patience' he had managed to get a hot shave.

When he opened the refrigerator there was no welcoming blast of cold air. He had left the grapefruit in the drip-tray below the ice-cube compartment. The grapefruit was awash, its sugar now a thin syrup in the tray. Water dripped dismally between the plastic-covered racks and a pool was forming on the floor. He cleared up the mess and then pecked at the soggy grapefruit with a bent teaspoon. Any taste had been washed out. He decided to fill up with bread and marmalade and opened the cupboard in which he had put the fresh loaf the day before. A brown rodent which could have been a large mouse or a small rat shot up into the top right hand corner of the cupboard then reappeared above it, making good progress up a pipe that disappeared, as did the rodent, into the roof space above the painted plywood ceiling. He gave the loaf to the horse which was already snuffling over the wire fence of the boundary beyond the kitchen door. It was cooler outside, so breakfast at the Captain's Arms seemed the right decision – one strengthened by the sound from next door of a guitar being plucked slowly and tunelessly by a hand seemingly determined to recover the party spirit.

After checking that all the louvres were wide open he set off for the dockyard. Two tall, paunchy whites in running shorts and vests were loping towards him along the dusty road, a tremendous amount of exertion going into very slow and unco-ordinated progress. Their faces were purple, their whole bodies poured sweat. Lips wide apart and drawn back over their teeth, they sucked and expelled air noisily, their agonized faces bearing painful witness to their dedication to the pursuit of radiant health. A black child less than half their height was accompanying them joyfully, sometimes imitatively, showing every strong, white, widely-spaced tooth in her head as she pranced by their side, not only keeping up with the suffering joggers but running beyond them and back again to absorb her excess of energy. Her orange skirt – to Matthew's eyes as well made as those a doting aunt had years earlier bought for Judy and Mary during a lavish pre-Christmas visit to Liberty's – was teamed with a bright blue top, white socks and red strap shoes. Her headful of thin plaits was topped by a toggle of cherry-red, cherry-sized beads which shared her bouncing exuberance.

Opposite Buck House, a few yards up the hill, the mother of Virgil and Ann-Marie was sitting below the Coca Cola notice plaiting the hair of a smaller child, equally well-dressed. At least, Matthew had assumed she was the mother of Virgil and Ann-Marie but would have laid bets with no one. Any number of women seemed to have responsibility for the children who played on the hill, and as they appeared to share it with equal pleasure and dedication the logical conclusion was that he was privileged to be living opposite a text-book example of the extended family. Who was mother, aunt, grand-mother or cousin seemed somewhat irrelevant.

Matthew smiled at the child who was sucking a finger with her toes turned in, gazing at him solemnly from under lowered lashes. She raised a cautious arm, just perceptibly wriggling her fingers in acknowledgment of his overture. Matthew waved and smiled again and the child's mother beamed delightedly.

'Tasha,' she ordered, 'yo' wave at dat man, now, 'n say goo' mornin'.'

In her candy-floss-pink dress Tasha looked like a commercial for an animated doll as her tiny fingers wriggled a little more positively, but it was clear that on such short acquaintance the relationship was not going to get any warmer. Respecting the wisdom of this inbuilt reserve Matthew went on his way.

By keeping to the windward side of the road he escaped the fine dust from every passing car. One of these was driven by Mrs Cornelius who slowed down to speak to him.

'You simply must come to dinner,' she said firmly.

He thanked the back of her car as she accelerated in a cloud of choking dust.

With his mind relieved of the logistics of living it returned to the party of the night before. He wondered why his remark about the house had gone down so big. Only a small detour was necessary to take a closer look at 'Jaws.' He turned off the road shortly before reaching the new and over-assertive police station that dominated the road to the dockyard. It was a stiff climb to reach 'Jaws'. Nearer inspection did nothing to improve his impression. From the closer viewpoint the effect was still that of a huge shark, its mouth half open, flashing great white teeth in its lower jaw and a hard pale line of gum in the upper. A lot of money had clearly been spent to achieve the disastrous result. Further along the road he could see another house, only just visible behind trees and a fence made of coconut matting. He walked towards it. Hand-painted notices, one on a tree, another against the matting, read: 'High voltage! Danger!! Power by accumulated solar energy. This property is protected electronically. Please take heed. Call out before entry,' and 'Danger! This house has a very high volt alarm.' Another notice near the high boarded gate read: 'You are warned! Savage dog patrols constantly.'

Lacking the least desire to put any of these warnings to the test, Matthew retraced his steps and came to a long drive on his left which he had noticed on the way up. A man was working on pot holes in the road and Matthew asked him where it led to. The man spoke broad bee-wee that was almost unintelligible, but Matthew gathered that at the end of the drive was a house called The Powder Magazine and that it was unoccupied. The reason for the man's gesture – a throwing up of his arms to indicate an explosion – he associated with the house's name. He walked down the drive which widened on to an unkempt drive beyond which, behind overgrown trees, he recognized a stone roof glimpsed earlier from the road to the dockyard. He walked round the building which clearly went back to the eighteenth or early nineteenth century and saw that it had been considerably added to and had then suffered a fire of major proportions. It came nearer to anything he had so far seen to merit the charge of raj-style. Although it was broad daylight the place had a depressing atmosphere and he was glad to leave.

At the Captain's Arms the few tables on the higher terrace were full except for one occupied by a thin, dark man of about twenty-five with quick eyes, a restless mouth and a problem of personal freshness. His friendliness was in no doubt. Matthew soon knew that his name was Sean, that he had crossed the Atlantic single-handed in a fibre-glass sloop, that he was going on round the world, and that he did some writing for the Irish newspapers. They swopped trans-Atlantic notes and Matthew was invited to inspect 'Morne Maid' later that day. Then Sean said he had to go into Campbelltown to renew his passport.

'If you decide to stay on after the date they stamp in your passport,' he warned, 'you can spend a day or two waiting around and being sent from one place to another; it'll cost you, too. Bureaucracy will have killed yachting by the time I'm thirty, so I'm holding out against the women for another five years.'

Matthew finished his breakfast and wandered along to 'Patience', admiring her thoroughbred lines alongside the beamier, larger craft strung along the quay. Sebastian was polishing the bright parts on deck.

'That's noble of you,' Matthew said. He left his sandals on the quay and went aboard.

'Coffee?' Sebastian invited.

'Just had some, thanks.'

'Sleep all right?'

'Not too brilliantly.'

'Ah! Rats in the roof?'

Matthew looked surprised.

'No, I don't think I noticed those until this morning when I found something eating a loaf.'

'They come and go,' Sebastian said. 'Engaging animals, rats; highly intelligent of course. I think the whole family go foraging for a day or so on end, then return for some home life. You hear them slithering about in the roof. Nothing to worry about, though. They don't attack.'

'There was quite a lot else going on,' Matthew said. 'Maybe I just didn't notice them in the general hubbub.'

'It takes a few days to get used to it,' Sebastian agreed. 'Even here I found the garbage smells and the neighbouring parties a bit tiresome last night, but one soon acclimatizes.'

'Perhaps I will have that coffee,' Matthew said.

'This is a lovely little yacht,' Sebastian said. 'I'm getting quite attached to her.'

'Tell me,' Matthew said, 'what was it I said last night?'

Sebastian grinned.

'You mean about "Jaws"?'

'How did you know that's what I'd named it?'

'It's been known as "Jaws" locally ever since it was put up,' Sebastian said. 'Great minds.'

'But that doesn't answer my question,' Matthew persisted.

'No. Well, I suppose I should have briefed you a bit before we went to the Watkins. "Jaws" was built by a black with the O.K. of the government. The go-ahead was given by Oslin Stedmore's planning control man, the small chap who turned up with the Minister last night.'

'Oh, Gawd!'

'Yes. What slightly complicates the issue is that whites who have been refused permission for more responsible developments have cited that monstrosity and pointed out that the man who built it is in Government himself. There's been quite a furore.'

'But I thought the Trust was here to prevent that kind of thing and that their relationship with the Government was so good.'

'It's good from the Government's point of view if it can tap the U.K. end through Bill Watkins or enlist his help to milk local whites' businesses, but when it comes to such matters as building applications and land it looks as though the right cash sum offered by the right person is the deciding factor. I suppose things aren't all that different back home.'

'Maybe not, but I doubt if even now anyone would get away

with plonking a "Jaws" in the middle of a National Trust landscape.'

'Well, there you are. Anyway, the Trust here is being kept just where the Government wants it to be, though I am not sure the Watkins realize this.'

'I got the impression of a bias towards the blacks.'

'Well, Bill is very strongly socialistic and Rosemary has a warm spot for all whom she can identify as the oppressed. I think she tends to be a little retrospective emotionally.'

'Are there grounds for their taking sides?'

'I don't know that it's fair to say they are taking sides exactly. The behaviour of some of the whites falls rather short of the admirable. Bill is very conscientious and well-meaning by his own lights and they both work like – well, hard – to run the Trust efficiently and responsibly. But strong party-political viewpoints make for naïvety, no doubt based on reluctance to find anything wrong with one's own team. Here, have a look at this.'

He fished a yachting magazine from a document case. The article he pointed to was headed: 'When you say Port St George, you've said Richardsons.'

'Read it,' Sebastian invited. 'I'll go on restoring your boat to her former glory.'

The article was sub-headed 'A unique man and his strong sons establish an industry and an empire.' It was a well-written account of the Richardsons' arrival in Port St George and of how the chartering business had been built up over the years. Captain Richardson had granted an interview to its author:

'The Captain stood and gestured through the large windows of his attractive house to the harbour below. "When we first came here there was nothing there but ruins. The Government was indifferent and we obtained permission to convert the old paymaster's office into our living quarters. We were charged no rent. In those days nobody thought Port St George was worth anything. They made us sign waivers of liability in case of injury. The floors were rotten and they didn't want to be responsible if we took a fall." Now times have changed. Not only does the Monesterion Government eagerly collect a substantial sum, but it is threatening to raise the rent again.'

There was a picture of Captain Richardson on the veranda of his home. Matthew recognized the smooth stone roof of the powder magazine overshadowing the modern addition. The caption read: 'Captain Richardson created an industry and still reigns as its czar'. The implication throughout the article was that everything that had happened in Port St George since the Richardsons arrived was due to their resourcefulness and dedication. It was not actually stated that they had restored the dockyard buildings, but the omission of any mention of The Port St George Trust could have given that impression.

'Beginning to get the picture?' Sebastian asked.

Matthew pulled a face.

'I can see such stuff must have been pretty irritating to the Watkins,' he said, 'but surely they must have realized that the Richardsons would have had no say about what went into print?'

'No doubt. But this association of the Richardsons with Port St George is long-standing, almost a legend. The article is only one example of the sort of thing that's been feeding the flames for a long time. The Watkins really have put their lives into the job here, as have the Richardsons.'

'But the Richardsons' and Tom Riley's stake is primarily commercial, which clashes with an outfit set up to restrain profit-motivated enterprise?'

'Right. But that doesn't excuse the *Labour's Voice* article which was packed with innuendo and un-supported allegations. As for the suggestion that Peter pretends an interest in the history and archaeology of the island, well that's just bloody ridiculous.'

'So I've realized. All right, so the Watkins are doing a job to the best of their abilities, but what on earth have the Richardsons done to justify the viciousness of the attack in *Labour's Voice*? And who wrote it?'

'Time may answer both those questions,' Sebastian said. 'I've made my guesses, but a friend is bringing the second instalment from Campbelltown this morning; it may give a firmer clue.'

'I had a look over old-man Richardson's house on the way here,' Matthew said. 'How did the fire start?'

'There was mention of a candle,' Sebastian said. 'It was a year or two back of course, after which the Captain retired to the land of his fathers. I think he had had enough. I know the battle with the insurers continues to this day.'

'So it must have happened after that article in the yachting mag.?'

'I suppose so. But I wouldn't draw too many conclusions from that. If the fire was no accident, other things could have sparked it off.'

'Who owns that house a bit further on up the track?' Matthew enquired. 'The maximum security outfit.'

'Oh, that. Tom and Nona Riley. Tom does the brokerage here.'

'Yes, I met him briefly. He must be a very frightened man.'

'I'm a firm believer that a shared sense of humour can overcome most problems. Tom's sense of humour is not on everyone's wavelength, and his manner can be rather unfortunate.'

'Arrogant?'

'Off hand and brusque, anyway.' Sebastian looked at him, a smile flickering. 'You're starting to sniff the air, aren't you?'

'How do you mean?'

'The war-horse syndrome. Your pro's nostrils, I suspect, are beginning to twitch.'

Matthew shrugged non-committally. 'It's interesting, certainly.'

Sebastian laid a finger against the side of his nose. 'Ah-*ha*!' he said.

'I've promised to see a chap about a boat,' Matthew said. 'Back soon.'

Sebastian grinned enigmatically and rubbed at a stanchion with renewed vigour.

'This is it,' Sean said proudly.

His patched and oddly twisted rubber dinghy had made the trip from the quayside, but Matthew felt it had been a close thing. He stood up in six inches of very dirty water and pulled himself on to 'Morne Maid' with the help of the starboard shrouds; they seemed as insubstantial as the thin metal mast they helped to support. The stern of the small yacht was a low scoop only inches above the water; useful for taking an outboard but a potential death trap in a big following sea.

'Did you start from the Canaries or the U.K.?' he asked.
'Cork,' Sean said. 'Then across the Bay. No problem.'

It seemed quite an understatement for an Irishman.

'Come into the cabin for a cup of tea,' Sean invited.

Until he dropped through the hatch Matthew had supposed that the stench was from the outfall of some drain. Below the cabin sole there was no doubt that it came from weeks of intensive and uninterrupted living. The cabin was in a state of total chaos. Apart from filthy cooking pots and pans stowed at random in whatever corner or on whatever flat surface had been handy at the time, there was a wide selection of such seemingly secondary needs as a large guitar, a chest expander, no less than six jock-straps, a totally inexplicable birdcage without bird, a heavy carved wooden cross of markedly Celtic influence, and a large number of empty bottles, their labels scrawled with messages from the guests of only imaginable send-off parties. The head was an evil green bucket of recent use. The chart table, which clearly served as a working surface, dining counter and workbench, was thick with a ripe mixture of congealed food, wax, oil and other substances Matthew did not try to analyse.

Sean poured some grey water from a grubby plastic container into a battered kettle that made the one in Buck House look lustrous and *avant garde*.

'In two seconds,' he promised, 'you'll be getting the finest cup of tea this side of the water. Would you like a bit of a bun to go with it?'

He reached for a half-open paperbag nestling against the green bucket. Matthew declined the bun with suitable if possibly overdone gratitude.

'There's a girl,' Sean said, as one unburdening a thought long in mind, 'who wants to come along with me on my way round.'

'Ah!' Matthew said. 'A girl? You could be a bit cramped.'

'Sure there's space for the donkey too,' Sean assured him. 'No problem.'

'Has she sailed with you?' Matthew asked. 'It's important to be sure about compatibility.'

Sean waved a dismissive hand.

'We had a bit of a sail yesterday,' he said. 'Just into the next bay. She'll do. Mind you, I've told her it's nothing permanent. I don't want her getting no ideas.'

He pumped the primus. 'Come on, you slow bastard, there's a crowd of us waiting on you.'

He was anxious for Matthew to read an article he had written about his trans-Atlantic trip. Matthew said he would take it away with him.

The tea lived up to expectations. His mug when empty revealed deposits rarely the aftermath of a Lipton's tea bag. They talked sailing and writing until Matthew felt he would not be showing premature eagerness to leave. Sean rowed him back to 'Patience', leaving him to leeward of the garbage area. It smelled pretty good after 'Morne Maid'.

'You must meet Suella,' Sean called out as he pushed off from the quay. 'She's moving in this afternoon.'

He rowed away, his misshappen dinghy heaving and crabbing like an arthritic shark.

Sebastian was deep in the second instalment of the 'rape' article. He held up an arm in greeting, his eyes on the page.

'Listen,' he said: '"Let it now be made abundantly clear that the dockyard was restored entirely through the efforts of the Port St George Trust and our late Governor Sir Frederick Glubb - God bless him! - and not by those squatters who profess to be lovers of history in order to achieve their own ends."'

'Hang on,' Matthew interrupted. 'That God bless Sir Frederick bit sounds rather odd from a rag like that.'

'Draw your own conclusions,' Sebastian said. 'Here's another sample for your files: "The dockyard czars, it is rumoured, have the Development Control Authority and the Central Housing Authority well under their thumbs, hence their undeniable recent offers of private housing plots to all sorts of Lords and Ladies and other overseas people at astronomical prices."'

'Sound, well-tried ingredients,' Matthew remarked. 'Is there any truth in what's being implied?'

'So far as I know, only that some of the people who have helped to make the dockyard what it is are now quietly trying to sell out before the island is given independence with all that may bring. Some of them may lack charm, but a number are in middle or late life and financially dependent on the businesses they have built up. They can't entirely be blamed for trying to get together some capital before the balloon goes up. The recent history of these islands is not exactly encouraging the whites to stay around.'

'I wonder who "Dockyard Dan" is?' Matthew said, skimming through the article.

'This much I know,' Sebastian said, 'there's a phrase in there that only one person I can think of would use in such a context. But I'm not going to jump the gun and start any rumours. Wherever the material came from, I suspect it was a collaboration and souped up by someone of low literacy or a fondness for pastiche.'

'They've certainly got it in for Tom Riley. I begin to see why his house is as placarded as a CND march.'

'I can see how you novelists get started,' Sebastian said. 'If I had any ability in that direction I daresay I'd be on my way into Campbelltown by now to see the editor.'

'You'd have to have a reason,' Matthew said. 'You can't corner editors out of idle curiosity.'

'Oh, well,' Sebastian said casually, 'I'm supposing that the politics of the dockyard had given me the urge to write a book.'

Matthew grinned. 'Never give up, do you?'

Sebastian's look of innocent surprise was not very convincing.

'Never give up what?'

'This campaign to get me back to the drawing board.'

Sebastian shrugged. 'It's just that every now and then I see your quivering nostrils. Seems a healthy sign. One to be encouraged. I'm one of your many readers, remember?'

Matthew had been well aware of the 'quivers' and had already succumbed to their demands more than Sebastian realized. He had been quietly, intensely excited by signs of an inspiration he had supposed would never return. But the other side of the coin was a deep-seated fear that the mood would disappear, the well run dry, before he was really under way. So he had determined not even to talk about the possibility of another book until he felt certain within himself that it was the real thing and not just a terminal twitch.

'If I pay for the petrol,' he said, 'how would it be if we went over to the Crescent Moon Hotel for a light lunch and a swim. I'm told the snorkelling there is fantastic and I'm feeling a bit tainted what with one thing and another.'

22

THE bay was half a mile long and contained only the one hotel. Nothing sullied the powder sand save drinking straws and the butts of Havanas. The blue-strapped loungers on which Matthew and Sebastian reclined were positioned beyond the range of the coconuts which hung in the palm tree above them. The ice in their lime squash was still in competition with the heat reflected from the sand. The warm breeze blowing directly off the turquoise sea was the catalyst that made all the other ingredients work.

'*Everyone* here is tanned,' Matthew said.

'I'm not aware of any competition,' Sebastian replied.

'But surely they are white when they arrive?'

'Not necessarily. This is Monesterio's most sought-after Mecca for pilgrims intent on the body fit and beautiful. And this is mid-January. The types who come here probably started their battle with winter way back in December. Come April they will be equipped to cope with the realities of a New York spring.'

'It's almost enough to make one a subscriber to *Labour's Voice*,' Matthew said.

'Almost,' Sebastian agreed, 'except that *Labour's Voice* is the Government's mouthpiece and the Government is all for attracting money into the island. Some of their ways of going about it may have struck you as somewhat self-defeating, but that's another story. Anyway, I have always had a soft spot for the rich.'

Matthew smiled. 'Friends with swimming pools and tennis courts can be handy.'

'No, I mean it,' Sebastian said. 'I know it sounds a cliché, but such a high proportion of rich people are so patently miserable that I have never been able to envy them. I suppose it's one of the factors which dissuaded me from taking a party-political stance.'

'Well, I think the concept of a world in which we have all been levelled down to a preconceived standard is a bloody depressing one,' Matthew said. 'The rich spend a lot of time being lonely and unloved, often with good reason, and I dare say it is the duty of every good Christian and humanist to try to save them from their fate; but what a colourless world it would be if we succeeded.'

'I tell myself that that's why I don't bother to try,' Sebastian said. 'Sheer selfishness, I fear.'

On loungers slightly to windward a couple was audibly agreeing that racial egalitarians were out of their tiny minds. *Labour's Voice* could have made use of their opinions. Matthew, looking at them, concluded that 'white' was a relative condition, more a state of mind than body. The man was the deepest mahoghany and further sun-bathing seemed pointless. His wife had a little way to go to catch up with him, but was already well beyond mulatto.

Between the loungers and the sea a Creole girl sauntered slowly past. She was the colour of a cup of creamy drinking chocolate and wore a wine-red, beautifully fitting beachrobe of towelling so fine it had the sheen of velvet; it stopped at hip level and was scalloped in the right places to reveal the full length of her perfect legs. She had the carriage of a queen who knew what it was all about, and on her slender wrists fine gold bracelets tinkled like temple bells heard from a long way off.

'Wow!' Matthew said, 'if I was twenty years younger...'

'I *am* twenty years younger,' Sebastian said, 'and I'm terrified.'

'She looks very very expensive.' Matthew drained his lime squash. 'Boy! Did that hit the spot!'

'I can see you are taking to all this decadence like a duck to water,' Sebastian said. 'How about salving our souls, or at least our minds, with a game of chess?'

With his pocket chess on a chair between them, they played a leisurely game. A hawk-faced couple stopped to watch their moves. It is not easy to suggest egregious wealth in nothing more than a bikini and a pair of bathing shorts, but the couple managed it.

'If you gentlemen felt like making up a four for bridge this evening...' the man said. His features were clearly not accustomed to making friendly overtures and the effort put his audience in mind of an amiable barracuda.

'It's a kind suggestion,' Matthew said, 'but we are not resident here.'

The couple wasted no more time on them.

'I wonder why chess should be thought any qualification for playing bridge?' Matthew remarked, castling for lack of any more positive ideas.

'Stark boredom makes strange bedfellows.'

'One doesn't realize how old most of them are until you see them close to.'

'It's only when they are over the top they can afford these places,' Sebastian said. 'See what I mean about the pity of it all?'

'I'm still not quite certain when to take you seriously,' Matthew said.

'Good,' Sebastian said.

'In some ways you seem older than your years, in others younger.'

'Immature?'

'I wouldn't say that. Unorthodox maybe.'

'Good again,' Sebastian said. 'I think we both have our doubts about orthodoxy.'

'Which is probably why we get on,' Matthew agreed. 'I suspect you are an only child too. It stays with one.'

'I had a brother, but he died young. I'm glad you feel we get on. It may be something to do with the frames of reference.'

His next move gave Matthew no choice but a dignified retirement.

'How about another dip?' Matthew said. 'Before lunch.'

They did two short lengths in different directions, their brisk British strokes singling them out from the other bathers who stood around like buoys in water deep enough to support their over-weight bodies. It was clear enough from the faces of the women why they did not choose immersion. Some of the men were a little more adventurous and dashed water into their faces boldly, clenching their eyelids and panting slightly with the effort.

Matthew and Sebastian pulled on shorts and light shirts, then walked across the rough crab-grass to the terrace by the swimming pool where lunch was being served.

'It's all flown in from the States,' Sebastian said. 'No question of trusting the local sources.'

The heightened adjectives in the menu almost disguised the fact that it was food that was being offered.

'A prawn,' murmured Sebastian, 'is not a prawn is not a prawn is not a prawn.'

The couple at the next table were irresistibly keen to get into conversation. They were younger and less conspicuously well-heeled than most of the hotel's guests.

'Both our families can be traced back to England,' the man said after the briefest of introductory pleasantries. He had a big frontal coif of hair and a face which seemed eager to please and to be accepted. His wife's short, nervous laugh was not quite a titter; it was clear she thought the world of her husband.

Matthew had grown accustomed to this opening.

'What part?' he enquired.

'Birkshire,' the man replied. 'Ethie here, her folks came from Devon-shire. That right, Ethie?'

'That's right, Vince,' his wife said. Her impeccable grooming did not quite go with the giggle which followed.

'I know Berkshire well,' Sebastian said. 'Nice county.'

'We're going there next year,' Vince said.

'If we can fix things at home,' his wife added.

'You have children?' Matthew enquired.

'Just one daughter,' Vince confirmed.

'What age?' Sebastian asked.

Ethie giggled again.

'Thirteen going on twenty-six,' she said.

'Shireen's a little precocious,' her husband explained.

'Vince travels a lot,' Ethie said. 'We've not had all that chance to make a family.'

It was confirmed that Vince was a junior executive in a real estate company, which had been one of Matthew's guesses.

'Why here *is* Shireen,' Ethie exclaimed. 'Shireen, come and meet these two gentlemen from England.'

The impression was one of high sophistication except for the face which, although tough and world-weary, had not really caught up. Shireen looked at Matthew and Sebastian with profound disinterest, her eyes spending a fraction longer eliminating the possibilities as they glided over Sebastian. She slumped into the chair between her parents, her face sulky with pending complaint.

'Did you have a nice swim, dear?' her mother enquired solicitously.

Shireen prodded a disgruntled toe at a small insect that was trying manfully to negotiate the stippled, slip-proof paving on the terrace. The place was remarkably free of minor fauna and Matthew concluded that the insect must have flown in since the terrace was last sprayed against all life which might diminish human enjoyment.

'It was a swim,' she said. A small flicker of animation passed over her face. 'I met this guy,' she added. 'Cool. Round thirty, maybe.'

'That's nice, dear,' Ethie said.

'Very societal,' Shireen added. 'I mean, you know, he's gotten flow, been around; like, lived; knows what it's all about.'

The implication that others had a long way to go hung heavily on the air.

'That's *very* nice, dear,' Ethie said with the abstracted sincerity of one on familiar ground.

'He showed me shots of his house in Virginia,' Shireen persisted. 'Real neat. And his horses. Stuff like that.'

'And of his wife, dear?' Ethie enquired gently.

'Yeah, well, that got busted. I mean, he went through it, but good. He's not letting it get him down or anything, mind. He's cool.'

'I'm sure he is, dear,' Ethie said.

'Yeah,' Shireen said, 'well, I mean, it's nice to meet a guy you can really talk to on, you know, the same level. Like, a person with the same vibes.'

'It must be, dear,' Ethie said.

'How about we eat?' Vince said.

He beckoned a waitress. She did not come with speed, but she came. They all ordered, which meant three large hamburgers, each containing meat, cheese and fish, with french fries and a whiff of salad, for Ethie, Vince and Shireen; a shrimp cocktail for Matthew; a cottage cheese salad for Sebastian. The shrimps, in the jumbo range, made an ample meal in the heat of mid-day. The cottage cheese salad, though it appeared to have nothing to do with the lyrical wording of the menu, satisfied Sebastian. Ethie, Vince and Shireen cleared their plates without difficulty, but found that two days' protein needs was no substitute for, nor argument against, the cream-heavy French pastries of 'No-Ingredient-Spared-Toothsomeness' which were offered as follow-ups. Matthew and Sebastian had coffees. Through the meal they heard a great deal more about Ethie, Vince and Shireen, and Vince asked Matthew's opinion of the Mediterranean for their next holiday.

'Spring and autumn are the best,' Matthew said. 'Provence is still beautiful and relatively unspoiled, but expensive. The beaches are much the same wherever you go these days. If you want good swimming you are not going to beat the Caribbean.'

'I appreciate your sharing that with us, Matthew,' Vince said.

'I want to go to Italy,' Shireen said in a complaining voice, as though to end a long-sustained argument.

'And we,' said Sebastian, rising, 'had better get back into the water, hadn't we, Matthew?'

They left to the accompaniment of a rising whine from Shireen.

'To have survived one's children's adolescence,' Matthew said, 'is to have greeted a dawn one never expected to see. You just don't know, my boy.'

They swam, basked and played another game of chess.

'Three-thirty,' Sebastian said. 'If we are to beat the sandflies we should pack it in.'

He had prudently left the Bustler facing downhill on the approach road through the hotel's surrounding golfcourse. They free-wheeled, then the engine puttered into life and they climbed back out of the grounds to the unpredictable surface of Monesterio's highway system. North of Wilberforce, some children leaving the school bus rushed into the road at the sight of the Bustler. Two of the boys spread their arms out dramatically, shouting 'A ride, a ride!' in their harsh, unchildlike voices. Sebastian waved and drove on.

'Adults are one thing, but kids are too much of a responsibility,' he said.

A little further on a boy in his teens signalled them to stop.

'I suppose he's old enough to look after himself,' Sebastian said.

The boy got into the back seat without a word and sprawled out lazily. They passed another boy and their passenger waved in a lordly manner. Near the centre of Wilberforce he said 'Here!'

Sebastian stopped. The boy said nothing but got out and headed towards timber bungalows up a rough lane.

'Hey!' Sebastian called. The boy turned. 'You too big a man to use that little word?' Sebastian enquired.

The boy sneered and turned away.

'Oick!' Sebastian growled, slamming the Bustler through the gears.

Matthew grinned.

'Nice to see you're human,' he said.

'There are times when some of them get me up to here,' Sebastian said, putting his hand across his Adam's apple, 'but our own lot can be just as odious in their way. However, charity begins abroad in this day and age, so I don't usually let them rattle me.'

Beyond Wilberforce an approaching car nearly struck a large bird which was flying across their path from behind trees on the other side of the road. The bird swerved to gain height, releasing something from its claws. The something was black and white and lay on the hot road, its small legs pushing ineffectually in the air, its far from small voice registering strident protest. Sebastian stopped alongside the creature and leaned out of the open side of the Bustler.

'Must have been a hawk,' he said.

He picked up the kitten. It had a large belly and a small head; its umbilical cord was still attached and it smelt frightful. It was the ugliest kitten Matthew could remember seeing. Sebastian put it in his straw hat which Matthew was holding in his lap in case the wind blew it out of the car.

'Here,' he said, 'a present from the skies. Poor little bleeder.'

'I seem to be dogged by bloody cats,' Matthew said, peering at the squealing object with a mixture of pity and distaste.

'Oh, well,' Sebastian said lightly, 'it's all part of the great loom of life, I suppose.'

Matthew grunted.

'I'm not sure I'm not revising some of my ideas about that. I went through some odd phases on the way over.'

'Odd?'

'Rationally, yes. I mean, to feel – when totally isolated from others – somehow more a part of life than before, that's surely odd.'

'You're not talking about loneliness?'

'No, I'm not. It was something much more deeply seated.'

'Maybe the voyage helped fill a gap. Most of us are bogged down in rigid routines allowing only a limited number of perceptions, which is why travel *should* develop the mind. It seldom does, of course, but that's another instance of how reason alone can be unreliable.'

'You're sceptical about rationalism, aren't you?'

'As an ultimate solution, yes. Aren't you? Sometimes?'

Matthew nodded.

'The past few months have raised a few doubts.'

'And planted some certainties?'

'I'm not so sure about that.'

'Maybe certainty is too strong a word; but I think we need more than doubt, fear and disillusionment to cope with this scheme of things.'

'All right,' Matthew said, 'but if one doesn't subscribe to notions of God, creation and the rest of it, one has to find some other explanation for what it's all about. Humanism fills that gap for a lot of people.'

'Well,' Sebastian said, 'I don't hold strong views about creation, destination, and so forth, because frankly I don't think our tiny human minds are on the right wavelength. I doubt whether we'll ever know about creation, and it seems a waste of time to argue about a possible hereafter when we're still making such a god-awful mess of the present and can't possibly understand something we've not experienced.'

'I'll go along with that.'

'But I have noticed one rather curious thing, which is that belief in a God, a sense of purpose, usually grows stronger with age. Whereas non-belief – or is it unbelief? – seems to weaken. Humanists always seem to be on guard rather than happy. I expect you've an answer for it.'

Matthew shrugged.

'I suppose if one only has one's reason to carry one along, the tendency is to safeguard it pretty jealously.'

'A character in a novel I was reading recently said something to the effect of there being a fierce need for the mystic to save us from the futility of a world we understand.'

'Who was the author?'

'Falling kittens and all that sun and sea have hammered my memory, but I know he wrote a lot of books earlier this century and I mean to get hold of some. I felt his way of looking at things may be coming back into favour.'

'With whom?'

Sebastian considered.

'Well, there's a fair number of people, maybe mostly younger than me, who take a dim view of the world we've made for ourselves. I don't mean the lay-abouts and difficult adolescents, I mean intelligent and, yes, rational people who feel out of tune with the violence and material gods of our age.'

'They don't make themselves very heard.'

'Maybe because they're less aggressive and ego-centred and so ignored by the media. But they're a growing section. Unfortunately they are often associated with those who for one reason or another can't cope with life and need the kind of anchors our welfare state is improperly equipped to provide.'

'Like my daughter's husband,' Matthew agreed gloomily.

'Possibly. But I think their spokesmen are beginning to pop up, sometimes in surprising places. Most get written off or conveniently forgotten, but maybe that's how it has to be until such time that their unity and maturity can make their influence felt.'

'Influence or power?'

'The power of influence, then. Even in my absurd role of "king" of Zafada I've gained through others' reactions to that dubious title new insights into how people tick and what our real problems are. The 'monarchy' may only have been a giggle among egg-heads to boost a fellow-writer's work by taking silly peerages and creating a literary so-called aristocracy, but perhaps because it now goes back a hundred years or more it's extraordinary how many people take it seriously.'

'Not really,' Matthew said, 'it's the stuff of history. What's any monarchy, if you go far enough back, but some mindless clash between greedy idiots, with the leader of the winning mob declaring himself "king" and rewarding the other thugs this or that title? All the panoply and structure which follows doesn't change the origins. Your "monarchy" has at least more civilized foundations.'

'For that little speech I should make you a grand-duke at the very least! Well, one of the lessons has certainly been that power is founded not on your own qualities or even on what you possess, but on the view others have of you. I suppose that's the kind of thing one would have recognized had it been pointed out, but so many facts of life don't really hit the target until one has lived with the actual experience. Even being a miniscule monarch can teach one a few things.'

'And from the sublime to the bloody ridiculous,' Matthew said, pointing to the still vociferous kitten in his lap, 'what the hell are we going to do with Fred?'

'Well, I don't suppose you want to spend several weeks giving it two-hourly feeds,' Sebastian said, 'so we have to find it a mother-cat or a very dedicated moggie-fancier. Rosemary Watkins is our next port of call. She's a girl with a big heart.'

'I hope she found room in it to forgive me for my gaff the other day,' Matthew said.

Sebastian pushed the Bustler up from twenty-five to a throaty thirty.

'I don't think you need fear antagonism from that direction,' he said. 'We ignorant honkies are always putting our feet in it one way or another.'

They drove on, Fred's demands for a more reliable feeding pattern obviating any need to use the Bustler's horn. It wasn't working, anyway.

23

'HAVE you done much sailing?' Matthew asked.

'Not a lot,' Suella admitted. 'Mind, my mommy and daddy took a charter last year and we sailed down through, you know, some of the islands. I wasn't sick much,' she added proudly.

'She'll be fine,' Sean said.

He picked at the plate of daintily arranged pieces of ham, salad, potato and sardine. He had lost something of his relaxed, devil-may-care bearing.

Suella replaced the paper napkin which had dropped from Sean's bare knee. The interior of 'Morne Maid' had been transformed. If there was an overall smell it was of disinfectant combined with fresh bread and a jasmine-like flower that sat in a pot on the now polished chart table. The evil green bucket had been replaced by one that was parlour pink and stowed discretely in the bow of the boat with a packet containing six rolls of matching toilet paper.

'So you're off on Tuesday?' Matthew said. The tide of conversation was not flowing strongly.

Sean nodded. Suella sighed and said 'Gee!' It was not a 'gee' of unqualified enthusiasm.

'Bit scared?' Matthew asked.

She nodded. 'Just a little, I guess.'

'Well, don't do anything silly,' Matthew said. 'The sea needn't be feared if one is sensible.'

Suella nodded again.

'Always wear a lifeline,' Matthew said. 'Even on the calm days. It is important to establish habit.'

'I've bought two more,' Sean said. 'One for her, one as a spare.'

'And eat plenty,' Matthew advised. 'You don't want to keep

off food because you may be afraid of being sick.'

'Gee!' Suella said with a sigh, 'it's sure great having you talk this way; it's like I was back home.'

'Well,' Matthew said, 'you *are* the same age as my younger daughter.'

Now that the generation gap had opened up between them like a chasm, he made his departure as soon as was politely possible. The meal had been a thank-you for commenting on Sean's article. Matthew hoped he had struck the right balance between a kind and a truthful assessment. When Sean rowed him to shore, Suella was using an aerosol air-freshener in the cabin.

He met Sebastian on the quayside.

'I have a feeling,' Matthew said, 'that that young man was happier living in a permanent state of capsize.'

'I got through on Peter's 'phone,' Sebastian said. 'Your appointment's at three-thirty, so be there by four.'

They walked across the green. Three dockyard workers finished their lunch on the steps of the officers' quarters and walked away, leaving plastic plates and beer cans to the whim of the wind which at once bowled a plate into an angle of the building.

'Not exactly litter-conscious, are they?' Matthew remarked.

The green was dotted with rubbish. Some cans and bottles had been rammed with faint concession to tidiness into the unhospitable centres of dagger plants.

'Another of the seeming insolubles. Trash collection is stoop labour. Stoop labour is synonymous with slavery.'

'Yet I thought there was massive unemployment.'

'There is. To give them their due, the Government has tried to reintroduce sugar cane cultivation, but islanders won't do work associated with the bad old days.'

'Surely that's all seen as history now?'

'Emancipation came only a century and a half ago, and the slave trade had been operating for three hundred years before that. Resentment and suspicion die hard.'

'I don't get the impression that the local radio does much to kill it. From some of the stuff I've listened to, you'd think the shackles were still cutting into the flesh. Doesn't the Government have some say in radio policy?'

'The radio's run by the Government.'

'I give up. Anyway, what's the answer to the sugar problem?'

'Workers may be brought in from another island.'

'While the locals stand round and watch and draw the dole?'

'They may go to some other island and work there.'

'Doing what?'

'Cutting cane, probably.'

'But...'

'I know. But it's cutting cane on their home ground they object to.'

'And the island is about to go fully independent from the British?'

'That's the idea.'

'Well, well,' Matthew said, 'I'm glad I've not invested in any raj-style properties out here.'

'The place is a mass on contradictions. Theoretically, the Labour Party here favours free enterprise.'

'But the work has to be acceptable?'

'Now, that's so even back home. Despite high unemployment, the blacks are proving fussier than the whites. The girls won't go into the factories and the boys want to be electricians, engineers, musicians, decorators; or take welfare until offered a job they think has dignity. Rastafarianism doesn't help either, promising a future in which black will have overtaken white.'

'Maybe the wheel will come full circle,' Matthew said, 'whites being exported from the U.K. to cut Monesterion cane.'

'If the old man dies, as he must one day, I don't rate the whites' chances when his sons have complete control.'

'The Premier?'

'Charlesworth Finch. He's not exactly a saint, but he's a lot better than what's waiting in the wings.'

'Are you saying blacks are inherently less capable?'

'I wouldn't use politicians as a gauge for anything. Plenty of white governments are just as short-sighted and corrupt. But the supreme idiocy of this bunch is that they cultivate resentment and negativity and can't see this must make a workable independence more difficult. Viz those hopelessly misjudged articles in *Labour's Voice*, trading on envy, greed and class – if not racial – prejudice. Whatever the people here may be capable of one day, their rulers have not prepared them to be capable of it now.'

They drank coffee in the cockpit. An elderly negress walked past, just beyond the iron rings by which the yachts were moored to the quay. She was tall and as loose-limbed as a girl fifty years her junior. The large bundle on her head was as steady as a rock without the help of hands.

'Hullo, Maisie,' Sebastian called, waving.

The woman stopped and smiled; her voice was deep and quiet, in keeping with the dignity of her carriage.

''Lo there, Mr Sebastian! I not know you a sailing man.'

'My friend's boat. Mr Braine.'

Matthew smiled and said 'Good afternoon.'

'How are the children, Maisie?' Sebastian asked.

'Chillun or gran'-chillun, Mr Sebastian?'

'I heard something about Christian having come back to the island.'

'That right, Mr Sebastian. All my chillun done return to the fold.'

'So now you can retire, Maisie, and let them look after you.'

The woman laughed.

'When you tired of work you tired of life, Mr Sebastian, and if I don't get this washing seen to I shall sure be in trouble.'

She walked on, her thin legs taking man-sized strides.

'She has seven sons,' Sebastian said, 'and all of them went to the States or the U.K. After sampling the glamorous opportunities offered on buses and undergrounds, and as washers up and street cleaners, they have returned to live on a fraction of their old earnings and an unassessable multiplication of happiness, for all that their masters are fast sowing the seeds of a fresh discontent.'

'But if nothing's done to limit the birthrate, surely emigration is inevitable?'

'Oh, sure. I stay unrepentantly convinced that the world's greatest and most ignored material problem is what someone rightly termed "the infestation of humanity."'

'Which one can hardly expect Monesterio to solve when the major powers themselves do nothing about it.'

'All right, but the real tragedy here, as doubtless you've seen, is not that the blacks lack ability to adjust to the West's lifestyle, but that they lack the sense to see that Western ways are not worth striving for. If Finch's sons Staffil and Desmore, both of whom had university education in the States, had any real concern for their people they'd have long ago taken credible steps to promulgate the sense and feasibility of self-sufficiency and containment. But no, they're as sold as the West on Westernizing the island while at the same time fostering hatred towards the society whose toys they covet.'

'Who is Maisie, anyway?' Matthew asked.

'The doyen of the dockyard's laundresses. She has looked after the Richardsons' washing since the day they sailed in here and now she has the pick of the boats. If there is anyone to be envied in this fool society of ours, it is the Maisies of this world, an equal in everything that matters and more content with her lot than a millionaire.'

'That is the kind of remark,' Matthew said with a smile, 'that would get some people I can think of hopping around like a hare on hot coals, but it so happens I know what you mean.'

'But then you're a Zafadan; they see things differently.'

'You gotta believe it,' Matthew said.

'What can I do for you, Mr Braine?' Desmore Finch enquired. He was a tall man with a powerful physique that had gone not so much to seed as to stomach.

'Your editor thought it better I talk to you,' Matthew explained, 'since you control the paper's policy.'

'Well, let's see if I can be of any help.'

A telex machine clattered in the corner. The painting behind the desk was the face of a healthy, nubile black girl. From one eye flowed a sensational stream of tears, prompting the thought that the other's duct must be blocked. What emotion the picture was designed to stimulate was less apparent.

'I was hoping you could put me in touch with the author of those articles you published recently - "The Rape of St. George".'

Finch's smile did not leave his broad, well-fed face, but it stiffened a little.

'That,' he said cautiously, fingering an expensive pen, 'might be a little difficult. You see, I was out of the country at the time. I have not even read the articles. What is your interest?'

'As your assistant may have mentioned, I am writing a book. The more I see of Monesterio, the more my interest grows in its history and future.'

'We are very conscious of both, Mr Braine.'

'It seems to me you are meeting many of the problems we have had to face back home. It is interesting to see such problems being dealt with in a relatively small area.'

'You feel we have problems?'

'The "rape" articles seem to point that way.'

Finch tapped the end of his pen gently against the leather blotter.

'These are problems we think we can solve, Mr Braine. The articles surely indicate the solutions.'

'Well, not to the outsider, frankly,' Matthew said. 'Quite apart from being, I'd have thought, inflammatory in a somewhat non-productive manner, they make certain allegations about the transfer of monies to foreign bank accounts, and about huge profits, which may or may not be true but seem to offer no solution other than to get rid of the people who have attracted business to the island.'

The smile was not holding. Desmore Finch leaned across the desk, pointing his pen at Matthew's head.

'Mr Braine, let me tell you, if I see any fault with those articles it is not that they are as you call it inflammatory but that they don't say nearly enough, nor with sufficient force. Had I written them, they would have been far more outspoken.'

'I'm concerned only to get at the facts so that anything I may write will reflect a true assessment,' Matthew said. 'I'm not taking sides. I genuinely want to understand why a seemingly rather unhappy situation has developed in a corner of the island that's of major importance to your economy.'

Its smile gone, Desmond Finch's face had lost any pretence to charm.

'You are saying, then, that Monesterio cannot get along without the help of certain commercial interests in the dockyard?'

'I'm not saying that, no.'

'Because let me tell you, Mr Braine, there is no problem. Monesterions can run any business they wish in the dockyard.' His hand swept the desk. 'Any business at áll.'

'You mean yacht business?'

'If I mean yacht business, are you suggesting Monesterions are less fitted to run yacht business than any other? Is that what you are saying, Mr Braine?'

'No!' Matthew replied with slight desperation. 'I am not saying anything of the kind. You are putting words into my mouth. I am merely seeking confirmation of certain allegations so that I can write a book based on fact rather than rumour.'

'We don't publish rumours, Mr Braine.'

The telephone on his desk rang. While Finch took the call, Matthew looked round the room. It was a lawyer's more than an editor's office. There was a long run of bound copies of *The All England Law Reports* and several other legal works including a thick volume on the law of libel.

Finch's caller clearly had a grievance. It was soon apparent that he was seeking a correction of some allegation made in *Labour's Voice*. Finch ended the conversation with a promise to look into the matter further, but as the receiver was replaced the caller's voice was still highly-pitched.

'Let me tell you this, Mr Braine,' Finch resumed, 'you do not know the half of what we could have published. For instance, it was alleged that for twelve years they stole our electricity in the dockyard.'

'Stole it?'

'Unauthorized use is stealing.'

'So the matter was brought to court and there may be records?'

'They settled outside.'

'There were meters, presumably? You mean they tampered with the meters?'

'I do not wish to open old sores by going into further details, Mr Braine. There is so much I could tell you. For instance, do you know that a man died in the dockyard? An overseer. It was alleged that he died because he knew too much.'

'Murdered?'

Finch nodded. 'That was the allegation. By drowning.'

'Who made the allegation?'

Finch spread his arms and shrugged.

'Does it matter? We have people whose business it is to keep their eyes open.'

'And what was the court's verdict in that case?'

'It did not come to court.'

'Oh!' said Matthew. 'I see. Well, I won't waste more of your time. If you could possibly put me in touch with the author of the articles I'm sure he could fill me in.'

'I don't know I could do that,' Finch said, 'but there are two people who maybe could help you. I'll 'phone them. Perhaps you would like to be in touch at the end of the week. I may have news for you.'

'That,' Matthew said, 'got me precisely nowhere.'

'I didn't really think it would,' Sebastian said. 'But it may have given you a clearer picture. Did he keep you waiting?'

'Fifteen, twenty minutes.'

'Not bad. His brother keeps honkies in the corridor for an hour or two, and *he* doubles up as the Minister of Tourism.'

'Sounds as though he needs a P.R. man.'

'He's that too. Oh, well, I think you're ready to pay a call on Charlie Schnitzler.'

'Charlie Schnitzler?'

'Charlie Schnitzler.'

24

FRED got more beautiful for being loved. Between them, Rosemary and her mother cat had done a good job. But the animal's name had been changed to Caesar, since Monesterion kittens did not often fall from the skies under the wheels of passing kings and survive to tell the tale.

The more Matthew saw of the Watkins, the more he liked them. They were so passionately involved in their work, so anxious to press for the right environmental decisions, so ready to spare their clearly over-extended time to entertain whoever dropped in, whether because of an interest in the work of the Trust or, as seemed more often the case, from personal loneliness or worry.

The party on Tabitha Heights was a good example of the trouble the Watkins would go to.

'I've been to a few cocktail sessions in my time,' Matthew said, 'but for originality without pretension this takes some beating.'

Angelique smiled. She was a beautiful girl with a figure-hugging dress that shimmered in the light of the setting sun. Matthew was not good at identifying dress materials; he suspected it was *lamé*; whatever its name, it would have looked vulgar on anyone but a woman with the carriage and colour of Angelique; on Angelique it produced no reservations in his mind whatsoever.

'You've not been here before, then?' she asked.

'Not at dusk and for such an intriguing reason.'

He wondered if she was mulatto or quadroon; it was not something he felt he should ask. With her strong yet fine hair, generous but delicately shaped lips, and slim figure, she had been fortunate in her physical inheritance.

'Don't be disappointed if the green flash is a little... well, disappointing,' she said.

Matthew looked at his watch.

'How long have we got?'

'A few minutes. The sun sinks very quickly once it reaches the horizon.'

'And the flash comes as it disappears?'

'That's the idea. Some complain that nothing happens. It's so quick that if one blinks one may miss it.'

'Sounds like the story of my life,' Matthew said. 'Oh, well, the anticipation is doubtless as pleasant as the event.'

'Is everyone's glass filled?' Rosemary called out.

The guests, most of them lightly but elegantly dressed, were grouped and wandering over the natural rock terrace below the ruined arches. Chilled hock had been served in slim stemmed glasses from the depths of the huge chest the Watkins had brought in their Landrover. Matthew and Angelique were standing on the edge of the terrace overlooking the dockyard hundreds of feet below; the shingled roofs of the old buildings shone silver and rose in the dying sun. The water was beginning to reflect the lights of the yachts as the sky filled with stars. Beyond the harbour the high southern hills stretched into the west, in silhouette more mountainous than by day.

'This place is quite ridiculously romantic,' Matthew said.

Angelique nodded.

'I hear you're a writer. You must be used to describing such things. I envy you. I think I would like to be able to portray beauty in words even more than in paint. I can do neither.'

Her voice lacked the harshness he had grown to expect from non-whites; her accent was a blend of American and European.

'I don't write very romantic books, I'm afraid.'

'Perhaps you will after your stay in Monesterio. It's a place that can change people.'

'You've known it for long?'

'Quite some time. I've worked here since my husband and I parted. I was born in Guadeloupe.'

'That explains your name. Angelique doesn't sound very Monesterion. But surely you were not educated in these islands? You seem - if it doesn't sound rude - so European.'

She smiled.

'I was brought up mostly in Europe; London and Paris, a spell in Rome; several years in America, north and south.'

'Don't you feel, at your age, rather... restricted living here?'

'Not really. I still move about a lot. And maybe I'm not as young as you suppose. Do you remember that song: "She may very well pass for forty-three in the dusk with a light behind her"?'

'I don't believe for a moment,' Matthew said stoutly, 'that you are anywhere near forty-three.'

She laughed.

'Tell me about your book.'

'Which one?'

'The one you are writing.'

'I'm surprised you know about it. Few people do.'

'You must have learned by now that Monesterio is covered by a very active vine. The smallest rumour misses no ears.'

'That's a quaint phrase.'

'A translation, but very true of this island.'

'Yes,' Matthew agreed. 'I'd noticed. If I forgot what I'd had for lunch I think I'd only have to ask the woman across the way.'

'Anyway, you are avoiding my question.'

'I'm not much good at talking about my work, especially before I've finished something.'

'Are you afraid your ideas might be used by someone else?'

'I doubt if they'd be so foolish. No, it's not that. My books usually write themselves. I seldom have a plot in my head before I sit down at the typewriter. As a rule I confront a blank sheet of paper without a clue as to what is going to go on to it.'

'Sounds nerve-racking.'

'It is, especially at my age when there's always the fear that inspiration may be drying up.'

'Oh, come on, who's being misleading about age now? You're in the prime of life with many books ahead of you.'

It was refreshing to discover she was not merely beautiful.

'Wait for it!' Bill called.

All eyes turned to the horizon as the very tip of the great orange globe sank below the seeming edge of the world, just to the east of the dark cone that was Zafada. Matthew stared at the horizon, trying not to blink. It was true, as the sun disappeared there was a split second of turquoise on the very rim of the sea. The guests raised their glasses and cheered and laughed, then resumed their conversations.

'But I suppose you have some idea by now what your book is going to be about?' Angelique resumed.

'Some, yes, but I'm no means clear about the ending.'

'You say it is not romantic, so what is its main theme? Historical? Political?'

'Political to some extent.'

'Present-day politics?'

'Very much so. Yesterday's are excruciatingly boring.'

'European politics?'

'No, here. I've been rather intrigued by... well, a lot of the things that are taking place on the island.'

'Yes, there's quite a lot going on.'

'But it's not just a political novel. In some ways it is proving autobiographical, at least to the extent of depicting some of the things that have happened to me recently, both physically and mentally. I suppose that sounds typical of author-egotism, but as it happens I've usually steered well clear of "me" themes.'

'It's philosophical, then?'

'You could say so. I seem to have shifted my priorities and viewpoints somewhat of late.'

She shivered.

'It's a little chilly, isn't it?'

For Matthew the steady trade wind blowing across the Heights provided perfect conditions, but he remembered the locals' belief that they were enduring winter.

'Why don't we drive down to the Captain's Arms and have a meal?' he invited. 'I see some of the guests are already leaving.'

'That would be lovely,' she said.

'My shack's on the way,' Matthew said. 'You could leave your car outside to spare it some of the worst stretches of road surface.'

He led the way. She backed her car down the side of Buck House.

'I'm feeling a bit blown about,' she said. 'Maybe I could tidy up before we go on?'

'It's not exactly palatial,' he apologized, turning the key in the front door. He switched on the light above the verandah, then went ahead of her, shutting the louvres of those windows whose screens he had learned to be the most punctured and ill-fitting.

'Oh, it's rather run,' Angelique said, 'and very handy for the dockyard.'

His typewriter was on the table, a pile of typed sheets by its side. Angelique touched the pile lightly.

'Your book?' she asked.

'Yes.'

'I'd love to read it,' she said.

She went into the bathroom. When she reappeared Matthew thought she looked even lovelier, despite the brighter, flatter light from the naked bulb overhead. Twenty years earlier he would have had the confidence to show his appreciation. As it was...

'She may very well pass for twenty-three,' he misquoted.

She laughed and tossed her hair. Her laugh was very musical and she had a way of looking at him, her head on one side, as though she found him special.

'You are very chivalrous, whatever your accuracy!'

It seemed all wrong that the difference in their ages should have reduced rather than strengthened his courage. He wanted to take her in his arms; instead, he opened the louvres after turning off the light.

As usual, the Captain's Arms was full. They sat at a table near the water, the only one Esterlyn could provide, but none the worse so far as Matthew was concerned for being well away from the high concentration of tables on the top terrace. It was a steel-band night and Matthew did his best to keep up with Angelique on the dance floor; but she was so much more experienced and mobile that they soon settled for doing their own thing, he, like several of the other white male dancers, stomping manfully in approximate time to the music, jabbing his elbows and lifting his hands above his head, confirming willingness.

'I'm sorry Sebastian isn't here,' he said, panting slightly as they returned to their table. 'I believe he's quite a good dancer when he can be persuaded to perform.'

'Sebastian?'

'Sebastian Rutherford, alias the king of Zafada.'

She laughed. 'Oh, yes, I've heard of him, but I don't think we've met. He keeps a rather low profile.'

'I think the tourists can be a little tiresome when they find out about the kingship bit. I gather even the Government is not entirely happy about someone claiming to be a king of one of the island's dependencies, so one way or another Sebastian has to be careful.'

'He's not very serious about it himself, then?'

'I don't see how he can be. It's a literary "monarchy", titular rather than territorial. All very lightweight and in keeping with a holiday island; or should be. I believe the original "ruler" tried to stake his claim seriously, but the British foreign office weren't having any.'

'Perhaps, with Monesterio's independence on the horizon, they think Sebastian might have ideas of reviving the claim?'

'I doubt it. He's surprisingly more serious about some things than his rather light-hearted view of life may suggest, but I'm pretty certain he's not planning a *coup* over Zafada!'

'I hope not. I think he'd be foolish to claim any territorial rights. There have been a lot of schemes for exploiting Zafada commercially and I suspect the Government in Campbelltown would take very firm action if Sebastian was to play along with some entrepreneur.'

'You sound as though you know something about it.'

She smiled. 'Like you, I've a mild interest in politics.'

She changed the subject and they talked until the band and the waitresses had left the terraces and the last guest had gone. He had found her very easy to get on with; well informed, eloquent, amusing. Good wine was not cheap at the Captain's Arms, but the bottles on the table proved he had grudged none of it. Her engaging laugh and mannerisms, her interest in himself and his ideas, had kept his mind off any thought of passing time. His rule about taking little or no alcohol during creative periods had gone heavily overboard.

'Do you realize,' she said, looking at her watch, 'that we are way past Monesterion bed-time?'

She reached down for her evening bag and took out a small *diamanté*-encrusted mirror; he seemed to remember his mother having something similar. He had not realized until that moment how much of the charm of the island lay in its failure to keep up with the present; it explained why the extroverted young off the yachts struck such a discordant note among the restored buildings of Port St George.

'I'm afraid I've kept you up,' Matthew said. 'I'd no idea it was so late.'

'And I've left my hair-brush in your bungalow,' she said. 'But I've enjoyed every minute.'

As they walked down the now dark approach road to the car park, she took his arm, not formally but leaning into him, her slim body seeming to retain contact with his from leg to shoulder, perfectly in time with his none too steady walk.

'Christ,' he said, 'did we drink two bottles or three?'

'The hock we started with was quite potent,' she said.

He drove the Bustler very slowly.

'You don't want your hair blown about,' he said.

If, as was perhaps improbable, Monesterio set any limit on a driver's alcohol intake, he guessed he must have exceeded it by a good margin. Though the potholes gave excuse enough for swerving, the still sober fraction of his brain was relieved to reach Buck House without incident. They had met no one on the road; except for the inevitable barking dogs in the distance, and the monotonous serenade of the frogs and crickets, the village was asleep.

'What we *ought* to do now is to go for a long walk to Tabitha Heights,' he said. 'To clear our heads.'

'What we are *going* to do is go to bed,' she said.

Her tone of voice left him to take it either of two ways. The recent closeness of her body helped choice.

'If that's an invitation,' he said, 'you're on.'

But with the diffidence of one unaccustomed to take such matters for granted, he made it sound as if he could be joking. He knew he should be making the running more aggressively, but the technique creaked with disuse.

'Would you *like* me to stay a little while?' she pressed.

She was very close to him again, her lips a little apart.

'God, yes,' he said thickly.

She pressed against him and kissed the point of his chin.

'Get into bed first,' she said, 'so that I can leave without disturbing you. I'll go and wash.'

He lay on the bed not believing his luck. When she came out of the bathroom the night sky was light enough to show her nakedness against the dividing curtain. She stood at the foot of the bed, then knelt on it and drew back the sheet he had pulled over himself, sliding beside him as though they shared a long-standing intimacy. A small part of his mind was for a moment a bystander, seeking an adjective less well-worn than sinuous to describe her body's approach; but his mind was not up to synonyms.

She kissed him firmly, seductively, before he had the chance to take the initiative, then felt the evidence of his arousal approvingly.

'No problem there,' she said, closing her mouth on to his once more.

Desire took him suddenly, urgently. He pushed her on to her back and her response was immediate; as he entered her she made a small low noise in her throat; half submission, half warning.

Then, 'Darling,' she said, 'darling, don't leave me behind. Kiss me. Kiss my titties. Hard. Harder! Kiss my...'

It was too late. He came, spending himself uncontrollably. She tried to follow him, but his flaccidity removed the edge of her passion and she lay back, her arms outstretched, resignation rather than satisfaction in her face.

'Oh, Christ!' he said. 'I'm sorry; I really am sorry.'

She smiled wanly, then more generously.

'It doesn't matter. Really. It doesn't matter. First times are often... not the best.'

'I was selfish.'

'It doesn't matter. Don't have a post-mortem. Let's lie quiet. I needn't go yet. When you're ready, kiss my pussy first. I should have said...'

He stroked her hips and legs, the skin baby soft. She was sweating; the odour was slightly sweet, not acrid or sour. He nuzzled her neck, apologizing again.

'Don't worry,' she said, 'don't worry.' Then as his hands stroked her once more, 'No, let's rest for a time. I'll turn over... until your're ready.'

She turned on her side, her body curved into but not quite touching his, her slim neck inches from his mouth. He willed a return of his desire, but his body felt as heavy as his mind. He closed his eyes, sighing deeply with weariness and self-disgust...

When he woke it was full daylight and Angelique had gone. The pillow next to his held a faint, sweet muskiness; a spoor for memory.

25

'HUMANISTS in the best mould,' Matthew said.

Sebastian nodded. 'Doing a very difficult job to the best of their ability. If Overseas Development offered me the Watkins job you wouldn't see my tail for dust.'

The Bustler was coping manfully with roads whose surface took all the driver's attention, but Matthew was able to enjoy the scenery to the full.

'To my mind,' Sebastian said, 'this is the most beautiful part of the island.'

Matthew grunted agreement, his neck twisted to study a passing tree laden with round green fruit the size of footballs.

'I can believe that. These hills looked magnificent last night.'

'Did you meet anyone new?'

'I spent most of the time talking to a rather lovely coloured girl.'

'The Watkins know a lot of people. What was her name?'

'Angelique someone-or-other. Come to think of it, I don't believe I was told her surname.'

Sebastian looked interested.

'Angelique Deshales, I expect. She uses her maiden name since her husband left her.'

'You know her, then?'

'I only met her once, briefly. I doubt if she knew who I was. Terrific figure and intelligent with it.'

Matthew sighed. 'Quite a package.'

Sebastian smiled. 'I can see she made an impression. Tell me more about her.'

Matthew frowned. 'I don't know that I can. We talked about a lot of things, including myself I'm afraid, but I know very little about her. What does she do on this island?'

'Good question. Rumour has it she's tied in with the Government at some level and that her husband left her because she was having it away with a certain Minister.'

'At what level? She certainly seemed informed on political matters.'

'I've no real proof, but I suspect she's the Government's one-woman Intelligence Service.'

'Good God, not the original beautiful spy!'

'Not the original, perhaps, but I can't imagine that on this island there can be another combination of such brain and beauty.'

'Well, it figures,' Matthew said reflectively. 'She knew about you and Zafada. Said you keep a low profile and wanted to know how serious you are about the king thing.'

'There you are, then,' Sebastian said. 'Now you know why even my friends find me reticent. One never knows when one of them may meet a beautiful creole.'

'I said I was pretty sure you had other things to do than fix a Cuban takeover.'

'Next time you see her you can tell her that's definite.'

'I doubt whether I shall. I suspect the Angeliques of this world are a little more than I can handle.'

'Did you..?' Sebastian began.

'Anyway,' Matthew added firmly, 'to return to the present, how far to Charlie Schnitzler's?'

'A few miles yet.'

Sebastian slowed almost to a halt for an exceptionally deep hole in the now concrete road. A tall young black passed them, his long arms flailing the air, his step so buoyant he might have been walking on powerful bed springs. He was singing: 'Ah'm feelin' high, high, high...'

'Wish I felt like he looks,' Matthew said.

'You probably did at his age. But not on grass.'

'Grass?'

'Marijuana.' He swerved sharply, causing Matthew to grab at the roof. 'This road is worse than when I last came this way. By the way, would it make the logistics of living a bit easier if you had use of this car?'

'I was very grateful for the loan of it last night.'

'I thought we might work it so that you had first call on it, keeping it at Buck House. I can't park it in the dockyard, and except for the weekly shop in Campbelltown I've little need of it now I'm stuck into my Port Painting period.'

'You're adjusting to the nautico-artistic life, then?'

'Very happily. Living on your boat has given me new eyes for the dockyard. Have you seen the shingles in the moonlight? I don't know if I shall be able to capture it, but the challenge is terrific.'

'Yes, I noticed the roofs last night. Well, all right then; many thanks; but on the basis that I pay my whack and that you have it whenever you want.'

The steep hills on either side opened out into broad lush valleys and then closed in again, the road winding, climbing and falling through jungle, pasture and plantations of great variety. The road surface was appalling, seldom allowing more than fifteen miles an hour, but it was no hardship to drive slowly through such a paradise.

A woman and three children were collecting weeds by the side of the road.

'I suppose up in these hills they have less money,' Matthew remarked. 'Their clothes are more... well, what one would expect.'

'Few of the blacks are exactly rolling,' Sebastian said. 'But you can't go by their clothes. Some of the houses are almost bare of furniture and what we would regard as basic needs, but there may be clothes hanging from every wall. They put nearly everything on their backs, particularly the women and children. Their judgments of others are based more on how they dress than on anything else. A reaction to the old image of the naked, ignorant savage of slavery days, maybe. Clothing is a symbol.'

The few houses they passed were almost as crowded together as those in the main-road villages. Some of the gardens were planted with vegetables, but many were a tangle of weeds or a bare patch of earth.

'You'd think everyone would grow their own food,' Matthew commented. 'Aren't they encouraged to do so?'

'The mechanics of "encouragement" throw up certain problems. Another is that growing food is not consistent with running all these animals over the land. The goats eat everything in sight.'

'Can't they wire their gardens?'

'Wire's expensive. Anyway, encouraged by the West's priorities, the locals increasingly see meat as a status food, so priority is given to animals rather than to plants; even in areas like this where drought is far less serious.'

'It seems crazy,' Matthew said. 'The place seems ready made for the "good life". What a spot for the lotus-eater!'

'Well, yes, if he wasn't all that hooked on the social life. But you're right in principle. I imagine the people in these parts still eat a lot of plant foods, but the trend is towards a higher proportion of animal products supplemented by supermarket importations from the States.'

'My daughter has strong views about the wastefulness of getting proteins through animals rather than direct from the plants. I must admit her statistics are fairly shaking; something like ten to twenty times as many people can be supported on direct consumption.'

'True enough. Old hat, in fact, to the environmentalists nowadays. In this as in some other respects Monesterio is the microcosm of the West. Yet we bemoan starving and malnourished nations while clinging to the old feeding patterns for no better reason than force of habit.'

'No better, but the strongest.'

The country opened out again into a broad valley in which cattle grazed convincing-looking grass. It could have been Hampshire or Sussex except that some of the trees bore huge green breadfruit and white tic birds stood close to the heads of the cattle, alert for what might be disturbed by the beasts' rasping mouths.

They left the road for a narrower but better maintained lane on the left.

'We're there,' Sebastian announced.

The car climbed steadily for over half a mile and Matthew glimpsed a large white house topping a high bluff. It had the air of a military installation, an impression heightened by a flagpole from which seven or eight flags streamed bravely in the strong breeze. Then they lost sight of the house entirely and passed through an impressive stone arch on whose lintel was cut the words FORT NELSON 1787. A huge rusty anchor hung incongruously from the centre of the arch, so low that it only just cleared the Bustler's roof. A red-lettered notice said 'Private property. Keep out'.

The lane had turned into a driveway which curved round a large stone-walled bed full of magnificent shrubs and flowers. Sebastian stopped the car at the foot of a long flight of ascending stone steps flanked by rusty cannons. The air was suddenly shattered by what sounded like the Hounds of the Baskervilles in full cry. Two powerfully built blacks appeared from nowhere, their scowling expressions a daunting accompaniment to the chilling chorus of the dogs.

'Mr Schnitzler is expecting us,' Sebastian said firmly, sliding out of the Bustler. 'You go tell him Sebastian Rutherford, please.'

One of the boys departed with the message. The other stayed nearby, picking at the leaves of the many-coloured hibiscus which grew in terraces stretching up to the almost hidden house; he was clearly watching their every move.

'Have a look at this,' Sebastian said.

He moved a few yards to where, fronting a large grassy area, a big bronze bell had been expensively hung in a low stone belfry in the base of which, deeply cut into a marble slab, an inscription paid fulsome tribute to Nelson and to his association with the property on which they now stood.

'I didn't realize he'd lived here,' Matthew remarked.

'It came as a surprise to many,' Sebastian replied.

The black reappeared and asked them to follow. They were led to the top of the stone stairs, then instead of entering through the portico over the main door, beside which a tablet confirmed that the fort had been built on the site of the first plantation house in the island, they were taken along winding stepped paths through more walled beds of glorious profusion. Matthew noticed that from the roof of the house a third boy was taking a photograph of them.

'Security,' Sebastian said. 'For the same reason, first-time visitors never get shown in through the main door.'

They ascended a further flight of stairs that led to a wide, curving verandah which extended to the far side of what appeared to be a newer building than the main house. They passed brand new wooden tables with built-in bench seats, a corner bar empty of bottles or other signs of use, and a large glass-walled tank containing not only a variety of many-coloured fish, but small working models of ships sunk, sinking, or firing off cannons in a final act of defiance. The verandah broadened into an open-sided terrace with tables to seat a hundred or more people. The view was breathtaking across mangrove swamps far below to a coconut-palm-fringed bay which might have been lifted from a film set. A plaque in the wall read:

> In Frigate Bay, which you see spread before you, the great Christopher Columbus first landed on Monesterio

Somewhat less breath-taking, but still compulsive viewing, was the man who sat at a table in the far corner of the terrace. Over his huge scarred stomach an open shirt hung to little point. His chest was reminiscent of heavy-duty coir matting, his head hair an unruly, tangled jungle dropping via wide sideburns to a full pirate's beard. His hirsuteness compelled a wide guess as to his age. He wore broad thick-rimmed sunglasses, smoked a cigar with the intensity of a man enjoying his last, and the table before him was laden with some eight or nine piled dishes of food. A doberman below the table was giving a passable imitation of a hunting dog at the feet of Henry VIII.

Charlie Schnitzler half rose and extended a large hairy hand like a cordial gorilla, then sank back panting slightly from the effort.

'Hi!' he said.

The expression and demeanour indicated that he had spoken with gentle friendliness, but the depth and resonance of the single utterance prompted speculation on the decibels had he really been trying.

Matthew eyed the doberman with slight apprehension, but the animal lowered the tone of the encounter by rolling on its back and offering a well-fed belly.

'You're still eating,' Sebastian said.

Charlie waved an amiable hand.

'I got a little hung up. Care to join me?' He gestured to the black. 'Hey, Hubert, get another coupla plates.'

'No, really, thanks,' Sebastian said. 'We've fed. You get on.'

'Tell you what,' Charlie said, 'why don't I get Hubert to show you round the gardens; your friend ain't seen them.'

'I'd like that,' Matthew said.

'Fine,' Charlie said. 'Fine. Hubert, hand 'em over to Humphrey; he knows more'n you do about the flowers and suchlike.'

The fort-like impression was strengthened by Humphrey's conducted tour. His earlier suspicion had given way to an engaging friendliness and he knew every flower by name. The terraces of hibiscus, plumbago, bougainvillaea and a host of less recognizable plants were divided by broad grassy pathways; the retaining walls were a blaze of colour from the trailing geraniums and periwinkle whose riotous but tidy growth spoke of devoted dead-heading and pruning. Humphrey showed them with pride some impressive specimens of amaryllis, billbergia, croton and amaranthus, the weird heliconia, and the even more strange crane flower, assuring them in each case that had they arrived earlier or later in the season the display would have been far more impressive.

'Humphrey grows plants that no one else on the island seems able to manage,' Sebastian said, 'and for him they will flower out of season.'

Humphrey beamed and Matthew felt they had a friend for life.

At every level, and with only a few feet between them, black cannons jutted truculently through the tangle of shrubs and flowers. Matthew made a rough count of several dozen before giving up. Humphrey then led them across the top of the drive and up a stone path at the end of which the flagstaff's base carried yet another marble slab offering further poignant thoughts about 'the greatest naval commander of all time'.

Beyond the flagstaff was a stone structure in one corner of which an engraved slab said 'Officers' Quarters. Built 1767. Rebuilt 1977'. Its roof was a lattice of metal slats on punched steel girders reminiscent of a hangar. The slats were not close-fitting, so allowed air, light and rain to penetrate to the thousands of plastic pots of cuttings and young shrubs stacked on racking all round the walls. An open bed in the centre had been planted with lettuce.

'Charlie was going to keep a helicopter here,' Sebastian said, 'but then his wife thought they had more need of a greenhouse, tropical style.'

'But all these notices,' Matthew questioned, 'and that

verandah, is it a home or a tourist trap?'

'For the present, the former. He's said to be still arguing the toss with bureaucracy as to whether and when it may be commercialized.'

'What does he do, otherwise?'

'He runs a chain of souvenir shops in several of the islands.'

'Must be some chain to have paid for this lot.'

'He has fingers in many pies,' Sebastian said. 'No one can quite keep up with it. Planes, property, fishing fleet, import, export... Rumours are rife.'

'The whole place is like a film set,' Matthew said.

'It's been that too. Twice. Charlie was a film director himself once.'

They followed Humphrey back to the house. Charlie had finished his meal and was drinking black coffee from a pint-sized cup with a fresh cigar. He looked flushed and was coping with a deep, ominous cough that seemed to involve his whole being in the problem of surviving it. His body stopped heaving. He breathed in deeply but carefully as though uncertain that his lung tissue would take the strain, said 'Jesus!' and wiped the back of his hand across his mouth.

'Ya seen it all?' he asked.

'Fantastic,' Matthew said. 'Quite fabulous.'

'O.K., so now I'll show you sump'n else.'

He took them up some more stairs and on to a narrow balcony running all round the top of the house. The large square room into which he led them housed scores of paintings. The colours were vivid, the subjects varied, but mostly people and plants. The pictures were painted with an intensity and vigour that sprang from the canvas and hammered the senses.

'Local artists?' Matthew enquired.

'Mostly Haitian. The bums on this island couldn't even produce the frames.'

'Incredible vitality,' Sebastian said.

'O.K., so now look at these.'

Charlie opened the glass doors of a cabinet which stood in the centre of the room. It was filled with a hundred or more stone effigies of birds, beasts, human faces, and other less discernible subjects, some of them clearly symbolic or erotic. They were all in perfect condition.

'Go on, handle them,' Charlie invited. 'You gotta feel these things.'

They felt heavy. They were beautifully done. They looked as though they were made yesterday.

'How did you acquire such a collection?' Matthew asked.

'Most, from a university museum. A very distinguished professor. I've been offered hundreds of thousands of dollars for 'em. U.S. dollars. I wouldn't sell for all the plunks in Texas. Here,' he added suddenly, rubbing his bare belly, 'I don't feel so good. Humphrey'll see you out.'

'That's how it often is with him,' Sebastian said as they drove away. 'Nothing personal.'

'What's the matter with him?'

'Quite a lot, I should think, but according to his wife, who shares the same roof when she isn't in Europe seeking cultural revitalization in her country of birth, he's obsessional, a manic depressive, and not to be taken in large doses. A book published recently makes him out to be a crook, a pornographer, a dope-pedlar, and a murderer of more people than most of us have hot dinners.'

'All that has been said about him in a book?'

'All that and much more.'

'But what about the libel laws?'

'Above all else, Charlie's a showman. He craves attention like an addict craves a fix. I fancy he has weighed the possible financial gains from instituting proceedings against frightening off publicity. He'd prefer to go on getting the publicity.'

'How much of the charges against him are true? That dog seemed soft enough. Where does he keep the brutes we heard on arrival?'

'He doesn't. That was a tape recording. He's sloppy about animals and they all go tame on him. He kept a leopard once, but it lost all its teeth from too many jelly-babies and got killed by a determined mongoose. A lot of things go wrong for Charlie. Even *he* isn't as feral as he'd make out. With Charlie you need to look below the surface.'

'The more I see of this island,' Matthew said, 'the more I feel like a drop of water on a sheet of hot blotting paper; as though I could disappear without trace any moment.'

'There are a few normal people about,' Sebastian assured him, 'but I must admit I haven't yet met them. By the way, the paintings were genuine.'

'You mean..?'

Sebastian nodded. 'Baloney. Pure codswallop. Cannons, bell, buildings, Nelson association. Eyewash. Even the stuff about Columbus landing in Frigate Bay. He never set foot on the island.'

'But what about the artefacts? The university professor?'

'He's doing time for flogging the biggest load of fakes since you-name-it.'

'Well,' Matthew said, 'at least the hibiscus were genuine.'

'They were Anneliese's doing. I'm sorry she wasn't there; she's the real power behind the throne; but you'll be meeting her later.'

'Shall I?'

'Yes, I forgot to tell you I'm letting you in for another small social occasion. Next Thursday. Back at Charlie's, in fact. I fixed it with Anneliese. I've also fixed you up with a bird.'

'Not Angelique?'

'No, not Angelique.'

'One never knows with you.'

'Listen, mate, if I was on those sort of terms with Angelique I'd probably be human enough to keep her to myself.'

'At your age,' Matthew agreed, 'I'd probably have felt the same.'

26

MORE than once he had thanked his lucky stars that to make his voyage from England convincing he had brought his typewriter. It had withstood the crossing well, not even the capsize doing any harm beyond remedy of oil and commonsense.

Considering the time taken coping with the bare logistics of the simple life, the novel was making good progress. Urge and inspiration had been sustained. He was no longer afraid of having to face up to the disappointment and frustration of a false start. It was still difficult to pin down just what shift of purpose was at work within himself, but there was no doubt at all that he had been given a fresh perspective, a new impetus, and that although still not certain of the book's final direction he had been able strongly and thankfully to submit to the intangible, elusive, often despairing agonies of the creative process. While there was no point in blazoning it about that he had embarked on another book, it need no longer be a secret.

Sebastian was delighted.

'Excellent!' he said. 'Now we can exchange notes. What is it the Quakers hold? Meetings for Sufferings?'

'I sometimes wonder,' Matthew said, 'what lies behind the mad masochism which drives one to wrest a living from a public reluctant to tackle anything more demanding than a magazine or a wine list; but if it's in the bloodstream one has just got to submit to it.'

The previous day had been exhausting, beginning with a visit to Mrs Cornelius's boutique in Campbelltown where he had paid a frightening sum to have a sea island cotton skirt sent to Rebecca for her birthday. As Mrs Cornelius gave him his receipt she had confirmed how much she was looking forward to having him round for dinner when the pressure eased a little.

The day had begun and ended with the car playing most of its almost inexhaustible repertoire of tricks. After a blockage in the feed pipe, a puncture and a slipped fan belt, the Bustler had crowned an afternoon spent exploring disused sugar mills in the centre of the island by developing a distributor neurosis which gave him an after-dark two-hour bunny hop through torrential rain. It stopped moments before he got to Buck House. Tired and tense, he decided to take a short walk before bed. He climbed to the top of the village, guided by music and singing to the church whose interior walls of celestial blue were bathed by such a concentration of electricity that the arrival of a few angels amidst the blue and gold and paeans of praise would have seemed more commonplace than miraculous. He stood in the road listening to the thumping and the singing. The open doors gave glimpses of the packed, swaying congregation, and their enthusiastic voices filled the warm night air with the command to 'Take joy, joy, joy in de Lord.'

When he returned to Buck House it was to discover that a less religious Saturday night celebration was beginning in the bungalow next door. He had a meal, then read in mounting heat behind closed louvres until his eyes could no longer focus on the page. He washed and turned out the lights before opening the louvres and lying in the dark with his pillow wrapped round his ears. The party ended at the unusually moderate hour of one in the morning. When the last door had been smashed joyfully into its frame by the retiring revellers, Matthew dozed off with the long sigh of a man well content to call it a day.

At one-thirty he was dragged from deep sleep by a frenzied rapping on the glass panel in the front door. His sleep had been so sound that as he surfaced he had time for a brief dream of being awoken by hysterical warnings of fire. He leaped out of bed, his heart pounding, his mind sorting dream from reality only when half way across the cool linoleum. He pulled the door open. A black man stood on the verandah.

'De blessins of de Lord be on yo', suh,' the man said.

'Eh?' Matthew said, squeezing his eyelids together and blinking.

'Suh, 'scuse me, but Ah'd 'preciate it if yo' could do me a small favour.'

Matthew shook his head in an attempt to clear it.

'It's the small hours of the morning,' he said with wary objectivity, stretching his lids and pushing his eyebrows towards his ears with weak fingers.

'Yes, suh, Ah 'preciate Ah've woken you, but mah family an' me, yo' see, we'd like it if yo' was to take us to de top o' de hill.'

There was a pause; a moment for digestion.

'To the top of the hill? What hill? Tabitha Heights?'

He switched on the verandah light, revealing in the road the Bustler on the verge and the faint outlines of a woman and some seven or eight children of various sizes, but all on their feet and showing no signs of crisis.

'Yes, suh, de Heights 'd do nicely.'

Encouraged by the signs of communication, the woman and children crowded on to the verandah and watched the negotiations hopefully, sixteen white eyeballs against the black background of the tropical night. The woman was alarmingly pregnant. Matthew felt in need of cross-checking. The night was fine and clear. As well as sixteen eyes his visitors had sixteen perfectly sound legs.

'You want me,' he said slowly, 'to dress and then take you all up to Tabitha Heights?'

Several mosquitoes surged purposefully through the doorway, no longer deterred by any residues from the aerosol.

'Ah'd 'preciate dat, suh.'

'Well, I can't,' Matthew said. 'It's out of the question. The car isn't working. It took me twenty minutes to cover the last thirty yards and I'm waiting for the blasted thing to be carted away by the sharks who hired out such garbage.'

The other looked shocked to hear of the deceit and insensitivity of which man was capable.

'Ah sure am sorry to hear dat, suh. Yo' mus' get Jenson Ford to fix it fo' yo' and den pass de bill on to dose pipple.'

'I don't want to know anything more about it,' Matthew said. 'It is cheaper, more reliable, and kinder on the nerves, to walk everywhere. To walk,' he repeated. 'Now, I'm sorry, but I'm trying to do a job and must get some sleep.'

The family retreated, saddened by the shafts of fate, but resigned.

He returned to bed, his nerves so jangled that sleep was once again far beyond reach. He passed futile minutes wondering what it could be about himself that should prompt a totally unknown family to expect a fun ride in the small hours of the morning. The only explanation he could think of was that they had been singing the praises of the Lord in the church up the hill and had left the service uplifted by expectation of the love of man.

The flight of mosquitoes had begun to zero in on him. He groaned, reached for the vinegar bottle, and covered himself from head to foot. The buzzing grew more angry but did not go away. The dogs and the cocks were in full chorus by the time sleep came.

When he woke at eight the life of the village was firing on every cylinder. The rats in the roof, who had not made their presence fully known until Sebastian had drawn his attention to them, appeared to be playing some form of rodent football before settling down to whatever routine normally occupied them during the day. They skittered and slithered on the thin plyboard ceiling, through the loosely battened joints in which showered a fine dust compounded, Matthew guessed, of the droppings and decay of decades.

Having cleared the table of his breakfast, Matthew sat at the typewriter and sought creative mood. But the night had left him exhausted and the sun was already topping up the heat inside the bungalow. He opened all the louvres, but the morning was windless and the nylon curtains hung limply to the floor. The past few days had produced breezes which, if not strong enough to attain the ideal conditions in which the curtains flew horizontally across the room, had at least made the place bearable.

On those days, also, the Monesterion Electricity Company's morning power cuts had kept the refrigerator mercifully quiet apart from the occasional thud of a falling slab of ice. Today the Company grudged the housewife nothing and the room thrummed to the ancient motor which added a degree or two to the sticky, airless heat of the room. It was but one noise among many, but its insistence got on his nerves.

He groaned and stuck his fingers into his ears, resting his elbows on the formica-topped table. This made matters worse. The vibration from the refrigerator passed along the wooden floor and up through the metal legs of the table whose surface acted as a kind of sound box, conducting through his arms and fingers a drumming that was not just audible but made physical attack upon his ear drums.

There was a knock on the door and two children asked him to sponsor them for a walk in aid of new sports equipment for their school. He had already learned that Monesterion sponsorship meant cash on signature, so he realistically parted with a couple of bee-wees and the children left happily. They were followed ten minutes later by a Jehovah's Witness who took fifteen minutes to get the message that she was working on a lost cause. Virgil and Ann-Marie appeared to be presenting precisely the same problems their mother had been coping with ever since Matthew moved into Buck House, and the cars, dogs and radios maintained the conviction of the villagers that anything in life worth doing is worth doing at maximum pitch.

Matthew had an idea. He would call on the Watkins.

'It's marvellous,' he told Sebastian. 'I just open the shutters at both ends of the room and the wind whips straight in off the water. I've got by with two showers a day instead of the usual five or six and my brain is twice as clear.'

The Watkins had found the solution. The old officers' quarters overlooking the main quay were being slowly rehabilitated as funds became available, and Matthew had been given free use of the south gallery which was earmarked to be turned into a library run by the Trust. The room was unfurnished except for a chart table, but the Trust's gift shop lent him a chair whose height he raised a few inches by standing it on bricks. He kept his papers from flying across the dockyard with the weight of an old shutter-bar and lumps of coral collected from the beach when taking the daily swim that was now part of his ritual.

'So the book's roaring along?' Sebastian enquired.

'At the moment, like that boy we passed the last time we came this way, I'm feeling high, high, high. When your painting's going well, do you get this sense of elation? Almost like the early stages of being sloshed?'

'Invariably. Maybe that's why we do it.'

'Would you believe it if I told you I left England with the intention of killing myself?'

Sebastian smiled. 'I believe most things,' he said, 'even if there is no apparent reason to do so. But was this just because your work was not going well?'

Matthew explained his mood prior to and during the early part of his voyage, though he found some difficulty seeing it in perspective, so overlaid was his past by the present creative euphoria.

'Maybe I could take my life if circumstances were bloody enough,' Sebastian said, 'but I'm not sure I could sustain a serious view of myself to the point of seeing it through. One has to be pretty solemn to get round to wrist-slitting. And, anyway, the thing with suicide is that one doesn't just reason oneself into it. There has to be despair.'

'I wish I'd more of your caustic attitude to life,' Matthew said. 'I've become a pretty gloomy sod over the years.'

'The best antidote to gloom is awareness of one's own absurdity.'

'In a way, that's what made up my mind. The best of jokes grow stale.'

'I wonder,' Sebastian said, 'how much of your decision was a kind of "I'll-show-you" defiance to a world not appreciating your talents?'

'The shrinks might say so. It's also a matter of age. You're nearer to my children in your thinking. Maybe an older generation can't cope with more than glimpses of a better pattern; can't sustain the incentive to go all out and attain it.'

'I certainly get depressed at times,' Sebastian admitted, 'but so far I haven't felt defeated by life.'

'We're both humanists in our way,' Matthew said, 'but yours is a slant I wouldn't exactly call religious, yet it seems something more than belief in the human mind to find all the answers.'

'A lot of people seem doubtful about humanism in its narrowest form; some of the young especially. All right, they see such material goals as controlled population, self-sufficiency, de-industrialization and so forth, but a number seem in tune with something more fundamental.'

Matthew nodded. 'You could be right. It may sound nonsense, but this book I'm on seems to be taking over. Its characters are having perceptions I can't really claim to be my own. Yet I've an irrational kind of faith in it I find it difficult to explain. I feel it may serve as some kind of bridge.'

'Between generations?'

'Partly. This division by generation thing needs tackling. I heard from Rebecca this morning, enclosing letters from the girls. Maybe distance is just making the heart grow fonder, but I feel I'm communicating with them more successfully now.'

'Or they with you?'

'If you like. But it goes deeper than that. I'm aware of changes in myself that are more than home-sickness or the revival of a tired mind.'

'Purpose regained? I haven't been through your single-hander experiences, but maybe personal danger, reminder of one's insignificance, time to reflect, survival disciplines, a goal however seemingly dead-end, can bring a kind of awareness; a sense of the underlying unity of life.'

'You don't half beat hell out of that concept,' Matthew said with a smile.

'A propos what you told me about that flying fish,' Sebastian said, 'I copied this out for you this morning. Old Josh. Slocum.'

The slip of paper read:

> In the loneliness of the dreary country about Cape Horn I found myself in no mood to make one life less in the world, except in self-defence, and as I sailed this trait of the hermit character grew till the mention of killing food animals was revolting to me.

'Hermit character?' Matthew said. 'Maybe. I think it was something more. It seemed to tie up with how I felt on top of Zafada. I'll never forget that.'

'Moments of breakthrough often seem a matter of timing,' Sebastian said.

'Breakthrough?' Matthew's voice was wary. 'I hope you're not going to spoil a beautiful friendship by selling me religion. You're up against a lifetime of consumer resistance. I've loathed the exclusiveness, humbug and intolerance of organized religion since an early age.'

Sebastian laughed. 'Don't worry. But this feeling you had at sea and on Zafada - I suspect it was what many people have known: a kind of felt understanding; a spiritual symbiosis if you like. Nothing to do with religion in any sectarian, organizational sense.'

'Certainly not in my case.'

'Fair enough. But the feeling you had - have maybe shared with others - is the important thing. From it, the others have taken a path leading to notions of a God, and finding it comforting have started sticking labels...'

'And that, as the Irishmen said, is where the trouble started.'

'Right. But where for them the ingredients of wonder, fear, the need for a sense of direction and a framework for behaviour, brought belief in a deity, for others it may have another meaning.'

'This more universal, more compassionate humanism you've been on about?'

'Well, something wider, certainly, than... what's that ringing phrase? ... anthropocentric humanism. As I see it, paying regard not just to man's rights but also to his obligations to all other life forms and to the possibility of there being something beyond our present vision.'

'There you are! God again.'

'No, why? That "something" could be a better concept of life, or a great blank, a limitless void of gunge. No one knows. And in our present crude state of evolution I don't think we can expect to know. It doesn't matter. We're too insistent on knowing, too little prepared to be shown by forces outside our circumscribed understanding. That's why the Christian religions have lost credibility. Like science, the Church is too clamorous with the answers; too certain of its monopoly.'

'I don't disagree with that; if the young are taught to use their minds, even in pursuit of unsatisfying goals, they must reject churchianity. But you're only saying that if superstition and blind faith is shown the front door, it will return by the back.'

'Not at all. Look, for decades, through two world wars and God knows how many smaller ones, the more thinking young have resisted such obvious contradictions as the conspiracy between Church and State in politics and war, and the Church has lost umpteen followers by its hypocrisy. At times the baby has doubtless been lost with the bath water. But to-day the gulf has been widened by a further factor; the environmental factor, if you like. The Church is being seen as out of touch not only with men - for all its self-defeating attempts to turn into an army of sociologists - but also with any remotely acceptable concept of a loving God.'

'Some might think you're for anarchy,' Matthew said.

'In which case I'd have proved a lousy communicator.'

'You still use the term "God".'

'Only in the sense of suggesting the unknown factor, the something that in the interests of purpose and sanity we must assume is greater than ourselves. But I agree. Words are hell – restricting, blinkering, division-making. Maybe that's another reason why the precepts of orthodoxy are no longer acceptable. We don't want to be tied down by words any more than by irrelevant rituals. There's more comfort in concepts.'

'Well,' Matthew said, 'if my novel gets published I hope you'll recognize some echoes.'

The Bustler's nearside front wheel took a pot-hole without fuss, but the nearside back gave a jarring 'clunk'.

'Have you noticed,' Sebastian said, 'how often when the answers to the world's problems are at the finger tips, some trifling example of our inadequacy brings us back to earth?'

They got out.

'Such as a flat tyre,' Matthew said.

The wheel took only minutes to change. The spare had no tread at all. They were between Freeman's Village and Wilberforce.

'We'd better to try to get it seen to,' Sebastian said.

He drove slowly on full beam. At the garage four youths were lying and squatting in the forecourt, twitching to the deafening output of a big black and steel radio-recorder with dozens of knobs and dials.

'Good,' said Sebastian. 'The boy in the red shirt works here.' He switched off the engine.

'No gas, man; we're closed,' the boy said.

'I've a puncture. Got to make Frigate Bay and back. You fix it? It's worth a ten.'

The boy shook his head. 'We're closed, man.'

'You've got the air there; it'd take you five minutes,' Sebastian said good-humouredly. 'A ten's good pay.'

The boy looked as though he might weaken, but one of the others, his Rasta dreadlocks bobbing to the music, led the rest in a half-chanted protest against the interruption, and the boy joined them.

'We'll just have to drive slowly and rely on that something or other that in the interests of purpose and sanity we must assume is greater than ourselves,' Matthew said drily.

Sebastian grinned.

'I don't think we're a bad example of a symbiotic relationship,' he said.

The Bustler chugged cautiously back on to the dark road, its puny headlights the only illumination in the moonless night. The tiny engine did its best to accompany the painfully unrehearsed rendering of 'Abide With Me' as they weaved through the potholes towards the bay Columbus never knew.

27

'I DON'T get it,' Matthew said. 'I thought Charlie hadn't opened this place to the public.'

'He hasn't, darling,' Brenda said. 'This is a Special Party night, by invitation only.'

'But he charges?'

'Sure he charges. Charlie's a nothing's for nothing man. He's got the setting, the service, the food, the wine. There's no place to touch it, and Charlie knows it.'

'It certainly seems the opposite of buying one's friendships.'

'The way he lives, he's not going to spurn a fast buck. Anyway, this is a P.R. exercise as much as anything. When you get to know this island a little better, it'll all begin to make sense.'

'I suspect there's more to Charlie than meets the eye,' Matthew said.

'That, darling,' Brenda said, 'is the understatement of the season.'

She had brought the Bishops in her reliable jeep and was Sebastian's idea; not a bad one, Matthew thought. By comparison with Angelique's, her voice was less like a courting dove than a chain-saw tackling seasoned teak, but her outward charms could have been overlooked only by a man of terminal indifference. By popular opinion in the region of forty, Brenda gave away nothing to Angelique in the way of figure and carriage. Matthew had noticed her soon after his arrival, admiring her wobble-free negotiation of the dockyard's rough stone paths in high-heeled shoes which matched her beautifully-cut powder-blue dress. The contrast with the casual and sparse coverings of the yachting crowd was more effective than any poster she might have erected for the sail-repair business she ran on the quay. Matthew had told her soon after his arrival that when his new mast was ready he hoped to do business with her. She had said 'That's all right, darling,' with the air of one who could wait for small favours. Her accent left no doubt of her South African background, and her grasp of the ways of men in a dockyard attracting an ever-changing stream of wealthy and lustily extroverted multi-nationals was soon apparent; management of both business and femininity had given her an aura that had something of the quality of high-tensile steel.

Matthew saw Mrs Cornelius and her husband at a table across the floor.

'Do you know them?' he asked Brenda.

'Of course, darling. Everyone knows everyone.'

'Does she do well with her shops?'

'She can't help but do well. She's a goer. She must be getting fifteen hundred a week for her Green Hills house.'

'I didn't realize she was letting it. I thought they'd moved out because the social life was too heavy.'

'Darling, do you write poems too?'

'Yes, all right,' Matthew agreed, 'I suppose it was naïve of me.'

He did not recognize the faces at the other tables, but their common bond was cragginess and arrogance with little distinction between male and female. It was clearly a gathering of those who were rich, powerful and intending to stay that way.

At their own table the Richardsons and the Schnitzlers completed the party. 'I thought the Bishops might like to be in on it,' Sebastian had said. 'Sir Alf may be doing some reporting when he returns to London.'

Charlie's staff were remarkably efficient. The service was impeccable, the food excellent, the measures of pina colada generous. Although Charlie's manner was relaxed, his eyes were everywhere, and the lift of a finger brought a black to their table. The waiters were large, healthy specimens dressed in white linen suits of almost military style, and in the rare moments when they had nothing to do they stood at ease on the perimeter of the verandah with their hands behind their backs and their attention on the needs of the diners. It was like another world.

'How on earth does he do it?' Matthew asked.

'Who, do what, darling?'

'How does Charlie get these boys to set such a high standard?'

'It's part of the package,' Brenda said. 'What has Sebastian told you about Charlie and Anneliese?'

'Not a lot.'

'Get him to fill you in sometime.'

'Why can't you tell me?'

'I'm making my living on this island, darling,' Brenda said cryptically.

An enormous black in trousers and shirt of the same colour moved into the centre of the verandah where he was lit by concealed lamps. His shirt was open to the waist and a thrice looped chain of fine gold gleamed across his wide chest. His huge fingers strummed a guitar and his deep strong voice left no doubt of his professionalism:

> 'Back to back,
> Belly to belly,
> I don't care a damn...'

The tables clapped his first song. The applause was as much invitation as response. He hummed and strummed before launching into another calypso:

> 'Yes, I have heard when you die after burial
> You have to come back as some insect or animal.
> Well, if is so, I don't want to be a donkey,
> Neither a goat, sheep or monkey.
> A fellow say he want to come back a hog.
> Not the Spoiler. I want to be a bed bug.'

Smiles and clapping encouraged him.

> 'Because I'm going to bite them young ladies, pardner,
> Like a hot dog or a hamburger,
> And if you know you are thin, don't be in a fright,
> It is only big fat women *I'm* going to bite.'

Two women at a table for four amply matched the bed bug's ideal. Their pink faces suggested recent importation as guests of the leathery-faced couple with them. They smiled self-consciously, but laughed, and others joined in to confirm the spirit of the thing. The singer's voice grew louder:

> 'Well, believe me, friends, so help me bless,
> I'll be a different bed bug from all the rest;

I ain't biting no ordinary people,
You have to be quite sociable and respectable,
Such as female doctors and barristers,
Duchesses, and Princesses with nice figures;
And when I bite them, friends, I going to boast,
I calling myself "King Bed Bug the First".'

Charlie thumped the table. 'Hey, boy,' he roared, 'that's the virgin-aunty version. Give 'em "Miss Muriel's Treasure".'

But the Spoiler was too much the artist to be told what to sing. He finished The Bed Bug and began a medley of songs, some calypsoes, some romantic favourites from the period most of the diners would know best. His voice was so powerful that his audience either drifted into glazed submission or competed by talking at the tops of their voices.

With Charlie and Sir Alfred leading the conversation at each end of the table, Matthew and Sebastian could give attention to either. Brenda was soon proving to Charlie that the ripeness of his stories left room for improvement. Sebastian was diverting a little of the respect being shown by Lady Bishop for Charlie's improbable evaluation of his own sexual prowess and inclinations, but it was an uphill fight consisting largely of putting Charlie down with ironical asides of which she was the more appreciative.

'Listen, *Sir* Bastian, kingo,' Charlie broke off, 'have you thought any more about that plan of mine for your island?'

'His island?' Lady Bishop queried.

'Sure, he's king of an island near here. Zafada. You didn't know?'

'I keep quiet about it, Charlie,' Sebastian said. 'You know why.'

'How exciting,' Lady Bishop said.

'I've told him how we can make a killing out of it,' Charlie said. 'Luxury restaurant and marina for the big yachts. Heliport. Casino. Tax-haven, even. But kingo here, he won't buy it. Can't figure why. I could make him a million.'

'It's all a fantasy, Charlie, and you know it. I don't own the island and I'm not a real king.'

'I could fix all that. You don't have to be a real anything around here. Don't get thrown by detail. Just leave it to me.'

'If ever you are tired of life, Lady B.,' Sebastian said, 'just apply to Charlie. He'll think up some fantastic scheme whereby he makes a fortune and you go on to better things in a blaze of publicity.'

'I'll remember that.'

'Trouble with you Brits,' Charlie growled, 'is you lost your spirit of adventure when you sent over that first boat-load. I'm tellin' ya, there's a gold-mine in that island out there.'

'And you'd doubtless find all the right seams, leaving me to sort out my credentials and motives with Campbelltown and London. No, thanks!'

'Pity,' Brenda said, 'I'd have liked to start a boutique on Zafada.'

'What a ghastly thought,' Matthew said. 'Places like that should be left to the birds. Literally.'

'Christ!' Charlie said, throwing his eyes to the ceiling. 'You Brits!'

Sir Alfred's end of the table was not doing so well. Conversation had cantered slowly down the more familiar course of where people lived, for how long they had been there, and whether they had family. Betty Richardson, employing with Sir Alfred the tactics he himself had used to establish rapport with Oslin Stedmore, was proving a sympathetic ear, and the talk turned without undue resistance on Sir Alfred's part to a résumé of his career. Anneliese Schnitzler also appeared to be hanging on his words.

Matthew studied her with interest. She was a tiny, soft-voiced woman, some years younger than her husband. Several of her remarks revealed a quaint grasp of the use and weight of English words. She was fair and wore her thin hair in a small, tight, rather untidy top-knot, and although her face was intelligent and mobile she was not the raving beauty Matthew had somehow expected. Her manner was so retiring and shy that she seemed almost to be apologizing for her existence, yet although her self-effacement implied guilt at the presumption of holding an opinion, what she actually said - though in the gentlest and most reasonable of voices - could seem a little out of character. The tone bore no relation to some of the things she came out with.

'Now that is almost what I said the other day to Charlie,' she remarked, her eyes big and frank when Sir Alfred had mentioned the impertinence of an Under-Secretary who had tried to tell him his job. 'I said it was not right that he should get so cross with the solar heating engineer who came to install the system.' Her hands fluttered in a submissive, defenceless gesture, like larks caught in lime. 'But Charlie said I should not be such a sodding bloody idiot. He said I was a stupid brainless cow and did not understand the ways of the world.' Her eyes and hands collaborated in a compound of helplessness and appeal. 'I feel sure he is wrong about me, Sir Alfred. I think I do know about the world. I really cannot understand him at times.'

Charlie spared Sir Alfred the need to reply.

'If you're on again about Rudy Mazlin, Annie,' he bellowed, 'jus' lay off, will ya? These folk are here to enjoy themselves. They don't want to hear a heap of crap about Rudy Mazlin.'

As Matthew had only just been able to hear what Anneliese had said, he supposed Charlie lip-read.

'I was going to amuse them by telling them what you had said, Charlie,' Anneliese rebuked gently with wide, hurt eyes. 'About how you told him that higher technology was nothing but advanced banana-peeling. Of course, it rather rude of you to talk to Rudy that way, seeing he was a guest in our house...'

'You're just getting at me again, Annie,' Charlie began.

'Shut up, Charlie,' Brenda said. 'Tell them how you first met Annie.'

He waved a hand impatiently.

'Aw, they don't want to hear all that balls.'

'All right,' Brenda said, 'I'll tell them.'

'Yes, go on, Brenda,' Peter said, 'they'll get a more accurate picture from you.'

'For Crissake,' Charlie said, 'there was nothing to it. I met her on the island. She decided I'd do. That was it.'

'You're missing out the best bits,' Betty said.

'Like the pussy allowance,' Brenda added.

'That was a tax gambit,' Charlie said dismissively.

'Charlie advertised in newspapers abroad,' Brenda explained. 'For girls.'

'As crew,' Charlie put in. 'For my yachts. Bona fide.'

'For his yachts. Bona fide. He gave this picture of a rich, husky, desirable male with his own yachts and plane. When they arrived he laid those who were willing and put the whole thing down to expenses.'

'I was chartering the yachts. It was legit.'

'And you were the one who stayed?' Matthew asked Anneliese.

'Oh, no,' she said softly, 'I was here already.'

'Yeah,' Charlie said, 'every day I'd see her. That was when I had a house the other side of the island. Every day she'd swim backwards and forwards in the bay with nothing on save that damn hat.'

'It was a very nice hat, Charlie,' Anneliese protested. 'Very becoming. You said so.'

'A bathing hat?' Lady Bishop asked.

'Straw. Black straw with a very wide brim. I bought it in Munich. With a red hibiscus pinned to the ribbon it was very pretty.'

'It must have been,' Lady Bishop said. 'But with the rest of you as you were, didn't you feel a little over-dressed?'

'To and fro, to and fro,' Charlie reminisced. 'Sundays she'd bring a leopard with her, on a leash, and give it over to some big blond buy while she swam. First, I thought she was screwy. Time came when if she missed a day I'd get worried. It got like it was a kinda fixation or something.'

'But it worked, eh, Charlie?' Sebastian said.

'Yeah,' Charlie agreed gloomily, 'she fixed me all right. But good.'

He seemed to have lost a lot of his ebullience.

'Our meeting was much less romantic,' Lady Bishop said with a sigh.

The two tangled clumps of coarse hair which divided Sir Alfred's powerful brow from the rest of his face, rose two inches then came down over his eyes like shutters, making them invisible. He said nothing.

The waiters were bringing to each table a small, whole pig on a huge silver dish. It had a persimmon in its mouth and its eyes had been replaced by purple passion fruit, turning what might have been pitiful into a creature both baleful and edible. It was garlanded with hibiscus and bougainvillaea and surrounded by fruits and vegetables of many colours and sizes. The guests murmured appropriately.

'Tell us, Lady B.,' Sebastian invited.

'I was in the Civil Service. I went to a meeting Alfred was addressing and got up and challenged what he had said.'

'Nothing like that had ever happened to me before,' Sir Alfred said mildly. The memory still seemed to hold an element of surprise. 'I found it most stimulating.'

'I think he felt from then on that he'd better keep an eye on me,' Lady Bishop said. 'You know, like inviting a leading Trade Unionist to dinner. Not because you necessarily want to...'

'*We* just met on a boat,' Betty said. 'Very ordinary I'm afraid.'

'What's ordinary about meeting on a boat in this part of the world?' Sebastian asked gallantly. 'I'll bet it was a snow-white schooner with coal-black sails.'

'Tan, actually,' Betty said. 'It belonged to Paul Getty or the Aga Khan or someone.'

Matthew decided that neither of his first meetings with his own wives bore comparison.

'We came to see the Schnitzlers' pictures the other day,' he said.

'They'd interest you, Cynthia,' Sebastian told Lady Bishop. 'A splendid collection.'

'You ain't seen nothing,' Charlie rumbled complacently. 'My private collection'd make your eyes fall out. Not only your eyes, either.'

'Now Charlie is going to boast about his voodoo masks and his erotica,' Anneliese warned. 'He can be so bloody boring. So childish.'

'Aw, shit!' Charlie said. He speared a piece of lobster and chewed it morosely.

'Really,' Anneliese said, 'why do American and English people have to *talk* about sex so much? If they're all that interested they should just get down to it, then think about something else. That's what I do. After all, it's not so different from having a good crap. Do it and forget it, that is what I would say.'

'What's this about Big Daddy?' Sebastian asked Peter.

'You mean about the cable?'

Sebastian nodded. 'Don't spare us the gory details. Big Daddy is always good for a story.'

Slices of the pig were being handed round, nestling pinkly in the centre of a variety of vegetables.

Peter grimaced.

'This one's quite nasty,' he said. 'Big Daddy,' he explained to Lady Bishop, 'is a nickname for Captain White, our dockyard policeman.'

'A corrupt black bastard,' Charlie supplied. 'And you can quote me.'

'Just be quiet, Charlie,' Anneliese murmured, 'there's a good boy.'

'Big Daddy can be a bit tiresome if he gets his knife into any of the visitors,' Peter continued, 'and yesterday he had a set-to with an American who came in on a big yacht and didn't see eye to eye on little matters like hanging around in Liberty Cove waiting to be cleared. He claimed he used to be able to send a boat out to collect the immigration people.'

'Which he could,' Charlie put in, 'before the Black Bureaucracy.'

'Anyway,' Peter went on, 'they had a flaming row and the American sent a cable to his embassy to complain of the treatment he was receiving in Port St George.'

'That's a serious move to make,' Betty said. 'Very political.'

'Where it's got nasty for us,' Peter said, 'is that the cable was sent through Tom Riley who sees to the telex and ship-to-shore side of things. Big Daddy, who's always quick to have a go at Tom, has accused him of complicity and God only knows what.'

'Black dirt,' Charlie said. 'That's what that guy is, black dirt. I could tell you...'

'Charlie...' Anneliese did not raise her voice, but her husband subsided again like a douched ember.

'He's saying more than that, Peter,' Betty added. 'Big Daddy is claiming that Tom prompted the cable; that it was his idea.'

'Listen,' Charlie said, the strain too much, 'and you can quote me: old man Finch told me with his own mouth that the biggest mistake he ever made was to educate the people of this island. Well, goddam it, he's right, though things could've been better if he'd made a job of it. All they've allowed on to the island have been fourth-grade teachers with fifth-grade notions of egalitarianism and all that cock. Not one of them with a better qualification than some crappy bit of paper to prove a pass in sociology or somesuch. But they all think they know what makes niggers tick, mind. So we've got a population of near-illiterates carrying half-baked chips about missing out and being owed a living and not doing anything demeaning like a day's hard work. I tell you, just look at this sodding place. It's no more than a crop-starved, under-irrigated, mis-managed niggers' breeding pen depending on the crutch of a resented tourist industry. That's no bloody basis for an economy.'

'What I can never understand,' Lady Bishop said firmly, 'is why people who dislike the blacks so often choose to live among them.'

Charlie hit his side plate with a spoon, breaking it in half.

'You got me wrong, lady,' he bellowed. 'Hating or loving the blacks don't come into it. Black's a good, clean word, make no mistake. If you don't like my talk about niggers, let me tell you that's what I call the servile phonies who earn hotel money, spitting in your soup and loathing your white guts, or who crawl to corrupt politicians who are only after power and use slave-consciousness to extort subsidies from Britain and the U.S. We're not in a simple black versus white situation out here. There's black and black same as there's white and white. The Government's blacks either toe the local line or leave the island to take punk jobs in the U.K. and the States, ending up ripe for black-minority agitation and disruption. *My* blacks know where they stand.'

'Your blacks?' Matthew queried.

'Sure. Listen, I'll tell you sump'n. Either you let these boys get corrupted by the stinking lifestyles of London and New York where they end up more bloody miserable than they ever were on the plantations, or you give them pride in their ability to do a decent job for decent pay and proper status. Discipline with status, that's what most of the world responds to.'

'But we're still not clear what you meant by *your* blacks,' Lady Bishop persisted.

'The blacks I employ. In my shops. On this estate. All over. They're the cream of the island, I'm tellin' ya. O.K., and of one or two other islands, maybe. And why? They know where they stand. They eat well, they dress well, they're fed well, they don't drink ... not on my land, anyways ... they've been taught their job, and they're into religion but heavy. I'm tellin' ya, I have no trouble from these boys. For why? Because I treat them better than anyone else on this island, and a whole way better than their own mob. Sure, they work and they work hard, for blacks that is, and they get paid and treated according. They've nothing to complain of. For the rest? I'll tell ya. Not one in one hundred has the spunk to earn an honest buck. For them it's wealth without work or they don't want to know. They're conditioned – by their own history and by the degenerates who are in power on this island. They'd rather lie around all day soaking up sunshine and racist garbage put out by myopic politicians. By Christ, if all that muck ever roused the bastards, it'd be a blood-bath. There's only Coca Cola and imported technology – and, all right, a whole load of natural idleness – between us and savagery. The blacks' brains are eidetic. No one seems to see that. They can visualize a skull split with a machette, and the day's coming when the commies and liberals'll kid 'em that violence will heal the slave scars and give 'em world status; that sacrificial retribution will create wealth for all without that most degrading of all things, hard work. You gotta believe it. I tell ya, they can't visualize liberty, liberalism, justice and other abstracts. But the cult of the anti-white is a specific they can comprehend, as it involves action and violence. They are pawns for violence, a fact that the liberals trying to coax them into Western lifestyles can't see for the rosy mists of equality. I'm tellin' ya, and you can quote me...'

'All right, Charlie,' Anneliese said, 'you've made your point.'

'My impression,' Matthew said carefully, 'is certainly that resentment is being deliberately fostered towards the whites; which is not to say the whites don't sometimes help it along.'

'Of course it's being fostered, for Pete's sake,' Charlie said, 'but what the jungle bunnies'll do to the whites and vice versa ain't nothing to what the blacks'll do to their own kind. The black élite keep the rest down financially, intellectually and socially for their own ends. The whole set-up's a kinda...'

'Slavery in indolence?' Sebastian suggested.

'Right. Token education, low wages, heavy unemployment, just enough service trade to keep the hotels running, but all the time a calculated balance between inertia and hate so as no-one gets too ambitious to rock the boat or too bolshy to upset the apple cart. The nature of the black is on their side, and because the politicians understand their own kind they are keeping some sort of balance. But tho' the black's too shittin' idle to want work, when the stirrers move in to rouse his blood-lust there'll be no stopping the massacre until the last white head is thrown into Newport Bay.'

'Or Frigate,' Sebastian said. 'You know, Charlie, I think Cynthia has a point. It beats me why you live on in this island. Those cannons of yours are past firing.'

'I'm not worried for myself,' Charlie growled. 'I'm just telling you. I ain't got no axe to grind. But these politicians...'

'I suppose they provide acceptable employment for the more intelligent,' Matthew said. 'The Ministries and so forth.'

'Sure,' Charlie said, 'sure. You been in any of those joints? So much black pussy running around you'd think you'd gotten involved in a chorus audition. But I'll tell ya. For a doll to get into Government service she needs one qualification only and that's not stenography. Politicians!'

'You sound almost jealous, Charlie,' Peter said.

'Listen, you know about their walkabout racket?'

'Business expenses?' Sir Alfred queried.

'O.K., I'll buy the euphemism. So all members of Government and Parliament get air fares, hotels, food paid when they're travelling. O.K. So they travel six months in the year, which is why you can never get hold of the bastards.'

'Be fair, Charlie,' Sebastian said. 'Show me the politician who isn't on to that kind of perk.'

'Yeah, but what you don't know is that this lot have voted themselves a hundred and seventy-five U.S. pocket money. Per day. On top. The premier and his deputy even more. And you can quote me. Know sump'n else? One of the ministers took fifteen of his friends and relations to a festival in Nigeria. Nigeria, mind. Story was it was a wedding party for his daughter who was marrying a professor out there. Professor of Emergent Economics, I'd guess. Cost the island tens of thousands. And the British pour aid into 'em. How can they do that? How can Monesterio, which has no income tax, seek aid from countries who have?'

'Ah, but wait a minute,' Sir Alfred began with the look of a man moving on to familiar ground.

'Listen...'

'Charlie,' Anneliese said.

He gestured impatiently.

'Some of you know this house. Right? You can guess what I spent on it. You'd be wrong. Treble it. When I bought the place it was a heap. Short lease; option to renew; same terms. Time came, when I'd near completed it and spent a mint, they said the lease was valueless, but they would graciously let me have the land at fifteen thousand U.S. an acre, short term, rising at each renewal. Big deal. I had old Finch out here; got the bugger by himself, face to face. Plenty of croc tears. Said his civil servants always get things wrong. Said he'd have a word with them. Has anything happened? Like hell it's happened. They're a bunch of two-timing, no-good thieves and hoodlums, and you gotta believe it. I could give you the names of ministers who have openly admitted their hatred of whites. Yet you still find people ready to invest in this island. I tell you, they're crazy. They don't see the writing. No more than they did in Jamaica, in Granada. And tell me, Pete, who have you got in the dockyard to stand up to them? The only guy who could show some muscle is that suck-arse Bill Watkins who spends his time picking the orchids which grow out of black bums. He won't last, but meantime the politicians'll take those soft-heads to the cleaners for every buck they can squeeze. Listen. You can quote me. Monesterio has the most beautiful climate in the world. What God gave us is just incredible. But don't look at the people. Take the hotels. All the hotel developments bar one were done by whites. O.K., I'll admit the best hotel of the lot is run by a sambo, but they hate his guts too because he's straight, clever, industrious and a mulatto. But what the black people have done is nothing.' He swept his hand over the table. 'Nothing.'

'All right, darling,' Brenda said, 'you've had your little moment, now how about we enjoy ourselves?'

'I recommend Anneliese's soursop ice cream, Matthew,' Betty said.

Anneliese smiled gently. 'People seem to like it after one of Charlie's monologues,' she said.

'Aw, to hell,' Charlie rumbled. 'One of these days you'll wish you listened to me, I'm tellin' ya.'

The Spoiler had gone full circle and was strumming behind Matthew's chair, riffling chords to claim the company's attention. The only serious competition was from Sir Alfred who had begun to reclaim his audience by explaining the British tax system to Anneliese whose expression suggested rapt attention. The Spoiler strummed louder.

'I asked my woman what can I do
to make her happy and keep her true...'

'... which is not to suggest,' Sir Alfred was saying, 'that at the top end the Government expect anything but a large slice of the cake. At the lower levels, however...'

'... she say only one thing I want from you
is a little piece of the big bamboo.'

Brenda gave a clap of recognition and some people on the terrace raised encouraging cheers. Lady Bishop registered tolerant anticipation. Sebastian was studying the faces round the table quizzically. Betty was listening respectfully to Sir Alfred.

'For de big bamboo it grows good and long,
de big bamboo it was always strong...'

'After all, profitability is the test of performance.'

'De big bamboo stands up straight and tall
and de big bamboo pleases one and all.'

'Mind you, the entire structure has been criticized for being top heavy.'

The Spoiler strummed, hoping for exclusive attention.

Sir Alfred appealed to his wife: 'Isn't that right, my dear?'

'Well, I give my woman a coconut;
She say "My friend, it O.K., but..."'

Lady Bishop had been giving only half an ear to her husband's explanations.

'About the tax structure?' she hazarded.

'Though you want to be good to me,
what good is de nuts without a tree?'

Sir Alfred nodded. 'You remember your own experience in the Civil Service?'

'Oh, of course, differentials,' Lady Bishop said, adjusting skilfully.

'Friends, I gave my woman a sugar cane,
sweet for de sweet she did explain.

'Have you always been an economist?' Anneliese asked. She gave the impression of really wanting to know.

'In one or other capacity. I've filled a variety of roles.'

'She handed it back and to my surprise
she likes de flavour but not de size.'

'I think it was most fun when he was in fibres,' Lady Bishop said. 'We travelled so much in those days, meeting such interesting people.'

'There was this Chinaman, whose name was Dick Kant Go,
he got married and went down to Mexico.'

'Ah, yes, travel,' Sir Alfred said, doing some quick up and down eyebrow work which Matthew had learned was a sign of jocular mood. 'Cynthia has always believed that somehow it would be better somewhere else. A common illusion.'

'You know his wife, she divorce him very quick,
she say she want bamboo and not chopstick.'

Lady Bishop smiled tolerantly. 'Alfred is very conventional. He is under-convinced of the value of variety.'

'What came after fibres?' Sebastian enquired.

'Say, Mr Gentleman, in that coat of black,
on you I will now launch this attack.'

'Oh, a fascinating period,' Lady Bishop said. 'Suddenly everyone seemed to appreciate his talents. He was in demand from all quarters.'

'The way you sitting I like yo' pose,
I hear yo' bamboo is the length of yo' nose.'

'You see, he'd always kept a very low profile. But then he gave a television interview, most reluctantly, and when the interviewer asked some leading questions he answered them absolutely honestly which completely threw the man who was expecting all the usual weavings and dodgings. Alfred had three sacks of fan mail and was offered a flood of appointments.'

'You over there in the shirt of white,
to sing on you it's my delight.'

Sir Alfred nodded. 'But Cynthia left me in no doubt what it was she expected of me.'

'Well, of course, dear, you'd have been wasted in any other capacity. Everyone knew it.'

'What I'm going to say, it's not a threat,
but I hear yo' bamboo is the size of yo' cigarette.'

'Possibly they didn't play the field,' Sir Alfred said modestly. 'There was Treadman and Runcibold. Both good men.'

'Yes, Alfred, but they weren't in your class. You can be too modest.'

The Spoiler thrashed his strings with climactic emphasis.

'Well, I agree Treadwell had no need to worry. He was a survivor. They offered him coal.'

'And you said yourself, Runcibold was never really on the inner track.'

'Anyway,' Sir Alfred said, confirming benevolence and modesty by some dexterous eyebrow play, 'things came out as you intended.'

'You seem not to hear tho' you listen o.k.,
but I not sure I believe all you say.'

'I remember quite clearly,' Lady Bishop said, 'the day he went to see the Government. I stood in the porch to see him off...'

'I don't know if you're tryin' to fool me,
but I hear yo' bamboo is just a memory.'

'... and I called out to him: "Now don't you come home and tell me you've taken steel".'

The terrace burst into applause as the Spoiler ended 'The Big Bamboo' in a thundering shower of descending chords before retiring behind a screen.

'I'm afraid he's a rather dominating singer,' Betty said to Sir Alfred. Her face had relaxed as the Spoiler left.

'Not at all,' Sir Alfred said. 'Splendid atmosphere here. But I thought that fellow's last verse rather weak. I heard a much better version years ago in Trinidad, but nowadays they don't let their hair down as they used to do.'

The Spoiler reappeared when coffee had been served. The lights had been dimmed and Matthew wondered if Sir Alfred had spoken too soon. But the Spoiler's mood had gone in a quite different direction and he sang a strange little song whose last line, lilting and fading in a whisper, haunted the brain, putting Matthew in mind of Zafada where the wind through the solitary peaks was like a far, massed singing:

'Sometime low,
sometime high,
I fly free,
my world the sky.
   Humankind they strive and strain
   - don't know why, nothing gain;
   pray to heaven, cling to earth
   - trouble and pain from hour of birth.
Not for me, man,
all this woe;
angels greet me
where I go.
   In my sky
   great choirs are heard
   - so say banana bird.'

There had been so much gentleness and nostalgic passion in the Spoiler's deep, slow rendering of the song, that it brought a huge burst of applause, perhaps intensified by an audience no longer obliged to show conspicuous broad-mindedness.

'A splendid evening,' Sir Alfred said. It was only ten, but he rose decisively as if closing a meeting with an agreed deadline. 'Really splendid.'

'Such fun,' his wife endorsed. 'Wonderful food, most amusing songs, and fascinating conversation. We shan't forget a moment of it.'

The Bustler hiccuped back across the island.
'Sir Alf seems to have enjoyed himself,' Matthew said.
'It's all grist to his mill, even Charlie's leadings off.'
'I think I'd rather have Charlie as friend than enemy.'
Sebastian nodded. 'Quite a few people feel that way.'

'Though how much of what he says you can believe...'
'More than a little.'
'How is it no one has had his guts for garters?'
'Like I said once before, with Charlie you've got to look below the surface. Literally, perhaps. He's a showman and an old softie, but also a shrewd cookie with a wife who by my book isn't the mouse she may appear.'
'Meaning?'
Sebastian hesitated.
'Look, you and I aren't islanders. We can afford a certain objectivity. Most of the residents can't, least of all if they are living off the area. If I tell you a bit more, keep it under your hat. Some not only don't know what's going on, but maybe wouldn't even want to know because ignorance can be more comfortable.'
'All right, I'm drooling at the ears.'
'For starters, then, did you notice how Charlie picked up what Anneliese was saying about some character who came to fix their solar panels?'
'Rudy Mazlin? Yes, I noticed.'
'Under every table on that verandah there's a bugging device which relays back to Charlie. The deaf-aid he was wearing this evening was a mike. He can overhear any conversation he chooses.'
'Just a naturally trustful, outgoing guy...'
'And take this Fort Nelson bit.'
'A load of eyewash, I think you called it.'
'Right, everyone except the tourists knows that. Or think they do. In fact, it's a double bluff. A fort is precisely what it is.'
'With fake cannon popping out of every hibiscus bush? Come on!'
'Below the house, deep down below the hibiscus and the fake cannon, there's an armoury. A real armoury with enough hardware to control not only this island but half the Caribbean.'
'How on earth do you know all this?'
'That's another story, all to do with this King of Zafada nonsense which, for all the wrong reasons, one or two people have taken far too seriously. Suffice it that one of Charlie's top brass told me some of it. After falling out with Charlie, and for rapid elevation to the Zafada peerage, he filled me in while waiting at the airport for his flight to New York. He was lucky

his plane was on time. Two Schnitzler heavies arrived just as it reached the runway. But Charlie himself has told me plenty in the course of trying to get me to lend the "kingdom" to his little plans for expansion.'

'I'm finding this a bit difficult to take. How the hell could Charlie create an armoury below the fort without the wrong people finding out?'

'I don't know if, originally, he even intended to. But the quick answer is mushrooms.'

'Mushrooms?'

'When he bought the Fort Nelson set-up – the old plantation house and the land – he played a straight bat and went into mushroom farming. Allegedly for reasons such as temperature and humidity control he built massive concrete underground caverns, improving on cellars and natural caves which had been used by smugglers or pirates centuries ago. The Government not only knew about it, but helped him recruit the best labour the island could provide. Charlie told them it would boost the island's economy, give employment, put Monesterio on the map.'

'And did it?'

'For a time. But then Charlie built Fort Nelson and everyone thought he was off on another of his enthusiasms. Which he was, of course. And the mushroom project dwindled and no one thought about the great concrete vaults under the more conspicuous growth of a tourist trap. But according to my ennobled subject there's not only an armoury down there, but sleeping quarters, trucks, a whole load of communications technology, and God only knows what. With his fingers in so many pies, it can't have been difficult to equip the place without raising a breath of suspicion.'

'To what end?'

'Only time will tell. But as I read it, the inspiration behind it is more Anneliese's than Charlie's, and that I find alarming. Anneliese doesn't monkey around. If she's after something, she gets it. Her family survived the second world war very comfortably, playing the rights cards with the outgoing as much as with the incoming, so to speak.'

'So Charlie's not aiming at a communist coup?'

Sebastian laughed.

'Certainly not that,' he said. 'Coup, maybe, but it won't be in league with the Castros of this world. The Labour Party's main platform is free enterprise – or freedom not to show it, if you like. Marxist activists have had little joy in the Windwards and Leewards. You can't sell "liberation" to people who are already as free as birds. There's no taste for regimes seeking to tamper with the process of changing governments by free ballot – which is not to say the Caribbean isn't getting its quota of bully boys who move in under the banner of democratic intent. No, my guess is personal dictatorship, with Anneliese calling all the best tunes.'

'Earlier, you said "top brass". You mean he's got a secret army stashed away below the fort?'

'Only a nucleus. Imported heavies from the States and elsewhere. The rest, mostly the men who built the caverns, live their own lives in the villages. But in each village there is one of Charlie's best men, in daily contact with Fort Nelson via – what do the radio buffs call it? – a private frequency.'

'I get the picture. So what is Charlie, a megalomaniac?'

'He may be. Or he may be a lot more calculating and on the ball than anyone imagines. Over the years there's been every kind of guess about him: C.I.A., F.B.I., mafia, an eccentric millionaire, you name it.'

'If he's so smart, how is it he can't get the Government to give him the go-ahead to let the public in on the Fort Nelson racket?'

'My guess is that that's another of his double bluffs. A red herring. I suspect he has no wish or intention to let the tourists in. I think he keeps a deliberate balance of antagonism between himself and the Government, and if ever they show a sign of relenting and co-operating, he drops another clanger in the right quarter so that they back-pedal and claw back any concession they might have made.'

'But he must have invested a fortune in the place.'

'He has, but if you think about it, nothing need be wasted. Even the restaurant...'

'An army canteen?'

Sebastian nodded.

'And tucked into the foot of the hills, half a mile away, is Charlie's private air strip and helicopter pad, patrolled round the clock, with good hard-standing that looks for all the world like a parade ground.'

'Wow! No wonder the knowing are keeping in with Charlie.'

'For "knowing" we should maybe read "suspecting", but there again I guess the Schnitzlers let out just what they want to let out, and no more.'

'And the Government is in ignorance of all this?'

'Good question. They could well be fully in the picture and playing along with Charlie. When their independence comes the Brits aren't going to lend any gun boats to an island that has been nothing but a painful drain on resources. The Government here may be glad, or anyway resigned, to come to terms with Charlie. For all I know they have already agreed their plan of campaign. You just cannot trust anyone out here.'

'Brenda said something about making her living on this island. I think I get the message now.'

The car swerved as Sebastian avoided a cow. It was tethered by a long rope to a stake on the verge and had ample freedom to get to the other side of the road.

'How does Brenda strike you?' he asked.

'May she never do so. As with Charlie, better as friend than enemy. A highly decorative flint with a good cutting edge, I'd say.'

'Brenda can be very friendly,' Sebastian said.

28

'WELL, darling, and how's the little book going?' Brenda enquired.

Their table was in the cool shade of the genip tree, overlooking green slopes between the huge phallic pillars of the long-fallen sail loft of Britain's naval heyday. The striped sail of a skilfully managed Sunfish dipped like a butterfly in the wash of a gleaming white schooner which was making for the harbour mouth. The near-predictable sun heightened the orgy of colour and light so soon taken for granted by those who live in the tropics.

Matthew sighed. No one but Sebastian had seen in authorship more than the faintly amusing whim of someone clearly lacking adult motivation.

'It's moving well,' he said.

His mind toyed with an analysis of his relationship with Brenda, only to conclude that perhaps it did not amount to one. She was beautiful, and rumour had it that she was available. The surroundings were romantic to the point of over-statement. But although for the third day running he was giving her a lunch-time shrimp cocktail at the Captain's Arms, he seemed to be making no progress. Correction: he was giving himself the shrimp cocktail while Brenda put away her usual menu consisting of the pumpkin soup, the scallop, and the baked banana dessert which, swimming in coconut cream, did nothing to explain the perfection of her figure.

'You don't look quite with it,' Brenda said, taking a teaspoon to the last few drops of the coconut cream. 'As though your mind was far away. Turning over ideas, I suppose?'

'Of a kind. But, yes, I'm happy about the book. I think it'll be the best thing I've done.'

'How long is it going to take you?'

'With any luck, only a day or two. Now I'm working in the officers' quarters I can go full out. The bungalow was too clammy. The physical side of things is important.'

'Too true, darling. Do you like living by yourself?'

'The evenings are a bit depressing. But I see Sebastian a good deal. He likes chess.'

'Each to his own, I always say.'

'Most nights I turn in early, then get up as soon as it's light.'

'No pussy?'

'I've not been inundated with offers.'

'It doesn't always come on a plate like a shrimp cocktail, darling. Anyway, I thought artists and writers didn't want it when they were being creative.'

'Folk lore put about by wives to keep the competition at bay. But it's true one needs to concentrate and, at my age, not dissipate the energies.' He thought for a moment. 'Not too much, anyway.'

'Is your wife coming out here?'

'I'm not in that financial bracket.'

'But you get on?'

'It's not a very vital relationship, but I suppose there is a lot to be thankful for.'

It sounded churlish, but to have modified the remark would not have helped. Rebecca's last letter had touched him. He wondered whether he was still feeding Brenda unreciprocated meals because of something more than a fear of rejection...

'Fine,' Brenda said with sincerity.

A tinge of regret would have been more flattering, but he felt slight relief.

'Coffee?' he invited.

'No, thanks, darling, I've got to go into town. They've managed to lose a consignment of sailcloth.'

'Sebastian has the Bustler today. Can you drop me at the shack?'

'No problem.'

It was a gauge of something that only then did he see the possibilities in a repeat invitation to coffee in Buck house.

'By the way,' Brenda added, 'I've brought you a little pressie.'

She fished an aerosol from the canvas bag at her feet. It had

'Scram' written on it in large red letters and a graphic picture of a mouse-sized mosquito in its death throes.

'It's back on the market, then? Thanks!' He read the small print. It promised four hours protection to sprayed skin.

'Four hours. What if I sleep from midnight until six?'

'Well, here *is* Sebastian,' Brenda said.

'Now you'll have to have a coffee,' Matthew said. He felt the relief which comes from not having to make a decision.

'No, I'm off,' Brenda said. 'Business before pleasure.'

'You know where you are with Brenda,' Sebastian said, sinking into her vacated chair and wiping his face. 'Phew! It's sticky.'

'Would you like to switch back to Buck House?'

'I'm easy. How about you?'

'Well, now I'm working in the dockyard it would somewhat simplify the domestic routine. Anyway, you must have collected a few reasons for having first call on the Bustler.'

'Not really, I'm rather enjoying freedom from the uncertainties of shore-based life. But I'll confess the artistic rapture is easing off a bit. How about Tuesday of next week? I should have finished the present sequence of sketches by then.'

'Splendid. It'll do me good to walk to Tabitha Heights instead of driving.'

'That's becoming quite a routine.'

'Tabitha Heights? Well, with all respect to your palace, it can be a blessed relief to get up there before turning in. To look out across the Atlantic from Magazine Hill, with the trade wind coming off countless miles of water, and the moon and the stars doing their stuff, is really something. When I take the other fork and look down over the dockyard from the Heights, it beats me why I'm nearly always alone up there. What's the matter with the young? It's one of the most romantic spots in the world on those hills, yet all the soulless young twits can do is swig beer before having it away in hot cabins. At their age...'

'They do say the young are never what they used to be. Hello! Tom looks a bit po-faced today.'

Tom Riley was sitting at a table under the awning with a man whose light but formal suit suggested business or officialdom. He was taking notes. Riley was talking fast and low between gulps of what looked like a very large whisky.

'I've still not really met him,' Matthew said.

'You wouldn't unless you're a potential buyer. No time for social chitchat. A tough cookie.'

'And an uneasy one, I'd guess.'

'He could have reasons,' Sebastian said, managing to convey to a passing waitress that coffee would be appreciated. 'That business about the cable to the U.S. embassy has not been forgotten.'

'God, what's the matter with our species?' Matthew said with sudden vehemence. 'Here we are in the nearest one can get to a physical paradise, bathed in almost constant sun, awash in natural beauty, life's necessities pruned to a minimum, within easy reach of the kind of life my daughter in her bleak Welsh commune is avid to attain, and still we are bugged by greeds and envies and hatreds. Shall we never learn?'

'Who was it said that most of us would rather be dead than sensible? Maybe middle-age is catching up with me, but I can't see any lasting improvement except through a radical change in values – the individual kind.'

'Which means re-education; not a quick process.'

'Nor is global population control, an equally vital part of the package.'

'No one wants to wait that long.'

'But where's the short-cut? Still, I envy writers, teachers. They can make some contribution, however small, whereas most of us can do little but fiddle around with the externals to keep the juggernaut on its same futile circuit.'

Matthew smiled. 'I've no illusion that one meaningful book from old Braine is going to be more than a drop in the ocean.'

'Study the Buddhists; they're very into drops.'

'You're fortunate; you seem to have a clear idea of alternatives.'

'It's pretty sketchy.'

'But you've some kind of inner conviction, some core. I can only see the truth of certain aspects. I can't see the whole... don't *feel* it, anyway.'

'Every book's a kind of milestone, surely? If one writes at the highest level of one's understanding, people at the same stage will respond. Better that than to cut corners and try to present the total package. That'd only scare them and bring instant crucifixion.'

'Instant neglect, more likely. Anyway, religious argument isn't my scene.'

'Nor mine in any sectarian sense. I distrust the isms, ologies and anities. All I know is that I believe I see certain things fairly clearly, and what stands out most of all is the extent of our ignorance – of science, medicine, notions of God, everything. Yet with all that incomprehension and insensitivity we have the arrogance to deny the possibility of matters, insights, other planes of awareness, infinitely more difficult of definition. It's the combination of ignorance and shut-mindedness that's so deadly.'

'Which,' Matthew said, stirring his coffee gloomily, 'is doubtless what Judy has many times said about me.'

'Be glad of it. The young are testing – words, themselves, their elders. If they readily accepted the world they're offered, the termitary would have arrived. Like us, they see aspects of the alternative pattern. Maybe an adequate minority will keep the ball rolling until the blueprint becomes a working reality.'

'Judy's obsession is with the environment. I used to suppose she just meant physical pollution and tearing down hedgerows. I think I understand her better than I did. There's a strong sense of inter-relationships, of the unity of life; your sort of thing.'

'Like you, though, I understand more than I practice. I respect those groups and individuals who live out their theories – or try to – and I don't mean the political hot-heads who are sick with the same values as the society they oppose.'

'When you're on the outside it's bloody difficult to distinguish one from the other.'

'Not really. The surface structuralists, as someone called them, believe that the structures have only to be changed for everything to come right, and that the publicity given to violent means will help achieve the ends. Their badges are pretty prominent.'

'Judy's certainly not that naïve.'

'As you say, she's more of an environmentalist, and apparently not in the camp that's seeking a modified technology and a more modest but still heartless exploitation of the environment. That lot's almost Establishment these days.'

'Definitely not Judy's mob.'

'Hers seems to have sensed something more important. It has its lunatic fringe, but I suspect that time will show them to be the only realistic environmentalists. They're aiming at a different kind of world, not to get the best of both by expedient adjustments. Sorry, I'm well into the saddle!'

'Saddles are for sitting in.'

'Anyway, for all their present inadequacies they could be the forerunners of more human, more humane, beings. They've seen that our cruelties and greeds – towards all life forms – can only brutalize and in the end be self-destructive. There's a girl I know – I may be marrying her...'

'Marrying? I like the way you slipped that in!'

'Well, she – Jane – changed course from the moment she saw that between exploitation of a child and any other living thing there's a link that can't be ignored. She realized that violence is indivisible and that this had to be built into us.'

'A concept not joyfully acceptable to State and Church.'

'Nor to most of us. But the realization is being handed down. It may be kept alive on a Welsh hillside, in a westcoast experiment in alternative lifestyles, in the books and little magazines that nowadays represent minority concerns and are finding readers in surprisingly orthodox quarters. The point is, it's catching on and I suspect its strength lies in its affinity with truths that the greatest minds have always subscribed to... Sorry, I got carried away a bit.'

'In this neck of the woods it's a welcome phenomenon.'

'By the way, I've some news for you.'

'Good?'

'Rather depressing. Firstly, permission has been given for twenty houses overlooking the dockyard. The no-skyline-building regulations have gone by the board. So much for the Watkins' political friends' integrity.'

'Vote-catching?'

'Naturally. Secondly, about those articles. I've heard from a source that's as near as one gets to the horse's mouth in this place that the material came from the Watkins.'

'They wrote them?'

'The draft, anyway. The Trust's files go a long way back, so they were able to draw on all sorts of letters and memoranda going way back beyond their own time here.'

'Surely Rosemary didn't have a hand in it? Bill, maybe, but Rosemary...'

Sebastian smiled. Matthew could read his unspoken comment.

'I told you Rosemary was very much on the side of the down-trodden,' Sebastian said.

'But the blacks on this island aren't down-trodden. There's not a sign of real poverty or hardship. They're just bone idle.'

This time Sebastian laughed.

'All right, but Rosemary was a nurse, don't forget, and she spent several years in Africa before coming here. Things were a lot grimmer in some of the places she worked. With the way some of the yachting fraternity behaves, Port St George is not exactly the best spot in which to disabuse an idealistic young woman of the idea that black is more deserving than white.'

'But the very language of those articles; they seemed to be written by a semi-literate, and several of the phrases were distinctly bee-wee, if you know what I mean.'

'Well, where they were naïve was in handing the articles over to Big Daddy. He has to go into Campbelltown most days and acts as go-between for Bill who has his work cut out in the dock-yard. It seems that Big Daddy did a spot of "improvement", doubtless with the help of the editor.'

Matthew tried to recall his exact words during a recent coffee-taking with the Watkins.

'Christ!' he said. 'I told Bill and Rosemary I thought the articles were vicious and libellous. I'm not sure I didn't add that they were the product of an unbalanced and ill-educated yob. And White was there!'

'Oh, well,' Sebastian said cheerfully, 'unsolicited testimonials can do a lot of good.'

'Do you suppose the Richardsons know?'

'If they don't, they soon will. An island of this size holds few secrets.'

Matthew felt a congestion, almost a nausea, in his throat.

'Oh, to hell with it!' he said. 'This place is beginning to get on my wick.'

'There's a lot to be said for coming over as a tourist for a comfortable, cocooned fortnight,' Sebastian agreed.

Enjoying the rare luxury of an evening shave, Matthew listened to the local news which followed the World Service. Although announced as regional, national and international, the local station seldom ranged beyond forthcoming cricket fixtures between the island's villages and a catalogue of social events and petty crime, though on this occasion the announcer gave lurid details of what he described as the island's first murder of the year. On the familiar principle that not even a split second's silence should tempt listeners to switch off and be left with their own thoughts, the newscaster's closing words were overlapped by the swelling organ music which heralded the 'Obits'. A suitably sepulchral voice took over:

'The death is announced of Helen Jarvis of Cashew Hill, aged eighty-nine, widow of Staffil Jarvis of Wilberforce. She leaves to mourn her sister Lorestine Henry, her brothers Tyrone and Glanfield Ford. She was mother of Debbie, Elroy, Charlotte, Claudena, Charlesworth and Eustace; grandmother of eleven including Esther, Andrea, Claxton, Conroy and Yvette; great-grandmother of fifteen including Emerson, Josabelle, Octavia, Jason, Lucilla, Elmer, Silver and Goldeen. She was the very good friend of Melva Pain of Liberty Town, of Leonora Daniel of Hosanna, of Ottoline Friday of Tabernacles, and of others too numerous to mention. The funeral will be...'

Normally the names alone were enough to make 'Obits' compulsive listening, but on this evening the programme merely added to Matthew's gloom. He switched it off and stood under the shower for longer than usual, seeking a state of chill that would calm thought and bring physical comfort for the rest of the evening. But it was a humid and windless night with the threat of thunder.

He turned the Bustler in the dark road and drove towards the dockyard. A torrential burst of rain had left small rivers on either side of the road, and trees dripped heavily. The seats in the Bustler were still quite dry, as there had been no breeze to blow the rain through its open sides. The road was empty of people.

Perhaps because the damp had affected its simple but neurotic electrics, the Bustler began to play up, bunny-hopping at first on the flat before giving up altogether as it felt the challenge of the small hill beyond which lay the final rutted stretch of road to the dockyard.

For a few moments Matthew sat in silence, listening despondently to the surrounding hiss of baked earth soaking up rain. Without any real expectation of a solution he got out and opened the flimsy plastic engine cover at the Bustler's rear. He had no torch and could see little, though the moon was trying to penetrate the recent storm cloud. He closed the cover and got back into the car to wait for more light.

Above the sibilance of the soil's thirst he heard what at first he took to be the scream of some bird or animal. The night was so still that the scream was sharp and clear and could have come from a long way off, but as his mind focused and analysed the sound he decided it could have been human. His conclusion was confirmed almost immediately by a man's voice, raised in anger or fear and followed at once by a harsh grating, metallic sound above the roar of an engine being highly revved. He got out and walked quickly up the short rise. Off to his left, no more than a hundred yards up the steep track, the headlights of some vehicle were plunging towards the road, their swerving and bumping motion suggesting the driver was out of control. Matthew could think of nothing to do but stand and watch the dancing lights, unconscious of the water dripping on to his thin open-necked shirt from the tree above him.

The end was rapid and predictable. He remembered the track's steepness and its deep ruts from the day he had gone to look more closely at 'Jaws'. The lights dipped suddenly and went out, and simultaneously a mingled crunch and rattle confirmed without help of sight that the vehicle had crashed. He stood for a moment, slightly stunned by the unexpectedness of the event, then walked down the slight incline towards the track to the left. The gleam of a torch suggested that the driver had escaped injury. As he approached, walking carefully over the soft sandy ground, he heard a voice. It was slightly familiar. As he came up behind the man who was holding the torch, he saw there was another, less heavily built man on his right; neither had heard his approach, being engrossed by the sight before them. In the torch's beam Matthew could see the body of a man crushed beneath the weight of a Landrover. He was as bent as an old fashioned hairpin, his back visibly, gruesomely broken, his head impaled by the broken shaft of a side mirror. Within six feet of the two men, Matthew now knew who they were.

'Well,' Captain White said to his companion with unmistakable satisfaction, 'dat's one shit-assed honky owder de way.'

Matthew recognized the dead man's face, though twisted and bloodied by the head injury. It was that of Tom Riley.

'Jesus!' he said.

The two men spun round.

'Who dat?' the Captain demanded angrily. He shone his torch into Matthew's eyes.

'Braine,' Matthew said. 'Matthew Braine. For God's sake, what happened?'

'Dere's been an accident.' The Captain's voice was under more control.

'So I see,' Matthew said. 'I could tell it was going to be nasty, but this . . .'

'Yo' saw it happen?' The Captain kept his torch beamed on to Matthew's face.

Matthew nodded. 'My car broke down just short of the police station. I heard a scream, then the engine. How on earth did you manage to get here so quickly?'

The Captain ignored the question.

'Yo' know de . . . victim?'

Matthew nodded. 'Tom Riley. God, what a ghastly business. He must have been out of control. Brake failure, I'd imagine.'

The torch was pushed nearer to his face, almost touching him. The Captain's voice rose again.

'Why yo' say dat? De man could've been drunk. Plenny of reasons.'

'Your enquiry will doubtless establish the cause.'

Captain White nodded slowly. 'Yeah, dat's right. We'll establish de cause, yo' can be sure o' dat. Corporal Winston an' me, we happen to be observin' de accident 'n we can put in our report.'

'An extraordinary thing to happen,' Matthew said. 'The brakes on these things are normally very strong.'

The Captain's voice was deep and measured.

'Look man,' he said, 'dis is pliss business. Yo' bes' be on yo' way.'

The corporal moved towards Matthew. Although the moon had broken through the cloud Matthew could not read his expression, but there was something in the bearing of both captain and corporal which suggested strongly that little good could come of hanging around.

29

'IT does smell fishy,' Sebastian agreed.

'It stinks,' said Matthew. 'I've turned it over half the night and it stinks to high heaven; like a lot of other things on this island.'

'Well, I don't know what the hell you can do about it,' Sebastian said. 'If there is anything dodgy about it, the cover-up will be unanimous and watertight.'

'I'll go to the Governor if necessary,' Matthew said. 'I feel in my bones it was not just a simple accident and I'm convinced Captain White had something to do with it. If ever I sensed guilt...'

'Watch it,' Sebastian murmured.

The waitress had come up behind Matthew's chair with their lunch. Matthew waited until she had gone.

'It was the way White said it,' he insisted. 'There was something... well, understood between them.'

'Do you think he knows you suspect?'

'If he doesn't he's thicker than he looks.'

Sebastian looked serious. 'Don't under-estimate him. He's not stupid. All the residents here know the sort of things he gets up to - some of them bloody well ought to, damn it; bribery's a two-way process - but he's never seriously been on the mat. He may look like a gorilla but he's got the skin of an eel.'

'Maybe an imported crime team and some British justice will sort him out.'

'My dear chap, by the time you organized that - even supposing you could - any possible evidence would have been spirited away. It's probably already gone. They may not move fast round here in the line of service to their fellow men, but when it comes to preserving their hides...'

'Then I'll confront him myself. Now. Tell him I'll...'

'Look,' Sebastian said patiently, 'take my advice. Forget it. This is not the Home Counties. I know just how you feel, but even if you proved something to your own or someone else's satisfaction, it won't bring Tom back to life.'

'I don't have any special feelings about Tom. I've hardly met him. It just riles me to see people getting away with... well, probably, murder.'

'I know, but be realistic. The only people who have any muscle won't be on your side. The police are controlled by the Government, and the Government is black-run and anti-white. The Governor's an obligatory figure-head who's due to be phased out anyway as soon as the island gets full independence. It's as simple as that.'

'Well, something ought to be done,' Matthew said stubbornly. 'I can't just sit back and do nothing.'

'Bad business,' Peter Richardson agreed. 'Very bad business. And without sounding heartless so soon after the event, it's going to leave us in a pretty pickle on the brokerage side. He had no number-two who really knows what's going on.'

'I saw him in the Captain's Arms only yesterday lunch-time,' Matthew said. 'I thought he looked scared of something.'

'Scared? Aren't you being a bit imaginative? Why should he be scared in the Caps?'

'He had someone with him; they were talking nineteen to the dozen. The other looked a bit official and was taking notes.'

'Could have been anyone. An owner's agent, probably. Tom has... had... a lot to do with agents.'

'All right, but I didn't get that impression. If you'd told me he'd been threatened, or had had a brick lobbed over his wire fencing, I wouldn't have been surprised.'

Peter laughed uneasily. 'You writers!' he said. 'Vivid imaginations.'

'But that business of the cable. We know White has had it in for Riley.'

Betty said: 'I'm sure Prue would have told me if Tom was in some kind of trouble. We're quite close.'

'What if... well, I don't want to make any suggestions about friends of yours... but what if White, rightly or wrongly, thought he had got some hold over Riley?'

'But now you're talking about a different ball game,' Peter pointed out. 'You've been suggesting murder, not blackmail.'

'You say yourself he has no number two who is fully in the picture. I've heard from several quarters that Riley kept a low profile. I'm not suggesting anything, of course, but it could all add up.'

'Well, I wish I could think of something useful to say,' Peter said, 'but quite honestly, on balance, and lacking anything more concrete to go on, I think we've just got to let matters take their course.'

Betty said nothing, but Matthew could tell by the set of her mouth that she would only echo Peter's unwillingness to become involved. Despite the refreshing breeze blowing through the Richardsons' bungalow, there was a slight atmosphere, a tenseness, in the room. They were distancing themselves, not with unfriendliness but by unspoken disinclination to probe or speculate.

'Oh, well,' Matthew said, 'I daresay I'm over-reacting a bit. But Tom wasn't a very pretty sight. It was a rather unsettling incident to get caught up in quite so intimately.'

'It must have been,' Betty agreed sympathetically. 'Beastly. Have some more tea before you go?'

'It didn't surprise me, darling,' Brenda said. 'Not one little bit.'

She looked up at the darkening sky through the frondy foliage of the casuarina tree and blew out a cloud of smoke.

'You mean you expected something of the sort?'

She shrugged slim shoulders and stubbed her cigarette.

'You learn to expect nothing and anything out here, darling. I just mean that Tom had it coming to him for one reason or the other. Things were stacking up against him.'

'Things?'

'That cable. Those articles. Government threats to offer brokerage concessions to break his monopoly. His heart. Something was going to give sooner or later.'

'Something giving is one thing. Bumping someone off is another.'

'Relax, darling. There's no evidence and you won't find any. Out here you just have to play by the rules or go under.'

'Close ranks and pretend nothing's happened?'

'You know how it is among the yachting crowd. Here today, gone tomorrow. Easy come, easy go.'

'"Don't rock the boat". Yes, I think I know.'

Brenda looked at him through eyes half-closed by the smoke of a fresh cigarette.

'You know, darling, Angelique was right about you.'

'Angelique? You know her, then?'

Brenda laughed. 'Well, of course, darling. We all know Angelique.'

Matthew shrugged. He felt slightly sick with distaste for the whole in-bred, nepotic, involved situation in which he had become enmeshed. He had begun to understand why barriers so soon came down.

'So what's she had to say about me?'

'Angelique? Oh, mostly quite nice things. She thought you rather a duck. But she did say there was a kind of innocence about you. I suspect that's what she found attractive. Angelique's short on innocent friendships.'

'Why were you discussing me?'

'We usually discuss dockyard matters when we meet. You may have noticed, women are almost as gossipy as men. As it happened, Tom and Prue came into the conversation and that somehow led to you.'

'How well did she know Tom?'

'About as well as she knows most people round here.'

'Would she have any ideas about his death, do you think?'

'God knows, darling. If she did, she'd not be likely to publish a broadsheet.'

'What's her job? I don't know much about her.'

'I think that's how she likes it to be. I suppose you could say she was something of a free-lance.'

'That covers a multitude of sins. Does she have Government connections?'

'Well, let's just say she lends her eyes and ears in a number of directions. One thing she did tell me was that Government has been none too happy about Tom for quite a time.'

'Meaning? That's a rather vague statement.'

'Darling, vagueness can be one of the most useful virtues. Just take it from aunty – leave well alone. Really, it pays in the long run.'

'So I'm learning.'

'We're all learning, darling,' Brenda said, finishing her martini. 'Some of us just take longer than others.'

'By the look of it, some of us don't have long enough.'

'Tom had the time. His antennae weren't quite sensitive enough, that's all. Look, why don't you come up to my house this evening and take pot-luck. That business rather spoiled things last night.'

He hesitated. 'Thanks, but I feel like cutting off for a time. Early night, that sort of thing. The writing didn't go very well today and I want to try to get it finished before moving back to "Patience."'

Brenda's pretty mouth registered a bearable resignation.

'Just as you wish, darling,' she said.

As he drove back to Buck House it crossed his mind that Brenda's invitation had been instinctively calculated, but his head was aching and in no condition for lateral speculation. He wanted a shower, some simple food, and peace. But although still churned up about the Riley incident, the writer in him had begun to respond as strongly as the bystander.

Showered and fed he lay on his bed and stared at the ceiling. His headache was almost gone, but he still felt restless. It was half an hour sooner than the time he usually set off for Tabitha Heights, but he felt drawn to go up there and walk around and let the cooling trade wind clear his mind.

The land was bathed in light by the almost full moon; the stars in closest attendance on her were dimmed by her brilliance. He could have driven the Bustler safely without headlights. The insect life was shrilling at full pitch. Along the road through the village a few people strolled, most of them elderly, and two children had enough light from the sky to be playing with a cricket bat and ball against the wall of a bungalow. The bungalow was built on piles, and down one side, spilling on to the foot-worn grass which passed for a lawn, was an advancing avalanche of used beer-bottles.

He left the village and wound up the deserted road towards the mile-long ridge that led to Tabitha Heights and Magazine Hill. The road had been spot-filled but still offered sudden surprises where rain had washed out the marl. Before the hairpin bend opposite the drive to Government House the Bustler started to bunny-hop, then recovered on the straight which followed and behaved itself at a modest twenty miles per hour in third gear. He passed the turning for the hotel that was the last habitation before the ridge was reached. As he climbed higher and passed the first block of ruined barracks, he felt the wind strengthen from the passenger's side of the Bustler.

But for the moon he might have missed the knot of men by the side of the road. It was a favourite spot for day-time tourists to stop and admire the view across the next but lower headland to Rodney Bay. The drop to the rather sinister intervening Serpents' Creek was bounded by a low wall, the remains of another military building of the eighteenth century. The ten or more blacks who were leaning against the wall with the wind coming from behind them did not hear the Bustler until it was almost upon them. At that point Matthew realized they were reacting to his arrival, moving to the side of the road excitedly, waving their arms and peering at the Bustler as though to identify it. Something about their demeanour prompted him to accelerate rather than slow down, and as he passed he saw that several men were carrying bush knives. One called out something that sounded like 'Dat's de man' and when he looked in the driver's mirror he saw dim evidence that the group was standing in the road. He could hear that they were shouting at him, but he could not make out their words. Then he saw that one of the men had detached himself from the rest and was running after the car at a tremendous speed. Matthew pressed the accelerator pedal flat against the plastic shell of the Bustler, and with the help of the slight fall in the road was able to widen the gap and pull away.

He felt suddenly chilled round the shoulders and neck. There was no doubt in his mind that the men had been expecting him. He drove on as fast as he dared over the often pot-holed surface, wondering what his next move should be. Tabitha Heights and Magazine Hill were headlands and, in a sense, *culs de sac*. Return had to be along the one and only road, from whichever headland he chose. He knew of no way of escaping by foot, for the tips of the headlands were precipitous, their flanks an impenetrable forest of thorn bush and cactus. If there was a way through it, the men waiting for him would know exactly where to go. He drove on, hoping that for once the Heights might have attracted others in whose company he could slip past the waiting mob. At the fork for Magazine Hill and Tabitha Heights he slowed, dithering as to which road to take. As it was a shorter distance to Magazine Hill, he went that way, but the headland was empty and white in the moonlight. The thought of coming across a bunch of hearty, well-muscled young yachtsmen, was attractive but vain. He turned round and drove at full speed past the beautiful arched remains of the old officers' quarters, now stirring imagination only as the perfect scene for the macabre and final encounter he was increasingly certain the men on the road below had in mind. He had never seen men carrying bush knives at night before; there seemed only one reason why they should do so, and one reason for their being on the road to the Heights.

At the fork he breathed a sigh of relief that there was no sign that the men had followed him. He turned sharply left for Tabitha Heights, calculating that even if the men ran at full pelt it would be some minutes before they caught up with him. Yet he was so prickling with fear and uncertainty that he peered fearfully into the bushes on either side of the road, though he knew that they had no need to have pursued him and that they must know this. He had no choice but to meet them again.

Tabitha Heights was equally deserted. He turned the Bustler round and faced it downhill, thankful that the ungrudging moon gave visibility for a hundred yards or more down the road. He switched the engine off and got out, leaning on the car's roof and listening intently for the sound of feet or voices. His heart was pounding and was the only noise he could hear apart from the faintly pulsing rhythm of a steel band some hundreds of feet and a thousand miles away. He did not waste time walking through the ruins to the rocky platform from which he had gazed on Port St George in the company of Angelique. There was no chance of his being heard at such a distance, or of anyone being able to reach him before it was too late.

The possibility struck him that the men would seek him on Magazine Hill and that if he timed his return correctly he could get past them before they returned to the fork. But then he reasoned that if their intentions were as serious as he feared, they would divide so as to cover both roads.

Facing the only solution, he felt a hard calm come into his brain. There was nothing for it but to drive the Bustler at the best speed he could raise and to maintain it at all costs.

Realization that this was his only chance calmed him a little. He got into the Bustler and turned on the ignition. There was no point in waiting for the men to appear. Better to hope to take them by surprise – or as much as the clattering engine would allow.

The engine whirred but did not fire.

'Sod it!' he muttered, fear returning like a blow on the nape of his neck.

He put the car into second gear and let off the handbrake, thanking his stars for the hill. He eased the clutch and the engine chunked reluctantly into life. Drawing a deep breath he put the Bustler through the gears as quickly as possible.

After about half a mile he wondered if he had allowed his imagination too much rein. Perhaps the men had given up, dispersed. The hope was short-lived. As he approached the straight where they had been waiting he saw they were still there, clustered in two groups by the low wall. The short downhill stretch that had enabled him to get away from them earlier now acted against him. After the approaching incline the Bustler would want a lot more wind-up time to achieve the speed he needed. But he put his foot down flat and beamed the headlights, pressing his palm on the horn and keeping it there, hoping without real hope that the lights would baffle identification for long enough to make his escape.

But the men had moved into a semicircle across the road and their intentions were all too clear. Five of them brandished bush knives and their threatening shouts and whoops were audible above the Bustler's engine. They were a waiting, hunting pack and there was not the slightest doubt that they meant final and bloody business.

Matthew began to swerve in deliberate long curves, conscious despite his fear of the absurdity of his James Bond situation in no more impressive an escape vehicle than an orange plastic beach buggy.

The group did not part, but the men at each end of the semicircle moved up the road towards him, forming a long funnel of threatening figures. The nearest man splayed his arms and danced absurdly, like a huge loose puppet, trying to wave him down. It was like being made to run the gauntlet at school, but with waiting weapons far more deadly than rolled newspapers or knotted handkerchiefs. He knew he must not let fear of hitting someone slow him down. The leading man leaped to one side as the Bustler's offside wing nearly ripped his shining black thigh, and Matthew heard the slap of the man's hand on the Bustler's roof as he pushed himself off from the vehicle, his feet dancing away from the threat of the wheels.

Then he was in the centre of the funnel, black figures springing away from the buggy's short bonnet with only inches to spare. One aimed a wild blow at the windscreen with his bush knife, but the weapon hit the steel framing and the glass held. The men's voices, strident and full of hate and over-excitement, were as frightening as their physical proximity. Two men, one each side of the Bustler, managed to grip the body on the corners where the roof joined the windscreen, and they pounded alongside, trying to slow the vehicle down. The one on the passenger's side attempted to jump into the seat, failed, nearly lost his hold, then carried on, keeping pace. The man on the driver's side was grunting with effort, his legs working like long lean pistons to keep up with the Bustler. Their joint pull was beginning to tell on the toy-sized engine and Matthew could hear the rest of the pack baying and screeching as they followed close behind. With desperation he clenched his right fist and hit out with all his strength at the groin of the nearest black. The man let go with a yelp of pain and fell back, doubling up in agony as he hit the ground. The man on the passenger's side had succeeded in gaining a crouching position on the broad edge of the buggy's frame, but for the moment his strength and balance were needed to keep himself from slipping back on to the road. A deep pothole appeared in the headlights and Matthew swerved towards it, driving the near-side front wheel into its centre. There was a metallic clunk, conjuring fear of a broken pinion, but as the Bustler bucked out of the hole the invader was jerked from his precarious perch and fell back into the road. As Matthew steadied the vehicle, thankfully aware he still had steerage, he felt a blow on the back of the seat followed by a clatter of something falling to the floor. He checked the rear mirror, fearful someone had succeeded in climbing in over the back, but his view of the road behind was uninterrupted and he realized that his attackers had given up. Intent only on putting as much distance as possible between himself and the mob, he pressed on down the now steepening hill, shaking his head and stretching his eyes like someone recovering from a blow on the head.

The Bustler was limping, an ominous clanking and vibration being transmitted from below the bonnet, but only when he reached the village did he slow, and by then he was shivering with reaction. When he stopped outside the bungalow and turned off the engine, his hand was shaking so much that he rattled the hanging bonnet key against the dashboard, and as he got out of the buggy his legs were weak and trembling. He leaned on the Bustler's low roof, resting his head in exhaustion on his arms, trying to collect his thoughts. He decided against driving on to the police station. If anyone was there at that time of the evening, it was not likely to be Captain White, and Matthew was in no mood to be fobbed off by some deputy. He wondered if it would be wise to spend the night by himself in Buck House. The mob would know where he was living. But the road was still fairly busy with walkers and the occasional car, and the bungalow next door was audibly filled by what sounded like the preliminaries of yet another party. For the first time he felt some comfort in being separated only by thin walls from a group of husky young men. He knocked on the door. It was opened by a large blond American.

'Sorry to trouble you,' Matthew said, 'but I have a little problem.'

The young man looked at him laconically.

'Join the club,' he said.

'I nearly got done over by a gang of thugs up the hill,' Matthew explained. 'It's just possible they may follow me.' He pointed to Buck House. 'I've taken that bungalow.'

'Yeah, I'd noticed.'

'I just wanted to say that if I should call for help I would be very grateful if you and your friends could give me a hand.'

'Sure,' the young man said, 'sure. No problem. Just give a shout and we'll come and fix 'em.'

'They may have bush knives.'

'No trouble.'

'Well, thanks very much indeed.'

'You're welcome,' the young man said, shutting the door.

It had been like borrowing a cup of sugar.

He went into Buck House, locking the front door and leaving the verandah light on, then made sure that the bolted back door off the kitchen was secure top and bottom. Then he took a stiff drink and went to bed. But he lay awake listening for anything more sinister than the mounting revels next door. Sleep filled very few of the ensuing hours.

'Yo' maht've killed someone,' the Captain growled.

'Jesus Christ,' Matthew said, slapping the table, 'someone might have killed *me*! I tell you, that gang wasn't thumbing a joy ride. They meant business.'

'What proof yo' got o' dat?' the Captain demanded.

'Proof? How much proof do you need? Do you imagine I would report such an incident if it was not true?'

'Ah ain't dealin' in specalation, man. Yo' can't come in here an' make dese allegations widout yo' have some proof.'

'I was by myself, I tell you. If I had proof it would be my headless body lying up there on Tabitha Heights.'

'So yo' haven't no proof,' the Captain confirmed with satisfaction. 'Listen, man, how Ah know yo' weren't up dere wid a skinful of liquor in yo'? What you tol' me soun's like dangerous drivin'. Runnin' down some high-spirited boys what was askin' yo' for a hitch.'

'I see,' Matthew said, his hands so tremulous with anger that he had to press them against the table. 'So now you have another useful alleged crime to quote. "Alleged attempted murder of innocent pedestrians by motorized raj-style honky." Your method of getting another "shit-assed honky out of the way".'

He knew he should not have said it, but his rage was in control of his reason. There was a pause and the Captain's small eyes narrowed.

'Yo' tryin' to provoke me, Mr Braine?'

'Seeing what you are capable of, that's hardly likely.'

'An' whaddya mean by dat?'

'You know damn well what I mean. Do you think I can't see the connection between last night and the death of Riley?'

The Captain did his best to portray injured amazement. It was a disappointing performance.

'Yo' crazy, man? Yo' know what yo' sayin'?'

'Yes, I do.' Matthew leaned across the table and his eyes blazed into the Captain's. The man's wary, shifty expression, and his lack of any genuine indignation, confirmed his suspicions. 'Now, look here, White, let's stop pretending. That bunch of thugs tried to kill me last night, and you knew about it long before I walked in here. Are you going to make some arrests and bring charges, or have I got to go above your head.'

'It's for yo' to make de charges, Mr Braine. Who yo' suggest Ah arrest? Yo' reckernize any o' yo' alleged assailants?'

'No, but I have something that should give you a lead.'

Matthew placed on the table the folded newspaper he had put beneath his chair. By design, it was *Labour's Voice* and contained the second article about the 'rape' of the dockyard. He opened the newspaper so that the article was the right way round for the Captain to see. On the newspaper lay a bush knife.

'Maybe something here is familiar to you,' Matthew said.

He could tell the Captain had recognized the article, but all he said was:

'Dat no knife Ah seen before.'

'Maybe you haven't, but it was thrown at me last night and landed in the back of my buggy. I don't doubt it was meant for my head. I suggest that the fingerprints on the handle should help you to narrow the field.'

The Captain picked the knife up by the blade and balanced it on is hand.

'An' dat's yo' only evidence for dis alleged attack?'

'It should be enough.'

The Captain smiled. Then he gripped the bush knife by the handle. Looking directly at Matthew and still smiling he slowly twisted the knife by the blade, making sure that every part of the handle was rotated in his large palm. He laid the knife on the paper.

'In dese cases, Mr Braine, it is gen'ally found dere is ver' liddle evidence.'

'You corrupt, murderous bastard!' Matthew exploded.

The Captain leaned across the table. His smile had turned into a triumphant leer. Their faces were within inches.

'Yo' don't seem ver' happy on dis island, Mr Braine. Ah dunno why yo' don' go back where you b'long, along o' dose lords 'n ladies who tink dis nigger island a fun place fo' bringin' dere bits 'n pieces in de winter time. No, suh, Mr Braine, Ah dunno why yo' stay on.'

'Is that a threat?'

'Ah don't t'reaten pipple, Mr Braine, but sometimes Ah promise dem tings.'

'Yes, I can guess,' Matthew said.

The corporal came into the room. Captain White's face took on an expression of concern.

'Ah tink, Mr Braine, dat mebbe dat ver' unpleasant incident de udder night affected yo' judgment a liddle. Why yo' not take a liddle vacation somewhere, or mebbe consider goin' back to de U.K.? Dis not de bes' place to be sick. Dat right, ain't it, corporal?'

'Dat's ri', Captain,' the corporal said. He was half the Captain's size and a head and a half shorter. Standing side by side they resembled a double-act, which Matthew reflected was precisely what they were.

'To hell with the pair of you,' he said lamely.

He picked up his copy of *Labour's Voice*.

'You'd better keep the knife,' he said. 'You'll doubtless find some use for it.'

He walked to the door.

'Don't imagine,' he said turning, 'that you have heard the last of this. There is a world beyond this island.'

As an exit line it left a lot to be desired.

30

ZAFADA, a grey cone on the horizon, was alternately masked and revealed by the dipping sails as 'Patience' ran before the steady breeze. It was perfect sailing weather with just enough cloud to give relief from the already burning sun. Only a one-cat protest committee struck a complaining note.

Although larger and more self-assured than the unsteady ball of fur which had joined ship in the Canaries, Seamew was rediscovering her sea legs with difficulty. Weeks of soft living in Port St George had taken their toll; the tolerant company of Sebastian had demoralized; for weeks she had basked unashamedly in conditions calculated to make her feel all cat. Now, each time 'Patience' pitched or tossed, she pronounced stridently upon those who meddle with the *status quo*.

Matthew's decision to return to 'Patience' sooner than agreed with Sebastian had been taken within half an hour of leaving the police station. Despite the assurance of the young American in the bungalow next door, he felt he would be safer back on the boat, sandwiched by two occupied yachts in an area where a mob of blacks would be conspicuous.

Sebastian, leaving Seamew in Matthew's care, had gone to Guadeloupe on a Brazilian ketch and would not be back for at least two days. So Matthew had made the move by himself, a trip each way in the Bustler completing the transfer of their belongings. He left a note for Sebastian in Buck House, vaguely worded in case it fell into the wrong hands.

He had decided against contacting the Richardsons or Brenda. The islanders' craving for non-involvement had been made fully apparent and he guessed he would only consolidate his reputation for fevered imagination if he recited the events of the past twenty-four hours.

He ate on board that evening, and despite his feeling of comparative security he fastened all hatches as soon as the crew of neighbouring boats had gone below. It was not until he was falling asleep, enjoying the yacht's gentle response to the wind which swept down from Tabitha Heights, that he was overwhelmed by desire to get away from the island as soon as he could and return to his first landfall in the Caribbean.

As 'Patience' ploughed steadily through the vivid blue water towards Zafada, he thought again and again from every angle about his escape from death, the events preceding it, his final encounter with Captain White. He asked himself whether fear had spurred his departure from Monesterio, telling himself it had not, any more than that fear alone had prompted him to leave England. If anything, Big Daddy's advice had at first stirred defiance and a determination to get Riley's death and his own near-escape investigated; but calmer reflection over a solitary coffee on the terrace of the Captain's Arms had given him a more realistic view of the odds. Reaction had set in, prompting a fierce need of change. The weeks on the island had underlined the unremitting sameness of human society – Monesterio and England, in all essentials microcosm and macrocosm – and the events of the past few days had only accelerated awareness that no sanctuary or heaven on earth could contain one's fellow men. The evidence of truth in Sartre's dictum that hell is other people lay in the bliss of escaping from them.

He recognized the negativity of his stance; that the idyllic circumstances of his flight from Monesterio should soften rather than harden his judgements of others; that he had found a likeable friend in Sebastian; above all, that he had been given the opportunity to write what he saw as his best book to date. There was reason for gratitude. He had no regret that his original plan had gone awry. His irritation with himself at abandoning his plan had been dispersed by absorption in his book. And Sebastian had been right – reason was not enough; 'there must be despair'. He had been short on despair. His creativity had been given just the breathing space and provocation it needed . . .

He filled his lungs with the pure air as an antidote to the tension of introspection and self-pity. The sea was empty save for a white yawl well away to port and heading south. He did not rebuke himself for the anthropomorphism of imagining that

'Patience' was equally enjoying being under sail again. The automatic pilot was disconnected. He was getting to know the yacht again, preferring the almost sensual pleasure of her response to the hand-held tiller.

'Quite like old times,' he told Seamew.

The kitten, tottering about on the coach roof, was too busy seeking survival with dignity to be communicative. Mounting queasiness out-distanced any nostalgia for the 'old times'. She staggered as 'Patience' negotiated an extra steep trough, her eyes taking conflicting sightings of the unsteady horizon. She was a fat kitten accustomed to good living and calm waters, and she didn't care who knew it.

Matthew's only regret was that the novel was not completed.

'I'll finish it before I make the climb,' he promised Seamew. 'After that, nothing will matter a fig.'

Seamew was already on the broad plateau of fatalism and in no mood to become emotional over literature. Her legs were spread as far as her tubby little body allowed, and she glared at the sea with unconcealed suspicion and dislike. Life had been more civilized with Sebastian.

Matthew scooped her off the roof with his free hand and pushed her unceremoniously below.

'Go and make some tea,' he said.

He had done no more than glance at the letter from Rebecca which he had collected before facing Captain White and then forgotten. The moment seemed right.

'Dearest Matt, We were all so glad to hear from you again and to know how happy you are about the new book. I rang the girls as soon as I got it - your letter, I mean - and both of them of course pretended to be frightfully blasé, claiming to have known all along that you would write a masterpiece as easily as you reached the Caribbean! But I could tell they were terribly pleased underneath.

You say you have nearly finished it. Of course that makes me wonder whether you will be coming back soon or whether you will want to stay on out there for a little holiday. I miss you an awful lot. I'm doing another day and a half in the shop to make the time pass more easily, and Vikki Morgan comes in quite a lot in the evenings because

Paul took the T.V. with him when he ran off with that air hostess and Vikki doesn't feel she should rent one with the uncertain financial future. *Our* set's playing up a bit these days and the man came and muttered darkly about the tube nearing the end of its useful life (isn't that anthropomorphism or whatever you call it?), but that seems absurd when you think that the Morgans have had that Jap set for nearly fifteen years without a moment's trouble.

Otherwise everything here goes on much as before. I've done what I can in the garden, but of course at this time of year there isn't a lot. The weather's been awful. Snow falling on to slush, then rain, then more freezing ... yuk! Old Bert Randall dug over the vegetable area before the worst of the weather and wants to know if you are going to have those stringless pole beans again this year or go back to the scarlet runners. It's obvious which he prefers!

Oh, and Simon Loewenstein rang, wanting to know whether you had made the crossing. It was rather satisfying being able to tell him you got there ages ago, and I hope it was all right I added you'd written most of a novel you felt might be the best thing you'd ever done. He said he was looking forward to reading it very much indeed ...

I was touched by what you said about my plant. Your rescuing it after the capsize, I mean. I'm so glad the cuttings took. I like to think of it still being with you, even unto the second generation as it were, though I suppose that's silly.

I've kept the most exciting news for last - Judy's having a baby, due in about five months. Goodness knows how they are going to manage in their commune, but I suppose everyone looks after everyone else like in a kibbutz, or isn't that quite the same? Anyway, she wants to call it Matthew if it's a boy and Rebecca if it's a girl, which is rather sweet, and I suppose names like that are quite suitable for the rather biblical sort of togetherness lifestyle they seem to have embraced.

Anyway, how do you feel about being a grand-father? Well, nearly. At least it will give you a new name to dedicate your book to. I've already seen the sweetest little one-piece woollen outfit, but the choice is (guess what?)

pink or blue, so of course I can't buy it until we know the sex. Really, they should arrange things better...'

The rest of the letter was entirely on a note of incipient grandmotherhood and he read it while sharing with Seamew the breakfast he had postponed in his anxiety to leave Port St George as soon as possible after daybreak. 'Patience' was making such good progress that it would not be long before he would want to concentrate on the approach to Zafada. He was curious to see the east face of the island near to. But first he wanted to get down to his novel, the final chapter for which was churning through his brain in an unusually complete form. He put 'Patience' on to automatic pilot and got down to work.

Before he went below, the even greyness of the island had already given way to tones. When he came on deck he could make out patches of distinct and differing colours where landslips and drifts of sparse vegetation lent character to the whale-shaped mass of rock. He decided to sail up the east coast and to clip the northern end as closely as possible before reaching his old anchorage. It seemed the quickest route, since he could lose wind on the lee shore, and he was intent on not wasting time. The last chapter had still to be completed and then there was revision of much that had gone before...

Zafada sloped upwards from south to north, and a shale-filled break in the cliffs on the south-east corner suggested easier access than the almost sheer face he had tackled on Christmas Day. But he judged from the breakers that even in still conditions the swell on the rocks would make landing on the windward shore impossible.

He felt again the pull of the formidably inaccessible and somehow mysterious great hump of rock. He wished he had questioned Sebastian more closely about his 'kingdom'. But the reluctance had been mutual, if for different reasons. Ever since Christmas Day Matthew had felt peculiarly possessive about the island, and in a curious way that possessiveness had increased, as though in some strange manner Zafada belonged to him or had, or was yet to have, some major part to play in his life. Whenever he had found – as was usually the case – that others did not know or care about its existence, he had felt an odd relief.

Keeping parallel with the island meant a broad reach. For fear of hidden rocks he stood a few hundred yards out to sea. He recalled that the water off the northern tip had looked deep, so he kept in as close to the tip of the island as the swell permitted, gybing 'Patience' before she was sailing by the lee, so that his view was not obstructed by the main and he could trim the sails to give maximum speed for the final rounding up into contrary or little wind.

It worked fairly well. 'Patience' lost way when only about fifty yards to the west of the rock on which he had nearly foundered those few but many-seeming weeks earlier. He decided to drop anchor rather than try to work further inshore. It was necessary to add an extra length of warp in order to get adequate hold on the deep and steeply shelving sea-bed. It had been a simple, pleasant sail. He furled the main on to the boom and resolved to get back to his book as soon as he had eaten. He felt slightly queasy, but Seamew recovered quickly in the gentle swell and demolished half a tin of cat food.

Because 'Patience' was anchored further out to sea than on the previous occasion, the view took in most of Zafada's western face. This was now reflecting the afternoon sun, and Matthew studied the island through his binoculars while he ate a light meal of bread, cheese and fruit. He was puzzled by what appeared to be a small building near the southern end of the island, but recalling that Zafada had once been mined for phosphates he supposed it to be a ruin on some abandoned wharf or jetty.

He rigged the awning which had long been a necessity for life at anchor in Port St George. Retrieving his typescript from beneath the cushion which Seamew, now torpid, had long made her own, he settled down to his typewriter.

The words flowed so effortlessly that he experienced the writer's familiar fear that what comes easily may not be coming well. The last page of the final chapter was finished before darkness fell. It was a short chapter, no more than five thousand words, and he worked up another small worry, fearful that it might give the impression of being rushed. He read it through carefully, finding little needing to be changed. He dipped back to earlier chapters, wondering if he would find their quality overshadowed by the final pages, but he saw nothing that minimal revision could not put right. The book was fit for retyping and submission.

He smiled at the trap he had set for himself, remembering that when he left England there was no thought that he would ever again write a book. He felt in his diaphragm the flutter which always came when a spell of writing proved totally satisfying – a quiver of fruition difficult to convey to those unaccustomed to the joys which seem to come so less often than the agonies of creativity.

He toyed with the title, uncertain whether *All Said and Done* was suitable; it might have been more fitting for an autobiography. Well, the novel was so autobiographical that perhaps it was exactly right. He tapped the sheaf of pages together along ends and sides to make a tidy rectangle. Unless he put the book out of mind he would tinker with it for the rest of the evening and then lie awake inventing doubts. So he slipped it into its folder, lifted cushion and somnolent kitten with one hand, and thrust it out of sight. Then he remembered what Rebecca had said in her letter, so he retrieved the folder, wound a blank sheet into his typewriter, and wrote on it:

'For Rebecca'

and in brackets, 'or Matthew because she/he may one day understand what made me write it.'

He inserted the sheet below the title page and replaced the folder beneath the cushion, humming a tune from *Salad Days*.

With a sudden craving for music, he chose a tape. The *New World Symphony*, it seemed exactly right. He prepared his evening meal in the dying light of the sun, peeling a yam in the cockpit, his body swaying to remembered passages. He felt wonderfully well, so fit he could have climbed a mountain. He grimaced, remembering that this was precisely what he had come to Zafada to do. Why? He looked up from his preparations at the island's jagged peaks. Through them the wind moaned softly and his binoculars showed that the gullies and crevices were alive with birds returning to their nests in the fading light.

His mind and body were in a rare harmony of quiet exhilaration. He was happy with his solitude, in no way missing the noisy bustle and unpredictability of Port St George village and dockyard. Yet a part of him wished to share his elation, and this turned his mind to Rebecca and to her letter and so to remembering that he had left her plant in Buck House. He wished it was on board, a kind of link across thousands of miles of ocean, but he told himself that Sebastian would attend with his usual efficiency to its every need.

The book's completion demanded some kind of formal celebration. He remembered that the bilge still contained Rebecca's bottle of champagne. He drank before his meal and then after, as an accompaniment for a heated tin of sponge pudding which was liberally coated with apricot jam. The evening passed pleasantly with a selection of Mozart and Debussy, and before turning in he re-played the *largo* from the *New World*. After the champagne this brought him to tears; it was one of the few pieces of music for which Rebecca, before marriage, had shared his enthusiasm.

To have lit the riding light would have been absurd. He gave Seamew the saucer of milk Sebastian had told him was now obligatory as a night cap. Sleep returned readily enough to Seamew, less easily to Matthew. The building he had glimpsed through his binoculars niggled at him. There was something about it he didn't like. He fell to sleep soon after midnight after resolving to clear up the mystery in the morning.

He had forgotten how steep the western face of Zafada looked when the morning sun was behind the island. The perils of his earlier ascent came back to him. The champagne had done nothing to put his metabolism into the peak of condition. As he shared breakfast with Seamew in the sunless near-chill below the great face of rock which towered a thousand feet into the sky, he wondered if he had been wrong to return to the highest end of the island.

He looked again through his binoculars at Zafada's tallest summit. The wind, such as it was, had backed in the night and was now variable from the north. He suspected it was in the process of changing, for it was an uncommon direction. With the mysterious building back in mind, he saw that he could solve more than one problem with a simple sail to the southern end of the island. He was under way within ten minutes of his decision, ghosting through the water in a breeze that was certainly too light to be relied upon for long.

The nearer they got to the other end of Zafada, the less happy he felt. It was increasingly clear that the building was of recent construction. Even more disturbing, there was evidence of human life. His heart sank, then lifted a little at the thought that he might have stumbled upon nothing more sinister than a fisherman's refuge. But his guess was soon demolished. The building proved to be a shingled timber hut built on stilts on the rocks at the foot of cliffs perhaps six hundred feet high, but not as sheer as those at the other end of the island. The hut's white-painted door faced to the north and was open, as was a small shuttered window looking west. Below the hut, between its stilts, two or three mattresses were airing. Worst of all, on the wall of the hut was a white notice board announcing absurdly, improbably, in red letters, ZAFADA POST OFFICE.

It was like an idiotic dream. He dropped anchor less than eighty yards offshore, feeling a surge of deflation he did nothing to analyse, preferring the all-out physical relief of anchoring, furling and preparing to go ashore. Disappointment gave way to anger. It was beyond his imagination to understand the ludicrous presence of a blow-away wooden hut parading as a post office on a deserted rock miles from the nearest inhabited island in the middle of the Caribbean. It was no figment of his imagination, no dream, though it should have been. It was unarguably, detestably there, and there had to be some explanation. The only consoling factor was the steep, shale-filled gorge which soared some five hundred feet above and a little to the north of the hut, ending in a slight valley which he judged might be a plateau offering an easier route to the summit.

Two young blacks were standing on the beach gazing at him. The narrow shore was massively cobbled by rounded rocks through which the surf creamed, leaving smooth gleaming hummocks which resembled a herd of basking seals of many sizes. Between the hut and the cliffs a washing line held a pair of shorts and a towel. The whole thing was so utterly incongruous that Matthew snorted with indignation as he assembled his coracle. He wrapped some food, two cans of beer, a flat tin of Elastoplast, and his binoculars in two plastic bags before putting them into a canvas holdall. He had considered leaving the binoculars behind, seeing no real need of them, but they were his most cherished possession apart from 'Patience' and he was not happy about leaving them on the boat which was an easy swim from the shore for the two boys on the beach. He made fast one end of a long, thin nylon rope to a stanchion at deck level, then tied the other round his waist and thence to an eye in the rim of the coracle. He coiled the rope and tucked it into his waist so that it would pay out as he paddled to the shore.

One of the boys shouted and pointed to a large rock which was further out in the surf than the rest. The boys clambered on to the rock, and when the coracle was lifting and falling in the swell within two or three yards of it one of them threw him a line. He saw what they had in mind. The boy kept the line almost taut between himself and Matthew, then when a particularly deep swell promised to carry the coracle up and towards the rock the boy timed the speed of his pull so that Matthew was taken to within grabbing distance at the maximum height of the water. The boy's strong wiry arm took Matthew's and hauled him on to the rock, while the other black recovered the coracle before it was drawn back into the sea. Apart from nearly losing his straw hat and scraping his left leg on the rock's slippery side, Matthew had made a remarkably smooth return to Zafada. His holdall was not even damp.

The blacks were as quick and wiry as goats. One, with the twiggy hair and wild eyes of a Rastafarian, carried the coracle to above the surf-line. The other took his satchel to the post office as he waded carefully between the rocks. He thanked them. The Rasta said nothing, but the other put his holdall inside the door of the hut and said to someone inside:

'Hey, Pete, yo' got a customer, man.'

He entered the hut up a short flight of open timber steps. It was bare inside except for a counter made of boards resting on trestles and a steel cabinet of much earlier vintage than the hut. A third man was behind the counter. He too was black, but old enough to be the boys' father. He was more formally dressed than the boys, which was to say he wore long dark trousers and a blue shirt with a battery of pencils and pens in its two breast pockets.

'Good morning, sir,' he said in a polite, matter-of-fact voice, as though Matthew had just stepped in off the High Street. He had an open, pleasant face.

Matthew offered him his hand, feeling his role to be more that of explorer than customer.

'This is a bit of a surprise,' he said.

'Surprise, sir?'

'A post office. Here. Zafada isn't inhabited, surely?'

'That's right, sir.'

'Does anyone ever call in?'

'Yes, *sir*! The day we opened was like race week out there. People from all over. New York, London, Paris, Rome. Some man even try to land up there in a chopper, but he go away and come by later from a boat.'

'But why the excitement? What's the point of coming out to a deserted rock when there are post offices on the islands?'

'The special stamps, sir. Ain't that what you come for?'

'Special stamps?'

The postmaster opened a cheap manilla folder.

'See here. Special Zafada issue. Very valuable first-day covers. Still worth buying, sir. Special Zafada over-stamp.'

'Well I'll be damned!' Matthew exclaimed. 'Do you man this hut... post office... right through the year?'

'No, sir, only two days a week if things are right for the mail boat. It not always possible to land here, you see.'

'So I've gathered.'

'If you want a set, sir, no problem. I'm short of the fifty cents right now, but all the others...'

'I'm not much of a philatelist,' Matthew said.

'You could send a letter to your wife or some friend,' the postmaster suggested. 'I can make up a very pretty envelope for you.'

'Well, maybe on my way back,' Matthew said.

'You coming back, sir?' The man looked surprised.

'Well, down. I'm going to climb to the summit.'

'To the top of this island?'

Matthew nodded.

'You got permission for that, sir?'

'Permission?' Matthew felt a prickling on the hairs of his neck.

'Yes, sir, like we say clearance. This is Government property and my instructions are that no one land here except in the way of business at this post office.'

Matthew laughed mirthlessly.

'Oh, for God's sake!' he said. 'You can't mean it. I've never heard of anything so ridiculous. What harm could I do climbing up a deserted rock in the middle of the sea?'

'It not a matter of harm, sir,' the postmaster said patiently, 'it a matter of my instructions. The Government make the rules.'

'They certainly do,' Matthew said angrily. 'It's small wonder these islands are riddled with tensions and hatreds between races when individual freedom can be curtailed to such absurd lengths.'

'If you'll pardon me saying so, sir, I don't go along with that. Too many folk they come to these places and see what they don't like and they say it the fault of that man because he black or that man because he white. I don't see that, no sir. I think we humans we just got it wrong all over. Governments they bad wherever you go, black, white, any colour. They just a bunch of humans, sir, and when humans get to tell others what to do it all go wrong. It just something about humans, that what I say. They ain't like other creatures. All this meddling and power and violence. We making a hell on this earth, sir, and that the truth of it. I can see that even just sitting on this island here with my stamps. Truth is, I seen it clearer since I first come.'

Matthew gestured with both hands, placatorily.

'I'm sorry, I didn't mean to sound off. I don't want to create trouble for you. But I've come a long way to make this climb. I'd be very disappointed not to be able to.'

'You see, sir, once I start letting people...'

'Has anyone else wanted to?'

The postmaster made a face and half lifted his arms.

'No, sir, I admit there ain't been no rush.'

'Then I don't understand why the Government are so jumpy.'

'They not very happy about that party what came over, sir. Since then I get my instructions.'

'Party?'

'The white men who come out with that fellow he say is the king. You not hear about that?'

Matthew had forgotten Peter Richardson's account of the 'assault'.

'Not in any great detail, no.'

'They go to the top and plant a flag, then put a proclamation on the wall here. The Government not like that, sir, I can tell you.'

'A proclamation? You're kidding!'

'Maybe those men were kidding, sir. They very light-hearted about it. But the Government they don't like it at all, sir, not one little bit.'

'What did the proclamation say?'

'Just one minute, sir, and I see if I find the copy they gave me. We have very nice little talk together and they gave me a copy of the proclamation.'

He rummaged in a drawer of the filing cabinet and produced the carbon copy of a typed sheet. It read:

PROCLAMATION

In 1865 the island of Zafada was claimed by Seumas Oliver Scully as a Kingdom for his son Patrick James. On July 21st 1880, his fifteenth birthday, Patrick James Scully was crowned King of Zafada by a member of the clergy at a correctly conducted ceremony of consecration.

King Patrick's claim was never contested, but soon after his coronation the British Government annexed the island and declared it a dependency of Monesterio. The British Colonial Office subsequently admitted that this act of annexation did not annul the sovereignty vested in King Patrick and his successors.

Patrick James Scully became a famous novelist. His book 'A World Without End' was acknowledged as a classic in early science fiction. He and his successor, the late King Kit 1st, created an intellectual aristocracy of well-known figures in literature and the arts. The ambitions of the present monarch, King Sebastian, like those of his predecessor, are cultural, not political.

This year is the realm's centenary. With the pending relinquishment of British control over Monesterio and her dependencies, it has seemed timely to issue a reminder of Zafada's abiding monarchy. To this end the flag of Zafada has today been planted on the island's summit.

The motive for this action is not to provoke or contest but to confirm our right and desire to invite friendly and fruitful collaboration with the Government of Monesterio on the eve of that country's independence.

The penultimate paragraph was asterisked, and a note at the foot of the proclamation read:

> The blue, brown and green of the Zafadan flag represent the sea, soil and plant life of the island. The flag reflects the reigning monarch's concern with environmental matters and is a reminder of the original ruler's Irish origins.

The proclamation was dated and signed by Sebastian and several others. Matthew recognized the names of Peter Richardson, a distinguished American scientist, and an official in the National Trust.

He laughed.

'Well, all right,' he said, 'but what was the Government getting steamed up about? This was obviously just a bunch of egg-heads letting their remaining hairs down and being a bit schoolboyish. Surely no one has been so po-faced as to take it seriously?'

The postmaster shook his head.

'They not like it, sir. Flags. Proclamations. That very political material, sir.'

'Yes, I do now remember hearing they weren't very pleased, but to forbid anyone to land on this island unless they are on post office business, it does seem to be taking things a bit far.'

'I guess they think one thing may lead to another, sir. There some very funny people around these days.'

'Well, I can promise you this,' Matthew said. 'I have no territorial claims or political intentions in wanting to climb to the top.'

'You a climber then, sir?'

'Not really. Not as an end in itself.'

'Then if I may ask, sir...'

Matthew shrugged.

'I don't know really; I can't explain it. I suppose I have a sort of strong wish to... get away.'

The postmaster nodded.

'I guess we all get like that from time to time, sir.'

'I came here once before,' Matthew said, 'but I landed at the other end of the island and reached the summit from there.'

The postmaster whistled.

'That must have been some climb, sir. Even the boys here

would find an easier way than that.'

'It was tough, but worth it when I reached the peak. What you said just now interested me – about seeing things more clearly since you came to Zafada. That's just how I felt when I was here at Christmas. I'd been in a pretty bad way mentally before I came here, and somehow on the summit of Zafada...'

The postmaster nodded again.

'There something special about this island. It can take folk one way or the other but no one forget Zafada.'

'Then you'll understand why I felt drawn to come back. Like a piece of iron being attracted by a magnet. I wanted to return, to be alone, to climb to the summit again, more than I wanted anything else. I'm afraid that's why I was put out to find this post office here.'

The postmaster closed his folder.

'If you happen to go out of here, sir, I ain't necessarily going to be watching where you go next.'

Matthew smiled.

'Thanks! You're a sport. But what about the boys?'

'I daresay they can go back along the shore and look to their fish lines – just until, maybe, you get started.'

'Perhaps you could have a couple of sets ready for me, and three envelopes stamped for the U.K.?'

The postmaster grinned.

'No problem, sir.'

'Make it four envelopes.'

It could do no harm to send Simon a casual note, mentioning that the book was now completed.

'My pleasure, sir.'

'If I should get back after you close, maybe one of the boys could go over to my boat in the morning with them and pick up the money. I haven't any on me.'

'Once we're here, sir, we never close.'

They shook hands.

'While you're up there, sir,' the postmaster added, 'keep your eyes open for the king's pyjamas.'

'His pyjamas!'

'Sure. He tell me the flag was made out of a pair of his pyjamas. The blue piece, anyways.'

Matthew smiled. 'I'll do my best. But I should think it blew into the sea long ago. Well, thanks again.'

The postmaster beamed.

'You're welcome, sir!'

The ravine rose at a sixty-degree angle, its treacherous volcanic shale and the often precariously-seated rocks giving no certain hold for hand or foot. At one point he lost his balance and slithered down some fifteen feet in a cloud of choking dust. A large rock which had been lying on the surface of the shale kept on down the gorge before shattering with an audible thump against a projecting ledge. He saw why the post office had been tucked away to the south of the ravine, hard up against the cliff face. Some of the rocks waiting for dislodgement could have demolished the hut like a matchbox.

After two hours he reached the most difficult part of the climb. At the top of the gully there was an overhang of smooth rock. From above it some twelve feet of rusty iron pipe dropped into the ravine. He guessed it had had something to do with the abandoned phosphate mining. It proved of no help in conquering the sheer ledge which confronted him, and in the end he had to edge round the side of the overhang, clinging like a beetle to the smooth yet friable rock, fighting the temptation to look down. Had he slipped there would have been nothing to break his fall until he reached the area of boulder-studded scree he had been careful to skirt for fear of precipitating a bone-breaking, flesh-stripping avalanche.

The last few feet were the worst. His body was curved round the overhang, his feet tense with their effort to retain a hold, his hands scrabbling for a root or outcrop of rock that would give his tired body the chance to haul itself the final vital inches. Not until the greater part of his body was on the ledge could he let his toes forgo their precarious hold, and he kicked and squirmed the last few inches until only the lower half of his legs overhung the gorge.

He was pouring sweat and too exhausted to go further until he had recovered his breath. His heart was hammering against his chest so violently that it almost hurt. After two or three minutes he was able to crawl a few feet and collapse again, lying on his back with his arms out-stretched, thankful for the return of the breeze after the still heat of the gorge.

He sat up and looked down at 'Patience', so small and still it was difficult to believe she was a real, ocean-going yacht. Except for the birds there was no other sign of life on land or sea. The post office was hidden far below by the cliff face to which it clung. Until that moment he had been concentrating too hard on surviving the climb to develop his reaction to the discovery that Zafada had become an outpost of Monesterion bureaucracy. Despite his cordial talk with the postmaster, and although he told himself not to be an idiot, he was bitterly disappointed. His plan to return to the island had had little shape beyond a strong desire to cut off from the affairs of men, though he had felt that once again to reach Zafada's summit, there to collect his thoughts in solitude, was for some indefinable reason the thing he had to do.

He stood up and examined himself gingerly for damage. He had escaped lightly with a few grazes and a place on the thigh which would doubtless turn a royal purple before the day was out.

The plateau was no more than a few hundred yards long and dipped again on the windward side of the island. It was thinly covered in grasses, sedges, lantana and less friendly shrubs. Almost as soon as he began walking he saw signs of the long-abandoned mining venture. Scattered among the thorn bushes was evidence of the cable-way that had traversed the gorge. Pulleys, carrier wheels, two great iron buckets, a boiler which looked as though it had come from Stephenson's 'Rocket', some chain, a quantity of wire hawser, and the remains of what might have been a trolley. A splendid winch handle, almost too heavy to carry in one hand, was proof enough that Peter Richardson had been one of very few souvenir hunters foolish or intrepid enough to penetrate Zafada's hidden hinterland.

On the south side of the saddle, built hard up against the rocky, thorn-covered bluff, were two stone-built structures resembling wartime pillboxes. Inspection suggested they were bake ovens. On the top of the bluff was another structure lacking a visible roof. Matthew climbed the bluff, his earlier disappointment eclipsed by his curiosity over the evidence of distant and somehow acceptable occupation. The roofless building was clearly a cistern for collecting or storing water, but its retentiveness must have been weathered away over the years, for when he peered over its edge, peered at in turn by a brace of basking black lizards, he saw two adult boobies huddled together in the far corner. They made no attempt to fly out of the cistern whose floor area provided too short a runway for clearing the high sides.

Sympathy for the birds' plight was heightened by its contrast with the vast, limitless freedom of sea and sky which lay only a wall's width away. It was somehow obscene that man's thoughtless interference had laid a cruelly effective trap in a place so patently the rightful home of creatures other than man.

Without further thought Matthew climbed on to the broad edge of the cistern and jumped down. The floor was a foot or two lower than the ground outside and was inches deep in a gruesome carpet of small bones which crunched beneath his feet. The boobies pressed themselves against each other, too weak to resist capture with anything but faint, slightly comical squawks that sounded like 'Oh, no!'

He grasped one of the birds with both hands from behind, in case of protest from the strong beak. It was like holding a bag of thin sticks and he wondered if rescue had come too late. He stood by the south wall of the cistern so that the booby would have a clear flight-path down the headland to the open sea, then swept the bird gently up and away over the wall. It used its wings immediately and he was glad to see that it had enough strength to keep a horizontal course until the top of the cistern wall hid it from view. The second bird followed it a few moments later.

Apart from the layer of bones the cistern was empty. Getting out was going to mean taking a run and a jump at one corner. In his exhausted state it seemed an eminently suitable moment to eat some of the food from the satchel he had left on top of the wall. It was already mid-day and the white heat of the sun was turning the cistern into an open-topped oven. He drank a can of the warm beer and ate a sandwich, crouched into one corner, gaining a little shade for his head by pressing hard back against the wall. There was a smell in the cistern which suggested that the last birds to die had not yet been fully cleaned by scavengers and the elements. It seemed pointless to have saved only two when thousands more must follow. He considered how to prevent further destruction of the foolish, rather endearing creatures, and decided that some form of ramp was the best answer.

Disinclined to contribute personally to the cistern's unsavoury carpet, he took as long a run as possible from one corner to the other, scrabbling furiously at the wall with his toes as his arms wrapped themselves painfully over the weather-worn rim. Knowing that a second attempt would find him weaker, he put every ounce of his strength into the assault, flinging his right leg sideways and upwards in a desperate bid to gain leverage.

It was touch and go. For a moment he seemed suspended in the air, uncertain of enough strength to improve the tenuous hold his foot had gained on the wall's edge. With desperation he forced his arms to give him just enough pull to bring the rough edge of the wall painfully level with his lower ribs. He heaved and rolled himself on to its flat top, almost falling on to the ground beyond. He sat there for a minute or two to recover, the hot hard rock burning through his shorts, convinced that his lacerations had been substantially augmented.

'You silly old fart,' he said, 'you're past this kind of thing.'

He thought of throwing rocks into the cistern to make a ramp, but at the top of the bluff there was none of a size he could handle. To have brought enough material up from below, one at a time, would have been beyond his physical ability or time. He descended to the plateau and searched for an alternative. Any timber there might have been from the mining days had long since succumbed to rain and sun. The man-made metal was unsuitable in shape and of unliftable weight. He decided that the only answer was to topple the dead fifteen-foot stem of an agave from the mini-forest of these riotously blooming plants at the east end of the plateau. This he did with some difficulty, avoiding the needle-sharp dagger-like leaves which grew from the base. He hauled the stem up the bluff, gasping and pouring sweat, positioning it as best he could inside the cistern, uncertain of the birds' skill as tightrope walkers. The stem was hard but brittle; it could not last long. He resolved to rig up something more satisfactory on his return from the summit.

The east face of the island was a gentle slope compared to the west, rising at an angle of some twenty degrees and finishing in an almost uninterrupted fringe of steep cliffs that made access to the eastern shore impossible. On the plateau's north side were more buildings – cisterns; an intact and puzzling rotunda with no door, slit windows and a pointed domed roof; the remains of a long, low house in which a cement-floored room containing a Victorian fireplace was much as it must have been left sixty or more years earlier when the island was abandoned. He was cheered by the lack of litter or any other sign of human visitation. The roof was intact, the room dry. With food and water he could have bivouacked in the house, but he wondered what night creatures there would be to contend with. A rat he had seen eating an egg had been of fair size.

A magenta bougainvillaea grew by the side of the house. Its white-eyed blooms seemed larger than any he had seen before. He picked three small clusters of petals and put them into the tin of Elastoplast, pressing them gently between the medicated strips, hoping to remember to enclose them in his letters to Rebecca and the children.

He moved on round the side of the hill, climbing steadily through terrain heavily populated by nesting boobies. They jerked and dipped their gannet-like heads at him, more enquiry than threat in the gesture. Had he wished, he could have grasped the birds by the neck, for they made no attempt to escape even when he was within two feet of their nests.

The greater threat was the exploding cacti which favoured the more gently sloping ground. He found what he judged was the same faint, disintegrating track he had discovered at Christmas, so he kept to this, not bothering to climb to either of the first two peaks that showed themselves. The heat was intense, but the ceaseless breeze and his hat made it bearable.

A young booby sitting on the track like a beaked powder-puff squawked at his approach. He lifted it up, conscious of the softness of its snow-white down and the vulnerability of its warm, tremulous body.

A few more hundred yards brought him to the summit. He was childishly pleased to see that the stick he had planted there was still in place. He told himself he should have tied a handkerchief to it, and now that this thought had come to him he did so, rather glad there was no one watching.

He sat below the staff, a few yards from the vertiginous edge, gazing westwards across the empty sea. How long he sat there he could not have said, for there came upon him a mood of such peace and timelessness it was as though he had arrived at a haven beyond which all ambition ceased. For a while he gazed through his binoculars at the wheeling birds, and north and east towards the larger islands, but the watching became pointless when he realized he had no wish to bring the world any nearer. He placed the binoculars on the flat rock which topped the summit behind him, then leant back with his head against the satchel, gazing from beneath the brim of his tilted hat at the lordly glide of a frigate bird in the high-clouded sky.

His mind roamed with objectivity and resignation, his thoughts centred mostly on the more pleasant memories, not the least the completion of his book. He recalled with amusement the character in *Humboldt's Gift* who was so apt to promise a Major Statement. Well, in his fashion and to the best of his ability he had made his own Major Statement. Not much of one, maybe, but all he was capable of telling in the way of what he had learned and sought and achieved in a life many shades and degrees below cause for satisfaction. If it was to be said against him that he had written of current values from the standpoint of an older generation, at least he was qualified to speak for those willing to admit that no one should claim age as reason for resisting change. If his own style of humanism had been inadequate, short in its awareness of the unity of life and of what that realization demanded, it may have served its purpose on the evolutionary ladder. Only time would show if he had at last 'got through'. He admitted to himself that he had not lost the vanity to hope that this time the world might place him among the ranks of writers who had contributed something more than acid entertainment at the expense of the minor follies of men. He smiled. Maybe, this time, Simon would ask him for a studio portrait...

His mind returning to Bellow's book, he recalled the second half of the passage where Charles Citrine had speculated on the Hereafter. At the time he had not chosen to ponder the further option which had been given. Now, for some reason, passages were coming into his mind. How had that paragraph gone? 'The option is to let the deepest elements in you disclose their deepest information. If there is nothing but non-being and oblivion waiting for us, the prevailing beliefs have not misled us, and that's that.' He could remember no more than the gist of the rest of it, to the effect that as the prevailing beliefs seldom make sense, the rationality and the finality of the oblivion-view were suspect. Another short sentence, one which came in a passage that had made him laugh out loud, had stuck in his mind and had kept recurring during his voyage from the Canaries. 'You were born trying to prove that life on this earth was not feasible.' Had it stuck because it was true of himself, or because he needed its healthy dismissal of his self-absorption? That was the trouble with Bellow. How much was maturity and depth, how much fireworks and professionalism disguising a magpie, mick-taking mind? Well, he had got his Nobel Prize, which was doubtless more than would be bestowed upon that blood bank lying beneath a cushion in the cabin of a small yacht on a blue, improbable sea.

He thought about Rebecca, Judy and Mary, and of the irony of his achievement of what they, but not himself, had supposed was his purpose in leaving them. He hoped that his book would give Rebecca a security that he, more than she, had realized would be threatened by his declining popularity as a writer. The royalties from a successful novel would provide a more satisfactory income than a claim for loss of life at sea...

The sun was rolling towards the horizon, gold turning orange, creating deep pools of shadow on the steep eastern slopes behind Zafada's peaks; throwing into sharp relief the massed summits of far-distant clouds fringing the visible world. It was Nature at her most impressive and assured, a quieter but no less firm statement than storm or hurricane of her eternal power of survival over the ways and will of men.

He drew in his breath and hunched his shoulders, as though a sudden but not unwelcome chill had bathed his skin; yet the air was still kind and his thin shirt adequate protection from the small drop in the warmth of a tropical evening.

From behind a veil of haze on the far horizon the sun's power did not hurt his eyes. He felt their blankness and it matched his mind's intoxication by the unsurpassable beauty of truths beyond human control.

And then, just as had happened once before, those few weeks earlier on the empty waters of the gale-torn ocean, his brain experienced a moment of doubt about the death of God. But on this occasion he was entertaining doubt free of fear.

It was enough to bring him back to the realities of the present.

The light was fading fast. He knew that if he did not hurry he would be descending the ravine in the dark. An impossible thought. Besides which there was the ramp to be improved in the cistern, and Seamew waiting to be fed... Then reason reasserted itself and he knew he could not possibly get back to the boat before the light had gone. It did not matter. He would sleep in the house at the other end of the island and return down the ravine in the cool of early morning. It was about time Seamew worked up a genuine appetite.

He got up and stretched, tired but at peace. Turning, intending to pick up his satchel and binoculars, he saw that he was not alone. The Rasta who had carried his coracle from the rocks was standing on the other side of the peak's small cairn. His right foot was on the binoculars' strap.

The boy's wiry body was glistening in the setting sun, the sinews below his dark skin as clearly defined as on a students' model. His head was thrown back, his legs apart, his arms at his side. Relaxed, confident, yet wary, his eyes were fixed on Matthew's, and something in them said more than speech. In his right hand he held a bush knife - not tensely nor with anger or challenge, yet in the very casualness of his grip there was evidence of an intention and an inevitability that both of them understood.

The man and the boy held each other's gaze for a matter of seconds, then the boy moved forward slowly, without overt threat, as though he had all the time in the world, as though he were the agent and the symbol of an event so preordained that there was no good reason under the wide sky for supposing things could be otherwise...

As the sun sank below the horizon the kitten left the coil of rope in which she had slept through another uneventful afternoon. She padded softly along the side deck of the yacht, then jumped down into the cockpit and so to her familiar cushion in the cabin below. She curled up and closed her eyes contentedly, secure in the felt knowledge that there were those who cared.

Who knew but that there might be cream for tea?